Polar Shift

Polar Shift

CLIVE CUSSLER
with PAUL KEMPRECOS

A NOVEL FROM
THE NUMA® FILES

MICHAEL JOSEPH
an imprint of
PENGUIN BOOKS

MICHAEL JOSEPH

Published by the Penguin Group
Penguin Books Ltd, 80 Strand, London WC2R ORL, England
Penguin Group (USA) Inc., 375 Hudson Street, New York, New York 10014, USA
Penguin Group (Canada), 90 Eglinton Avenue East, Suite 700, Toronto, Ontario, Canada M4P 2Y3
(a division of Pearson Penguin Canada Inc.)
Penguin Ireland, 25 St Stephen's Green, Dublin 2, Ireland (a division of Penguin Books Ltd)
Penguin Group (Australia), 250 Camberwell Road,
Camberwell, Victoria 3124, Australia (a division of Pearson Australia Group Pty Ltd)
Penguin Books India Pvt Ltd, 11 Community Centre,
Panchsheel Park, New Delhi – 110 017, India
Penguin Group (NZ), cnr Airborne and Rosedale Roads, Albany,
Auckland 1310, New Zealand (a division of Pearson New Zealand Ltd)
Penguin Books (South Africa) (Pty) Ltd, 24 Sturdee Avenue,
Rosebank, Johannesburg 2196, South Africa

Penguin Books Ltd, Registered Offices: 80 Strand, London WC2R ORL, England

www.penguin.com

First published in the United States of America by G. P. Putnam's Sons Ltd 2005
First published in Great Britain by Michael Joseph 2005

1

Set in 13.5/16 pt Monotype Garamond
Typeset by Rowland Phototypesetting Ltd, Bury St Edmunds, Suffolk
Printed in Great Britain by Clays Ltd, St Ives plc

A CIP catalogue record for this book is available from the British Library

ISBN-13: 978–0–718–14788–4
ISBN-10: 0–718–14788–X

Prologue

EAST PRUSSIA, 1944

The Mercedes-Benz 770 W150 Grosser Tourenwagen weighed more than four tons and was armored like a Panzer. But the seven-passenger limousine seemed to float like a ghost over the cushion of new-fallen snow, gliding with unlit headlights past slumbering cornfields that sparkled in the blue light of the moon.

As the car neared a darkened farmhouse that lay in a gentle hollow, the driver gently touched the brakes. The car slowed to the speed of a walk and approached the low-slung, fieldstone structure with the stealth of a cat stalking a mouse.

The driver gazed thoughtfully through the frosted windshield with eyes the color of arctic ice. The building appeared to be abandoned, but he knew better than to take chances. White paint had been hastily slapped over the car's sculpted black steel body. The crude attempt at camouflage made the automobile practically invisible to the Stormovic ground attack planes that prowled the skies like angry hawks, but the Mercedes had barely escaped the Russian patrols that materialized out of the snow like wraiths. Rifle bullets had cratered the armor in a dozen places.

So he waited.

The man stretched out on the spacious backseat of the four-door sedan had felt the car decelerate. He sat up and blinked the sleep out of his eyes.

'What is it?' he asked, speaking German with a Hungarian accent. His voice was fuzzy from sleep.

The driver hushed his passenger. 'Something's not –'

The rattle of gunfire shattered the glassy stillness of the night.

The driver mashed the brake pedal. The massive vehicle hissed to a skidding stop about fifty yards from the farmhouse. He switched off the engine and snatched the 9 mm Lugar pistol from the front seat. His fingers tightened on the Lugar's grip as a burly figure dressed in the olive uniform and fur hat of the Red Army staggered out the front door of the farmhouse.

The soldier was clutching his arm and bellowing like a bee-stung bull.

'Damn fascist whore!' he bawled repeatedly. His voice was hoarse with rage and pain.

The Russian soldier had broken into the farmhouse only minutes before. The farm couple had been hiding in a closet, huddling under a blanket like children afraid of the dark. He had put a bullet in the husband and turned his attention to the woman, who had fled into the tiny kitchen.

Shouldering his weapon, he had crooked his finger and crooned, *'Frau, komm,'* the soothing prelude to rape.

The soldier's vodka-soaked brain failed to warn him that he was in danger. The farmer's wife hadn't begged for mercy or burst into tears like the other women he had raped and murdered. She had glared at him with hot eyes, whipped a carving knife out from behind her back and slashed at his face. He had seen a flash of steel in the moonlight streaming through the windows and had thrown up his left arm to defend himself, but the sharp blade sliced through his sleeve and forearm. He punched her to the floor with his other

2

hand. Even then she had lunged for the knife. Consumed with white-hot fury, he cut her in half with frenzied bursts of his PPS-43 machine gun.

As he stood outside the farmhouse, the soldier examined his wound. The cut was not severe, and the blood flow was down to a trickle. He pulled a pint of homemade vodka from his pocket and drained the bottle. The fiery hundred-proof liquor trickling down his throat helped numb the searing pain in his arm. He tossed the empty bottle into the snow, wiped his mouth with the back of his glove and set off to rejoin his comrades. He would brag that he'd been wounded fighting a gang of fascists.

The soldier trudged a few steps in the snow only to stop as his sharp ears picked up the *tick-tick* sound of the car's engine cooling down. He squinted at the large grayish smudge in the moon shadows. A suspicious scowl appeared on his broad peasant face. He slipped his machine gun from his shoulder and brought it to bear on the vague object. His finger tightened on the trigger.

Four headlights blazed on. The powerful in-line eight-cylinder engine roared into life and the car sprang forward, its rear end fishtailing in the snow. The Russian tried to dodge the oncoming vehicle. The corner of the heavy bumper caught his leg, and he was thrown to the side of the road.

The car slid to a stop, the door opened and the driver got out. The tall man walked through the snow to the soldier, his black leather overcoat slapping softly against his thighs. The man had a long face and a lantern jaw. His close-cropped blond hair was uncovered even though the temperature was below zero.

He squatted next to the stricken man.

'Are you hurt, *tovarich?*' he said in Russian. His voice

was deep and resonant, and he spoke with the detached sympathy of a physician.

The soldier groaned. He couldn't believe his bad luck. First that German bitch with the knife, now this.

He cursed through spittle-covered lips. 'Damn your mother! Of *course* I'm hurt.'

The tall man lit a cigarette and placed it between the Russian's lips. 'Is there anyone in the farmhouse?'

The soldier took a deep drag and exhaled through his nostrils. He assumed that the stranger was one of the political officers who infested the army like fleas.

'Two fascists,' the Russian said. 'A man and a woman.'

The stranger went inside the farmhouse and emerged minutes later.

'What happened?' he said, again kneeling by the soldier's side.

'I shot the man. The fascist witch came after me with a knife.'

'Good work.' He patted the Russian on the shoulder. 'You're here alone?'

The soldier growled like a dog with his bone. 'I don't share my loot or my women.'

'What is your unit?'

'General Galitsky's Eleventh Guards army,' the soldier replied with pride in his voice.

'You attacked Nemmersdorf on the border?'

The soldier bared his bad teeth. 'We nailed the fascists to their barns. Men, women and children. You should have heard the fascist dogs scream for mercy.'

The tall man nodded. 'Well done. I can take you to your comrades. Where are they?'

'Close by. Getting ready for another push west.'

The tall man gazed toward a distant line of trees. The

rumble of huge T-34 battle tanks was like distant thunder. 'Where are the Germans?'

'The swine are running for their lives.' The soldier puffed on the cigarette. 'Long live Mother Russia.'

'Yes,' the tall man said. 'Long live Mother Russia.' He reached into his overcoat, pulled out the Lugar and placed the muzzle against the soldier's temple. '*Auf Wiedersehen*, comrade.'

The pistol barked once. The stranger slid the smoking pistol into its holster and returned to the car. As he got behind the wheel, a hoarse cry came from the passenger in the backseat.

'You killed that soldier in cold blood!'

The dark-haired man was in his mid-thirties, and he had the handsome chiseled face of an actor. A thin mustache adorned a sensitive mouth. But there was nothing delicate about the way his expressive gray eyes burned with anger.

'I simply helped another Ivan sacrifice himself for the greater glory of Mother Russia,' the driver said, speaking in German.

'I understand this is war,' the passenger said, his voice tight with emotion. 'But even you must admit the Russians are human, like us.'

'Yes, Professor Kovacs, we are *very* much alike. We have committed unspeakable atrocities against their people, and now they are taking their revenge.' He described the horrors of the Nemmersdorf massacre.

'I'm sorry for those people,' Kovacs said in a subdued tone, 'but the fact that the Russians behave like animals doesn't mean that the rest of the world must descend into savagery.'

The driver heaved a heavy sigh. 'The front is beyond that

ridge,' he said. 'You are welcome to discuss the goodness of mankind with your Russian friends. I won't stop you.'

The professor drew in on himself like an oyster.

The driver glanced in the rearview mirror and chuckled to himself.

'A wise decision.' He lit a cigarette, bending low to shield the light from his match. 'Let me explain the situation. The Red Army has crossed the border and blown through the German front as if it were made of fog. Nearly all the inhabitants of this lovely countryside have fled their homes and fields. Our valiant army has been fighting a rearguard action as it runs for its life. The Russians have a ten-to-one advantage in men and arms, and they are cutting off all land routes west as they race toward Berlin. Millions of people are on the move to the coast, where the only escape is by sea.'

'God help us all,' the professor said.

'*He* seems to have evacuated East Prussia as well. Consider yourself a fortunate man,' the driver said cheerfully. He backed the car up, threw the shift into low gear and drove around the Russian's body. 'You are seeing history.'

The car headed west, entering the no-man's-land between the advancing Russian juggernaut and the retreating Germans. The Mercedes flew along the roads, skirting deserted villages and farms. The frozen countryside was surreal, as if it had been tilted on its side and emptied of all human life. The travelers stopped only to refuel from the spare gas tanks the car carried in its trunk and to relieve themselves.

Tracks began to appear in the snow. A short while later, the car caught up with the tail end of the retreat. The strategic withdrawal had become a full-fledged rout of army trucks and tanks that lumbered along through the falling snow in a slow-moving river of soldiers and refugees.

The luckier refugees rode on tractors or horse-drawn carts. Others walked, pushing wheelbarrows piled with personal possessions through the snow. Many had escaped with only the clothes on their backs.

The Mercedes rode up on the edge of the road, and its deep tire treads dug into the snow. The car kept moving until it passed the head of the retreat. Around dawn, the mud-splattered car limped into Gdynia like a wounded rhino seeking shelter in a thicket.

The Germans had occupied Gdynia in 1939, expelled fifty thousand Poles and renamed the bustling seaport Gotenhafen, after the Goths. The harbor was transformed into a navy base, primarily for submarines. A branch of the Kiel shipyard was established to turn out new U-boats that were matched with crews trained in nearby waters and sent to sink Allied ships in the Atlantic.

Under orders from Gross Admiral Karl Doenitz, an eclectic flotilla had been assembled at Gdynia in preparation for the evacuation. The fleet included some of the finest passenger liners in Germany, cargo ships, fishing boats and private vessels. Doenitz wanted his submarine and other naval personnel rescued so they could continue to fight. Eventually, more than two million civilians and military personnel would be transported west.

The Mercedes made its way through the city. A bitterly cold wind was blowing in from the Baltic Sea, whipping snowflakes into clouds of icy, stinging nettles. Despite the frostbite conditions, the city's streets were as crowded as on a summer's day. Refugees and prisoners of war slogged through deep drifts in futile search of shelter. Relief stations were overwhelmed with long lines of hungry refugees waiting for a crust of bread or a cup of hot soup.

Wagons piled high with passengers and goods clogged

the narrow streets. Refugees streamed from the train station to join the throngs who had arrived on foot. Muffled under layers of clothing, they resembled strange snow creatures. Children were pulled along on makeshift sleds.

The car was capable of speeds reaching 170 kilometers per hour, but it soon became bogged down in traffic. The driver cursed and leaned on the horn. The heavy steel bumper failed to nudge the refugees out of the way. Frustrated at the glacial pace, the driver brought the car to a complete halt. He got out and opened the rear door.

'Come, Professor,' he said, rousting his passenger. 'Time for a stroll.'

Abandoning the Mercedes in the middle of the street, the driver bulled his way through the crowd. He kept a firm hand on the professor's arm, yelled at people to make way and shouldered them aside when they didn't move fast enough.

Eventually, they made their way to the waterfront where more than sixty thousand refugees had gathered, hoping to get aboard one of the vessels lined up at the piers or anchored in the harbor.

'Take a good look,' the driver said, surveying the sight with a grim smile. 'The religious scholars have been all wrong. You can plainly see that it is *cold,* not hot, in Hell.'

The professor was convinced he was in the hands of a madman. Before Kovacs could reply, the driver had him in tow once more. They wove their way through a snow-covered settlement of tents fashioned from blankets and dodged scores of starving horses and dogs abandoned by their owners. Wagons cluttered the docks. Lines of stretchers carried wounded soldiers brought in from the east aboard ambulance trains. Armed guards stood at each gangway and turned away unauthorized passengers.

The driver cut in front of a passenger line. The steel-helmeted sentry manning the checkpoint raised his rifle to bar the way. The driver waved a sheet of paper printed in heavy Gothic type under the sentry's nose. The guard read the document, snapped to attention and pointed along the dock.

The professor didn't move. He had been watching someone on board the ship anchored at the dock throw a bundle down to the crowd on the pier. The throw was short and the bundle fell into the water. A wailing went up from the crowd.

'What's happening?' the professor said.

The guard barely glanced in the direction of the commotion. 'Refugees with a baby can get on board. They toss the baby back down and use it as a boarding pass over and over. Sometimes they miss and the baby goes in the water.'

'How gruesome,' the professor said with a shudder.

The guard shrugged. 'You'd better get moving. Once the snow stops, the Reds will send their planes to bomb and strafe. Good luck.' He raised his rifle to bar the next person in line.

The magic document got Kovacs and the driver past a pair of tough-looking SS officers who were looking for able-bodied men to press into duty on the front. They eventually reached a ramp leading onto a ferry crammed with wounded soldiers. The driver again showed his documents to a guard, who told them to hurry aboard.

As the overloaded ferry left the dock, it was watched by a man wearing the uniform of the naval medical corps. He had been helping to load the wounded on board, but he slipped through the mob and away from the waterfront to a maritime junkyard.

He climbed onto a rotting derelict of a fishing boat and went below. He pulled a crank-operated radio from a galley cupboard, fired it up and muttered a few sentences in Russian. He heard the reply against the crackle of static, replaced the radio and headed back to the ferry dock.

The ferry carrying Kovacs and his tall companion had come around to the seaward side of a vessel. The ship had been drawn several yards from the dock to keep desperate refugees from sneaking aboard. As the ferry passed under the ship's bow, the professor looked up. Printed in Gothic letters on the navy-gray hull was the name *Wilhelm Gustloff.*

A gangway was lowered and the wounded were carried aboard the ship. Then the other passengers scrambled up the gangway. They wore smiles of relief on their faces and prayers of thanks on their lips. The German fatherland was only a few days' cruise away.

None of the happy passengers could have known that they had just boarded a floating tomb.

Captain Third Class Sasha Marinesko peered through the periscope of the Submarine S-13, his dark brow furrowed in a deep scowl.

Nothing.

Not a German transport in sight. The gray sea was as empty as the pockets of a sailor returning from shore leave. Not even a stinking rowboat to shoot at. The captain thought of the twelve unused torpedoes aboard the Soviet sub and his anger festered like an open sore.

Soviet naval headquarters had said that the Red Army offensive against Danzig would force a major sea evacuation. The S-13 was one of three Soviet subs ordered to wait for the expected exodus off Memel, a port still held by the Germans.

When Marinesko learned that Memel had been captured, he called his officers together. He told them he had decided to head toward the Bay of Danzig, where the evacuation convoys were more likely to be found.

Not one man objected. Officers and crew were well aware that the success of their mission could mean the difference between a hero's welcome and a one-way ticket to Siberia.

Days earlier, the captain had run afoul of the secret police, the NKGB. He had left the base without permission. He was out whoring on January 2 when orders had come down from Stalin for the subs to sail into the Baltic and wreak havoc among the convoys. But the captain was on a three-day bender in the brothels and bars of the Finnish port of Turku. He returned to the S-13 a day after it was supposed to sail.

The NKGB was waiting. They became even more suspicious when he said he could not remember the details of his drunken binge. Marinesko was a cocky and tough submarine skipper who had been awarded the orders of Lenin and the Red Banner. The swashbuckling submariner exploded in anger when the secret police accused him of spying and defection.

His sympathetic commanding officer put off the decision on conducting a court-martial. That ploy fell apart when the Ukrainians who served aboard the sub signed a petition asking that their captain be allowed to rejoin his boat. The commander knew that this display of simple loyalty would be seen as potential mutiny. Hoping to defuse a dangerous situation, he ordered the sub to sea while a decision was made about a court-martial.

Marinesko reasoned that if he sunk enough German ships, he and his men might avoid being severely punished.

Without telling naval headquarters of their plan, he and his men quietly put the S-13 on a course that would take it away from the patrol lanes and toward its fateful rendezvous with the German liner.

Friedrich Petersen, the *Gustloff*'s white-haired master captain, paced back and forth in the wardroom, sputtering like a walking pyrotechnics display. He stopped suddenly and shot a red-hot glare at a younger man dressed in the spit-and-polish uniform of the submarine division.

'May I remind you, Commander Zahn, that I am the captain of this ship and responsible for guiding this vessel and all aboard to safety.'

Bringing his iron discipline to bear, Submarine Commander Wilhelm Zahn reached down and scratched behind the ear of Hassan, the big Alsatian dog at his side. 'And may I remind *you,* captain, that the *Gustloff* has been under my command as a submarine base ship since 1942. *I* am the senior naval officer aboard. Besides, you forget your oath not to command a ship at sea.'

Petersen had signed the agreement as a condition of his repatriation after being captured by the British. The oath was a formality because the British thought he was too old to be fit for service. At the age of sixty-seven, he knew his career was washed up no matter the outcome of the war. He was a *Leigerkapitän*, the 'sleeping captain,' of the *Gustloff*. But he took some comfort in the knowledge that the younger man had been withdrawn from active operations after he botched the sinking of the British ship *Nelson*.

'Nonetheless, Captain, under your supervision the *Gustloff* has never left the dock,' he said. 'A floating classroom and barracks anchored in one place is a far cry from a ship at sea. I have the highest regard for the submarine service, but you cannot argue that I am the only one qualified to take the vessel to sea.'

Petersen had commanded the liner once, on a peacetime voyage, and would never have been allowed to take the helm of the *Gustloff* under ordinary circumstances. Zahn bristled at the thought of being under the command of a civilian. German submariners considered themselves an elite group.

'Still, I am the ranking military officer aboard. Perhaps you have noticed that we have antiaircraft guns mounted on the deck,' Zahn retorted. 'This vessel is technically a warship.'

The captain replied with an indulgent smile. 'An odd sort of warship. Perhaps *you* have noticed that we are carrying thousands of refugees, a mission more fitting of the merchant marine transport.'

'You neglected to mention the fifteen hundred submariners who must be evacuated so they can defend the Reich.'

'I would be glad to acquiesce to your wishes if you show me written orders to do so.' Petersen knew perfectly well that in the confusion surrounding the evacuation, no orders existed.

Zahn's complexion turned the color of a cooked beet. His opposition went beyond personal animosity. Zahn had serious doubts about Petersen's ability to run the ship with the inexperienced polyglot crew at his command. He wanted to call the captain a burned-out fool, but his stern discipline again took hold. He turned to the other officers, who had been witnessing the uncomfortable confrontation.

'This will be no "Strength Through Joy" cruise,' Zahn

said. 'All of us, navy and merchant marine officers, have a difficult task and bear heavy responsibility. Our duty is to do everything possible to make things easier for the refugees, and I expect the crew to go out of their way to be helpful.'

He clicked his heels and saluted Petersen, then strode from the wardroom followed by his faithful Alsatian.

The guard at the top of the gangway had glanced at the tall man's document and handed it to an officer supervising the boarding of the wounded.

The officer took his time reading the letter. Finally, he said, 'Herr Koch thinks highly of you.'

Erich Koch was the murderous *Gauleiter* who had refused to evacuate East Prussia while preparing his own escape on a ship carrying looted treasure.

'I like to think that I have earned his respect.'

The officer hailed a ship's steward and explained the situation. The steward shrugged and led the way along the crowded promenade deck, and then down three levels. He opened the door to a cabin that contained two bunks and a sink. The room was too small for the three of them to enter at the same time.

'Not exactly the *Führer* suite,' the steward said. 'But you're lucky to have it. The head is four doors down.'

The tall man glanced around the cabin. 'This will do. Now, see if you can get us some food.'

A flush came to the steward's cheeks. He was tired of being ordered about by VIPs traveling in relative comfort while ordinary mortals had to suffer. But something in the tall man's cold blue eyes warned him not to argue. He returned within fifteen minutes with two bowls of hot vegetable soup and chunks of hard bread.

The two men devoured their food in silence. The

professor finished first and put his bowl aside. His eyes were glazed with exhaustion, but his mind was still alert.

'What is this ship?' he said.

The tall man scraped the bottom of his bowl with the last of his bread, then lit up a cigarette. 'Welcome to the *Wilhelm Gustloff*, the pride of Germany's "Strength Through Joy" movement.'

The movement was an ongoing propaganda stunt to demonstrate the benefits of National Socialism to German workers. Kovacs glanced around at the spartan accommodations. 'I don't see much strength or joy.'

'Nonetheless, the *Gustloff* will again one day transport happy German laborers and party faithful to sunny Italy.'

'I can hardly wait. You haven't told me where we're going.'

'Far beyond the reach of the Red Army. Your work is too important to fall into Russian hands. The Reich will take good care of you.'

'It looks as if the Reich is having trouble taking care of its own people.'

'A temporary setback. Your welfare is my utmost priority.'

'I'm not concerned about *my* welfare.' Kovacs hadn't seen his wife and young son for months. Only their infrequent letters had kept hope alive.

'Your family?' The tall man regarded him with a steady gaze. 'Have no worry. This will soon be over. I suggest you get some sleep. No, that's an order.'

He stretched out on the bunk, hands clasped behind his head, and shut his eyes. Kovacs was not deceived. His companion seldom slept and could snap fully awake at the slightest provocation.

Kovacs examined the man's face. He could have been in

his early twenties, although he looked older. He had the long head and craggy profile portrayed in propaganda posters as the Aryan ideal.

Kovacs shuddered, remembering the cold-blooded way the Russian soldier had been dispatched. The past few days had been a blur. The tall man had arrived at the lab during a snowstorm and produced a document authorizing the release of Professor Kovacs. He had introduced himself only as Karl, and told Kovacs to gather his belongings. Then came the madcap dash across the frozen countryside and the narrow escapes from Russian patrols. Now this miserable ship.

The food had made Kovacs drowsy. His eyelids drooped, and he drifted off into a deep sleep.

While the professor slept, a squad of military police swept the *Gustloff* in search of deserters. The ship was cleared for departure, and a harbor pilot came aboard. At around one in the afternoon, the deckhands cast off the mooring lines. Four tugs came alongside and began to pull the ship away from the dock.

A fleet of small boats, loaded mostly with women and children, blocked the way. The ship stopped and took the refugees aboard. The *Gustloff* normally carried 1,465 passengers, served by a crew of four hundred. As she began this voyage, the once-elegant liner was carrying eight thousand passengers.

The ship headed into the open sea, and dropped anchor late in the afternoon to rendezvous with another liner, the *Hansa,* to wait for their escorts. The *Hansa* had developed engine trouble and never showed up. Naval Command was worried that the *Gustloff* would be exposed to danger in open waters and told the ship to go it alone.

The liner plowed into the whitecapped waters of the Baltic, fighting a stiff northwest wind. Hailstones rattled the windows of the bridge, where Commander Zahn seethed with anger as he looked down at the two so-called escorts that had been sent to protect the liner.

The ship was built for southern climes, but, with any luck, it could survive bad weather. What it could not survive was *stupidity*. Naval Command had sent the liner into harm's way with an old torpedo boat called the *Lowe,* or 'Lion,' and the T19, a worn-out torpedo recovery vessel, as escorts. Zahn was thinking that the situation could not get any worse when the T19 radioed that it had developed a leak and was returning to the base.

Zahn went to Captain Petersen and the other officers gathered in the bridge.

'In view of our escort situation, I suggest that we pursue a zigzag course at high speed,' he said.

Petersen scoffed at the suggestion. 'Impossible. The *Wilhelm Gustloff* is a twenty-four-thousand-ton ocean liner. We cannot go from one tack to the other like a drunken sailor.'

'Then we must outrun any U-boats with our superior speed. We can take the direct, deepwater route at the full speed of sixteen knots.'

'I know this ship. Even without the bomb damage to the propeller casings, there would be no way we could reach and maintain sixteen knots without blowing out our bearings,' Petersen said.

Zahn could see the veins bulging in the captain's neck. He stared through the bridge windows at the old torpedo boat leading the way. 'In that case,' he said in a voice that seemed to echo in a tomb, 'God help us all.'

*

'Professor, wake up.' The voice was hard-edged, urgent. Kovacs opened his eyes and saw Karl bending over him. He sat up and rubbed his cheeks as if he could squeeze the sleep out of them.

'What's wrong?'

'I've been talking to people. My God, what a mess! There are two captains and they fight all the time. Not enough lifeboats. The ship's engines are barely keeping us up to speed. The stupid submarine division ordered the ship to sail with an old torpedo boat escort that looks as if it was left over from the last war. The damned fools have got the ship's navigation lights on.'

Kovacs saw an uncharacteristic alarm in the marble features.

'How long have I slept?'

'It's nighttime. We're on the open sea.' Karl shoved a dark blue life jacket at Kovacs and slipped into a similar jacket.

'Now what do we do?'

'Stay here. I want to check the lifeboat situation.' He tossed Kovacs a pack of cigarettes. 'Be my guest.'

'I don't smoke.'

Karl paused in the open doorway. 'Maybe it's time you did.' Then he was gone.

Kovacs spilled a cigarette from the pack and lit up. He had quit smoking years ago, when he got married. He coughed as the smoke filled his lungs, and he felt dizzy from the strong tobacco, but he recalled with delicious pleasure the innocent debauchery of his college days.

He finished the cigarette, thought of lighting up another but decided against it. He had not had a bath in days, and his body itched in a dozen places. He washed his face in the sink and was drying his hands on a threadbare towel when there was a knock at the door.

'Professor Kovacs?' a muffled voice said.

'Yes.'

The door opened, and the professor gasped. Standing in the doorway was the ugliest woman he had ever seen. She was more than six feet tall, with broad shoulders straining the seams of a black Persian lamb coat. Her wide mouth was painted in bright red lipstick, and, with such heavily rouged lips, she looked like a circus clown.

'Pardon my appearance,' she said in an unmistakably male voice. 'This is not an easy ship to get aboard. I had to resort to this silly disguise, and a few bribes.'

'Who are you?'

'Not important. What is important is *your* name. You are Professor Lazlo Kovacs, the great German-Hungarian electrical genius.'

Kovacs grew wary. 'I am Lazlo Kovacs. I consider myself to be Hungarian.'

'Splendid! You are the author of the paper on electromagnetism that electrified the scientific world.'

Kovacs's antenna quivered. The paper published in an obscure scientific journal had brought him to the attention of the Germans, who kidnapped him and his family. He said nothing.

'Never mind,' the man said genially, the clown smile even broader. 'I can see that I have the right man.' He reached under his fur coat and pulled out a pistol. 'I'm sorry to be rude, Professor Kovacs, but I'm afraid I'm going to have to kill you.'

'*Kill* me? Why? I don't even know you.'

'But *I* know you. Or, rather, my superiors in the NKGB know you. As soon as our glorious Red Army forces crossed the border we sent a special squad to find you, but you had already left the lab.'

'You're *Russian?*'

'Yes, of course. We would love to have you come and work for us. Had we been able to intercept you before you boarded the ship, you would be enjoying Soviet hospitality. But now I can't get you off the ship, and we can't let you and your work fall into German hands again. No, no. It just wouldn't do.' The smile vanished.

Kovacs was too stunned to be afraid, even when the pistol came up and the muzzle pointed at his heart.

Marinesko could hardly believe his good luck. He had been standing on the S-13's conning tower, oblivious to the freezing wind and spray that stung his face, when the snow cleared and he saw the enormous silhouette of an ocean liner. The liner appeared to be accompanied by a smaller boat.

The submarine was riding on the surface in heavy seas. Its crew had been at battle stations since sighting the lights from boats moving against the coast. The captain had ordered the submarine's buoyancy reduced so that it would ride lower in the water and thus evade radar.

Reasoning that the ships would never expect an attack from shore, he ordered his crew to bring the sub around the back of the convoy and run a course parallel to the liner and its escort. Two hours later, Marinesko turned the S-13 toward his target. As it closed in on the port side of the liner, he gave the order to fire.

In quick succession, three torpedoes left their bow tubes and streaked toward the unprotected hull of the liner.

The door opened, and Karl stepped into the cabin. He had been outside, listening to the murmur of male voices. He was puzzled when he saw the woman standing with her back to him. He glanced at Kovacs, still holding the towel, and he read the fear in the professor's face.

The Russian felt the blast of cold air through the open door. He whirled and shot without aiming. Karl was a millisecond ahead of him. He had put his head down and rammed it into the Russian's midsection.

The blow should have cracked the assassin's rib cage, but the heavy fur coat and the stiff corset he wore were like padded armor. The head butt only knocked the wind out of him. He crashed into a bunk, landing on his side. His wig fell off to reveal short black hair. He got off another shot that nicked Karl's right shoulder muscle at the base of the neck.

Karl lunged at the assassin, and with his left hand groped for the throat. Blood from his wound spattered them both. The assassin brought his foot up and kicked Karl in the chest. He reeled back, tripped and fell onto his back.

Kovacs grabbed the soup bowl from the sink and threw it at the assassin's face. The bowl bounced harmlessly off the man's cheekbone. He laughed. 'I'll tend to you next.' He aimed the pistol at Karl.

Va-room!

A muffled explosion thundered off the walls. The deck slanted at a sharp angle to starboard. Kovacs was flung to his knees. Unused to the high-heeled boots on his feet, the assassin lost his balance. He fell on top of Karl, who grabbed the man's wrist, pulled it to his mouth and sank his teeth into cartilage and muscle. The pistol clunked to the deck.

Va-room! Va-room!

The ship shuddered from two more massive explosions. The assassin tried to rise, but again lost his balance when the ship lurched to port. He teetered on the verge of standing. Karl kicked him in the ankle. The Russian let out an unladylike yell and crashed to the floor. His head came to rest against the metal base of the bunk.

Karl braced himself against the sink pipes and drove his hobnail boot into the man's throat, crushing his larynx. The man flailed at Karl's leg, his eyes bulged, his face went dark red, then purple, and then he died.

Karl staggered to his feet.

'We've got to get out of here,' he said. 'The ship's been torpedoed.'

He muscled Kovacs from the cabin into the passageway, where there was pandemonium. The corridor was filled with panic-stricken passengers. Their screams and shouts echoed off the walls. The ringing of alarm bells contributed to the din. The emergency lights were on, but a pall of smoke produced from the explosions made it difficult to see.

The main stairway was clogged with an unmoving crush of panicked passengers. Many of them had stopped in their tracks as they gagged from the throat-burning fumes.

The mob was trying to push against the river of water that spilled down the stairs. Karl opened an unmarked steel door, dragged Kovacs into a dark space and shut the door behind them. The professor felt his hand being guided to the rung of a ladder.

'Climb,' Karl ordered.

Kovacs dumbly obeyed, ascending until his head hit a hatch. Karl shouted from below to open the hatch cover, and to keep climbing. They went up a second ladder. Kovacs pushed another cover open. Cold air and wind-driven snow-flakes lashed his face. He climbed through the hatch, and helped Karl into the open.

Kovacs looked around in bewilderment. 'Where are we?'

'On the boat deck. This way.'

The icy, sloping deck was eerily quiet, compared to the

horror in the third-class section. The few people they saw were the privileged passengers whose cabins were on the boat deck. Some were clustered around a motorized pinnace, a sturdy boat built to cruise in the Norwegian fjords. Crew members had been chipping away with hammers and axes at the ice on the davits.

With the davit fastenings finally freed, the crewmen surged aboard, pushing aside women, some of them pregnant. Children and wounded soldiers didn't have a chance. Karl drew his pistol and fired a warning shot in the air. The crewmen hesitated, but only for a second, before they continued to fight their way onto the lifeboat. Karl fired another shot, killing the first crewman who had climbed into the boat. The others ran for their lives.

Karl lifted a woman and her baby into the boat, then gave the professor a hand before climbing in himself. He allowed some crewmen aboard, so they could throw the dead man out and lower the boat to the water. The hooks attached to the lowering lines were unfastened and the motor started.

The heavily burdened boat wallowed as it moved slowly across the sea toward distant lights from a freighter that was headed their way. Karl ordered that the lifeboat stopped to pick up people floating in the water. Soon it became even more dangerously overloaded. One of the crewmen protested.

'There's no room in the boat,' he yelled.

Karl shot him between the eyes. 'There's room now,' he said, and ordered the other crewmen to toss the body overboard. Satisfied that the short-lived mutiny was under control, he squeezed next to Kovacs.

'You're well, Professor?'

'I'm fine.' He stared at Karl. 'You're a surprising man.'

'I try to be. Never let your enemies know what to expect.'

'I'm not talking about that. I saw you help the wounded and women. You cradled that baby as if it were your own.'

'Things are not always what they seem, my friend.' He reached into his coat and brought out a packet wrapped in a waterproof rubber pouch. 'Take these papers. You are no longer Lazlo Kovacs but a German national who has lived in Hungary. You have only a slight accent and will easily pass. I want you to disappear into the crowd. Become another refugee. Make your way toward the British and American lines.'

'Who are you?'

'A friend.'

'Why should I believe that?'

'As I said, things are not always what they seem. I am part of a circle that has been fighting the Nazi animals long before the Russians.'

Light dawned in the professor's eyes. 'The *Kreisau Circle*?' He had heard rumors of the secretive opposition group.

Karl brought his finger to his lips. 'We are still in enemy territory,' he said with a lowered voice.

Kovacs clutched Karl's arm. 'Can you get my family to safety as well?'

'I am afraid it is too late for that. Your family is no more.'

'But the letters –'

'They were clever forgeries, so you would not lose heart and give up your work.'

Kovacs stared into the night with a stunned expression on his face.

Karl grabbed the professor by the lapel and whispered in his ear. 'You must forget your work for your own good and the welfare of mankind. We cannot risk that it will fall into the wrong hands.'

The professor nodded dumbly. The boat banged up

against the freighter's hull. A ladder was lowered. Karl ordered the reluctant crewmen to take the boat out again to pick up more survivors. From the freighter's deck, Kovacs watched the boat push off. Karl gave one last wave and the boat disappeared behind a veil of falling snow.

In the distance, Kovacs saw the lights of the liner, which had turned onto its port side, so that the funnel was parallel to the sea. The boiler exploded as the ship slipped below the surface about an hour after being torpedoed. In that short time, five times more lives were lost on the *Gustloff* than on the *Titanic*.

I

Those who laid eyes on the *Southern Belle* for the first time could be forgiven for wondering whether the person who had named the huge cargo ship possessed a warped sense of humor or simply bad eyesight. Despite a genteel name that suggested eyelash-fluttering, antebellum femininity, the *Belle* was, simply put, a metal monstrosity with nothing that hinted at female pulchritude.

The *Southern Belle* was one of a new generation of fast, seaworthy vessels being built in American shipyards after years of the United States taking a backseat to other ship-building countries. She was designed in San Diego and built in Biloxi. At seven hundred feet, she was longer than two football fields put together, with room enough to carry fifteen hundred containers.

The massive vessel was controlled from a towering super-structure on its aft deck. The hundred-foot-wide deckhouse, which resembled an apartment building, contained crew and officer quarters and mess halls, a hospital and treatment rooms, cargo offices and conference rooms.

With its glowing ranks of twenty-six-inch touch display screens, the *Belle*'s bridge, on the top level of the six-deck superstructure, resembled a Las Vegas casino. The spacious center of operations reflected the new era in ship design. Computers were used to control every aspect of the integrated systems and functions.

But old habits die hard. The ship's captain, Pierre 'Pete' Beaumont, was peering through a pair of binoculars, still trusting his eyes despite the sophisticated electronic gadgetry at his command.

From his vantage point on the bridge, Beaumont had a panoramic view of the Atlantic storm that raged around his ship. Fierce, gale-force winds were kicking up waves as big as houses. The waves crashed over the bow and washed halfway across the stacks of containers tied down on the deck.

The extreme level of violence surrounding the ship would have sent lesser vessels scurrying for cover and given their captains sweaty palms. But Beaumont was as calm as if he were gliding in a gondola along the Grand Canal.

The soft-spoken Cajun loved storms. He reveled in the give-and-take between his ship and the elements. Watching the way the *Belle* blasted her way through the seas in an awesome display of power gave him an almost sensual thrill.

Beaumont was the vessel's first and only captain. He had watched the *Belle* being built and knew every nut and bolt on the ship. The ship had been designed for the regular run between Europe and America, a route that took it across some of the most cantankerous ocean on the face of the earth. He was confident that the tempest was well within the forces that the ship had been built to withstand.

The ship had loaded its cargo of synthetic rubber, fiber filaments, plastics and machinery in New Orleans, then sailed around Florida to a point halfway up the Atlantic coast, where it began on a straight-line course to Rotterdam.

The weather service had been right on the nose with its forecast. Gale-force winds had been predicted, developing into an Atlantic storm. The storm caught the ship about two hundred miles from land. Beaumont was unperturbed, even when the winds intensified. The ship had easily survived worse weather.

He was scanning the ocean when he stiffened suddenly and seemed to lean into the lenses. He lowered the binoculars, raised them again and muttered under his breath. Turning to his first officer, he said:

'Look at that section of ocean. Around two o'clock. Tell me if you see anything unusual.'

The officer was Bobby Joe Butler, a talented young seaman who hailed from Natchez. Butler had made no secret of his wish someday to command a ship like the *Belle*. Maybe even the *Belle* itself. Following the captain's lead, Butler surveyed the ocean around thirty degrees off starboard.

He saw only the gray, mottled water stretching toward the misted horizon. Then, about a mile from the ship, he sighted a white line of foam at least twice as high as the sea in the background. Even as he watched, the mounding water grew rapidly in height as if it were drawing power from the surrounding waves.

'Looks like a real big sea coming our way,' Butler said in his Mississippi drawl.

'How big do you estimate it to be?'

The younger man squinted through the lenses. 'Average seas have been running around thirty feet. This looks to be double that. Wow! Have you ever seen anything this big?'

'Never,' the captain said. 'Not in my whole life.'

The captain knew his ship could handle the wave if the *Belle* faced into it bow first to cut down the area of impact. The captain ordered the helmsman to program the autosteer to face the oncoming wave and keep it steady. Then he grabbed the mike and flipped a switch on the console that would connect the bridge with speakers all over the ship.

'Attention all hands. This is the captain. A giant rogue wave is about to hit the ship. Get to a secure location away from flying objects and hold on. The impact will be severe. Repeat. The impact will be *severe*.'

As a precaution, he ordered the radioman to broadcast an SOS. The ship could always send out a recall, if needed.

The green, white-veined wave was about a half mile from the ship. 'Look at that,' Butler was saying. The sky was lit up by a series of brilliant flashes. 'Lightning?'

'Maybe,' the captain said. 'I'm more concerned about that damned sea!'

The wave's profile was unlike anything the captain had ever seen. Unlike most waves, which slope down at an angle from the crest, this one was almost straight up and down, like a moving wall.

The captain had a peculiar out-of-body sensation. Part of him watched the advancing wave in a disinterested, scientific fashion, fascinated by the size and power, while another part stood in helpless wonder at the immense, menacing power.

'It's still growing,' Butler said with unabashed awe.

The captain nodded. He guessed the wave had grown to a height of ninety feet, nearly three times as high as it was when it was first sighted. His face was ashen. Cracks were starting to appear in his rock-hard confidence. A ship the size of the *Belle* couldn't turn on a dime, and it was still facing the oncoming sea at an angle when the gigantic wave reared up like a living thing.

He was expecting the shock from the wave but was unprepared when a trough big enough to swallow his ship opened up in the ocean in front of him.

The captain looked into the abyss that had appeared before his eyes. 'It's like the end of the world,' he thought.

The ship tilted into the trough, slid down the side and buried its bow in the ocean. The captain fell against the forward bulkheads.

Rather than strike head-on, the wave collapsed on top of the ship, burying it under thousands of tons of water.

The pilothouse windows imploded under the pressure, and the entire Atlantic Ocean seemed to pour into the bridge. The blast of water hit the captain and the others on the bridge with the force of a hundred fire hoses. The bridge became a tangle of arms and legs. Books, pencils and seat cushions were thrown about.

Some of the water drained out through the windows, and the captain fought his way back to the controls. All the control screens were dead. The ship had lost its radar, gyro compasses and radio communication, but, most seriously, its power. All the instrumentation had become short-circuited. The steering gear was useless.

The captain went to a window and surveyed the physical damage. The bow had been destroyed, and the ship was listing. He suspected that the hull plating may have been penetrated. The lifeboats on the foredeck had been swept from their davits. The ship wallowed like a drunken hippo-potamus.

The big wave seemed to have stirred up the seas around it like a demagogue rousing a mob. Waves rolled across the foredeck. Worse, with its engines having failed, the ship was lying transversely to the seas, drifting in the worst possible position.

Having survived the wave, the ship lay with its side exposed, in danger of being 'holed,' in the colorful jargon of the sea.

The captain tried to remain optimistic. The *Southern Belle* could survive even with some compartments flooded.

Someone would have heard the SOS. The ship could float for days, if necessary, until help arrived.

'*Captain.*' The first officer interrupted the captain's thoughts.

Butler was staring through the broken window. His eyes were locked in an unbelieving stare on a distant point. The captain's gaze followed Butler's pointing finger, and he began to tremble as the thrill of fear went through him.

Another horizontal line of foam was forming less than a quarter of a mile away.

The first airplane arrived two hours later. It circled over the sea and was soon joined by other planes. Then the rescue ships began to arrive, diverted from the shipping routes. The ships lined up three miles apart and combed the sea like a search party looking for a lost child in the woods. After days of searching, they found nothing.

The *Southern Belle*, one of the most advanced cargo ships ever designed and built, had simply vanished without a trace.

2

The arrow-slim kayak flew across the sapphire surface of Puget Sound as if it had been shot from a bow. The broad-shouldered man in the snug cockpit seemed at one with the wooden craft. He dipped his paddles in the water with an easy, fluid motion, concentrating the power of his brawny arms into precise strokes that kept the kayak moving at a steady speed.

Sweat glistened on the kayaker's rugged, sun-burnished features. His piercing, light blue eyes, the color of coral under water, took in the broad expanse of the sound, the fog-shrouded San Juan Islands and, in the distance, the snowcapped Olympic Mountains. Kurt Austin gulped the salty air into his lungs and spread his lips in a wide grin. It felt good to be home.

Austin's duties as the director of the Special Assignments Team for the National Underwater and Marine Agency constantly took him to far-flung parts of the world. But he had acquired his taste for the sea on the waters around Seattle, where he was born. Puget Sound was as familiar to him as an old flame. He had sailed boats on the sound almost from the day he could walk, and had raced boats since he was ten. His big love was racing boats; he owned four of them: an eight-ton catamaran, capable of speeds of more than a hundred miles an hour; a smaller, outboard hydroplane; a twenty-foot sailboat; and a scull that he liked to row early in the morning on the Potomac.

The latest addition to his fleet was the custom-made Guillemot kayak. He had bought it on an earlier trip to Seattle. He liked its natural wood construction and the graceful design of the thin hull, which was based on an Aleut craft. Like all his boats, it was fast as well as beautiful.

Austin was so intent absorbing the familiar sights and smells that he almost forgot that he was not alone. He glanced over his shoulder. A flotilla of fifty kayaks trailed a few hundred feet behind his ribbonlike wake. The heavy, fiberglass, double-cockpit kayaks each carried one parent and one child. They were safe and stable, and no match for Austin's racehorse. He removed a turquoise NUMA baseball cap, revealing a jungle of prematurely gray, almost platinum hair, and waved it high above his head to urge them on.

Austin had not hesitated when his father, the wealthy owner of an international marine salvage company based in Seattle, had asked him to lead the annual benefit kayak race he sponsored to raise money for charity. Austin had worked six years for Austin Marine Salvage before being lured into a little-known branch of the CIA that specialized in under-water intelligence gathering. After the Cold War ended, the CIA closed down the investigative branch, and Austin was hired by James Sandecker, who headed NUMA before becoming vice president of the United States.

Austin dipped his paddles in the water and steered the kayak toward two boats anchored about a hundred feet apart, less than a quarter of a mile ahead. The boats carried race officials and press people. Stretched between the boats was a huge red-and-white plastic banner with the word FINISH written on it. Rafted together on the other side of

34

the finish banner were a barge and a chartered ferryboat. At the end of the race, the kayaks would be pulled up on the barge and the participants would be treated to lunch aboard the ferry. Austin's father was watching the race in a forty-eight-foot white-hulled powerboat named *White Lightning*.

Digging his paddle in, Austin was preparing for a sprint to the finish when he noticed a flicker of movement out of the corner of his eye. He turned to his right and saw a tall curved fin cutting through the water in his direction. As he watched, at least twenty more fins popped up behind the first one.

Puget Sound was home to several pods of orcas, who fed on salmon. They had become local mascots, and a big boom to the economy, attracting tourists from all over the world who flocked to Seattle to come out on whale-watch boats or take part in kayak adventures. The killer whales would come right up to the kayaks and often put on a show, breaching partially or jumping clear out of the water. Typically, the orcas would glide harmlessly past, often within a few feet of a kayak, without disturbing it.

When the first fin was about fifty feet away, the orca stood on its tail. Nearly half its twenty-five-foot length was out of the water. Austin stopped paddling to watch. He had seen the maneuver performed before, but it was still an awesome sight. The whale inspecting him was a big bull, probably the leader of the pod, and must have weighed at least seven tons. Moisture glistened on its sleek, black-and-white body.

The whale splashed back into the water, and the fin again moved rapidly in his direction. He expected from experience that at the last second the orca would duck under the kayak. But when it was only a few feet away, the whale again reared up and opened its mouth. The rows of razor-sharp teeth set in the pink mouth were close enough to touch. Austin stared in disbelief. It was as if a beloved circus clown had morphed into a monster. The jaws began to close. Austin jammed the wooden paddle into the creature's maw. There was a loud snap as the teeth closed on the paddle.

The whale's massive body came down on the front part of the thirty-five-pound kayak and smashed it to splinters. Austin went into the cold water. He sank for a second, then bobbed to the surface, buoyed by his personal flotation device. He spat out a mouthful of water and spun around. To his relief, the fin was moving away from him.

The pod of whales was between Austin and a nearby island. Rather than head in that direction, he began to swim farther out into the bay. After a few strokes, he stopped swimming and rolled onto his back. The chill that danced along his spine was not caused by the cold water alone.

A phalanx of fins was chasing after him. He kicked his water shoes off and slipped out of his cumbersome flotation vest. He knew that the gesture was a futile one. Even without his vest, he would have needed an outboard motor strapped to his back to outrun an orca. Killer whales can swim at speeds up to thirty miles per hour.

Austin had faced many human adversaries with an icy coolness, but this was different. He was driven by the primeval horror his Stone Age ancestors must have experienced: the fear of being eaten. As the whales neared, he could hear the soft watery sound they made as air was expelled through their blowholes.

Souf-souf.

Just as he expected sharp teeth to sink into his flesh, the chorus of steamy exhalations was drowned out by the roar of powerful engines. Through water-blurred eyes, he saw sun reflecting off a boat's hull. Hands reached down to grab his arms. His knees banged painfully against the hard, plastic side of the boat, and he flopped onto the deck like a landed fish.

A man was bending over him. 'Are you okay?'

Austin gulped in a lungful of air and thanked the unknown Samaritan for his help.

'What's going on?' the man said.

'A whale attacked me.'

'That's impossible,' the man said. 'They're like big, friendly dogs.'

'Tell that to the whales.'

Austin scrambled to his feet. He was on a well-appointed powerboat around thirty feet long. The man who had pulled him from the water had a shaved bald head with a spider tattoo on the scalp. His eyes were hidden behind sunglasses with reflective blue lenses, and he wore black jeans and a black leather jacket.

Set into the deck behind the man was a strange, cone-shaped, metal framework about six feet high. Thick electrical cables sprouted from the framework like vines. Austin stared at the weird construction for a second, but he was more interested in what was happening out on the water.

The pod of orcas that had chased him like a pack of hungry sea wolves was swinging away from the boat and was now headed toward the other kayakers. A few people had seen Austin go over, but they had not been close enough to witness the attack. With Austin gone, the racers were in a state of confusion. Some continued to paddle slowly. Most had simply stopped dead in the water, where they sat like rubber ducks in a bathtub.

The orcas were closing in fast on the bewildered racers. Even more frightening, other pods of whales had appeared around the kayak flotilla and were gathering around for the kill. The racers were unaware of the sharp-toothed danger headed their way. Many of them had paddled the sound and knew that the orcas were harmless.

Austin grabbed the boat's steering wheel. 'Hope you don't mind,' he said as he punched up the throttle.

The man's reply was lost in the roar of twin outboard motors. The boat quickly got up on plane. Austin pointed the bow at the narrowing gap between the kayakers and the moving fins. He hoped that the noise of the engines and hull would disrupt the orcas. His heart sank when the whales split into two groups and went around him, still intent on their targets. He knew orcas communicated with each other to coordinate their attacks. Within seconds, the pod hit the kayak fleet like a spread of torpedoes. They rammed the light boats with their huge bodies. Several kayaks went over and their passengers were thrown into the water.

Austin slowed the boat's speed and steered between the bobbing heads of children and their parents and the knife-like orca fins. The *White Lightning* had moved closer to some capsized kayaks, but the situation was too chaotic for it to be of any help. Austin saw one of the tallest fins bearing down on a man who was floating in the water holding his young daughter in his arms. Austin would have to run over the other kayakers to get to them. He turned to the boat's owner.

'Do you have a rifle speargun on board?'

The bald man was fiddling frantically with an instrument box that was connected to the framework by a cable. He looked up from what he was doing and shook his head.

'It's okay,' he said. 'Look!' He pointed toward the mass of overturned kayaks.

The big fin had stopped moving. It remained stationary,

playfully wobbling in place, only feet from the man and his daughter. Then it began to move *away* from the broken kayaks and their hapless paddlers.

The other fins followed. The surrounding pods that had been closing in broke off their attack and meandered back into the open waters. The big bull breached in a high, playful leap. Within minutes, none of the orcas was in sight.

A young boy had become separated from his parent. His flotation vest must have been donned improperly, because his head was slipping below the surface. Austin climbed up on the gunwale and launched his body into the air. He hit the water in a shallow racing dive and stroked his way to the boy. He reached him just before he went under.

Austin treaded water, holding the youngster's head above the surface. He only had to wait a few moments. The *White Lightning* had launched its inflatable life rafts, and racers were being plucked from the water. Austin handed the boy up to his rescuers and pivoted in the water. The bald man and his boat had disappeared.

Kurt Austin Senior was an older mirror image of his son. His broad shoulders had a slight sag, but they still looked fully capable of battering their way through a wall. His thick, platinum-silver hair was worn shorter than that of his son, who tended to be away from barbers for long periods of time.

Although he was in his mid-seventies, a strict regimen of exercise and diet had kept him trim and fit. He could still put in a workday that would have exhausted men half his age. His face was tanned from sun and sea, and his bronze skin was laced with a fine network of wrinkles. His blue-green eyes could blaze with lionlike ferocity, but, like those

39

of his son, they usually looked out at the world with gentle amusement.

The two Austins were seated in plush chairs in the *White Lightning*'s luxurious main cabin, nursing oversize shots of Jack Daniel's. Kurt had borrowed a tailored sweat suit from his father. The waters of Puget Sound had been like a bathtub filled with ice cubes, and the liquor trickling down Kurt's throat was replacing the chill in his outer extremities with pleasing warmth.

The cabin was furnished in leather and brass and decorated with polo and horse-racing prints. Kurt felt as if he were in one of those exclusive English men's clubs where a member could die in his overstuffed chair and not be discovered for days. His hard-driving father was not exactly the English gentleman type, and Kurt guessed that the atmosphere was designed to smooth the rough edges brought on by his hardscrabble fight to get to the top in a competitive business.

The old man replenished their glasses and offered Kurt a Cuban Cohiba Lanceros cigar, which he politely refused. Austin lit up, and puffed out a purple cloud that enveloped his head.

'What the hell went on out there today?'

Kurt's mind was still a blur. He reconsidered the cigar offer, and as he went through the manly ritual of lighting up he ordered his thoughts. He took another sip from his glass, and laid out the story.

'Crazy!' Austin said, summing up his reaction. 'Hell, those whales never hurt anyone. You know that. You've sailed the sound since you were a kid. You ever hear of anything like that happening?'

'Nope,' Kurt said. 'Orcas seem to *like* being around humans, which has always puzzled me.'

40

Austin replied with a loud guffaw. 'That's no mystery. They're smart, and they know that we're badass predators just like them.'

'The only difference is that they kill mainly for food.'

'Good point,' Austin said. He went to pour another shot, which Kurt waved off. He knew better than to try keeping up with his father.

'You know everyone in Seattle. Ever come across a bald guy with a spider tattoo on his head? Probably in his thirties. Dresses like a Hell's Angel, in black leather.'

'The only one who meets that description is Spiderman Barrett.'

'Didn't know you were into the comics, Pop.'

Austin's face crinkled in laughter. 'Barrett's a whiz kid computer geek who made it big out here. Sort of a minor-league Bill Gates. Only worth three billion bucks, maybe. He's got a big house overlooking the sound.'

'I feel for him. Do you know him personally?'

'Only by sight. He was a fixture on the local nightclub circuit. Then he dropped out of circulation.'

'What's with the head art?'

'Story I heard is that when he was a kid, he was a big Spiderman fan. Cut his hair, had his scalp tattooed and let his hair grow back. As he got older and started to go bald, the tattoo showed, so he shaved his head. Hell, with the kind of money Barrett has he could decorate his body with the Sunday funnies and nobody would blink an eye.'

'Eccentric or not, he saved me from becoming whale bait. I'd like to thank him, and apologize for commandeering his boat.'

Austin was about to tell his father about the metal structure on Barrett's boat, but a crewman came into the cabin and announced, 'Someone from Fish and Wildlife is here.'

A moment later, a petite, young, dark-haired woman dressed in the green uniform of the US Fish and Wildlife Service entered the cabin. She was in her mid-twenties, although her black-rimmed glasses and serious expression made her look more mature. She identified herself as Sheila Rowland, and said she wanted to ask Kurt about his whale encounter.

'Sorry to barge in on you,' she said in apology. 'We've closed off further kayak expeditions in Puget Sound until we can get to the bottom of this incident. Whale watching is a big part of the local economy, so we've put the investigation on the fast track. The vendors are starting to scream about the ban, but we can't take chances.'

Austin told her to take a seat, and Kurt went through his story for a second time.

'That's so strange,' she said with a shake of her head. 'I've never known orcas to hurt anyone.'

'What about attacks in marine parks?' Kurt said.

'Those are whales that are held in captivity and put under pressure to perform. They get angry at being cooped up and overworked, and sometimes they take out their frustrations on the trainers. There have been a few cases in the wild where an orca has grabbed a surfboard, thinking it's a seal. Once they discover their mistake, they've spit the surfer out.'

'I guess the whale I encountered didn't like my face,' Austin said with dry humor.

Rowland smiled, thinking that with his bronzed features and intense, light blue eyes, Austin was one of the most attractive men she had ever met. 'I don't think that's the case. If an orca didn't like your face, you wouldn't *have* one. I've seen a whale toss round a five-hundred-pound sea lion as if it were a rag doll. I'll see if there is any video coverage of the incident.'

'That shouldn't be a problem, with all the cameras focused on the race,' Kurt said. 'Is there anything you could think of that would stir up the whales and make them more aggressive?'

She shook her head. 'Orcas have extremely fine-tuned sensing systems. If something gets out of whack, they might want to take it out on the nearest object.'

'Like the overworked whales in the marine parks?'

'Maybe. I'll talk to some cetologists and see what they have to say.' She rose and thanked the two men for their time. After she left, Austin's father went to pour another round, but Kurt put his hand over the glass.

'I know what you're doing, you old fox. You're trying to shanghai me onto one of your salvage ships.'

Kurt Senior had made no secret of his desire to lure his son from NUMA and bring him back into the family business. Kurt's decision to stay with NUMA rather than take over the reins of the business had been a sore point between the two men. Through the years, what had been a bitter source of friction became a family joke.

'You're turning into a sissy,' Austin said with mock disgust. 'You've got to admit that NUMA hasn't cornered the market on excitement.'

'I've told you before, Pop. It's not all about excitement.'

'Yeah, I know. Duty to country and all that. Worst thing is, I can't blame Sandecker anymore for keeping you in Washington now that he's vice president. What are your plans?'

'I'll stick around a couple more days. I've got to order a new kayak. What about you?'

'Got a big job raising a sunken fishing boat off Hanes, Alaska. Want to come along? I could use you.'

'Thanks, but I'm sure you can handle the project yourself.'

'Can't blame me for trying. Okay, then, I'll buy dinner.'

Austin was sawing through a manhole-sized slab of beef at his father's favorite steak house when he felt his cell phone vibrating. He excused himself and took the call in the lobby. Looking at Austin from the video phone's tiny display screen was a dark-complexioned man with thick black hair combed straight back. Joe Zavala was a member of Austin's Special Assignments Team who had been recruited by Sandecker right out of the New York Maritime College. He was a brilliant marine engineer whose expertise in designing submersibles had found a ready niche at NUMA.

'Glad to see you're still in once piece,' Zavala said. 'The orca attack on your kayak race is all over the news. Are you okay?'

'I'm fine. In fact, you might say I had a *whale* of a time.'

Zavala cracked the tips of his lips in a slight smile. 'I lead such a dull life. Who else but Kurt Austin could turn a charity kayak race into a life-and-death struggle with a bunch of loco killer whales?'

'The last time I looked you were well along in your goal of dating every eligible woman in Washington. I'd hardly call that dull.'

The gregarious Zavala was much in demand by many of the single women around Washington who were attracted by his charm, his soulful dark brown eyes and Latin good looks.

'I'll admit that life can get interesting when I run into an old date when I'm out with a new one, but that's nothing compared to your race. What happened?'

'I'm having dinner with my father, so I'll have to fill you in when I get back in a couple of days.'

'Looks like you'll be back in Washington sooner than that. We've been ordered to sail out of Norfolk tomorrow night. Do you know Jerry Adler?'

'The name sounds familiar. Isn't he a wave guy out at Scripps?'

'He's one of the foremost ocean wave experts in the world. We're going to help him find the *Southern Belle*.'

'I remember reading about the *Belle*. She's the big containership that went down last March.'

'That's right. Rudi called me. Adler wants you on the project. Apparently, he's got some clout, because Rudi agreed to his request.' Rudi Gunn was in charge of NUMA's day-to-day operations.

'That's odd. I've never even met Adler. Sure he didn't make a mistake? There are a dozen guys at NUMA who've worked searches. Why me?'

'Rudi said he didn't have a clue. But Adler has an international reputation, so he went along with his request to help find the ship.'

'Interesting. The *Belle* went down off the mid-Atlantic coast. How close is the search area to where the Trouts are working?' Paul and Gamay Trout, the other members of the Special Assignments Team, were in the midst of an ocean survey.

'Close enough so that we can raft up and have a party,' Zavala said. 'I've already packed the tequila.'

'While you line up a caterer, I'll change my plane reservations, and let you know when I'm coming in.'

'I'll meet you at the airport. We'll have a plane waiting to fly us to Norfolk.'

They discussed a few more details and hung up. Kurt pondered the request from Adler, then went back to his table to tell his father he would be leaving in the morning.

If Austin was annoyed about his son's change in plans, he didn't show it. He thanked Kurt for coming to Seattle for the kayak race, and they vowed to get together again when they had more time.

Kurt caught an early flight out of Seattle the next morning. As the plane took off and headed east, he thought about his father's muted reaction to his change in plans. He wondered if Austin Senior really wanted him to join the family business. To the old man, it would be admitting that he was on the road to retirement. Both men tended to have strong opinions, and it would be like having two captains on a rowboat.

In any case, his father was plain wrong about Kurt's attachment to his NUMA work. It wasn't the excitement that kept him at the huge ocean science agency. Every opportunity for an adrenaline rush meant many long hours of reports, paperwork and meetings, which he tried to avoid by staying in the field. The siren call that lured him back again and again was the unfathomed *mystery* of the sea.

Mysteries like the strange encounter with the killer whales. He pondered the incident with the orcas. He wondered, too, about the man with the weird tattoo and the purpose of the electrical setup he'd seen on Barrett's boat. After a few minutes, he put his formless thoughts aside, picked up a pad and a ballpoint pen and began to sketch out specifications for a new kayak.

3

Before Frank Malloy had become a high-priced consultant to the nation's police departments, he'd been the quintessential cop. He loathed disorder of any kind. His uniforms were always pressed and sharply creased. In a holdover from his Marine Corps days, his salt-and-pepper hair was cut close to the scalp, military style. Frequent workouts kept his compact body fit and muscular.

Unlike many police officers who found stakeout tedious, Malloy enjoyed sitting for hours in a car, watching the ebb and flow of traffic and pedestrians, ever alert for the slightest rent in the fabric of society. It also helped that he had an iron bladder.

Malloy was parked on Broadway, checking out the steady parade of fast-walking pedestrians and gawking tourists, when a man cut away from the crowd and made his way straight for the unmarked NYPD cruiser.

The man was tall and slim, and looked to be in his thirties. He wore a tan, lightweight suit, wrinkled at the knees, and scuffed New Balance running shoes. He had red hair and beard, and his goatee was cut to a point. His shirt collar was unbuttoned and his tie hung loose. Years as a beat cop had honed Malloy's ability to size up people at a quick glance. Malloy pegged the man as a reporter.

The man came over to the car, bent down so his face was level with the window and flashed his photo ID.

'My name is Lance Barnes. I'm a reporter with the *Times*. Are you Frank Malloy?'

The question spoiled Malloy's triumph.

'Yeah, I'm Malloy,' he said with a frown. 'How did you make me, Mr Barnes?'

'Easy,' the reporter said with a shrug of his shoulders. 'You're sitting alone in a dark blue Ford in a neighborhood where it's practically impossible to get parking.'

'I must be losing my touch,' Malloy said dolefully. 'Either that or I've still got cop written all over me.'

'Naw, I cheated,' Barnes said with a grin. 'They told me at the MACC that you'd be here.'

MACC was shorthand for the Multi-Agency Control Center, the entity in charge of security for the international economic conference that was being held in New York City. Political and business leaders were converging on the Big Apple from all over the world.

'I cheated too,' Malloy said with a chuckle. 'MACC called and said you were coming over.' He studied the reporter's face and decided he looked familiar. 'We met before, Mr Barnes?'

'I think you gave me a jaywalking ticket.'

Malloy laughed. He never forgot a face. It would come to him. 'What can I do for you?'

'I'm doing a story on the conference. I've heard you're the top consultant in the field when it comes to dealing with sophisticated techniques of disruption. I wondered if I could interview you about how you plan to deal with the planned protests.'

Malloy owned a firm in Arlington, Virginia, that advised police departments around the country on crowd control. He was on the boards of a number of companies that made riot-control equipment, and his business and political connections had made him relatively rich. A favorable story in *The New York Times* could mean even bigger bucks for his consulting business.

'Slide in,' he said and reached over to open the passenger door. Barnes got in the car, and they shook hands. The reporter shoved his sunglasses onto his forehead, revealing intense green eyes and sharply angled eyebrows that formed a V similar to the shape of his mouth and chin. He pulled a notebook and a miniature digital recorder from his pocket. 'Hope you don't mind if I record this. It's insurance, to make sure my quotes are right.'

'No problem,' Malloy said. 'You can say anything you want about me, but just spell my name right.' Since he'd left law enforcement and started his consulting company, Malloy had become a pro at handling reporters. 'You were at the press conference?'

'Oh yeah,' Barnes said. 'Quite the arsenal! The Long Range Acoustic Devices you've got mounted on the Humvees just blow my mind. Is it true those things were used in Iraq?'

'They're considered nonlethal weapons. They can let out an earsplitting screech that drowns out even the loudest demonstrators.'

'If someone blasted one hundred and fifty decibels in my ear, I'd stop chanting about peace and justice.'

'We'll only use the screamers to communicate with large crowds. We tested them the other day. Good for four blocks at least.'

'Uh-huh,' the reporter said, jotting down a few notes. 'The anarchists will get the message, all right.'

'My guess is that we won't need the big artillery. It's the little stuff that counts, like the scooter patrols and mechanical barriers.'

49

'I've heard you've got a lot of high-tech stuff too.'

'True,' Malloy said. 'The most effective way to control the crazies is with *software*, not hardware.'

'How so?'

'Let's take a ride.' Malloy turned the key in the ignition. As the car pulled away from the curb, he got on the radio. 'This is Nomad. Heading north on Broadway.'

'*Nomad?*' Barnes said after Malloy had signed off.

'I wander around a lot. Keeping an eye on things. The crazies know I'm on the move, but they don't know where I am. Keeps them on edge.' He turned east, drove a short distance on Park, then made his way back to Broadway.

'Who are these "crazies," as you call them?'

'When it comes to anarchists, you never know who or what you're dealing with. Back in Seattle, we had enviro nuts and peace nuts. We had Wiccans and feminist neo-pagans, yelling about the WTO and the Goddess, whoever *she* is. Most of your mainstream anarchists are against the world economic order. They're nonviolent when it comes to people, but some of them say corporate property is fair game. Chaos is their main weapon. They're usually organized in autonomous collectives or affinity groups. They act by consensus and avoid any kind of hierarchy.'

'Given their lack of organization, what exactly are you looking for?'

'Hard to describe,' Malloy said. 'Pretty much the same stuff I did when I was on the street. The crazies will split up into small groups. Pairs or singles. I just look for patterns of behavior.'

'I've read about the Seattle protests. Sounds like that was a nightmare.'

Malloy let out a low whistle. 'I've still got the scars to prove it. What a *mess*!'

'What went wrong?'

'The crazies targeted the World Trade Organization. What they call the "power elite". I was a district supervisor in charge of crowd control. We got caught with our pants around our ankles. Ended up with a hundred thousand demonstrators pissed off at what they said was an oppressive world trade system. There was looting, curfews, cops and National Guard running around shooting rubber bullets or tear gas at the nonviolent as well as violent protesters. The city ended up with an international black eye and a pile of lawsuits. Some people said the police overreacted. Others said they didn't do enough. Go figure.'

'As you said, a major mess.'

Malloy nodded. 'But the Battle of Seattle was the turning point.'

'In what way?'

'The protesters learned that marching down the street wasn't enough to get attention. Only *direct* action worked. You had to break things up, inconvenience people, disrupt the focus of the people in your bull's-eye.'

'From what I've seen around the city today, the power elite have come a long way since Seattle.'

'Hundred percent,' Malloy said. 'I was in Philly for the GOP convention when the anarchists made us look silly again. They'd raise hell, then run down the streets with a bunch of overweight cops chasing them. Created chaos and confusion. They stirred up the pot at the WTO conference in Miami too. We finally began to get a handle on things at the World Economic Forum here in 2002, and pretty much had our strategy in place for the Republican Convention in 2004.'

'You kept disruptions to a minimum, but there were complaints about civil rights being violated.'

'That's part of the protest strategy. These guys are sophisticated. It's mostly a small group of hard-core instigators that moves from city to city. They provoke authority hoping we'll overreact. Whoops!'

Malloy pulled off to the side, double-parking near a group of people carrying musical instruments, and barked into his hand radio.

'Nomad to MACC. Guerrilla musicians gathering for an unpermitted march from Union Square to Madison Square Garden.'

Barnes scanned the sidewalk on both sides of the street. 'I don't see anyone marching.'

'They're walking in two-by-twos now. Nothing illegal about that. They'll start coming together in a minute – no, wait, there they go now.'

The musicians were coalescing into larger groups, stepping off the curb into the street to form a procession. But before the parade began, police officers on bicycles and scooters swooped in from both sides and began to make arrests.

Barnes furiously scribbled notes.

'I'm impressed,' he said. 'That went off like clockwork.'

'It should. That little maneuver was the result of years of experience. We're only dealing with an in-between economic conference, but there are hundreds of guests and protesters, so there's the potential of big trouble. The crazies are always trying to stay one step ahead of us.'

'How do you tell the real fanatics from people who simply want to protest?'

'Pretty hard. We just arrest anyone who's a troublemaker and sort things out later.' He took a ringing cell phone from its dashboard cradle and handed it to Barnes. 'Check this out.'

The reporter read the text on the phone's message screen. 'It says that the scooter goon squad is wrapped around the guerrilla musicians. Telling people to avoid this neighborhood. Calling for cameras. Medics and legal observers. Says to blockade cops from arresting demonstrators harassing people in the Theater District. Who's this from?'

'The *crazies*. The cops aren't the *only* ones who learned from Seattle. The anarchists have their own MACC-type media center. They tell the activists what routes to take to stay away from the cops. While we shut down one operation, they're starting another.' He laughed. 'We're spending multimillions each year on security measures, and they use technology that's practically free.'

'Don't they know you can read the same messages?'

'Sure. But the demonstrations are more spontaneous, so we're always playing cat-and-mouse games with each other. *Intel* is the name of the game. They're fast, but it comes down to numbers. We've got thirty-seven thousand cops, a blimp, helicopters, video cameras and two hundred of our guys have helmet video cameras connected to the security nerve center.'

'Can't they monitor the police scanners?'

'We *know* that they do. Rapid response is the key. You know what they say in a fight, a good big guy can beat a good little guy any day. On a level playing field, we're going to win.'

Barnes handed the phone to Malloy. 'This appears to be for you.'

The text printed on the message screen had changed.

GOOD MORNING, NOMAD. OR SHOULD WE CALL YOU FRANK, MR MALLOY?

'Huh?' Malloy said. He looked at the phone in his hand as if it had turned to a snake.

'How the hell are they doing this?' he said, turning to Barnes. The reporter shrugged and made some notes. Malloy tried to clear the screen, but a new message came on.

PLAY TIME.

The screen went blank. Malloy snatched up the radio and tried to call MACC, but the call wouldn't go through. The cell phone rang again. Malloy listened a few moments, and said, 'I'll get right on it.' He turned to Barnes, his face pale. 'That was MACC. They say that the air-conditioning broke down in the nerve center. The communications are going haywire. No one knows where the squads are. Traffic lights have gone red all over town.'

They were approaching Times Square. Hundreds of demonstrators, apparently unimpeded by the police, were pouring into the square from the side streets. The square was as crowded as New Year's Eve.

Malloy's cruiser moved slowly through the mob that surged around it. As they approached the old *New York Times* Building, the huge video screen stopped showing a Disney character and went black.

'Hey, look at that,' Barnes said, pointing at the screen.

Big letters had appeared in white, streaming across the ABC News Spectacular sign.

GREETINGS, NEO-ANARCHISTS, FELLOW TRAVELERS AND TOURISTS. WE HAVE SHUT DOWN THE OPPRESSIVE ARMIES OF THE POWER ELITE. THIS IS A SMALL TASTE OF THE FUTURE. TODAY IT'S NEW YORK. NEXT WE'LL SHUT DOWN THE WORLD. CONVENE A SUMMIT CONFERENCE TO DISMANTLE THE FRAMEWORK OF GLOBALIZATION OR WE'LL DISMANTLE IT FOR YOU.

HAVE A NICE DAY!

A smiley face with horns appeared, then a single word: LUCIFER.

'Who the hell is *Lucifer*?' Malloy said, staring through the windshield.

'Beats me,' Barnes said. He reached for the door handle. 'Thanks for the ride. I've got to file a story.'

Then the word disappeared, and FRANK MALLOY appeared simultaneously on every sign of every size on the square. Panasonic. LG. NASDAQ.

Malloy cursed and scrambled out of the car. He scanned the milling crowd. Barnes had been swallowed up among the thousands of protesters. He muttered the name 'Lucifer' and a chill ran up his spine. It came to him where he had seen the reporter's face. The pointed beard, the red hair and the V-angled brows and mouth and the green eyes had subconsciously reminded him of renderings he had seen of Satan.

As Malloy stood there wondering if he had gone crazy, he was unaware that he was under the gaze of those same jade eyes. Barnes had stepped into the doorway of an office building where he could watch Malloy. He held a cell phone to his ear, and he was laughing.

'I just wanted you to know that your plan went off like clockwork. The city is in total breakdown.'

'That's great,' said the voice on the other end of the line. 'Look, we've got to talk. It's important.'

'Not now. Come out to the lighthouse, so I can thank you in person.'

He tucked the phone in his pocket and gazed out at Times Square. A young man had thrown a brick through the front window of the Disney store. Others followed his example, and within minutes the sidewalks were littered with broken glass. A car was set on fire, sending black billowing smoke toward the heavens. The acrid stench of burning plastic and fabric filled the air. A guerrilla band was marching down the street, playing the theme from *Bridge on the River Kwai*. The music could barely be heard over the cacophony of honking car horns.

Barnes gazed at the scene with a beatific smile on his satanic face.

'Chaos,' he murmured like a monk chanting his mantra. 'Sweet, sweet chaos.'

4

The deck lights were ablaze when the NUMA car carrying Austin and Zavala pulled up to the dock at Norfolk. Austin climbed the gangway with a jaunty step. He was happy to be going back to sea, and excited about sailing on the research vessel *Peter Throckmorton*, one of the newest ships in the NUMA fleet. He owed the mysterious Dr Adler a debt for inviting him on the search expedition.

The 275-foot ship was named after one of the early pioneers in nautical archaeology. Throckmorton had proven that archaeological methods could work underwater, spurring a whole era of discovery. The ship was a seagoing workhorse. It was designed with versatility in mind, and its remote-sensing equipment could just as easily explore an underwater city as a field of hypothermal ocean vents.

Like most research vessels, the *Throckmorton* was a seagoing platform from which scientists could launch vehicles and probes to carry out their experiments. Sprouting from the fantail and foredeck were the booms and cranes that could be used to deploy the various undersea probes and submersibles the ship carried. Power winches were located on the port and starboard sides.

One of the ship's officers greeted the NUMA men at the top of the gangway.

'Captain Cabral welcomes you aboard the *Throckmorton* and wishes you a pleasant trip.'

Austin knew the captain, Tony Cabral, from other NUMA expeditions, and looked forward to seeing him again.

'Please thank the captain, and tell him we're pleased to be sailing under his command.'

With the brief formalities over, a crewman escorted them to their comfortable cabins. They dropped off their duffel bags and went to find Adler. At the suggestion of the crewman, they looked for him in the vessel's survey control center.

The center was a spacious semidark room on the main deck. The walls were lined with banks of monitors that served as the eyes and ears for the ship's remote-sensing gear. When a probe was launched, the information it gathered was transmitted to the center for analysis. With the ship still in port, the room was deserted except for a man who sat at a table pecking away at a computer keyboard.

'Dr Adler?' Kurt said.

The man looked up from his keyboard and smiled. 'Yes. And you must be the folks from NUMA?'

Austin and Zavala introduced themselves and shook hands with Adler.

The wave scientist was a rumpled, big-boned man who had the physique of a lumberjack and a mop of shaggy, silver hair that looked like Spanish moss growing on an old oak. His upper lip was adorned by a crooked mustache that looked as if it had been pasted on his face as an afterthought. He had a rumbling voice and a grumpy way of talking, as if he had just got up from a nap, but the alert, gray eyes that squinted at them through wire-rimmed glasses sparkled with good humor. He thanked them for coming, and pulled over a couple of chairs.

'You don't know how glad I am to see you gentlemen. I wasn't sure Rudi Gunn would go along with my request to have you on the expedition, Kurt. Getting Joe here is an unexpected bonus. I was probably being a bit persistent.

Blame my Quaker background. Friendly persuasion and all that. We don't push; we sort of lean on people until they notice us.'

The professor would never have to worry about going unnoticed, Austin thought. 'No apologies needed,' he said. 'I'm always up for a sea cruise. I was surprised that you specifically wanted me on board. We've never met.'

'But I've heard a lot about you. And I know that NUMA likes to tout its accomplishments without specifically attributing them to the work of your Special Assignments Team.'

The team had been the brainchild of Admiral Sandecker, who ran NUMA before Dirk Pitt took over as director. He wanted a group of experts for undersea assignments that sometimes took place outside the realm of government oversight. At the same time, he used the team's more spectacular missions to leverage funds out of Congress.

'You're right. We prefer to minimize our role.'

Adler responded with a big-toothed grin. 'It's very hard to minimize the discovery of the body of Columbus in an underwater Mayan pyramid. Or to belittle the prevention of a methane hydrate tsunami off the East Coast.'

'Dumb luck,' Austin said. 'We were only doing some troubleshooting.'

Zavala rolled his eyes. 'Kurt says that the only problem being a troubleshooter is that trouble sometimes shoots back.'

'I'll concede that the Special Assignments Team has taken on some odd missions, but NUMA has dozens of technicians far more capable than I am at search and survey. Why did you ask for me?'

Adler's face grew solemn. 'Something very strange is going on in the ocean.'

'Nothing new there,' Austin said. 'The sea is more alien than outer space. We know more about the stars than the planet under our feet.'

'I'd be the first to agree with you,' Adler said. 'It's just that, well, I've got some crazy ideas banging around the inside of my skull.'

'Joe and I learned a long time ago that there's a thin line between crazy and rational. We'd like to hear what you have to say.'

'I'll run them by you in due time, but I'd prefer to wait until we find the *Southern Belle*.'

'No hurry. Tell us about the *Belle*'s disappearance. As I recall, she was sailing off the mid-Atlantic coast. She sent out an SOS, saying she was in trouble, then she vanished without a trace.'

'That's right. An intensive search was launched within hours. The sea seemed to have swallowed her up. It's been tough on the crew's families not knowing what happened to their loved ones. From a practical point of view, the owners would like to get their legal house in order.'

'Ships have disappeared without a clue going back hundreds of years,' Austin said. 'It still happens, even with instantaneous and worldwide communication.'

'But the *Belle* wasn't simply *any* ship. It was about as close to an unsinkable vessel as possible.'

Austin grinned. 'That sounds vaguely familiar.'

Adler raised his finger. 'I know. The same thing was said about the *Titanic*. But the science of shipbuilding has made huge leaps since the *Titanic* went down. The *Belle* was an entirely new type of oceangoing cargo vessel. It was built strong enough to withstand the most severe weather. You said that this isn't the first time a well-made vessel has vanished. Absolutely right. A cargo ship named the *Munchen* disappeared in a storm while crossing the Atlantic in 1978. Like the *Belle*, it radioed an SOS, saying it was in trouble. No one could understand what could have happened to such a modern ship. Twenty-seven crewmen were lost.'

'Tragic. Was any trace of the ship ever found?' Austin asked.

'Rescue attempts started immediately after the SOS. More than a hundred ships combed the ocean. They found some wreckage, and an empty lifeboat that provided a valuable clue. The boat would have hung by pins on the starboard side more than sixty feet above the waterline. The steel pins attached to the boat were found to be bent from forward to aft.'

Zavala's mechanical mind immediately saw the significance of the damage to the ship. 'Easy call,' he said. 'A violent force at least sixty feet tall knocked the lifeboat off its pins.'

'The Maritime Court said the ship sank when bad weather caused an "unusual event".'

Austin chuckled. 'Sounds as if the Maritime Court was dancing around the real conclusion.'

'The mariners who heard the court's findings would agree with you. They were outraged. They knew *exactly* what sunk the *Munchen*. Sailors had been talking for years about their encounters with waves eighty or ninety feet tall, but the scientists didn't believe their stories.'

'I've heard the stories about monster waves, but I've never experienced one firsthand.'

'Be thankful, because we wouldn't be having this conversation if you had run into one of these creatures.'

'In a way, I don't blame the Maritime Court for being cautious,' Austin said. 'Sailors do have a reputation for stretching the truth.'

'I can vouch for that,' Zavala said with a wistful smile. 'I've been hearing about mermaids for years without seeing one.'

'No doubt the court was leery of headlines about vampire killer waves,' Adler said. 'According to the conventional scientific wisdom at the time, waves like the ones the mariners reported were theoretically impossible. We scientists had been using a set of mathematical equations, called the Linear Model, which said that a ninety-foot wave occurs only once every ten thousand years.'

'Apparently, after the loss of the *Munchen*, we don't have anything to worry about for the next hundred centuries,' Austin said with a wry grin.

'That was the thinking before the Draupner case.'

'You're talking about the Draupner oil rig off Norway?'

'You've heard of Draupner?'

'I worked on North Sea rigs for six years,' Austin said. 'It would be hard to find anyone on a rig who hadn't heard about the wave that slammed into the Draupner tower.'

'The rig is about one hundred miles out to sea,' Adler explained to Zavala. 'The North Sea is infamous for its lousy weather, but a real stinker of a storm came in on New Year's Day 1985. The rig was getting battered by thirty- to forty-foot waves. Then they got slammed with a wave that the rig's sensors measured at ninety feet. It still leaves me breathless to think about it.'

'Sounds like the Draupner wave washed the Linear Model down the drain,' Zavala said.

'It blew the model out of the sea. That wave was more than thirty feet *higher* than the model would have predicted for the ten-thousand-year wave. A German scientist named Julian Wolfram installed a radar setup on the Draupner platform. Over four years, Wolfram measured every wave that hit the platform. He found twenty-four waves that exceeded the limits of the Linear Model.'

'So the tall tales weren't so tall,' Austin said. 'Maybe Joe will meet Minnie the Mermaid after all.'

'I don't know if I'd go that far, but Wolfram's research showed that the legends had a basis in fact. When he plotted out the graph, he found that these new waves were steeper, as well as bigger, than ordinary waves. Wolfram's work hit the shipping industry like a, well, like a freak wave. For years, marine architects had used the Linear Model to build ships strong enough to handle a wave of no more than forty feet or so. Weather forecasts had been based on the same flawed premise.'

'From what you're saying, every ship on the sea was vulnerable to being sunk by a killer wave,' Zavala said.

Adler nodded. 'It would have meant billions in retro-fitting and redesign. The potential for an economic disaster spurred more research. The attention focused on the coast off South Africa where many mariners had encountered freak waves. When scientists plotted ship accidents off the African cape, they found that they lay on a line along the Agulhus current. The big waves seemed to occur primarily when warm currents ran against cold currents. Over a ten-year period in the 1990s, twenty ships were lost in this area.'

'The shipping industry must have breathed a big sigh of relief,' Austin said. 'All a ship had to do was steer clear of that neighborhood.'

'They learned it wasn't that simple. In 1995, the *Queen Elizabeth II* encountered a ninety-foot wave in the North Atlantic. In 2001, two tourist cruisers, the *Bremen* and the *Caledonian Star*, were slammed by ninety-foot waves far from the current. Both ships survived to tell the tale.'

'That would imply that the Agulhus current isn't the only place these waves occur,' Austin said.

'Correct. There were no opposing currents near these ships. We paired this information with the statistics and came to some unsettling conclusions. More than two hundred supertankers and containerships longer than six hundred feet had been sunk around the world over a twenty-year span. Freak waves seemed to play a major role in these losses.'

'Those are pretty grim statistics.'

'They're horrendous! Because of the serious implications for shipping, we have set out to improve ship design, and to see if forecasting is possible.'

'I wonder if the research project the Trouts are working on has anything to do with these steroid waves,' Zavala said.

'Paul Trout and his wife, Gamay Morgan-Trout, are our NUMA colleagues,' Austin explained to the professor. 'They're on the NOAA ship *Benjamin Franklin*, doing a study of ocean eddies in this area.'

Adler pinched his chin in thought. 'That's an intriguing suggestion. It's certainly worth looking into. I wouldn't rule *any*thing out at this point.'

'You said something about forecasting these freak waves,' Austin said.

'Shortly after the *Bremen* and *Caledonian Star* incidents, the Europeans launched a satellite that scanned the world's oceans. In three weeks, the satellites picked out ten waves like the ones that nearly sank the two ships.'

'Has anyone been able to figure out the cause of these killer waves?'

'Some of us have been working with a principle in quantum mechanics called the Schrödinger equation. It's a bit complicated, but it accounts for the way things can appear and disappear with no apparent reason. "Vampire wave" is a good name for the phenomena. They suck up energy from other waves and, *voilà*, we have our huge monster. We still don't know what triggers these things in the first place.'

'From what you've said, every ship whose hull is built to withstand seas based on the Linear Model could suffer the same fate as the *Southern Belle*.'

'Oh, it gets better than that, Kurt. *Much better.*'

'I don't understand.'

'The *Southern Belle*'s designers incorporated the newer data on giant waves into their work. The *Belle* had a covered forecastle, a double hull and strengthening of the transverse bulkheads to prevent flooding.'

Austin stared at the scientist for a moment. Choosing his words carefully, he said, 'That would mean that the ship may have encountered a wave *larger* than ninety feet.'

Adler gestured toward his computer screen. The image showed a series of wave lines and measurements.

'There were actually *two* giant waves, one hundred and one hundred twelve feet high, to be exact. We captured their pictures on satellite.'

Adler had expected his dramatic pronouncement to make an impression, but both men responded with expressions of intense interest rather than the gasps of disbelief that he had expected. Adler knew he had done well in coaxing a favor from Rudi Gunn when Austin turned to his friend and, without missing a beat, calmly announced:

'Looks like we should have brought our surfboards.'

5

Big Mountain, Montana

The old man pushed off from the chairlift and skied with strong skating steps to the top of Black Diamond run. He paused at the brow of the hill, and his cobalt eyes took in the panoramic sweep of sky and mountain. From seven thousand feet, he had an eagle's-eye view of the Flathead Valley and Whitefish Lake. The snowy peaks of Glacier National Park glistened in the east. Stretching out to the north were the jagged teeth of the Canadian Rockies.

No fog shrouded the bald summit. Not a wisp of cloud marred the luminous blue sky. As the warm sunlight toasted his face, he reflected on the debt he owed the mountains. There was no doubt in his mind. Without the clarity offered by the brooding peaks, he would have gone insane.

When World War II ended, Europe began to pull itself back together, but his mind was a jungle full of dark murmurings. No matter that he had lent his deadly skills to the cause of the Resistance. He was still a robotic killer. Worse, he had a fatal defect – humanity. Like any fine-tuned machine with a flawed mechanism, in time he would have flown apart.

He had left the war-ravaged continent for New York, and pushed west until he was thousands of miles from the smoldering European slaughterhouse. He had built a simple log house, cutting and hewing each log with hand tools. The backbreaking labor and the pure air cleansed the shadowed recesses of his memory. The violent nightmares became less frequent. He could sleep without a gun under his pillow and a knife strapped to his thigh.

With the passage of years, he had evolved from a remorseless, polished killing machine into an aging ski bum. The close-cropped blond hair of his youth had turned to a pewter gray that now grew over his ears. A shaggy mustache matched his wild eyebrows. His pale features had become as weathered as buckskin.

As he squinted against the sun-sparkled snow, a smile came to his long-jawed face. He was not a religious man. He could not muster enthusiasm for a Maker who would create something as absurd as Man. If he chose a religion, it would be Druidism, because it made as much sense to worship an oak tree as any deity. At the same time, he regarded each trip to the top of the mountain as a spiritual experience.

This would be the last run of the season. The snow had held late into the spring as it did at higher altitudes, but the light, fluffy champagne power of the winter had given way to wet, heavy corn. Patches of exposed brown earth showed through the thin cover, and the smell of damp earth hung in the air.

He adjusted his goggles and pushed off with his poles, schussing straight down the North Bowl face to gain speed before initiating his first turn. He always started his day with the same trail, a fast bowl run that wound in between silent snow ghosts – strange, phantasmagoric creatures that formed when cold and fog coated trees with rime. He made the smooth, effortless turns he had learned as a child in Kitzbuhl, Austria.

At the bottom of the bowl, he shot down Schmidt's Chute and into a glade. Except for the most dedicated skiers and boarders, most people had hung up their skis to work on their boats and fishing gear. It seemed that he was the master of the mountain.

But as Schroeder broke out of the trees into the open, two skiers emerged from a copse of fir trees.

They skied a few hundred feet behind him, one on either side of the trail. He moved at the same steady pace, making short radius turns that would give the newcomers room. Instead of passing, they matched him turn for turn, until they were skiing three abreast. A long-dormant mental radar kicked on. Too late. The skiers closed on him like the jaws of a pair of pliers.

The old man pulled over to the edge of the trail. His escorts skidded to hockey stops in sprays of snow, one above him and the other below. Their muscular physiques pushed tightly against the fabric of their identical, one-piece silver suits. Their faces were hidden by their mirrored goggles. Only their jaws were visible.

The men stared at him without speaking. They were playing a game of silent intimidation.

He showed his teeth in an alligator smile. 'Mornin',' he said cheerfully in the western accent he had cultivated through the years. 'They don't make days better than this.'

The uphill skier said in a slow, Southern drawl, 'You're Karl Schroeder, if I'm not mistaken.'

The name he had discarded decades before sounded shockingly alien to his ears, but he held his smile.

'I'm afraid you *are* mistaken, friend. My name is Svensen. *Arne* Svensen.'

Taking his time, the skier planted his ski poles into the snow, removed one glove, reached inside his suit and extracted a PPK Walther pistol. 'Let's not play games, *Arne*. We've authenticated your identity with fingerprints.'

Impossible.

'I'm afraid you've confused me with someone else.'

The man chuckled. 'Don't you remember? We were standing behind you at the bar.'

The old man combed his memory and recalled an incident at the Hell Roaring Saloon, the après-ski watering hole at the bottom of the mountain. He had been pounding down beers as only an Austrian can. He had come back to his stool from a restroom break and found his half-filled beer mug had vanished. The bar was busy, and he assumed another customer had mistakenly walked off with his drink.

'The beer mug,' he said. 'That was you.'

The man nodded. 'We watched you for an hour, but it was worth the wait. You left us a full set of fingerprints. We've been on your ass ever since.'

The *schuss-schuss* of skis came from up-trail.

'Don't do anything stupid,' said the man, glancing uphill. He covered the gun with his gloved hand.

A moment later, a lone skier flew by in a blur and disappeared down the trail without slowing.

Schroeder had known that his transformation from cold-blooded warrior to human being would leave him vulnerable. But he had come to believe that his new identity had successfully insulated him from his old life. The gun pointed at his heart was persuasive evidence to the contrary.

'What do you want?' Schroeder said. He spoke with the world-weariness of a fugitive who had been run to ground.

'I want you to shut up and do what I say. They tell me you're an ex-soldier, so you know how to follow orders.'

'Some soldier,' the other man said with undisguised scorn. 'All I see from here is an over-the-hill guy crapping his pants.'

They both laughed.

Good.

They knew he had been in the military, but he guessed they didn't know that he had graduated from one of the world's most notorious killing schools. He had kept his martial arts and marksmanship skills honed, and, although he was pushing eighty, constant physical exercise and strenuous outdoor pursuits had maintained a body many men half his age would have envied.

He remained calm and confident. They would be on his turf, where he knew every tree and boulder.

'I was a soldier a long time ago. Now I'm just an old man.' He lowered his head, hunching his shoulders to project an attitude of submission, and injected a tremor into his deep voice.

'We know a lot more about you than you think,' said the man with a gun. 'We know what you eat, where you sleep. We know where you and your mutt live.'

They had been in his house.

'Where the mutt *used* to live,' said the other man.

He stared at the man. 'You killed my dog? Why?'

'Your little wiener wouldn't stop yapping. We shut him up.'

The friendly little female dachshund he had named Schatsky was probably barking because she was glad to see the intruders.

A coldness seemed to flow into his body. In his mind, he heard his classroom mentor, Professor Heinz. The cherubic psychopath with the kindly blue eyes had been rewarded with a teaching sinecure at the Wevelsburg monastery for his work designing the Nazi death machine.

In skilled hands, nearly any ordinary object can be a lethal weapon, the professor was saying in his soft-spoken voice. *The hard end of this newspaper rolled into a tight coil can be used to break a man's nose and drive the bone splinters into his brain. This fountain*

70

pen can penetrate the eye and cause death. This metal wristwatch band worn across the knuckles is capable of breaking facial bones. This belt makes a wonderful garrote if you can't quickly remove your boot laces . . .

Schroeder's grip tightened on the pole handles.

'I'll do whatever you say,' he said. 'Maybe we can work this out.'

'Sure,' the man said with the flicker of a smile. 'First, I want you to ski slowly to the base of the mountain. Follow my dog-loving friend. He's got a gun too. I'll be right behind you. At the end of the run, take your skis off, stick them in the rack and walk to the east parking lot.'

'May I ask where you're taking me?'

'We're not taking you anywhere. We're *delivering* you.'

'Think of us like FedEx or UPS,' the other man said.

His companion said, 'Nothing personal. Just business. Move it. Nice and easy.' He gestured with the gun, then he tucked it back into his suit so he could ski unhindered.

With the downhill man in the lead and Schroeder in the middle, they skied the trail single file at a moderate speed. Schroeder sized up the man ahead as an aggressive skier whose muscle partly made up for his lack of technical skill. He glanced back at the other man and guessed from his free-form technique that he was the less accomplished skier. Still, they were young and strong, and they were armed.

A snowboarder flew by and disappeared down the trail.

Gambling that his escort would reflexively glance at the moving object, Schroeder made his move. He made a wide turn, but instead of traversing he spun his body around 180 degrees so that he was facing uphill.

His escort didn't see the maneuver until it was too late. He tried to stop. Schroeder jammed his downhill ski into the snow. He grasped his right ski pole with both hands, letting the other pole hang by its strap, and drove the steel tip into the small fleshy part of the man's neck above the turtleneck.

The man was still moving when the tip punched a ragged hole in his throat below the Adam's apple. He let out a wet gurgle, his legs went out from under him and he crashed to the snow where he writhed in terrible agony.

Schroeder sidestepped the flailing body like a matador evading a stricken bull.

The lead man glanced over his shoulder. Schroeder yanked back his improvised spear. He dug his poles in and swooped down the trail. He drove his right elbow into the man's cheek and knocked him off balance. With knees bent and head low in a tuck, he schussed straight down the trail until he neared the bottom of the run, where the trail made a sharp turn to the right.

The second skier must have been carrying a machine pistol under his jacket because the burp of automatic gunfire shattered the mountain stillness.

The shots harmlessly shredded the overhead tree branches.

A second later, Schroeder was safely out of the line of fire.

He turned onto a narrow, double-black expert run that twisted down the side of the mountain like a corkscrew. The ski patrol had strung yellow tape and put up a sign, saying the trail was closed.

Schroeder ducked under the tape. The trail dropped into an almost vertical run. The snow had a brownish tinge, showing that the cover was thin. The surface was broken by large patches of bare ground. Rocks that normally lay under the snow base were exposed.

He heard gunfire behind him, and miniature fountains of mud erupted a few feet away. The shooter was at the top of the ridge, firing down.

Schroeder slalomed between bare ground and rocks. His skis hit slush and almost ground to a stop, but there was just enough of a skim coat to allow the skis to keep sliding.

Schroeder wove his way through a field of short moguls and got onto a steep pitch where the snow cover was adequate. He heard gunshots off to his right. His pursuer was skiing down a trail that was parallel to Schroeder's, firing through the glade that separated them. Most of the shots hit trees. The gunman saw that he was missing his mark and went into the woods separating the two trails.

The man's form resembled a kangaroo on steroids, but he powered his way through the woods in leaps and bounds. Schroeder saw that the man would break out of the trees below him, where he could rake the trail with killing gunfire.

The man fell once, and quickly got back on his skis. The delay would give Schroeder time to ski past the gunman before he broke back into the open. He'd still be an easy target. Instead, as the gunman broke from the woods on the side of the trail, Schroeder charged down on him.

The man saw Schroeder hurtling at him and fumbled for his gun under his suit.

Schroeder slashed with his ski pole at the man's exposed face like a Cossack on a rampage. The blow went high and smashed the man's goggles. He lost his balance, skiing first on one ski, then the other. The gun flew out of his hand. Weaving drunkenly, arms flailing, he pitched over the edge of the trail, where it dropped down steeply for about twenty feet into the woods.

He ended up upside down in the snow depression around the trunk of a large fir tree. His skis were tangled in the lower branches. He struggled to get out of his bindings, but they were out of reach. He hung there helplessly. His breathing was labored.

Schroeder sidestepped his way down the slope. He picked the Uzi out of the snow, where the man had dropped the weapon, and held it loosely in one hand.

'Who are you working for?' Schroeder said.

The man managed to push his smashed goggles onto his head. 'Acme Security,' the man said, speaking with effort.

'Acme?' Schroeder said with a smile.

'They're a big outfit down in Virginia.'

'You knew who I was, you must have known why they wanted me.'

The man shook his head.

'What were you going to do with me?'

'We were going to deliver you to people at the bottom of the mountain. There was supposed to be a car waiting.'

'You've been watching me for days. You know more than you're saying. Tell me what they said,' he said soothingly. 'I give you my word I won't kill you. See?' He flung the Uzi into the woods.

A suspicious expression came to the man's face, but he decided to take his chances. 'There was something about a girl's picture we found in your house. They think you know where she is.'

'Why do they want her?'

'I don't know.'

Schroeder nodded. 'One more thing. Who killed Schatsky?'

'Who?' The man looked at Schroeder as if he were insane.

'My little dachshund. The noisy wiener dog.'

'My partner killed him.'

'But you didn't stop him.'

'I *like* dogs.'

'I believe you.' Schroeder backed off and began to herringbone up the slope.

'You can't leave me here!' the man shouted with panic in his voice.

Schroeder stopped. 'I only said I wouldn't *kill* you. I never said I would pull you out. Don't worry. I'm sure they'll find you when the snow melts.'

The temperature would drop down to zero that night. The human body's vital organs were not meant to function upside down, and the man would probably die soon from suffocation.

Schroeder skied to the base of the mountain to a spot that offered a view of the parking lot. He picked out the black Yukon SUV with the tinted windows. Three men stood beside it, looking up the mountain. He wondered who they were, but decided it didn't matter. For now.

He removed his skis, left them on a rack and went to the locker room. He grabbed his fanny pack, stuck the boots in the locker, quickly changed into his walking shoes and headed to the lot where he had parked his truck.

Schroeder checked out the lot and saw nothing suspicious. He walked quickly to the truck and got in. As he drove out of the parking lot, he reached under the seat for a pistol and placed it in his lap.

He contemplated his next move. It would be dangerous to go back to his house. He headed out of town toward Glacier National Park. Twenty minutes later, he pulled up in front of a small, ramshackle building. The sign outside said: GLACIER PARK WILDERNESS TOURING COMPANY AND CAMPS. It was one of a number of businesses and real estate holdings Schroeder had invested in using straw companies. Behind the building were several camps he rented out in the warm season.

He parked behind the building, went inside a cabin he reserved for his own use and removed a moth-eaten moose head from over the fireplace to reveal a wall safe. He opened the safe with a few twists of the combination lock. Inside was a strongbox stuffed with cash, which he jammed into his parka pockets along with fake driver's licenses, passports and credit cards.

Schroeder went into the bathroom and shaved off his mustache. He tinted his hair brown to match the picture in his ID, and from a closet he pulled a prepacked suitcase. The change of identity took less than thirty minutes. Haste was of the essence. Anyone who could find a way through the web of fake identities that he had woven had to have considerable resources. It was only a matter of time before they tracked down the wilderness camps.

Someone might be watching the small airport in Kalispell. He decided to drive to Missoula and rent a car. Halfway to his destination, he stopped at a pay phone. Using a phone card, he called a long-distance number. As the phone rang, he held his breath, wondering if she would even remember him. It had been a long time. A man answered. They exchanged a few words and hung up. There was disappointment in his eyes.

Montana has no speed limit. As Schroeder pushed the truck to its limits, he wondered how the genie had once again escaped from the bottle. He was much younger the first time it had been contained, and he wondered if, at his age, he was still up to it.

He thought about the girl. Her portrait in his bedroom was taken by a commercial studio. They could trace it back. He thought his computer files were clean, but one could never tell. Then there were the phone records. He had grown careless in his old age. It was only a matter of time before they found her. He wondered what she looked like. The last time he had seen her was at her grandfather's funeral. He let his mind drift back, recalling the events that linked him to the young woman.

It was 1948. He was living in his log cabin in Montana. Although he had access through Swiss bank accounts to vast amounts of money, he eked out a living doing odd jobs and guiding tourists through Glacier National Park. One client, a businessman from Detroit, had left a magazine in his cabin. Schroeder did all the cleanup work himself, and he had glanced idly through its pages. That's when he discovered what had happened to Lazlo Kovacs since the night the *Wilhelm Gustloff* went to the bottom.

The magazine article described a company set up by Dr Janos, an enterprising World War II Hungarian refugee. His corporation was bringing an innovative array of consumer products to the market, all based on electromagnetic properties, making him a millionaire in the process. Schroeder smiled. There was no photograph of the reclusive inventor, but the Kovacs genius came through on every item.

It was the mud season in between skiing and trekking, so one day he packed a bag and took the train to Detroit. He found the Janos lab in an unmarked building. He had to ask several people in the neighborhood where the lab was.

He watched the front door from a parked car. The patience he had learned when stalking human beings was eventually rewarded. A Cadillac limousine pulled up to the building. Instead of stopping in front, it went around to an alley in the back. It took off before he could see who got in the car. He followed the car to the exclusive Grosse Pointe section of Detroit, where many auto executives lived. He lost the limo when it went through the gate of a walled estate.

*

The next afternoon, he was at the lab again. He parked where he had a clear view of the back alley. When the limo showed up, he got out of his car and walked over to the alley. The chauffeur, who was holding the door open, glanced at him but probably throught Schroeder was a bum to be ignored.

A man emerged from the back door and walked to the limo. He glanced in Schroeder's direction, started to get in the car, then he looked again. A wide grin came to his face. To the puzzlement of the limo driver, his wealthy employer went over and put his arms around the bum in a great hug.

'After all these years. What in God's name are you doing here?' Kovacs said.

'I thought you might like to take a ride in the snow,' Schroeder said with a grin.

Kovacs responded with a look of mock horror. 'Not if you are at the wheel.'

'You're looking well, old friend.'

'Yes, you too. Different, however. I wasn't sure at first. But it's the same old Karl.'

'I shouldn't have come here,' Schroeder said.

'Please, my friend, it was fated that we would meet again. I have so much to thank you for.'

'Knowing that you are well and prosperous is thanks enough. Now I must go.'

'We must talk first,' Kovacs said. He told his driver to wait, and led the way back into the lab. 'There is no one here,' he said.

They passed through rooms filled with electrical contraptions that would have been at home in Dr Frankenstein's lab and settled in a luxurious office.

'You've done well,' Schroeder said. 'I'm glad to see that.'

'I've been very fortunate. And you?'

'I am happy, although my home isn't as rich-looking as yours.'

'You've been to my house? Of course, I should have known. You touch all the bases, as they say in our adopted country.'

'You have a family?'

A cloud passed over Kovacs's brow, but then he smiled. 'Yes, I remarried. And you?'

'There have been many women, but I continue to be a loner.'

'Most unfortunate. I'd like to introduce you to my wife and daughter.'

Schroeder shook his head. This was as far as it goes, he said. Kovacs said he understood. Schroeder's presence would raise too many questions. Both of them still had enemies in the world. They talked for another hour, until Schroeder finally asked the question that had been on his mind.

'I assume you have buried the frequencies?'

Kovacs tapped his forehead. 'Up here, now and forever.'

'You are aware that there was an attempt to capitalize on your work. The Russians found material at the lab and tried to make it work for them.'

Kovacs smiled. 'I am like the aunt who writes down her cookie recipe for the family but leaves out an important ingredient. Their experiments would have taken them only so far.'

'They tried. Our adopted country conducted similar research, once the government found out what was going on. Then the experiments stopped.'

'There is no need to worry. I haven't forgotten what my work did to my first family.'

Satisfied with the answer, Schroeder said he had to go.

They shook hands and embraced. Schroeder gave Kovacs an address to get in touch with him, if needed. They vowed to talk again, but years passed without contact. Then one day, Schroeder checked his blind box and found a message from the Hungarian.

'I need your help again,' the message said.

When he called, the scientist said, 'Something terrible has happened.'

This time, Schroeder went directly to the Grosse Pointe mansion. Kovacs greeted him at the door. He looked terrible. He had aged well, the only visible change a graying of his hair, but there were dark circles under his eyes, and his voice was hoarse, as if he had been crying. They sat in the study, and Kovacs explained that his wife had died a few years before. Their daughter had married a wonderful man, he said, but they were both killed in a car crash a few weeks before.

When Schroeder offered his condolences, Kovacs thanked him, and said there was one way he could help. He spoke into an intercom, and a few minutes later a nursemaid came in. She was holding a beautiful, blond baby girl.

'My granddaughter, Karla,' Kovacs said, proudly taking the baby. 'She is named after an old friend who, I hope, will soon be her godfather.'

He handed the baby to Schroeder, who held her awkwardly in his arms. Schroeder was touched by the invitation and accepted the responsibility. As the girl grew up, he made several trips to Grosse Pointe, where he was referred to as Uncle Karl, and had become entranced by her grace and intelligence. On one occasion, she and her grandfather had spent several days in Montana. They were sitting on the porch of his log cabin, watching the girl chasing butterflies, when Kovacs revealed that he had a fatal illness.

'I am going to die soon. My granddaughter is well provided for. But I want you to pledge that you will watch over her as you once watched over me and protect her from all harm.'

'It will be my pleasure,' Schroeder said, never dreaming that one day he would have to honor his pledge.

The last time he had seen Karla was at her grandfather's funeral. She had started college and was busy with studies and friends. She had developed into a lovely and intelligent young woman. He checked in with her from time to time to make sure she was well, and followed her career with pride. It had been years since they had seen each other. He wondered if she would recognize him.

He clenched his teeth in renewed determination.

Whatever it took, he knew he must get to her before *they* did.

6

The intruder slithered through the dark water in an explosion of bubbles that scattered schooling fish like windblown leaves. As the five-foot-long torpedo flew through the sea, the transducer pulsing under its metal skin bounced high-speed bursts of energy off the bottom. An electronic ear collected the returning echoes, and the data from the sonar tow fish flew at the speed of light along an armored fiber-optic cable hundreds of feet long. The thick cable snaked onto the deck of the turquoise-hulled ship plowing a foamy wake through the ocean about two hundred miles east of the mid-Atlantic coast of the US.

The cable terminated in the survey control center on the ship's main deck. Austin sat in front of a glowing screen, analyzing the side-scan sonar images. A revolutionary undersea exploration tool invented by the late Dr Harold Edgerton, side-scan allowed the quick survey of vast areas of ocean bottom.

A dark vertical line running from the top to the bottom of the screen showed the path of the survey ship. Broad color bands to either side of the line represented the port and starboard areas being probed by the side-scan sonar. Navigational data and time were displayed on the right side of the screen.

Austin stared at the screen, his face bathed in its amber light, alert to every visual nuance. It was a tiring job, and he had been at it for two hours. He had glanced away from the screen and was rubbing his eyes when Zavala and

Adler stepped through the door. Zavala was carrying a thermos of coffee and three mugs that he had picked up in the mess hall.

'Coffee break,' he said. He poured the mugs full and handed them around.

The hot coffee burned Austin's lips, but it gave him a welcome wake-up lift. 'Thanks for the caffeine pick-me-up,' he said. 'I was getting bleary-eyed.'

'I can take the next shift,' Zavala volunteered.

'Thanks. I'll put the scan on autopilot for now, and show you and the professor what we've been doing.'

Austin set the sonar monitor to buzz if it picked up an object larger than fifty feet in size, and the three men gathered around a chart table.

'We're running a medium-range search to cover the most ground possible without distorting the results,' Austin said. 'The ocean depth here is about five hundred feet. We've marked out twelve-mile squares along the assumed course of the missing ship.' He drew his finger along the perimeter of a rectangle marked in grease pencil on a transparent overlay. 'The survey ship follows imaginary parallel lines in each square like someone mowing a lawn. We're about halfway through this square. If we don't locate the ship in this spread, we'll continue to probe a series of overlapping squares.'

'Anything interesting turn up?' Zavala said.

Austin made a face. 'No mermaids, if that's what you mean. Lots of flat ooze with hard sediment mixed in here and there, boulders, dips and depressions, school fish and sea clutter. No sign of our ship – or *any* ship, for that matter.'

Adler shook his head in frustration. 'You wouldn't think it would be so damned difficult with all these electronic gizmos to find a vessel that's longer than two football fields put together.'

'It's a big ocean. But if any ship can find the *Belle*, it's the *Throckmorton*,' Austin said in reassurance.

'Kurt's right. The instrumentation on this ship can tell you the color of a tube worm's eyes at a thousand fathoms,' Zavala added.

Adler chuckled. 'Deep-ocean biology isn't my area of expertise, but I wasn't aware those remarkable creatures *had* eyes.'

'Joe is exaggerating, but only a little bit,' Austin said with a smile. 'The stuff available on the *Throckmorton* makes a strong case for those who argue that humans can explore the deep ocean without getting their feet wet. Instead of being crammed into a submersible vehicle, here we are sipping coffee while the side-scan fish does all the work for us.'

'And what do *you* think, Kurt?'

Austin pondered the question. 'There is no doubt that someone like Joe can build an underwater robot vehicle that can be programmed to do everything but bring you your newspaper and slippers.'

A brilliant mechanic as well as engineer, Zavala had designed and directed the construction of numerous underwater vehicles, manned and unmanned, for NUMA.

'Funny you should mention that,' Joe said. 'I'm working on a design that will do all that and mix a damned good margarita too.'

'Joe makes my point.' Austin gestured at the screens lining the walls of the survey center. 'But what's missing in the comfortable confines of this room is the hunger for the one quality that will keep the human race from atrophying like an unused limb. *Adventure.*'

Adler smiled with pleasure at having made the right

decision in going to NUMA for help. Austin and Zavala were obviously sharp-minded scientists, knowledgeable in arcane areas of ocean research. But with their athletic bearing, quick humor and good-natured camaraderie the two NUMA men seemed like throwbacks. They were more like eighteenth-century swashbucklers than the seagoing academics he was used to, with their fussy intensity and taciturn personalities. He lifted his coffee mug in a toast.

'Here's to adventure,' he said.

The others raised their mugs. 'Maybe it's time we had a wave scientist on the Special Assignments Team,' Austin said.

An urgent buzzing from the sonar monitor cut short Adler's laughter.

Austin set his coffee aside and stepped over to the sonar screen. He watched the display for a few seconds. His lips widened in a smile and he turned to the professor. 'You said earlier that you'd like to assess the damage to the *Southern Belle* before you tell us about the theories you've been toying with.'

'Yes, that's right,' Adler said. 'I'm hopeful that I can learn why the *Belle* went down.'

Austin swiveled the screen so that the professor could see the spectral image of a ship lying on the ocean bottom five hundred feet below.

'You're about to get your chance.'

The sea had wasted no time taking over ownership of the *Southern Belle.*

The ship caught in the powerful spotlights of the remote-operated vehicle was no longer the magnificent vessel that had once plowed across the ocean like a moving island. Its blue hull was covered with a greenish-gray growth that gave the ship a shaggy-dog appearance, as if it had grown fur. Microscopic organisms had taken up residence in the seaweed, attracting schools of fish that nuzzled for food in the nooks and crannies of what had become a huge incubator for marine life.

The ROPOS ROV had been launched from the *Throckmorton*'s A-frame stern soon after Austin had notified the bridge that the sonar scan had picked up the ship's image. The vehicle was around six feet long, three feet wide and high, and shaped like a seagoing refrigerator. Despite its boxy shape, the ROV's design had gone far beyond the 'dope on a rope' function of the earlier remote vehicles. It was a moving ocean laboratory capable of a variety of scientific functions.

The ROV carried two video cameras, twin manipulators, sampling tools, sonar and digital data channels. The vehicle was attached to the ship by a fiber-optic tether that provided communication and the transmission of live video and other data. Driven by a forty-horsepower electric motor, the ROV had rapidly descended the nearly five hundred feet to where the ship lay on the bottom in an upright position.

Joe Zavala sat at the control console piloting the boxy undersea robot with a joystick. Zavala was an experienced pilot who had logged hundreds of hours in helicopters, small jet and turboprop aircraft, but controlling a moving object hundreds of feet away required the deft hand of a teenage video-game addict on the controls.

Keeping an eye on the video picture in front of him, Zavala guided the ROV as if he were sitting inside it. He used a firm yet gentle hand on the joystick, giving the vehicle subtle commands to compensate for shifts in current. With each move of the joystick, he had to be careful that the ROV didn't get tangled in its umbilical.

The mood was somber in the crowded remote-sensing center. Crew and scientists had squeezed into the room after word of the *Southern Belle*'s discovery had spread throughout the ship. The silent spectators gazed at the ghostly images of the dead ship like mourners at a funeral bier.

Reality had set in after the initial excitement of the ship's discovery. Those who follow the sea know that the solid deck under their feet rests on an undulating liquid foundation of ocean water that is as treacherous as it is beautiful. Everyone on the *Throckmorton* knew that the sunken ship had become a tomb for its crew. All were aware that they could suffer the same fate. There was no sign of the men who had gone down with the *Southern Belle*, but it was impossible not to contemplate the last terrifying moments of the cargo ship's doomed crew.

Totally focused on his task, Zavala brought the ROV down to deck level and ran it over the deck from bow to stern. Normally, he would have to be careful that the vehicle didn't get tangled in the masts and radio antennae, but the *Belle*'s deck was as level as a billiard table. The camera picked up ragged metal stubs where the cranes and booms used to handle cargo containers had been snapped off like toothpicks.

As the ROV soared over the aft end of the ship, its lights picked out a large rectangular opening in the deck.

Zavala murmured an exclamation in Spanish. Then he said, 'The deckhouse is gone.'

Austin was leaning over Zavala's shoulder. 'Try searching the area immediately around the ship,' he suggested.

Zavala worked the joystick, and the vehicle rose higher above the deck. It moved around the ship in an expanding spiral, but there was no sign of the deckhouse.

Professor Adler had been watching the show in stony

silence. He tapped Austin lightly on the arm and led him to the far end of the room, away from the crowd clustered around the ROV monitor.

'I think it's time we talked,' the professor whispered.

Austin nodded and returned to the control console. He told Joe he would be in the ship's recreation room, then he and the professor left the survey center. With the rest of the ship's complement working or watching the pictures of the *Belle*, they had the rec room to themselves. It was a comfortable space, with leather furniture, a television set and DVD-player, movie cabinet, pool table and Ping-Pong table, some board games and a computer.

Austin and Adler settled into a couple of chairs. 'Well,' Adler said, 'what do you think?'

'About the *Belle*? You don't have to be Sherlock Holmes to deduce why it went to the bottom. The deckhouse was blasted off.'

'We have the satellite pictures showing wave activity. There's no doubt in my mind that she was hit by one or more killer waves far bigger than anything we've seen before.'

'Which brings us back to your theories. You were reluctant earlier to talk about them. Has finding the ship changed your mind?'

'I'm afraid my theories are out of the ordinary.'

Austin leaned back in his chair and folded his hands behind his head. 'I've learned that nothing is ordinary when it comes to the ocean.'

'I've hesitated up to now because I didn't want to be labeled a humbug. It took years for the scientific community to accept freak waves as fact. My colleagues would rip me to shreds if they knew what I was thinking.'

'We couldn't let that happen,' Austin said reassuringly. 'I'll respect your confidence.'

The professor nodded. 'When the empirical evidence of these waves became too strong to deny, the European Union launched two high-resolution-image satellites. The project was called MaxWave. The goal was to see if these waves existed, and examine how they might influence ship and offshore platform design. The European Space Agency satellites would produce "imagettes," covering an area just ten by five kilometers. Over a three-week period, the satellites identified more than ten freak waves all higher than eighty-two feet.'

Adler went over and sat in front of the computer. He tapped the keyboard until an image of the globe appeared on the screen. The Atlantic Ocean was speckled with annotated wave symbols. 'I'm using the census data from Wave Atlas. Each symbol denotes the location of a giant wave, its height and the date it was formed. As you can see, there has been an increase in wave activities over the last thirteen months. And in the size of these monsters as well.'

Austin pulled up a chair next to the professor. He scanned the wavy symbols. Each symbol was annotated with the height and date of the event. The waves were randomly scattered around the world, except for several clusters.

'Do you notice anything unusual?'

'These four circular patterns are each spaced the same distance apart in the Atlantic, including the area we're in now. Two in the North Atlantic. Two in the South. What about the Pacific?'

'I'm glad you asked me that.' He manipulated the globe until the Pacific Ocean came into view.

Austin whistled. 'Four similar clusters. Strange.'

'That's what struck me as odd too.' A faint smile crossed his lips. 'I've measured the clusters and found that they are exactly equidistant in each ocean.'

'What are you saying, Professor?'

'That there appears to be a conscious plan at work here. These waves are the work either of man or God.'

Austin pondered the implications of the professor's statement. 'There is a third possibility,' he said after a moment. 'Man acting as God.'

Arching a bushy eyebrow, Adler said, 'That's out of the question, of course.'

Austin smiled. 'Not necessarily. Mankind has a history of trying to control the elements.'

'Controlling the sea is another matter.'

'I agree, although there have been crude but effective attempts. Dikes and storm barriers go back hundreds of years.'

'I was a consultant on the Venice tidal gate project, so I know what you mean. Stopping the ocean involves a relatively simple concept. It's the engineering that becomes the challenge. The creation of giant waves would be far more difficult.'

'But not impossible,' Austin said.

'No, not impossible.'

'Have you given any thought to means? Something like huge underwater explosions?'

'Highly unlikely,' Adler said with a shake of his head. 'You'd need an explosion of a nuclear level, and it would be detected. Any other ideas?'

'Not offhand,' Austin said. 'But it's definitely something that NUMA should investigate.'

'You have no idea how happy I am to hear you say that,' Adler said with relief. 'I thought I was going crazy.'

A thought occurred to Austin. 'Joe wondered if the Trouts' work might shed some light on this mystery,' he said.

'Sure, I remember. You mentioned that a couple of your

NUMA colleagues are working on another research project in this area.'

Austin nodded. 'South of our position. They're with a group of scientists on the NOAA ship *Benjamin Franklin*, looking into the biological implications of the giant eddies in the Atlantic Ocean.'

'As I said, I wouldn't rule anything out. It's certainly worth looking into.'

'We can talk to them about their findings when we get back to port.'

'Why wait?' Adler said.

Adler's fingers played over the keys and a Web site popped up on the screen, followed by a satellite image showing the mid-Atlantic coast. 'The ocean satellite taking this picture can pick up an object as small as a sardine.'

'Amazing,' Austin said, leaning close to the screen.

Adler clicked the computer mouse. 'Now we're seeing ocean water temperature. That wavy band of reddish brown is the Gulf Stream. The blue area is cold water, and those circular blobs in tan are warm water eddies. I'll zoom in on our ship.'

He worked the computer mouse so that one of the tan-colored swirls filled the screen. The outlines of two vessels were now visible near the whorl.

'That blip is the *Throckmorton*. The other one must be your NOAA ship. Wow! This stuff still amazes me.'

Austin leaned over Adler's shoulder. 'What's that smaller circle in the southeast quadrant?'

Adler enlarged the image. 'It's a separate eddy. Acting real funny. The numbers in the little boxes show water movement speed and level. The level within the swirl seems to be dropping while the water is moving at increasing speed.' Adler's eyes were glued to the screen. The swirl, now almost a perfect circle, continued to grow. *'Migod,'* he said.

'What's the problem?'

The professor tapped the screen. 'We seem to be looking at the birth of a gigantic whirlpool.'

7

Gamay Morgan-Trout carefully lowered the Van Dorn sampler over the port rail of the NOAA survey ship and watched the nine-liter plastic cylinder sink beneath the foamflecked waves. She played out the thin connecting cable as the sampler plunged hundreds of feet to the ocean bottom.

After the bottle filled with water and automatically sealed, she began to winch it back on board with the help of her husband. Paul Trout hauled the dripping bottle the last few feet from the water, detached the sampler from the cable and held it to the light, as if he were testing the color of a fine glass of wine.

Trout had a twinkle in his hazel eyes. 'This is absurd,' he said.

'What's absurd?'

'Consider what we're doing.'

Still puzzled, Gamay said, 'Okay, we've just tossed a fancy bottle over the side and hauled it up filled with seawater.'

'Thank you for making my point. Look around at this ship. The *Benjamin Franklin* is loaded with cutting-edge research gear. We've got stuff like specialized echo sounders, multibeam and side-scan sonar and the latest in computer hardware and software. But we're no different from the ancient mariners who smeared wax on their sounding lead to check out the composition of the ocean bottom.'

Gamay smiled. 'And now we're about to collect plankton using an old-fashioned fisherman's net. I draw the line when it comes to transport. No rowboat. How's the Zodiac coming?'

'Ready to go,' Trout said. He read the surface of the sea with an experienced eye. 'Wind's freshening. Could get choppy. We'll have to stay sharp.' He pronounced it 'shaap,' betraying his New England roots.

Gamay glanced at the whitecaps starting to dot the grayish-blue water. 'We might not be able to go out again for days if we wait.'

'My thoughts exactly.' He handed her the Van Dorn sampler. 'I'll meet you at the Zodiac davit.'

Gamay delivered the sampler to the wet lab. The water sample would be analyzed for trace metals and organisms. She went to her cabin, pulled a hooded, foul-weather suit on over her jeans, Icelandic wool sweater and chamois shirt, and tucked her long, dark red hair under a multicolored 'Friends of the *Hunley*' baseball cap. Slipping into her personal flotation device, she went out to the stern deck.

Trout was waiting next to the davits that held the twenty-three-foot-long, rigid inflatable boat. He was dressed impeccably as usual. Under a full suit of yellow commercial-grade, foul-weather gear, he wore designer jeans specially tailored to fit his six-foot-eight frame and a navy sweater made of cashmere wool. One of the colorful bow ties to which Trout was addicted adorned the button-down collar of his Brooks Brothers oxford-weave blue shirt. As a counterpoint to his casual elegance, he wore scuffed work boots, a holdover from his days at the Woods Hole Oceanographic Institution, where functional footwear was de rigueur. He wore a navy wool cap to protect his head.

The Trouts climbed aboard the rigid inflatable boat and the Zodiac was lowered into the sea. Paul started the Volvo Penta diesel inboard/outboard engine as Gamay cast off the

94

tether line. They stood side by side at the steering console with legs braced in a charioteer's pose, knees bent to absorb the shock of the flat-bottomed hull slapping the waves.

The rugged inflatable craft planed over the seas like a playful dolphin. Trout steered toward a Day-Glo orange sphere that was bobbing in the water about a quarter mile from the ship. They had set the buoy earlier in the day to provide a reference point for the phytoplankton survey.

It was not the most hospitable work environment. Glowering clouds were moving in from the east, and the horizon line was barely visible where gray sea met gray water. The easterly wind had come up a few knots. The thick cloud layer blocking the sunlight was starting to spit light rain.

But as they prepared for the survey, Paul and Gamay wore that particular expression of bliss people born to the sea have when they are in their natural element. Paul had climbed aboard a fishing boat with his fisherman father as soon as he could walk. He had fished commercially out of the Cape Cod village of Woods Hole until he went off to college.

Gamay was unfazed by the gloomy weather, although her background was somewhat different from Trout's. Born in Racine, Wisconsin, she had spent many of her younger years sailing the sometimes cantankerous waters of the Great Lakes with her father, a successful developer and yachtsman.

'You must admit this is a lot more fun than wallpapering,' Paul said as he maneuvered the boat closer to the buoy.

Gamay was readying the survey gear. 'This is more fun than almost *anything* I can think of,' she said, ignoring the cold spray that splashed her face.

'Glad you qualified your statement with "almost,"' Paul said with a leer.

Gamay gave him a sour look that didn't match the

amusement in her eyes. 'Pay attention to what you're doing or you'll fall overboard.'

The Trouts hadn't expected to be back to sea so soon. After wrapping up their last mission with the Special Assignments Team, they had planned to catch some R & R. Trout had once observed that Gamay's relaxation technique must have been learned from a French Foreign Legion drillmaster. A fitness and exercise nut, she was only home a few hours before embarking on an Olympic-level running, hiking and biking schedule.

Even that wasn't enough. Gamay had a habit of making a top priority of whatever happened to come into her mind at a given moment. Trout knew he was in trouble when, after a day together cruising through the Virginia countryside in their Humvee, she eyeballed the living-room wallpaper of the Georgetown town house they were constantly remodeling. He had nodded with learned patience as Gamay ticked off the remodeling projects she had piled on their plate.

The remodeling frenzy lasted only a day. Gamay was slapping wallpaper on a wall with typical ferocity when Hank Aubrey, a colleague from Scripps Institute of Oceanography, called and asked if she and Paul would like to take part in an ocean eddy survey off the mid-Atlantic coast aboard the *Benjamin Franklin*.

Aubrey didn't have to twist their arms. Working with Austin and the Special Assignments Team was a dream job that took them on adventures to exotic parts of the world. But sometimes they yearned for the pure research of their college years.

'Ocean eddies?' Trout had said after they accepted the invitation. 'I've read about them in the oceanographic science journals. Big, slow-moving swirls of cold or warm water that are sometimes hundreds of miles across.'

Gamay nodded. 'According to Hank, there's a lot of new interest in the phenomenon. The whorls can hamper offshore drilling operations and affect weather. On the good side, they can churn up marine microorganisms from the ocean floor to the surface and cause an explosion up the food chain. I'll be studying the flow of nutrients and the impact on commercial fishing and whale populations. You can look into the geological components.'

Noting the growing excitement in his wife's voice, Paul said, 'I love it when you talk dirty.'

Gamay puffed away a strand of hair that had fallen over her face. 'We scientist types are a bit odd when it comes to the things that turn us on.'

'What about the wallpapering?' Paul teased.

'We'll *hire* someone to finish it.'

Paul tossed the wallpaper brush into a bucket. 'Finest-kind, cap,' he said, using a phrase from his fishing days.

The Trouts worked together with the precision of a fine Swiss watch. Their teamwork was a quality former NUMA director James Sandecker recognized when he hired them for the Special Assignments Team. Both were now in their mid-thirties. From outward appearances, they were an un-likely couple.

Paul was the more serious of the two. He seemed con-stantly in deep thought, an impression that was heightened by his habit of speaking with his head lowered, eyes peering up as if over glasses. He seemed to reach deep inside himself before saying anything of importance. His seriousness was tempered by a sly sense of humor.

Gamay was more open and vivacious than her husband. A tall, slender woman who moved with the grace of a fashion model, she had a flashing smile with a slight gap between her upper front teeth, and, while not gorgeous or overly sexy, was appealing to most men. They had met at Scripps, where he was studying for his doctorate in deep-ocean geology, and Gamay was switching her field of interest from nautical archaeology to marine biology.

A few hours after receiving the call, they were packed and boarding the *Benjamin Franklin*. The *Franklin* had a highly trained crew of twenty, plus ten scientists from various universities and government agencies. Its primary mission was to conduct a hydrographic survey along the Atlantic coast and the Gulf of Mexico.

On a typical trip, the ship made thousands of precise depth measurements to create a picture of the ocean bottom and any wrecks or other obstructions that happened to be present. The information was used to update nautical maps for NOAA, the National Oceanic and Atmospheric Administration.

Aubrey had greeted them at the top of the gangway and welcomed them aboard the ship. Aubrey was a slightly built man whose flighty energy, sharply pointed nose and nonstop chatter made him resemble an English sparrow. He led them to their cabin. After dropping off their bags, they headed to the mess hall. They settled at a table, and Aubrey brought them cups of tea.

'Damn, it's great to see you,' he said. 'I'm really pleased you could join our project. How long has it been since we've seen each other, three years?'

'More like five,' Gamay said.

'Ouch. Much too long, in any case,' he said. 'We'll make up for it on this trip. The ship's due to leave in a couple of hours. I often think of you working at NUMA. It must be fascinating,' Aubrey said in a voice tinged with envy. 'My work on big swirling masses of water pales by comparison with your adventures.'

'Not at all, Hank,' Gamay said. 'Paul and I would kill for the opportunity to do pure science. And from what we've read, your research affects a great many people.'

Aubrey brightened. 'I suppose you're right. There will be a formal scientific orientation session tomorrow. What do you know about the phenomenon of ocean eddies?'

'Not a lot,' Gamay said. 'Mostly, that the swirls are a largely unexplored scientific area.'

'Absolutely right. That's why this survey is a matter of great importance.' He plucked a napkin from its holder and produced a ballpoint pen from his pocket in a gesture the Trouts had seen on a dozen other occasions.

'You'll get to see the satellite images, but this will show you what we're dealing with. We're headed to a site close to the Gulf Stream, about two hundred miles out. This swirl is a hundred miles across, located east of New Jersey, on the edge of the Gulf Stream.' He drew an irregular circle on the napkin.

'Looks like a fried egg,' Trout said.

Trout liked to kid Aubrey about his penchant for working out scientific problems on restaurant napkins, even suggesting once that he compile them in a textbook.

'Artistic license,' Aubrey said. 'It gives you an idea of what we're dealing with. Ocean eddies are basically giant, slow-moving whirlpools, sometimes hundreds of miles across. They seem to be cast off by ocean currents. Some rotate clockwise. Others move counterclockwise. They can transport ocean heat or cold, and move nutrients from the bottom of the ocean to the top, affecting weather and creating an explosion of marine life up the food chain, depending.'

'I've read somewhere about fishing trawlers working the edges of these things,' Trout said.

'Humans aren't the only predators that have discovered the biological implications of eddies.' Aubrey sketched out a few more pictures on the napkin and held it up.

'Now it looks like a fried egg being attacked by giant fish,' Trout said.

'Actually, as anyone with eyes can see, these are whales. They've been known to feed along the edges of eddies. There are a couple of teams trying to track whales to their feeding grounds.'

'Using whales to find whorls,' Trout observed.

Aubrey grimaced at the wordplay. 'There are better ways to find these puppies than tagging sperm whales. Thermal expansion causes the water inside an eddy to create a bump in the ocean that can be traced by satellite.'

'What causes ocean currents to shed these eddies?' Trout said.

'That's one of the things we hope to learn on this expedition. You two are ideally suited for the project. Gamay can apply her biological expertise to the question, and we're hoping you can come up with some of the computer models you're so good at.'

'Thanks for inviting us aboard. We'll do our best,' Gamay said.

'I know you will. This goes beyond pure science. These big swirls can be real weathermakers. A stalled ocean eddy off the California coast can produce cold temperatures and rain in LA. Similarly, in the Atlantic an eddy spinning off the Gulf Stream can produce thick fog.'

'Not much we can do about the weather,' Trout said.

'That's true, but knowing what to expect will allow us to adapt to it. The ocean eddy survey could be vital to the nation's economy. The safety of commercial shipping and the flow of petroleum, coal, steel, cars, grain and computerized cargo depend on accurate weather forecasting.'

'Which is why NOAA is so interested in what we're doing,' Trout said.

Aubrey nodded. 'That reminds me, I've got to talk to the captain about our schedule.' He rose from his seat and pumped their hands. 'I can't tell you how pleased I am to be working with you guys again. We're having a get-to-know-each-other party tonight.' He slid the napkin across the table to Trout. 'There will be a quiz on this material in the morning, wise guy.'

Luckily for Trout, Aubrey was only joking about the quiz, although the orientation was comprehensive. And by the time the survey ship dropped anchor, both Trouts had become well versed in ocean eddy science. From the vantage point of the ship's deck, the sea in the vicinity of the swirl looked no different from any other part of the ocean, but satellites and computer models had shown it to be moving at approximately three miles per hour.

Trout had done some computer graphics of the ocean bottom in the vicinity of the swirl, and Gamay concentrated on the biological applications. The phytoplankton survey was a vital piece of her research, which was why she was so anxious to get it out of the way.

With the Zodiac rocking in the troughs between waves, they lowered a Neuston net over the side. The net had a rectangular, tubular frame, and the ten-foot cloth net itself was long and tapering, which allowed it to sample large volumes of water. They let out the line so that the net floated partially out of the water. Then they made several tows straight out in a radius from the marker buoys, keeping an eye on the white-hulled NOAA ship to maintain their bearings. The results were good. The net was bringing in solid samples of plankton.

Trout had put the motor at idle and was helping Gamay make a last haul when they looked up at the same time at a strange rushing sound. They exchanged puzzled glances and stared off at the ship. Nothing seemed amiss. People were visible, moving about on the deck.

Gamay had noticed a flickering sparkle on the surface of the sea as if the sun were a fluorescent bulb on its last legs. 'Look at the sky,' she said.

Trout glanced up and his jaw dropped down to his knees. The clouds seemed to be enveloped in a canopy of silver fire that pulsated in brilliant bursts of radiance. He gazed, awestruck, at the heavenly display, and responded with a very unscientific observation.

'Wow!' he said.

The noise they had heard repeated itself, only it was louder this time. It seemed to be coming from the open sea away from the NOAA ship. Trout wiped the drizzle out of his eyes and pointed at the ocean.

'Something's happening at about two o'clock, maybe an eighth of a mile away,' he said.

A roughly circular patch of ocean was going dark as if a cloud were casting a shadow.

'What is it?' Gamay said.

'I don't know,' Trout said. 'But it's getting bigger.'

The dark patch was expanding, forming a circle of puckering, wrinkled water. One hundred feet in diameter. Then two hundred feet. And rapidly growing. A glittering band of white appeared at the edge of the dark circle and rapidly developed into a low wall of spume. A low moan rose from the depths as if the sea were crying out in pain.

Then the center of the darkness dropped suddenly and a massive wound appeared in the ocean. It was quickly expanding in size, and would reach them within seconds.

Trout's hand instinctively reached for the throttle just as invisible fingers of current reached out from the widening gyre and began to pull them back toward the yawning black void.

8

The great gaping cavity that had opened in the sea was visible only for an instant before it disappeared behind a mounding circle of foam. Tatters of spume flew off the top of the sudsy crest. An intense, briny odor saturated the air as if the Zodiac were suddenly in the midst of a huge school of fish.

The NOAA ship was moving toward the Zodiac. People lined the rail. They were pointing and waving their hands.

The boat was on the verge of extricating itself from the sticky currents when a big sea broke over the blunt bow and they lost headway. Trout's jaw tightened. He cranked the throttle up as far as it would go and pointed the bow away from the cauldron. The motor revved to near-valve-popping levels. The boat lurched as if it had been given shock treatment. The Zodiac gained a yard or two before being snatched again by the powerful tentacles of current that were generated around the huge whirl.

A rumble issued from the bowels of the sea, the sound so overpowering that it drowned out the desperate roar of the straining motor. The air was filled with a great vibration as if hundreds of pipe organs were set on low end. Thick, milky mist issued from the hole in the water. Making the scene even more unreal was the laser show overhead. The dancing lights had changed in color from silver to blue and purple.

The boat scudded into a tightening spiral as it was dragged into the encircling belt of foam. There was no chance of escape. The Zodiac was lifted to the top of the roiling ridge of white water, now around six feet high, where it was buffeted and rocked with such violence that Gamay was almost thrown into the sea.

Trout released the wheel and lunged for Gamay. His strong fingers caught the fabric of her foul-weather jacket and he pulled her back into the boat. It was no longer safe to stand. They dropped to their hands and knees and grabbed onto a safety line attached to one of the inflatable-hull tubes.

The Zodiac was fully in the grip of the moving ridge of gleaming white water. As if the constant pitching and yawing weren't enough, the boat spun like a drunken ballet dancer.

The punishment continued as the boat was carried along the roiling ridge of foam. On one side was the sea. On the other, a great whirling funnel whose black walls sloped at a forty-five-degree angle. The sides of the whirlpool looked as hard as glass.

The boat teetered dangerously at the top of the foaming wall and then slid into the great whirling funnel of black water. The fierce current whipping around the wall of the whirlpool surpassed the pull of gravity. The boat's descent ended about twenty feet below the shiny rim of froth. Caught by the centrifugal force like the ball in a spinning roulette wheel, the boat began to go round and round the funnel.

The Zodiac hung at a forty-five-degree angle, its flat bottom parallel to the slanting surface, with the port side lower than starboard. The bow pointed forward as if the boat were still moving under its own power.

The Trouts twisted their bodies around so that their boots were wedged under the downhill pontoon. They looked down into the whirlpool. It was at least a mile in diameter. The funnel slanted sharply, and the bottom was hidden behind the swirling clouds of thick mist that rose from the churning water. Light passing through the mist had created a rainbow that arced over the maelstrom as if nature was trying to moderate its raw display of power with delicate beauty.

Without a stationary reference point, it was impossible to determine how fast they were moving or how many times the Zodiac had made the circle. But after several minutes had passed, the rim seemed higher. It became painfully obvious that the boat was descending even as it was hurled forward.

Trying to reorient herself, Gamay glanced up at the circle of sky wheeling far above. She saw movement at the rim of the whirlpool and pointed with her free hand.

Trout wiped the water out of his eyes. 'Oh hell,' he said. 'It's the *Franklin*.'

The vessel was at the edge of the gyre, its stern protruding into thin air from the ridge of foam. The ship disappeared after a moment. Seconds later, it returned to view, only to disappear again.

The Trouts forgot about their own misfortune. From the ship's peekaboo performance, it was apparent that the *Franklin* had been caught in the swirling currents generated by the vortex and was being drawn into the funnel.

The ship oscillated back and forth in a deadly game of tug-of-war as the propellers came out of the water and the vessel lost way. The ship would tilt, the propellers would catch and the vessel would rise up and over again in a bucksaw motion that went on for several minutes. Then the entire length of the vessel was drawn over the lip and into the cauldron. The ship's bow was higher than the stern. It hung there as if stuck by glue.

'Go, baby, *go* . . . !' Trout yelled.

Gamay gave him a quick glance, even smiling briefly at the unusual display of emotion, before she, too, joined in the cheering.

The smooth water behind the ship boiled as if someone had turned the burner on high. The engines were doing their work. The propellers biting into the slanting sides of the funnel, the ship inched its way painfully toward the rim again, settled back, shot upward at an angle, was buried by the foam, then gave a mighty surge that carried it over the lip.

This time, the ship disappeared for good. The Trouts cheered, but their celebration was tempered by their own sense of loneliness and impotence against an unstoppable force of nature.

'Any ideas about how *we* get out of here?' Gamay shouted.

'Maybe the whirlpool will end on its own.'

Gamay glanced down. In the few minutes they had watched the ship struggle, the boat had dropped at least another twenty feet.

'I don't think so.'

The water had lost its India ink cast, and the slick black sides had picked up a brownish tinge from the mud being scooped up from the bottom. Hundreds of dead or dying fish whirled in a great circle like confetti caught in a wind-storm. The damp air was thick with the smell of brine, fish and bottom muck.

'Look at the debris,' Paul said. 'It's rising from the bottom.'

Wreckage was being churned up from the floor of the sea in the same way a tornado picks up objects and lifts them in the air. There were splintered wooden cartons, plywood, hatch covers, scraps of ventilators, even a damaged lifeboat. Much of the material sank back into the vortex, where it was regurgitated and destroyed with the same effect as if it were at the bottom of Niagara Falls.

Gamay noticed that some pieces, mostly small, were heading up toward the rim. 'What if we jump into the water?' she said. 'Maybe we'd be light enough to rise to the top like that stuff.'

'No guarantee we'd ascend. More likely, we'd get sucked farther into the whirlpool, to be ground up like hamburger. Remember that the first rule of the sea is to stick with your boat – if possible.'

'Maybe that's not such a great idea. We've dropped lower.'

It was true. The boat had slipped farther into the whirlpool.

A cylindrical object was working its way up the side of the whirlpool. Then several more followed.

'What's that?' Trout said.

Gamay wiped away the moisture from her eyes and looked again, at a point twenty feet ahead and slightly below the Zodiac. Before becoming a marine biologist, she had been a nautical archaeologist, and immediately recognized the tapered ceramic forms with their greenish-gray painted surfaces.

'They're amphorae,' she said. 'And they're moving *upward.*'

Trout read his wife's mind. 'We'll only have one chance to go for it.'

'Our weight may change the dynamics, and there will only be one chance to go for it.

'Do we have a choice?'

The three ancient wine vessels were maddeningly close. Trout pulled himself up to the steering console and pressed the starter button. The engine caught. The boat moved ahead at its crazy angle, and he had to compensate with its tendency to fishtail by creative handling of the wheel. He wanted to get above the amphorae to block their way.

The first amphora in the group started to drift across the bow. In another second, it would be out of reach. Trout gunned the motor, and the boat passed just above the moving object.

'Get ready,' Trout yelled. The leap would have to be perfectly timed. 'It will be slippery, and it's going to roll. Make sure you grab on to the handles and wrap your arms and legs around it.'

Gamay nodded and climbed onto the bow. 'What about you?' she said.

'I'll catch a ride on the next one.'

'It's going to be hard to keep the boat steady.' She knew that without someone to keep the boat under control, Trout's leap would be even more hazardous.

'I'll figure it out.'

'Like hell, you will. I'm not going.'

Damned stubborn woman. 'This is your only chance. Someone's got to finish that damned wallpapering. *Please.*'

Gamay gave him a hard stare, then shook her head and crawled farther out onto the bow. She bunched her legs under her and was preparing to make the leap.

'Stop!' Trout shouted.

She turned and glared at him. 'Make up your mind.'

Trout had seen what Gamay hadn't. The whirlpool's glassy sides above them were clear of debris. The wreckage that had been kicked up by the churning seemed to have reached an invisible barrier beyond which it failed to rise. The debris was moving back down into the funnel as quickly as it had risen.

'Look,' he yelled. 'That sea trash is being pulled down again.'

It took Gamay only a few seconds to see that he was right. The amphorae were as high as they were going to go. Trout stretched his hand out and pulled her back into the boat. They held on to the safety line, unable to do anything more than watch helplessly as their boat descended farther into the abyss.

9

The spherical figure on the computer screen reminded Austin of the membrane, cytoplasm and nucleus of a malignant cell.

He turned to Adler. 'What exactly are we dealing with here, Professor?'

The scientist scratched his shaggy head. 'Hell, Kurt, you got me. This disturbance is growing by the second, and it's moving in a circle at thirty knots. I've never seen anything like it, in size or speed.'

'Neither have I,' Austin said. 'I've run into rough swirling currents that gave me sweaty palms. They were comparatively small and short-lived. This seems more like something out of Edgar Allan Poe or Jules Verne.'

'The vortices in *Descent into the Maelstrom* and *Twenty Thousand Leagues Under the Sea* are largely literary inventions. Poe and Verne were inspired by the Mokstraumen maelstrom off Norway's Lofoten Islands. The Greek historian Pytheas described it more than two thousand years ago as swallowing ships and throwing them up again. The Swedish bishop Olaus Magnus wrote in the 1500s that it was stronger than Charybdis from *The Odyssey* and that the maelstrom smashed ships against the bottom of the sea and sucked in screaming whales.'

'That's the stuff of fiction. What about reality?'

'Far less frightening. The Norwegian whirlpool has been scientifically measured, and it isn't even close to the violent cauldron described in literature. Three other significant whirlpools, Corryvreckan, Scotland, Saltstraumen, also off Norway, and Naruto, near Japan, are far less powerful.' He shook his head. 'Odd to see any whirlpool action on the open sea.'

'Why is that?'

'Whirlpools usually appear in narrow straits where there is fast-moving water. The whirling confluence of tides and currents, combined with the shape of the sea bottom, can create substantial disturbances on the surface.'

The image on the screen showed the distance shrinking between the whirlpool and the *Benjamin Franklin.* 'Could that thing be a danger to the ship?'

'Not if earlier scientific observations are any indication. The Old Sow whirlpool off the coast of New Brunswick is approximately the same strength as Moskstraumen, with speeds of about twenty-eight kilometers per hour. It's the largest ocean whirlpool in the Western Hemisphere. The turbulence near the phenomenon can be dangerous to small boats, but it poses no hazard for larger vessels.' He paused, staring in fascination at the screen. '*Damn!*'

'What's wrong?

He stared at the malignancy on the screen. 'I wasn't sure at first. But this thing is growing rapidly. In the time we've talked, it has almost doubled in size.'

Austin had seen enough.

'I'd like you to do me a great favor, Professor,' he said, keeping his voice cool and calm. 'Get to the survey control center, fast. Tell Joe to pull the ROV immediately and come to the bridge as soon as possible. Tell him that it's urgent.'

Adler glanced at the screen once more, then hurried off. While the professor went on his errand, Austin climbed to the bridge.

Tony Cabral, the *Throckmorton*'s skipper, was a genial man in his late fifties. His tanned face was dominated by a strong nose, he had an upturned black mustache and his mouth was usually stretched in a crooked grin that made him look like a benevolent pirate. But he wore an expression of dead seriousness that changed to one of surprise when he saw Austin.

'Hey, Kurt, I was just about to send someone looking for you.'

'We've got a problem,' Austin said.

'You know about the SOS we received?'

'First I've heard of it. What's going on?'

'We picked up a Mayday from the NOAA vessel a few minutes ago.'

Austin's worst fears were realized. 'What's their status?'

Cabral frowned. 'Most of the message was garbled. There was a lot of background noise. We recorded the call. Maybe you can make sense of it.'

He flicked a switch on the radio console. The bridge was filled with a cacophony that sounded like an oratorical contest at a madhouse. There was wild shouting, but the words were mostly incomprehensible except for a hoarse male voice that cut through the pandemonium.

'*Mayday!*' the voice said. 'This is the NOAA ship *Ben Franklin. Mayday.* Come in, anybody.'

Another voice, more garbled, could be heard in the background, bawling: '*Power!* Damnit, more power . . .'

Then came a quick phrase. It was only caught for an instant, but that was all that was needed to convey the unmitigated terror.

'*Damnit!* We're going in!'

Cabral's recorded voice came on. He was trying to respond to the SOS.

'This is the NUMA ship *Throckmorton*. What is your situation? Come in. What is your situation?'

His words were drowned out by a dull, churning roar as if a monsoon were howling through a cavern. Then the radio went dead. The silence that followed was worse than any noise.

Austin had tried to imagine himself on the *Franklin*'s bridge. The scene was obviously one of chaos. The voice calling the Mayday was probably the captain's. Or, more likely, he was the one urging the engine room to give them more power.

The unearthly swirling roar was beyond anything in Austin's experience. He realized that the hair on the back of his neck was standing up like soldiers at attention. He glanced around the bridge. Judging from the apprehensive faces of captain and crew, it was clear that he was not alone in his thoughts.

'What's the *Franklin*'s position?' Austin said.

Captain Cabral stepped over to a blue-glowing radar monitor.

'That's another crazy thing. We picked them up on radar eighteen miles away. They were moving in a southwest direction. Then they disappeared from the radar screen.'

Austin watched the radar sweep line go around a couple of times. There was no sign of the ship, only some patches of scatter where the radar beam touched the wavetops. 'How long will it take to get there?'

'Less than an hour. We've got to haul in the ROV first.'

'Joe's doing it now. He should have the vehicle aboard by now.'

Cabral gave the order to get under way and head toward the *Franklin* at top speed. The *Throckmorton* pulled anchor, and its high bow was starting to cut through the ranks of waves when Zavala showed up with Professor Adler.

'The professor told me about the whirlpool,' Zavala said. 'Any word from the *Franklin*?'

'They sent an SOS, but the radio transmission got cut short. And we lost them on radar.'

Cabral heard the brief exchange. 'What's this about a whirlpool, Kurt?'

'The professor and I were checking satellite images and picked up a big, spinning water disturbance near the *Franklin*'s position. Maybe a mile or two across.'

'Isn't NOAA doing a study of ocean eddies?'

'This is no slow-moving eddy. It's probably hundreds of feet deep, and spinning at more than thirty knots.'

'You're not serious.'

'Deadly serious, I'm afraid.'

Austin asked the professor to describe what they had seen. Adler was filling the captain in on the details when they were interrupted by the radio operator.

'We're picking them up on radar again,' the operator said.

'Captain,' the radio operator said a second later. 'I'm getting a transmission from the *Franklin*.'

Cabral took the microphone. 'This is Captain Cabral of the NUMA ship *Throckmorton*. We have received your Mayday. What is your current status?'

'This is the *Franklin*'s captain. We're okay now, but the ship was almost sucked into a big hole in the sea. Damnedest thing I've ever seen.'

'Anyone injured?'

'Some bumps and bruises, but we're dealing with them.'

Austin borrowed the microphone. 'This is Kurt Austin. I've got a couple of friends aboard your ship. Could you tell me how Paul and Gamay Trout are doing?'

There was a heavy silence, and at first it seemed that the

radio transmission had again been cut short. Then the voice came on. 'I'm sorry to tell you this. They were making a plankton survey in the Zodiac inflatable when the whirlpool pulled them in. We tried to go to their aid, and that's when we got in trouble.'

'Did you actually *see* them in the whirlpool?'

'We were pretty busy, and the visibility is practically nil.'

'How close are you to the whirlpool now?'

'We're about a mile away. We don't dare get any closer. The currents flowing around that thing are still pretty strong. What do you want us to do?'

'Stay as close as you're able. We're coming over to take a look.'

'Will do. Good luck.'

'Thanks,' Austin said, turning to Cabral. 'I'd like to borrow the ship's helicopter. How soon can you have it ready to fly?'

Cabral was aware of Kurt's reputation at NUMA. He knew that despite Austin's easy smile and casual manner, this self-assured man with the battering ram shoulders and pale hair could handle whatever weirdness was going on. Cabral was a seasoned mariner, but the developing situation was beyond his ken. He would keep the ship going and let Austin deal with the rest.

'It's all fueled and ready to go. I'll tell the crew to meet you there.' He picked up the intercom microphone.

Austin suggested that the NUMA ship stay at its present course and speed. Then he and Zavala raced down to the helicopter pad on the main deck, stopping first at the ship's supply room for a few items. The deck crew had the engine warming up in the McDonnell Douglas light utility helicopter. They climbed into the cockpit and buckled up.

The rotors thrashed the air and the chopper lifted off the deck, then scudded low over the water.

Austin scanned the sea through a pair of binoculars. After the helicopter had been in the air for several minutes, he spotted the antennae and then the superstructure of the NOAA ship. It was near a circle of dark ocean that dwarfed the ship in size. The whirlpool seemed to have stopped growing, but he had to admire the gutsiness of those on the *Franklin* for staying close to the maelstrom.

Zavala moved the helicopter a couple of hundred feet higher, keeping the aircraft on a straight-line course headed directly for the vortex. As they drew nearer, he said:

'It looks like a volcano caldera.'

Austin nodded. There were some volcanic similarities, mainly having to do with the funnel shape of the hole, and the mist issuing from it. The steamy exhalation was the source of the haze that covered much of the ocean.

The slick, black sides of the funnel glimpsed through gaps in the steam cloud were far smoother than those of any volcano Austin had ever seen. Nothing of the image transmitted from the satellite could convey the simple awfulness of the phenomenon. It looked like a big, festering puncture wound in the sea.

'How big do you figure this pothole to be?' Austin said.

'Too *damned* big!' Zavala measured with his eye. 'But, to be precise, I'd say it's about two miles across.'

'That's my estimate too,' Austin said. 'From the angle of the sides, it could go down all the way to the ocean bottom. Hard to tell, with the swirling mists. Can we get closer?'

Zavala obliged, until they were directly above the whirlpool. From this vantage point, the gyre looked like an immense, steam-filled cone. The chopper hovered a couple of hundred feet above the vortex, but they were still unable to see deep inside of it.

'What now?' Zavala said.

'We can go in, but we might not come out.'

'What's your point?'

'I'm giving you an option. From the looks of that mess below us, we may already be too late to do anything for our pals. You may be risking your life for nothing.'

A grin crossed Zavala's dark face. 'Like I said, what's your point?'

Austin would have been surprised at any other answer. There was no way either one of them would have deserted their friends. He jerked his thumb downward. Zavala nodded and worked the controls. The helicopter started its descent into the black heart of the maelstrom.

10

The infernal noise was the worst part of the descent into the abyss.

The Trouts could clamp their eyes shut to avoid having to look into the deep, whirling pit, but it was impossible to block out the deafening waves of sound that battered them with no interruption. Every molecule in their bodies seemed to be vibrating from the aural onslaught. The sound took away their last small comfort: the ability to talk. They communicated with gestures and hand squeezes.

The crashing waters at the base of the vortex produced a rolling thunder, as if a hundred lightning storms were in progress. The clamor was amplified by the megaphone shape of the whirlpool. Even more terrifying were the loud snorts and chortles that came from the bottom, as if the Zodiac were being drawn into the hungry maw of a giant pig.

The Zodiac and its two passengers had slipped about two-thirds of the way down the steep sides of the funnel. As the cone narrowed in diameter, the speed of the whirling current increased until the inflatable boat spun around like a scrap of lettuce headed down the kitchen drain.

The lower the boat descended, the darker the Stygian atmosphere around them became. The thick mists being churned up at the bottom of the whirlpool had thickened and further cut down the meager sunlight from the surface. Both Trouts were suffering from vertigo induced by the constant spinning. The moisture-soaked air would have been hard to breathe even without the choking exhalations from the pit: a foul combination of brine, fish, dead things and muck that smelled like the inside of a fisherman's boot.

The boat had remained at the same slanting attitude with its bottom parallel to the side of the vortex. Gamay and Paul sat side by side, so close they seemed to be joined at the hip. They were holding on to the boat's safety line, and to each other. They were numb with exhaustion from riding in a half-standing, half-sitting position, with their bodies angled and feet wedged under the lower pontoon. Moisture had seeped in around their rain gear, soaking their clothes, and the cold added to their misery.

At their accelerating rate of descent, it was clear that their suffering would end soon. They were minutes away from plunging into the thickest part of the billowing mists. Gamay glanced upward for one last look at the sun. She blinked, unable to believe her eyes.

A man was dangling above the Zodiac. He was silhouetted against the dull sunlight, and she couldn't make out his face, but there was no mistaking the broad shoulders.

Kurt Austin.

He hung from a line attached to the helicopter. He'd been waving his arm and shouting himself hoarse, but the noise from the whirlpool had drowned out his voice as well as the sound of the whirling rotors.

Gamay dug her elbow into Paul's side. He managed a grim smile when he followed her pointing finger with his eyes and saw Austin doing his Peter Pan imitation above their heads.

The helicopter was matching the Zodiac's speed around the inside of the whirlpool. In an amazing example of stunt flying, Zavala flew the chopper at a banking angle to keep its rotors from touching the funnel's watery walls. A miscalculation, a drift of a few feet, and the helicopter would come crashing down on the Zodiac in a whirl of broken rotors.

The rescue had been hastily improvised. As the helicopter descended into the whirlpool, Austin had spotted a small flash of bright yellow more than halfway down the side of the funnel. He recognized Trout's foul-weather gear immediately and pointed it out to Zavala.

The helicopter chased after the whirling Zodiac like a cop pursuing a speeding car. Austin quickly tied a series of man-harness hitches in the rescue line. He had his foot in one of these loops and his hand in another as he swung back and forth in the turbulence caused by the rotor downwash and the updraft from the whirlpool.

Trout motioned for Gamay to go first. She waved at Austin to signal that she was ready. The helicopter dropped lower until the bottom loop of the ladder was about a foot from her outstretched hands.

Austin had climbed to the lower end of the makeshift ladder in the hope that his weight would stabilize it. But the line still jerked and snapped like a bullwhip.

The lifeline grazed Gamay's fingertips, only to evade her grasp. She tried two more times to grab the loop, but the same thing happened. In a desperate move, she stretched her body to every inch of its five-foot-eight height and pulled herself up until she was onto the higher pontoon.

The line came down again. She balanced herself precariously, threw her hands up like a volleyball player trying a block and this time she grabbed the lower loop with both hands.

She became airborne. With the weight of two people holding it down, the line became more stable. She hung on with one hand, grabbed the next loop and pulled herself higher. The rope spun as she climbed, increasing the effects of vertigo.

She faltered for a moment and might have fallen, but Austin saw that she was in trouble. He reached down, grabbed her wrist and hauled her to the next loop. She raised her chin, saw Austin's fierce grin a few feet above her and mouthed a silent thanks.

With the bottom loop free, it was Trout's turn to abandon the Zodiac. He reached above his head to signal that he was ready. The line dropped to within inches of his outstretched hand. As Trout went to grab the line, turbulence battered the helicopter, and it shifted toward the slanting water wall. Trout's fingers grasped at air, and he almost lost his balance.

Zavala had been struggling to compensate for the added weight on one side of the chopper. With a cool hand at the controls, he moved the helicopter back into position. Trout concentrated his full attention on the lowest loop, estimated its distance, then, using the springiness in the pontoon of the rubberized boat, he lunged up and grabbed the line. He held on to the single loop with one hand, unable to grab on to a higher handhold as he twisted in the wind.

The helicopter began a slow, steady ascent, moving up at an angle roughly parallel to the whirlpool's sloping side. The water walls fell away as the aircraft gained altitude. They had reached the funnel's midpoint when the Zodiac made one last revolution around the funnel and dis- appeared into the seething cauldron. Soon the helicopter was even with the water level at the surface, then above it. Zavala began to move the helicopter laterally, away from the vortex.

Trout had been unable to pull himself up to another loop. He still dangled with one outstretched arm. His fingers were raw from rope burn. He felt as if his elbow socket would pop at any second. Throughout the entire ascent, he had twisted at the end of the swinging line.

Zavala was trying to balance the need to put distance between the helicopter and the whirlpool with the added strain that would be placed on his human cargo by an increase in the chopper's speed.

The helicopter was about two hundred feet from the whirlpool's edge when Trout's strength gave out. He lost his grip and fell into the sea, hitting the water with a mighty splash.

He was fortunate that he hit the surface feetfirst. His legs cushioned the shock, but his knees came up into his chest and knocked the wind out of his lungs. He plunged several feet under the surface before the buoyancy in his flotation vest took hold. He came up spitting seawater. Trout didn't think his body could get much colder, but the frigid Atlantic immediately penetrated to his bones.

Zavala had felt a slight jounce when the load lightened and suspected he had lost one of his passengers. He brought the helicopter around in a banking turn, hovered for an instant, then dropped down so his friend could reach the rope ladder. For the second time that day, Trout was reaching for the rope. But as his stiff, sore fingers came within inches of the loop, he found himself dragged away by a strong current. Trout was a strong swimmer who had been around the ocean all his life, but the more he stroked, the farther from the rope he found himself.

The helicopter tried to keep pace.

The current was pulling Trout with such force that he found it impossible to stay in place long enough to reach for the loop. Time and again, he tried. He was rapidly drawn back to the edge of the whirlpool, sucked into the ring of breakers and swept under the wall of foam.

It was all he could do to keep his head above water to breathe. The whirlpool seemed to be trying to drag back at least *one* of the humans who had the audacity to escape its clutches.

The current carried him around the rim. Trout struggled to keep his head above water in the surflike conditions around the whirlpool.

Austin had no intention of giving up on his friend. He pulled himself up the line hand over hand and back into the helicopter. Then he braced his legs, grabbed the rope in two hands and hauled Gamay aboard.

He gave her a quick peck on the cheek, then threw the line back through the open door and climbed down to the end of the crude ladder.

Zavala was following Trout around the frothing rim. Again he brought the helicopter down until the rope was close enough for Trout to reach. Trout made a feeble grab for the line but it again eluded his grasp.

Austin guessed that Trout was too exhausted to pull himself out. He saw Gamay peering anxiously down at him from the helicopter. He gave her a wave, took a deep breath and jumped from the helicopter.

He came down in the water several feet from Trout and stroked his way closer to his friend. Trout croaked like a bullfrog with a bad cold:

'What . . . the . . . hell . . . are . . . you . . . doing . . . here?'

'You looked like you were having fun, so I thought I'd join you.'

'You're crazy!'

Austin gave him a soggy grin. He struggled to buckle their flotation vests together. With that task finally accomplished, he looked up and saw the helicopter swooping back and forth over their heads.

Austin waved, and Zavala brought the helicopter in for another rescue attempt. After several tries, Austin saw that he would have to have the speed of a rattlesnake to grab the flapping rope. The cold water had sapped his energy, and he knew there was little chance he'd be able to pull them both from the water. But he kept on trying for the line, and didn't notice right away that something odd was occurring.

They were moving more slowly around the whirlpool. The angle of the water in the great watery pit was less steep than it had been. He thought it was his imagination, or simply an optical illusion, but after a moment or two he saw that the bottom of the whirlpool was rising, giving the gyre a bowl shape.

Around the rim of the gyre, the raging circle of breakers seemed to be subsiding. The water was dropping back to ordinary sea level.

The bottom continued to rise. At the same time, their forward motion slowed, until they were moving at the pace of a walk.

Zavala had seen the change in the whirlpool's configuration, and once more brought the helicopter in low over the struggling figures.

Austin felt a surge of adrenaline-fueled energy. He reached up and his fingers closed around the line. Gamay was tending it and giving him plenty of slack. His cold, fumbling fingers slipped the line under Trout's armpits, then around himself, and he signaled Zavala to haul them out.

As they rose above the wavetops, Austin could see the NOAA ship and the *Throckmorton* cutting the distance in their direction.

He glanced down, and his eyes grew wide at the sight that greeted them. The whirlpool had virtually vanished, and in its place was a great, dark circle of slowly rotating water filled with every kind of ocean debris imaginable.

At the center of the puckered area was a massive

bubbling, like that made when a scuba diver is about to surface, only much bigger. Then the water rose in a greenish-white mound, and a huge object emerged from the sea and wallowed in the waves.

In its death throes, the maelstrom had disgorged a ship.

II

The LA-250 Renegade amphibious airplane had followed the rocky Maine coast to Camden, where it wheeled above a line of swanlike windjammers leaving the picturesque harbor and then headed east over Penobscot Bay. Its destination was a pear-shaped island easily identified by the candy-striped red-and-white lighthouse that stood on a high promontory at its narrower end.

The plane made a water landing near the lighthouse and taxied up to a mooring buoy. Two men got out of the plane, climbed into an outboard skiff that was tied up at the mooring and headed toward a wooden dock, where a cigarette boat and a forty-eight-foot schooner were tied up. They left the skiff and walked along the dock to a steep flight of stairs that led up the side of a rugged cliff.

The bright Maine sunshine reflected off Spider Barrett's shaved head and colorful tattoo. Barrett looked as if he could single-handedly cause a biker riot. He wore black jeans and a black T-shirt that revealed thick arms covered with skull tattoos. His eyes were hidden behind round-framed, reflecting blue sunglasses. A gold ring dangled from one ear, he had a silver stud in his nostril and an Iron Cross hung from a silver chain around his neck.

The Hell's Angel look was deceiving. Although Barrett owned a fortune in classic Harley-Davidson motorcycles, he was an honors graduate of the Massachusetts Institute of Technology where he had majored in quantum physics.

The pilot was named Mickey Doyle. He was a compactly

built man who looked like a walking sports bar. He wore a Celtics T-shirt and a New England Patriots zippered sweatshirt. A Red Sox baseball cap was jammed down on a thatch of unruly hair the color of carrot juice. He was chewing on a thick cigar stub. Doyle had grown up in tough, working-class South Boston. He had a quick, street-smart intelligence and antic Irish sense of humor, and a disarming smile that charmed the unwary but failed to soften the hardness in his blue eyes.

A man carrying an automatic rifle materialized from a thicket of low-growing blueberry bushes. He was dressed in a camouflage uniform and wore a black beret at a rakish angle. He gave the two men a hostile stare, jerked the gun barrel toward the base of the cliff and followed a few paces behind, his weapon cradled in his arm.

At the foot of the bluff, the guard clicked a remote and a door disguised as rock facing opened. On the other side was an elevator that whisked them up to the lighthouse.

As they stepped from the lighthouse they saw Tristan Margrave, who had been chopping wood and stacking it into a neat pile. He put his ax down, waved the armed man away and walked over to greet the newcomers with a handshake.

'So much for my peace and quiet,' he said, a mock frown on his thin, satanic face.

He was taller than the other two men by a foot. Although his hands were callused from cutting wood, he was neither a laborer nor a *New York Times* reporter named Barnes, as he had introduced himself to the detective Frank Malloy. He had met Barrett at MIT, where he had graduated with a degree in advanced computer science. Working together, they had developed innovative software that had made them millionaires many times over.

Barrett watched the departing guard disappear into the

trees. 'You didn't have the guard dog the last time I was here.'

'Guy from the security company I hired,' Margrave said dismissively. 'There's a contingent of them camped farther down the island. Gant and I thought it might be good to hire them.'

'And what Gant wants, Gant gets.'

'I know you don't like the guy, but Jordan is vital to our efforts. We need his foundation to negotiate the political agreements we're going to get after our work is done.'

'Lucifer's Legion not good enough for you anymore?'

Margrave chuckled. 'My so-called legion began to fall apart as soon as there was any hint of discipline. You know how anarchists hate authority. I needed professionals. They call themselves "consultants" these days, and charge an arm and a leg for their services. That guard was just doing his job.'

'What *is* his job?'

'To make sure no unauthorized visitors come onto the island.'

'Were you expecting visitors?'

'Our enterprise is too important to fail.' Margrave grinned. 'Hell, what if someone saw a guy with a spider tattoo on his head and began asking questions?'

Barrett shrugged and glanced at the woodpile. 'Glad to see you're living your retro philosophy, but cutting all those logs would be a lot easier with a chain saw. I know you can afford one.'

'I'm a neo-*anarchist*, not a neo-Luddite. I believe in technology when it's for the good of mankind. Besides, the chain saw is broken.' He turned to the pilot. 'How was the flight from Portland, Mickey?'

'Smooth. I flew over Camden, hoping the pretty sailboats would cheer your partner up.'

'Why should he need cheering up?' Margrave said. 'He's about to enter the pantheon of science. What's going on, Spider?'

'We've got problems.'

'That's what you said on the phone. I thought you were kidding.'

Barrett gave him a bleak smile. 'Not this time.'

'In that case, I think we all need a drink.' Margrave led the way up a flagstone walkway that led to the big, two-story, white clapboard building attached to the lighthouse.

When Margrave bought the island three years earlier, he had decided to preserve the keeper's house as it had been in the days when it quartered the taciturn men who manned the lonely station. The pine-board walls had bead-board wainscoting, and the worn linoleum flooring was original, as were the slate sink and hand pump in the kitchen.

Margrave gave Doyle's shoulder a squeeze. 'Hey, Mickey, Spider and I have some stuff to discuss. There's a bottle of Bombay Sapphire in the pantry. Rustle up a couple of drinks, like a good fellow. There's beer in the fridge for you.'

'Aye-aye, Captain,' the pilot said with a grin and a brisk salute.

The other two men ascended a painted wrought-iron spiral staircase to the second floor. The upper level, which once housed bedrooms for the keeper and his family, had been gutted to create one large room.

The clinical minimalist décor stood in stark contrast to the preservation on the ground floor. A laptop computer sat on a black teak table on one side of the room. A chrome-and-leather sofa and a couple of armchairs were the only furniture on the other side. Windows on three walls offered views of the island, with its tall pine trees, and the sparkling waters of the bay. Flowing through the open windows was the salty scent of the sea.

Margrave motioned Barrett to the sofa and settled into a chair. Doyle arrived a few minutes later and served the drinks. He popped a can of Budweiser for himself and took a seat at the table.

Margrave raised his glass in a toast. 'Here's to you, Spider. The bright lights of New York City will never be the same. Too bad your genius must go unrecognized.'

'Genius had nothing to do with it. Electromagnetism runs almost every part of our lives. Fiddle around with the magnetic fields and it's easy to mess stuff up.'

'That's the understatement of the century,' Margrave said, roaring with laughter. 'You should have seen the look on that cop's face when his name was plastered all over Times Square and Broadway.'

'Wish I could have been there in person, but it was easy enough to do from my house. The locator you carried in your recorder did its job. The big question is whether our demonstration put us anywhere nearer our goal.'

A cloud seemed to pass over Margrave's brow. 'I've been checking the media reports,' he said with a shake of his head. 'The spin machine is going full steam. The Elites are saying it was a fluke that the disruptions coincided with the world economic meeting. They're worried, but the fools haven't taken our warning seriously.'

'Time for another shot across the bow?'

Margrave got up and went over to the table. He came back with the laptop computer, settled in his chair again and tapped on the keys. The sole blank wall glowed and displayed a huge electronic map of the oceans and continents.

The global composite image was made from data fed into it from orbiting satellites, ocean buoys and dozens of ground stations around the world. Continents were silhouetted in black against the bluish green of the sea. Numbers from 1 to 4 blinked in the Atlantic Ocean; two were above the equator, two below it. A similar pattern was displayed for the Pacific Ocean.

'The numbers show where we made experimental probes of the ocean floor. The computer modeling I've programmed indicates that if we bring all our resources to bear in this area of the South Atlantic, we'll get the desired effect. The time for warnings is past. The Elites are either too dumb or too arrogant. In either case, we should go for the big enchilada.'

'How soon are you talking about?'

'As soon as we can get things set up. The only language that the Elites understand is money. We've got to hit them hard in their pocketbooks.'

Barrett removed his sunglasses and stared into space, apparently deep in thought.

'What's going on, Spider?'

'I think we should call the whole thing off,' Barrett said.

Margrave's face underwent an amazing transformation. The V-shaped eyebrows and mouth deepened. The expression of devilish mischief was gone. In its place was a look of pure malevolence. 'You've apparently got some issues.'

'We're not talking college pranks, Tris. You know the potential for damage if this thing gets out of hand. Millions could die. There would be huge economic and natural disruptions that the world might not recover from for decades.'

'How could it get out of control? You said you had a handle on it.'

Barrett seemed to sink into himself.

'I was kidding myself. It's always been a crapshoot. After that business with the cargo ship on Site Two, I went back to the drawing board. I tested a miniaturized version of the equipment in Puget Sound. The orcas went crazy. They attacked a whole bunch of kids. They would have eaten one guy if I hadn't pulled him out of the water.'

'Someone saw the zapper?'

'Yeah, a guy named Kurt Austin. I read about him in the paper. Works for NUMA, and was leading the kayak race that got busted up. He only saw the setup for a second. He wouldn't have known what it was for.'

A dark cloud seemed to pass over Margrave's face. 'I hope you're right. Otherwise, we'd have to eliminate Mr Austin.'

Barrett looked horrified. 'You're *kidding*!'

Margrave smiled. 'Of course I was just joking, old pal. I saw the reports of the orca attack. What are you telling me, Spider, that orcas are predators?'

'No, I'm saying that my experiment messed with their sensory abilities because I was unable to control the electromagnetic field.'

'So what?' Margrave said. 'No one got hurt.'

'Have you forgotten that we lost one of our own ships?'

'It was a skeleton crew. They knew the dangers involved. They were well paid to take the risk.'

'What about the *Southern Belle*? Those people weren't paid to take part in our experiments.'

'Ancient history. It was an accident, my friend.'

'Hell, I know that. But we're responsible for their deaths.'

Margrave leaned forward in his chair. His eyes burned with smoldering intensity.

'*You* know why I feel so passionate about this enterprise.'

'Guilt. You want to atone for the Margraves who built up your family fortune on the blood of slaves and opium addicts.'

Margrave shook his head.

'My ancestors were small-time compared to what we're facing. We're battling a concentration of power that is unlike anything the world has ever seen. Nothing can rival the multinational corporations that are taking over the world with the help of the WTO, the World Bank and the IMF. These unelected, undemocratic entities ignore civilized laws and do anything they want, no matter what impact it has on everyone else. I want to reclaim power over the earth for its inhabitants.'

'Spoken like a classic anarchist,' Barrett said. 'I'm with you, but killing innocent people doesn't seem to be the way to do it.'

'I am truly sorry about the loss of those ships and their crew. It's unfortunate, but it couldn't be helped. We're not bloodthirsty or crazy. If we pull this thing off, that ship is a small price to pay. Some sacrifices are necessary for the greater good.'

'The end justifies the means?'

'If necessary.'

'Thank you, Mr Karl Marx.'

'Marx was a charlatan, an overblown theorist.'

'This project is based upon some pretty unconventional theories, you'll have to admit. Marxism was only a half-baked idea before Lenin read *Das Kapital* and turned Russia into the workingman's paradise.'

'This is a fascinating discussion, but let's get back to something we both agree on. *Technology.* When we started this gig, you said you could keep a rein on all the power we're unleashing.'

'I also told you it would be an imperfect system without the proper frequencies,' Barrett said. 'I've done the best I could without those numbers, but there's a big difference between a rifle shot and a shotgun blast, which is what we're using. The waves and gyres we created far exceed anything we saw in the computer models.' He paused and took a deep breath. 'I'm thinking of pulling out, Tris. What we're doing is too dangerous.'

'You *can't* pull out. The project would go down the drain.'

'That's not true. You could plunge ahead on the basis of the work I've done. As your friend, I'm urging you not to continue.'

Instead of reacting with anger, Margrave laughed. 'Hey, Spider, *you're* the one who discovered the Kovacs Theorems and brought them to my attention.'

'Sometimes I wish I hadn't. The man was brilliant, his theories dangerous. It may have been a blessing that his knowledge died with him.'

'If I told you Kovacs had come up with a way to neutralize the effect of his theorems, would you reconsider your decision to leave the project?'

'Having a fail-safe option would make a big difference. But it's a moot point. The knowledge died with Kovacs at the end of World War Two.'

A sly look came into Margrave's eyes. 'Pretend, for the sake of discussion, that he *didn't* die.'

'Not a chance. His lab got overrun by the Russians. He was killed or captured.'

'If he was captured, why didn't the Russians expand on his work and make superweapons?'

'They *tried* to,' Barrett said. 'They caused the Anchorage earthquake and screwed up the weather.' He paused, and light dawned in his eyes. 'If the Russians had Kovacs, they would have done better. So he *must* have died in 1944.'

'That's the common assumption.'

'Wipe that smug grin off your face. You *know* something, don't you?'

'The story was true, as far as it went,' Margrave said. 'Kovacs publishes the paper about electromagnetic warfare. The Germans kidnap him to develop a weapon that will save the Third Reich. The Russians capture the lab and take the scientists back to Russia. But one of those German scientists left Russia after the Cold War ended. I located him. Cost me a fortune in bribes and payoffs.'

'Are you telling me he had the data we need?'

'I wish it were that easy. The project was strictly compartmentalized. The Germans held the Kovacs family hostage. He held back crucial data hoping to keep his family alive.'

'Makes sense,' Barrett said. 'If the Germans were aware there was an antidote to his work, they would no longer need him.'

'That's my guess too. He didn't know that the Nazis disposed of his family almost immediately, and forged letters from his wife urging him to cooperate for the sake of the children. Hours before the Russians arrived at the lab, a man showed up and took Kovacs off with him. Tall, blond guy driving a Mercedes, according to our scientist.'

Barrett rolled his eyes. 'That description would fit half the population of Germany.'

'We got lucky. A few years after he left Russia, our German informant came across a picture of the blond man in a ski publication. Sometime in the sixties, the guy who snatched Kovacs won an amateur ski race. He had a beard and was older, but our source was certain this was the guy.'

'Have you tracked him down?'

'I sent some of our security guys to invite him for a talk. Same company that supplies the island guards.'

'Who is this company, Murder Incorporated?'

Margrave smiled. 'Gant suggested them. I'll admit that the security company we're using is hard-assed. We wanted pros who wouldn't be shy about pushing the boundaries of the law.'

'Hope you're getting your money's worth from these law pushers.'

'Not so far. They blew their big chance to talk to the Kovacs contact. He smelled them coming and took off.'

'Cheer up. Even if you find him, there's no assurance he knows anything about Kovacs's secrets.'

'I came to the same conclusion. So I went back to Kovacs. I programmed a massive search of everything written and said about him. I started with the premise that if he had lived, he would have continued his research.'

'Quite the leap of faith. His work destroyed his family.'

'He'd be careful, but his fingerprints would be hard to hide. My program combed every scientific publication written since the war. It found a number of articles mentioning unique commercial uses of electromagnetic fields.'

Barrett leaned forward in his chair. 'You've got my attention.'

'One of the pioneers in the research was a company incorporated in Detroit by a European immigrant named Viktor Janos.'

'Janus was the two-faced Roman god who looks to the past and the future. Interesting.'

'I thought so. The parallels with Kovacs's work were too weird to be true. It's as if Van Gogh copied Cézanne. He might master impressionistic light, but he couldn't stop himself from using colors that were bold and basic.'

'What do you know about Janos?'

'Not a lot. Money can buy anonymity. He was supposedly Romanian.'

'Romanian was one of the six languages Kovacs was fluent in. Tell me more.'

'His lab was in Detroit, and he lived in Grosse Pointe. He must have run whenever he saw a camera, but he couldn't hide the fact that he was a generous philanthropist. His wife was mentioned in the local society pages. There was a birth notice of their child, a son, who died with his wife in a car crash.'

'A dead end, literally?'

'That's what I thought. But Janos had a granddaughter. I referenced her name and struck gold. She had done a graduate thesis about woolly mammoths.'

'The ancient elephants? What's that got to do with Kovacs?'

'Stay with me. She maintains that the mammoths were wiped out by a natural catastrophe that was a more devastating version of what we're trying to do. Here's the interesting part. In her writing, she said that had this happened today, science would have been able to neutralize the catastrophe.'

'The antidote?' Barrett snorted. 'You're kidding.'

Margrave retrieved a portfolio from the table and tossed it into Barrett's lap. 'After you read this, I think you'll change your mind about the project.'

'What about the granddaughter?'

'She's a paleontologist, working with the University of Alaska. Gant and I decided to send someone up there to talk to her.'

'Why not hold off on the project until we find out what she knows?'

'I'll wait, but I want to get all the pieces in place so that we can hit the ground running.' Margrave turned to Doyle, who had been quietly absorbing the discussion. 'What do you think about all this?'

'Hell, I'm just a dumb air jockey from Southie. I go with the flow.'

Margrave winked at Barrett. 'Spider and I will be busy for a while.'

'I got you. I'll grab another beer and go for a walk.'

After Doyle left, the two other men huddled over a computer. When they were satisfied their plan had gone as far as it could, they agreed to meet again. Doyle was puttering around the dock when the meeting broke up.

'I appreciate you changing your mind about leaving the project,' Margrave said to Barrett. 'We've been friends a long time.'

'This goes beyond friendship,' Barrett said.

They shook hands, and minutes later the plane was skimming across the bay for takeoff. Margrave watched until it became a speck in the sky, then he went back into the lighthouse. He stared out the second-floor window for a moment with a smile on his strange face. Barrett was a genius, but he was unbelievably naïve when it came to politics.

Despite his assurances, Margrave had no intention of delaying the project. If ever a time existed when the end justified the means, it was *now*.

12

'Incredible!' Barrett said with a shake of his head.

He sat in the seaplane's passenger seat, his nose buried in the portfolio Margrave had given him.

Doyle looked over. 'Good stuff Tris gave you?'

'*Good!* This material is fantastic!'

Barrett raised his head from the papers he had been engrossed in and glanced out the window. He had paid little attention to the world outside the cockpit and expected to see the same rocky coastline they had followed on the flight to the lighthouse island. There was no sign of the Gulf of Maine. Instead, thick pine forest spread out in every direction.

'Hey, Mickey, did you have one beer too many back there?' Barrett said. 'Where's the water? This isn't the way we came in. We're lost.'

Doyle grinned as if he'd been caught playing a practical joke. 'This is the scenic route. I wanted to show you where I go deer hunting. It will only add a few minutes to the trip. Sounds like there's good stuff in the homework Tris gave you.'

'Yeah, it's pretty amazing material,' Barrett said. 'Tris is right. The subject is arcane, and the author generalizes a lot. And there's a difference between naturally occurring phenomena and the kind of thing we're trying to stir up. But she writes with firsthand knowledge about this so-called antidote. She sounds as if she had talked to Kovacs personally.'

'Good man. Guess that means you're sticking with the project.'

'Naw.' Barrett shook his head. 'There's nothing here that will make me change my mind. Even if we talked to this woman, there's no telling how much she actually knows or how much is simply theoretical. This craziness can't go forward. The only way to head off a disaster is to go public.'

'What do you mean?'

'I've got a friend on the science desk at the *Seattle Times*. I'm calling him as soon as we land, and I'm going to lay out the whole story.'

'Hey, Spider, you can't tell people the skinny on this deal,' Doyle said with a vigorous shake of his head. 'You sure you want to go public? You could get in one hell of a big mess.'

'I'll have to take that chance.'

'This will wreck Tris as well as the project. He's your partner.'

'I've given it a lot of thought. It will be better for him in the long run.'

'I dunno about that.'

'*I* do. He may end up thanking me for scuttling this crazy scheme.'

'Why not wait? He said he would hold off until someone talked to Kovacs's granddaughter.'

'I've worked with Tris a long time. He only said that to calm me down,' Barrett said with a smile. 'The world has got to know what we've been hatching, and, unfortunately, I'm the one to spill the beans.'

'Ah hell.'

'What's wrong, Mickey? You said I was the one being gloomy.'

'How long have we known each other, Spider?'

'Since our MIT days. You were working the cafeteria. How could you forget?'

'I haven't. You were the only one of those smart-assed college kids who didn't treat me like scum. You were my friend.'

'You paid me back, big-time. You knew the best bars to find girls in Cambridge.'

'I *still* do,' Doyle said with a grin.

'You've done okay for yourself, Mickey. Not everyone can be a pilot.'

'I'm small potatoes compared to the Man.'

'Tris? I guess he is larger than life. I've always been a tinkerer. I'm like the architect who builds one house. He's like the developer who sells thousands of those houses. His vision was what made us both fortunes.'

'You believe all this anarchy stuff he talks about?'

'Some of it. Things are way off balance in the world, and I'd like to shake up the Elites, but I was more interested in the scientific challenge. Now that's turned to crap, and I have to set things straight.'

'And I'm telling you, like a friend, that's not a good idea.'

'I appreciate that friendship, but I have to say I'm sorry.'

Doyle paused a moment before answering, then said, 'I'm sorry too,' with sadness in his voice.

With the matter apparently settled, Barrett went back to the portfolio, occasionally glancing out the cockpit window. They were flying over dense forest when Doyle cocked his ear. 'Whoops! What's that?'

Barrett looked up from his reading. 'I don't hear anything except the engine.'

'Something's not right,' Doyle said with a frown on his face. The plane dipped several feet. 'Damn, we're losing power. Hold on. I'm gonna have to set her down.'

'Set her down?' Barrett said with alarm. He craned his neck, looking at the thick woods below. 'Where?'

'I used to know the countryside pretty well, but it's been a while since I hunted up in these parts. I think there's a lake not far from here.'

The plane lost more altitude.

'I see something,' Barrett said, pointing at a flash of reflected sunlight.

Doyle gave Barrett the thumbs-up sign and steered toward the patch of blue water. The aircraft descended rapidly at an oblique angle that looked as if it would end in the tall pines. At the last second, Doyle pulled the plane up, skimming the treetops before making a pancake landing on the lake.

The plane coasted on its momentum toward shore and scraped up onto a narrow beach. Doyle was laughing. 'That was a hell of a ride. You okay?'

'My ass is up around my ears, but other than that I'm fine.'

'Getting in was easy,' Doyle said, glancing at the surrounding woods. 'Getting out will be the hard part.'

Barrett pointed at the radio. 'Shouldn't we be calling for help?'

'In a minute. I want to check for damage.' He climbed out onto the pontoon and stepped onto the beach. He stooped a couple of times to look under the fuselage. 'Hey, Spider, take a look at this.'

Barrett got out of the plane. 'What's up?'

'Here, under the fuselage. It's amazing.'

Barrett started to get down on his knees. He was still carrying the portfolio.

'I don't see anything.'

'You will,' Doyle said. 'You will.' He slipped a pistol out from under his windbreaker.

Barrett bent lower, and the leather folder dropped from his hand. The thick wad of papers spilled out onto the ground. Some of the sheets were caught by a lake breeze and scattered across the clearing as if they had a life on their own.

Barrett bolted after the wayward portfolio, scooping up the papers with the skill of a shortstop. He managed to gather all the papers before they blew into the trees. He tucked them back into the folder and hugged it close to his chest. He had a grin of triumph on his face as he started to walk back to the plane.

He saw the gun in Doyle's hand.

'What's going on, Mickey?'

'Good-bye, Spider.'

He could tell from the tone of Doyle's voice that his friend wasn't joking. His grin vanished. 'Why?'

'I can't let you sink the project.'

'Look, Mickey. Tris and I can talk this out.'

'It's got nothing to do with Tris.'

'I don't understand.'

'I'll hoist a beer in your name the next time I get back to Cambridge,' Doyle said.

The .25-caliber pistol in his hand went *pop-pop*.

The first bullet buried itself in the leather folder. Barrett felt the thud against his chest, but he was still in a state of disbelief when the second bullet grazed his head. Survival reflexes took over. He dropped the folder, turned and bolted into the woods. Doyle got off a couple more shots, but the bullets dug harmlessly into a tree trunk. He swore and gave chase.

Barrett ignored the low-lying tree branches that slashed at his face and the briers that grabbed at his jeans. His surprise and dismay at being shot by a friend had given way to sheer terror. Blood was trickling down the side of his head and neck. As he crashed through the forest, he saw a silver shimmer ahead. *Oh hell.* He had circled back toward the lake, but there was no going back.

He burst from the woods onto a sandy beach a hundred yards or so from the plane. He could hear Doyle crashing through the brush just behind him. Without hesitating, he slogged into the water, and then took a deep breath and dove under the surface. He was a strong swimmer, and, even with his boots on, he got several yards from shore by the time Doyle arrived at the water's edge. He went as deep as he could go.

Doyle stood on the shore and carefully aimed at the ripples marking the surface where Barrett had disappeared. He peppered the water with bullets, patiently reloaded and shot off another clip.

The water was crimson where Barrett had disappeared. Doyle decided to wait five minutes until he was sure Barrett wasn't holding his breath, but he heard someone yelling from the other side of a patch of tall weeds growing in the water off to his left.

He glanced back at the stain growing on the surface of the lake and tucked the gun in his belt. Walking briskly, he made his way through the woods and back to the clearing. He gathered up the papers that Barrett had dropped and slipped them into the folder, first noticing the bullet hole in the leather binding. He cursed. Served him right for using a popgun. Minutes later, he was in the plane, flying over the treetops.

As soon as he thought he had telephone service, Doyle punched out a number on his cell phone. 'Well?' said a man's voice at the other end.

'It's done,' Doyle said. 'I tried to talk him out of it, but he was determined to spill the beans.'

'Too bad. He was brilliant. Any problems?'

'Nope,' Doyle lied.

'Good work,' the voice said. 'I want to see you tomorrow.'

Doyle said he would be there. As he clicked off, he experienced a twinge of Irish sentimentality at having to kill his old friend. But Doyle had grown up in a neighborhood where a friendship could end with a nighttime burial over a drug deal gone wrong or an imprudent comment. This was not the first time he had dispatched a friend or acquaintance. Business, unfortunately, was business. He put Barrett out of his mind and began to think of the riches and power that would soon be in his grasp.

He would have been less at ease if he knew what was going on back at the lake. A canoe had rounded the weed patch. The two fly fishermen in the canoe had heard the pop of Doyle's handgun. They wanted to warn whoever was hunting that people were in the area. One of the men was a Boston lawyer, but, more important, the other was a doctor.

As they emerged from the weeds, the lawyer pointed toward the water and said, 'What the hell is that?'

The doctor said, 'It looks like a melon with a spider on it.'

They paddled until they were a few feet from the object. The melon disappeared, and in its place were eyes, a nose and a gaping mouth. The lawyer raised his paddle and prepared to bring it down on the floating head. Spider Barrett looked up at the two astonished faces. His mouth opened.

'Help me,' he pleaded.

13

With a hull displacement of twenty-three thousand tons and seventy-five thousand horsepower produced by its powerful engines, the Yamal-class Russian icebreaker *Kotelny* was capable of continuously breaking through seven feet of ice. Its sharply angled bow sliced through the slushy spring ice pack like a warm knife through sherbet. As Karla Janos stood in the bow and surveyed the fog-shrouded island that was her destination, she felt as if someone had walked across her grave.

The involuntary shudder that passed through her willowy body had nothing to do with the rawness of the weather in the East Siberian Sea. Karla was bundled in a down parka, and she had become inured to biting cold after two winters with the University of Alaska at Fairbanks, where temperatures routinely dropped to forty degrees below zero. She was well enough acquainted with the territory around the Arctic Circle to know that there was little chance Ivory Island would live up to the image of warm whiteness evoked by its name, but she was totally unprepared for the total bleakness of the isolated place.

As a scientist, Karla knew that her reaction was emotional rather than objective, but the island had a forbidding aspect that she couldn't easily shrug off. The most prominent feature of the island was a dead volcano that still had patches of snow around its truncated summit. The overcast skies drained all traces of color from the sunlight so that the sea and land appeared to be bathed in a depressing gray light. As the ship moved closer to the island, she saw that the low rolling hills and tundra around the volcano were broken by a network of ravines whose twisting cliffs, combined with a trick of the slanting sunlight, created an optical illusion, as if the surface of the island were writhing in pain.

'Excuse me, Miss Janos. We'll be dropping anchor in fifteen minutes.'

She turned and saw the ship's commander. Captain Ivanov was a sturdily built man in his sixties. His broad face was weathered from the arctic elements, and a white sailor's beard fringed his chin.

The captain was a kindly man who had spent much of his life sailing the frigid waters around the archipelago. Karla and the avuncular Ivanov had forged a strong friendship since she had boarded the icebreaker at its home base on Wrangel Island. She had enjoyed their wide-ranging chats over dinner. The captain had impressed her with a scope of knowledge of history, biology and meteorology that went beyond the tools necessary to command a large ship on unfriendly seas. She had made him blush when she called him a Renaissance man.

Karla reminded the captain of his daughter, a dancer with the Bolshoi Ballet. She was tall, slim and long of leg, and she moved with the easy grace of someone who is confident in her body. Her long blond hair was tied tight at the back of her head in dancer style. She had inherited the best features of her Magyar and Slavic ancestry: a wide forehead, high cheeks, wide, sensuous mouth, a creamy complexion and smoky gray eyes whose almond shape hinted at an Asian forebear. Although Karla had studied dance briefly, she tended more toward athletic pursuits. She had been a track standout at the University of Michigan, where she earned a degree in paleontology with a minor in vertebrate biology.

'Thank you, Captain Ivanov,' she said. 'My bags are packed. I'll collect them from the cabin right away.'

'Take your time.' He gazed at her with kindly blue eyes. 'You seem distracted. Are you all right?'

'Yes, I'm fine, thank you. I've been watching the island, and, well, it's rather sinister-looking. My imagination, obviously.'

He followed her gaze. 'Not entirely. I've sailed these waters for years. Ivory Island has always seemed different. Do you know much about its history?'

'Only that it was found by a fur trader.'

'That's right. He established the settlement on the river. He killed some of the other traders in a fight over furs, so they couldn't name it after a murderer.'

'I've heard that story. I'm not so sure, even if I were a murderer, that I'd like my name attached to such a lonely and unattractive site. Besides, Ivory Island seems more poetic. And from what I know about the island as a source of ivory, accurate as well.' She paused. 'You said the island was different. In what way?'

The captain shrugged. 'Sometimes, when I've passed the island in the dark, I have seen lights moving about near the old fur-trapper settlement on the river. What they call Ivorytown.'

'That's the expedition's headquarters, where I'll be staying.'

'They were probably pockets of gas luminescence.'

'*Gas?* You said the lights were moving.'

'You're very observant,' the captain said. 'I apologize. I haven't been trying to frighten you.'

'On the contrary, you're *interesting* me.'

Karla was so much like his daughter. Intelligent. Headstrong. Fearless. 'In any event, we'll be back in two weeks to pick you up,' he said. 'Good luck with your research.'

'Thank you. I'm optimistic that I'll find something on the island to bolster my theory about the cause of the woolly mammoth's extinction.'

The captain's lips curled into a wry smile. 'If your colleagues on the island are successful, we may be seeing mammoths in the Moscow zoo.'

Karla heaved a heavy sigh. 'Maybe not in our lifetime. Even if the expedition manages to find mammoth DNA from an ancient specimen and it can be used to artificially impregnate an Indian elephant, it could take more than fifty years to develop a creature that is mostly mammoth.'

'I hope it never happens,' the captain said. 'I don't think it's wise to tamper with nature. It's like the sailors say about whistling on board a ship. You might whistle up a wind.'

'I agree, which is why I'm glad I'm engaged in pure research.'

'Again, I offer my best wishes. Now, if you'll excuse me, I must tend to my ship.'

Karla thanked him for his hospitality, and they shook hands. Karla felt a sense of loneliness as the captain walked off, but she braced herself with thoughts of the work ahead. With a defiant glance at the island, she headed off to her cabin, where she collected her bags, and came back on deck to wait for her ride to shore.

The ship made a sweep close to the shore of a natural harbor to break a channel through the ice. Karla piled her bags into the ship's launch, then got in herself. The open boat was lowered to the water, the two crewmen aboard cast off the lines and they headed toward the island, weaving their way around chunks of ice as big as cars. As the boat made its way toward land, she could see a figure on shore waving at them.

Minutes later, the launch pulled up to shore a few hundred feet from a river that emptied out into the harbor and Karla stepped out onto the gravelly beach. The middle-aged woman who had been waiting on the beach came over and gave her an unexpected hug.

'I'm Maria Arbatov,' she said, speaking with a Russian accent. 'I'm so glad to meet you, Karla. I've heard many good things about your work. I can't believe someone so young has done so much.'

Maria had silver hair tied up in a bun, high, rosy cheekbones and a broad smile that took the chill out of the arctic air.

'I'm pleased to meet you too, Maria. Thanks for the warm welcome.'

Maria excused herself and supervised the unloading of some supplies that had been carried in on the boat. The boxes were neatly piled on the beach, where they would be retrieved later. Maria said there was nobody or nothing around to disturb them. Karla thanked the boat crew. She and Maria climbed a slight hill and hiked along the bank of the river. A path had been trampled by boot prints, suggesting that it had been the major traffic artery to and from the beach for a long time.

'How was your trip?' Maria asked as their feet crunched in the permafrost.

'*Great.* Captain Ivanov is a sweet man. The *Kotelny* regularly takes tourist groups around the islands, so my cabin was quite comfortable.'

'Captain Ivanov was very gracious to us as well when he brought the expedition in. I hope you didn't get too comfortable. We have done our best, but our accommodations are far more primitive than those on the ship.'

'I'll survive. How is the project going?'

'As you Americans say, do you want the good news first or the bad?'

Karla gave her a sidelong glance. 'I'll leave it up to you.'

'First, the *good* news. We have gone out on several expeditions and collected many promising specimens.'

'That *is* good news. Now the bad?'

'You have arrived in the middle of a new Russo-Japanese war.'

'I wasn't aware that I was stepping into a combat zone. What do you mean?'

'You know that this expedition is a joint venture?'

'Yes. It's a consortium of Russian and Japanese interests. The idea is to share the findings.'

'As a scientist, you know that what's important is not so much *what* you find but how much credit you get for it.'

'Credit equals stature, career and, ultimately, money.'

'Correct. And, in this case, there is a great deal of money at stake, so it is even more important who will get the credit for our findings.'

They were about a half a mile from the beach and had climbed a low rise when Maria announced: 'We are almost there. Welcome to Ivorytown.'

They followed the path across the tundra to several buildings clustered near the river. The biggest structure, the size of a single-car garage, was surrounded by several windowless buildings that were a third as big. The roofs were constructed from rusty corrugated steel. Two large tents had been set off to the side. Karla walked up to the nearest building and ran her hand over the rough, gray surface of the outside wall.

'This is made almost entirely of bones and tusks,' she said in wonderment.

'The people who lived here made use of the most

152

plentiful material on the island,' Maria said. 'The fossils are bound in some sort of homemade concrete. It's quite sturdy, and fulfills its main function, which is to keep the cold wind out.'

The weathered wooden door in the side of the building swung open and a heavyset man with a beetling brow emerged. He shouldered Maria aside, hugged Karla like a long-lost uncle and kissed her wetly on both cheeks.

'I'm Sergei Arbatov,' he said. He gave Karla a gold-toothed smile. 'I'm the leader of this project. It's so nice to have such a lovely creature working with us.'

Karla couldn't help but notice the shadow that crossed Maria's brow. She had done her homework on the expedition members and knew that while Sergei was the project leader, his wife was his senior in the number of academic degrees she had. Karla constantly had to butt heads against the male academic establishment, and didn't like the way he patronized her and ignored his wife. Karla stepped past Arbatov and put her arm around Maria's shoulders.

'And it will be nice working with someone of such scientific achievement,' she said.

Maria's frown disappeared and she beamed with pleasure. Arbatov's glower indicated that he didn't appreciate the snub. It's not certain what would have happened next if two more people had not stepped out of the building. Without hesitating, Karla stepped over and bowed slightly before one of the men.

'Dr Sato, my name is Karla Janos. I'm pleased to meet you,' she said to the older of the two men. 'I've heard so much about the Gifu Science and Technology Center and Kinki University.' She turned to the younger man. 'And you must be Dr Ito, the veterinarian, with Kagoshima University in southern Japan.'

The men's mouths widened in toothy smiles, and their heads bobbed, almost in unison, in polite bows.

'We hope you had a good trip,' Dr Sato said. 'We're very pleased you could join our expedition.'

'Thank you for allowing me to be here. I know you must be busy with your own work.'

Karla chatted with the two men about mutual scientific acquaintances, and then Maria came over and took her by the arm.

'Let me show you where you'll be staying.' She led the way to one of the smaller buildings, and they stepped inside the dim and musty interior. 'This was built by some of the old fur traders, and the camp was expanded by ivory hunters. It's more comfortable than it looks,' Maria said. 'The big tents are used as our kitchen and dining room. The little tent set off by itself away from the camp is a unisex bathroom. It gets breezy out there, so you'll learn to be quick. There's no shower. You'll have to be happy with sponge baths. We've got an electric generator, but we use it sparingly because of the limited amount of fuel.'

'I'm sure I'll be quite happy,' Karla said, although she wondered for an instant if any of the fur trader murders had taken place in the building. She unrolled a foam pad and bedding on the floor.

'I must compliment you. You had our Japanese friends eating out of your hand when you brought up their affiliations.'

'It was easy. Once I had their names, I looked them up on the Internet. I saw their pictures and read about their backgrounds. I think my charm was lost on Sergei, though.'

Maria let out a whooping laugh. 'My husband is a good man at heart or I would have gotten rid of him a long time ago. But he can be a toad sometimes, especially when it comes to women, and his ego is like a big balloon.'

'I read about the both of you as well. He doesn't have half the scientific credentials you have.'

'Yes, but he's got the *political* connections, and that's what counts. He will respect you for standing up to him, but if you don't mind flattering the old man he'll be eating out of your hand too. He's really quite insecure, and I do it all the time.'

'Thanks for the advice. I'll butter him up. What's our schedule?'

'Everything's up in the air right now.'

'I don't understand.' She saw a glint of amusement in Maria's eye. 'Is there something you haven't told me?'

'Yes. The good news is that we have found something quite wonderful. The bad news is that the others are deciding whether to let you in on the discovery now or whether they should wait until they know you better.'

Karla's curiosity was piqued by the tantalizing hint, but she said, 'Whatever you decide is fine with me. I've got my own work to keep me busy.'

Maria nodded, and led the way back to where the other scientists were gathered outside the large building.

Addressing Karla in a stern voice, Arbatov said, 'You have arrived on the island at a very awkward, or fortunate, time, depending on you.'

'I don't understand.'

'We have taken a vote,' Arbatov said in a stern voice. 'We have decided to bring you into our confidence. But first you must swear not to divulge what you have seen to anyone, now or later, without the express consent of the members of this expedition.'

'I appreciate that,' Karla said. 'But I don't understand.' Karla glanced at Maria for help.

155

Arbatov gestured toward the shed, whose thick wooden door was flanked by the Japanese men. They looked like sculptures on an Asian temple. At the signal from the Russian, Sato opened the door and swept his arm in the air, inviting her to step inside.

Everyone was smiling. For a moment, Karla wondered if she had blundered into a den of lunatics who'd been driven mad by the arctic isolation. But she tentatively stepped forward and entered the big shed. The atmosphere was far less musty than her sleeping quarters, and she detected an animal, barnlike odor. Its source was a tangle of brownish red fur that lay on the table illuminated by the generator-powered floodlights. She took another step closer and began to make out details.

The creature looked as if it were sleeping. She half expected the eyes to pop open or the tail or short trunk to twitch.

Lying in front of her, as lifelike as it must have looked twenty thousand years ago, was the most perfectly preserved baby mammoth she had ever seen.

14

Jordan Gant was like a Chimera, the mythical Greek monster of antiquity that was an assemblage of different, incongruous parts.

He was as disciplined as a fasting monk, and he projected an ascetic air, but the black, tailored suit and matching turtleneck that emphasized his pale skin and silver hair cost more than many people make in a week. His Washington office on Massachusetts Avenue was spartan compared to the luxurious lairs of the other high-powered foundations in the neighborhood, yet he owned a palatial Virginia farmhouse, a stable of horses and a garage full of fast cars. He had made a fortune off multinational investments, but he was the director of an organization whose stated goal was to hobble corporations like those that had made him rich.

His ears were small and close to his head, giving him the streamlined look of a hood ornament. His facial features were smooth, as if they had been formed before any character – good or bad – was etched on them. His expressions were no more substantive than images projected on a screen. In its relaxed, natural state, his face lacked emotion of any kind. He had mastered the politician's smile to perfection, and he could turn it on as if he had a built-in electrical switch. He could feign sincere interest in the dullest of conversations, and project sympathy or joy, donning a mask like an actor from antiquity. At times, he seemed more an illusion than a man.

Gant was wearing his most congenial façade as he sat in his office talking to Irving Sacker, a middle-aged man with jowls and thinning black hair. With their manicured finger-nails, respectable haircuts and conservative suits, Sacker and the other three attorneys from his influential Washington law firm looked as if Georgetown Law School had punched them out of legal dough with a cookie cutter. Although they differed in facial features and physiques, they all had the sharp-eyed expressions of hunting raptors ready to swoop down on a legal technicality.

'I see that you've brought along the casework and disks as I requested,' Gant said.

Sacker handed him an attaché case. 'Normally, we would keep a backup of our files at the office, but since you've paid so generously for privacy we have cleaned all the data from our computers and files. It's all here. It's as if we never handled your case.'

'On behalf of the Global Interests Network, I'd like to thank you for all your hard work. Thank you for keeping this entire project a secret.'

'We were simply doing our job,' Sacker said. 'It was an interesting challenge. What we've created on paper for you is a megacorporation that would control every possible means of electronic communication on the planet. Cell phone networks. Satellites. Telecommunications. The whole enchilada.'

'You'll have to admit that this is the way that things have been heading, with all the buyouts and mergers in the industry.'

'Those arrangements are like lemonade stands compared to the entity we've set up for you.'

'Then you've done exactly what you've been asked to do.'

'In that case, I hope you'll retain us for any antitrust suits that arise,' Sacker said with a grin.

Gant chuckled. 'You'll be the first on our list.'

'Would you mind if I asked you a question, Mr Gant?'

'Not at all. Fire away.'

'These agreements and contracts would, under a highly unlikely set of circumstances, position someone to assume control over the major communications systems of the world. Correct me if I'm wrong, but your foundation is at odds with what you see as oppressive world trade, market system and capitalism.'

'That's right. GIN is pro-democracy and nonpartisan. We agree that free trade can be beneficial to developing countries and the promotion of peace. But we're campaigning against the current free-trade model. We're concerned when corporate interests are put above safety standards, and environmental regulations are seen as barriers to free trade. We're against a concentration of power in the hands of a few multinational corporations. We oppose the spread of investments across corporate boundaries, allowing them to evade local laws. We see the World Bank, the WTO and IMF as superseding local government.' He picked up a red-white-and-blue brochure and handed it to Sacker. 'You can read all about our Freedom Project campaign in this handsome little pamphlet.'

'I've read it,' Sacker said, 'and I don't disagree with some of your positions.' He looked up at posters on the wall showing the WTO as a giant octopus. 'Why would a foundation like yours spend a lot of money setting up the kind of thing you're against?'

'Simple. We think the megacorporation you've designed will be a reality in the near future. If you want to fight your enemy, you have to know it. We're primarily a think tank.

The blueprint you prepared will give us the chance to probe the weaknesses, as well as the strengths, of a globalized communications network.'

'Very clever. It seems as though GIN is pretty good at the communications business already. I can't turn on the TV news without seeing one of your talking heads pontificating on the subject of the day.'

'Thank you. Our public outreach is pretty impressive, but you're talking about *influence*, not power.'

Sacker glanced at his watch and heaved himself out of his chair. Gant shook hands with the team of attorneys and ushered them to the door. 'Thank you again. We'll be in touch.'

When the lawyers had left, Gant went over to his telephone, punched the intercom button and said a few words. The side door to the office opened and Mickey Doyle came in.

'Hello, Mickey,' Gant said. 'You heard?'

Doyle nodded. 'Sacker's a smart guy. He was getting at something; he just didn't know what it was.'

'I think I deflected him with my explanation, but I'm not sure he believed me completely. No matter. Have you talked to Margrave since the incident with Barrett?'

'This morning. He said he tried to call Spider but couldn't get him. I told him that when I dropped Barrett off at the Portland airport, he said he wanted to get away for a few days to think things over.'

'Good work.' He opened a desk drawer and pulled out a leather-bound folder. Rather than risk questions over the bullet hole in the old folder, Doyle had replaced it with a new one. 'I've read the material from Karla Janos. She definitely knows something.'

'That's what Spider said. What do you want me to do about her?'

'It's already in the works. When you called me from the island with the news about an antidote that might neutralize what we're doing, I decided to move quickly. Our security arm traced the woman to the University of Alaska in Fairbanks. We just missed her, unfortunately. She's gone off on a scientific expedition to Siberia.'

'Siberia! Jeezus! Why not the moon?'

'Don't worry. The people who pay the bills here at the foundation have a long reach. They frequently do business in Russia and were able to put me in touch with a gentleman in Moscow. He notified his people in Siberia, and they tracked Ms Janos down to a remote island. They'll kidnap and hold her. In the meantime, a team is on its way to interrogate her to see what she knows.'

'Do you think she knows something that can kill the project?'

'It's of no consequence,' Gant said. 'We simply want to learn if she's talked to anyone else. Then we'll dispose of her. We may have another problem to deal with. Kurt Austin, the NUMA man that Barrett mentioned. I don't like the idea that he saw the coil mechanism.'

'We'll keep an eye on him.'

'Good. I've run up a CV on Austin. He's got an impressive background. We don't want him causing problems. If we see him as a threat, he'll have to be eliminated quickly. In the meantime, stay close to Margrave, and immediately report anything important. We want him to pursue this project to the end using his own fortunes and energy.'

'It will be a pleasure.'

Gant was a master at hiding his own emotions, but he

had a talent for reading the expressions of others. Doyle looked like a bulldog about to be served a slab of steak.

'You don't like him, do you?'

'Tris? Naw. He's always treated me like crap. He thinks I'm his monkey. Tells me to fetch coffee and drinks, and pop a beer as my reward. I'm pretty invisible to a guy like him.'

'That's what makes you so valuable to the Freedom Project. You're better than a fly on the wall. You'll be rewarded far beyond your dreams. If it's any consolation to you now, for all Margrave's brilliance he doesn't have a clue about what's going on under his nose. He has no idea that the security company working for him is a private army for the very "Elites", as he calls them, whom he wishes to humble. He thinks his little project is going to forward the goals of his neo-anarchist friends. He doesn't realize that what he is doing will destroy him and his unwashed fools, and solidify the power of those he would like to defeat.'

'What do you want to do about the old guy in Montana?'

Gant chuckled. 'My philosophic ravings must bore you.'

'Not at all. I just need some direction.'

'I wouldn't think that you'd want to tangle with that old grizzly bear again after he mauled two of your men.'

'He was smart. They were dumb.'

'I don't like loose ends, but he is no longer a priority. With the information on the girl, we don't need him anymore. One more thing. Those lawyers who were in my office. I'd like you to dispose of them. Do your best to make it look accidental. An explosion in their office, perhaps.'

Doyle rose from his chair. 'I'll get on it right away.'

After Doyle left, Gant went to his window and looked out at Massachusetts Avenue. The fools in this city thought that they were living in the most powerful country in the world. They never understood that military power was limited. The organization of Elites that he was part of knew that political ends were not achieved by guns alone but by close surveillance and total control of all communication.

Goals that would soon be realized.

15

Austin leaned against a rail on the *Throckmorton* and peered through binoculars at the ship that had suddenly appeared from the heart of the sea. The vessel listed drunkenly to one side, and sat so low in the water that the three-foot seas were splashing onto the deck. By some miracle, the ship somehow managed to stubbornly resist being pulled back to its watery grave.

As an experienced salvage expert, Austin had pulled objects of every size and shape off the bottom, ranging from atomic bombs to submarines. He knew that simple physics suggested that the ship should not be afloat at all. At the same time, he was aware that strange things happen at sea. He was not a superstitious man, but years sailing the world's oceans had made the unexplainable commonplace. He was no different from many sailors who bestowed vessels with human qualities. The ship seemed determined to tell its story. And Austin was just as determined to hear what it had to say.

'What's keeping her afloat?' said Zavala.

'I don't know what's keeping her up or why she popped to the surface,' Austin said. 'She could have been stuck in the muddy bottom or weighted down by cargo. Maybe the whirlpool shook things loose, and she rode to the surface like a wood chip.' He noticed Zavala's skeptical expression, and said, 'Okay, I don't have the foggiest idea why she came to the surface and why she hasn't sunk. Are you up for taking a closer look at her?'

Like Austin, Zavala was wrapped in a blanket that the crew had supplied when they came aboard after rescuing the Trouts. 'I was hoping to settle in with a bottle of *reposada*, but I can be ready to get up in the chopper again as soon as I change into some dry clothes.'

Austin had forgotten that his clothes were soaking wet from his ocean dip.

'I was thinking of going over by boat so we could go aboard and look around,' he said.

'I'm always up for a boat ride. Besides, tequila tastes better as it ages.'

Austin suggested that they meet at the boat launcher. He went to his cabin and exchanged his soggy clothes for dry ones. Before hooking up again with Zavala, he stopped at the sick bay to check on the Trouts. They were sleeping. The medical tech said they were suffering from exposure and exhaustion but after a few hours of rest they would be fine.

On the way out of sick bay, he encountered Professor Adler, who was anxious to talk to the Trouts about their firsthand experience in the whirlpool. The professor was disappointed that he couldn't see them, but he seemed happy when Austin suggested that he speak instead to some of the crew of the *Benjamin Franklin*, who had been transported to the *Throckmorton* to have their injuries treated. The *Franklin* was anchored near the *Throckmorton* while recovering from its battering.

Austin met Zavala at the launch boom as planned, and minutes later their boat was cutting a foamy way toward the mystery ship. Austin steered the inflatable around the vessel in a big circle while Zavala snapped photographs. The sea was covered with dead fish and debris of every kind. Austin measured the vessel with his eye, comparing it to the NOAA and NUMA ships.

'She looks fairly new. I'd say she's around three hundred feet long,' he said.

'She looks like I feel after a night out on the town,' Zavala said. 'She's fairly wide in the beam. Built to take a sizable load of cargo. But I don't see any cargo booms. They must have been knocked off in the whirlpool.'

'There's no name or registration numbers on the hull,' Austin said.

'Maybe we're looking at a pirate ship.'

Zavala's suggestion was not as bizarre as it sounded. Modern-day piracy was a big problem on the seas of the world. Like their ancient counterparts, pirates captured ships and used them to attack other vessels.

'Maybe,' Austin said, but he sounded unconvinced. The vessel was in fairly good condition, considering that she had lain on the bottom of the sea. 'From the look of her, she was only submerged a short while. I don't see any unusual rust, although it might have been blasted off.' He slowed the boat down to a crawl. 'We've seen everything we can from sea level. Let's go aboard?'

'Proper protocol says we should wait for an invitation from the captain?' Zavala said.

'Yes, under ordinary circumstances. But he seems to be otherwise occupied. I think I see the cocktail flag flying,' Austin said.

'You've got better eyesight than I have. All I see is a hulk that looks as if it would roll over if a seagull landed on the deck.'

'In that case, we'd better make sure we're wearing our water wings.'

While Zavala contacted the *Throckmorton* on a hand radio and asked the ship to stand by in case of an emergency, Austin brought the boat around to the lower side of the ship. He waited for a wave to roll in, then gunned the motor. The boat rode up on the crest and the power of the sea carried the Zodiak onto the deck. Zavala quickly tied the boat to a metal stub projecting from the deck. Leaning forward like roofers to compensate for the ship's list, they half walked, half crawled up the slanting deck. The broad expanse was clear except for a twisted tangle of metal that protruded from the deck at the ship's midpoint.

They made their way across the deck using their loping, bent-over walk. Four girders had been bolted to the deck to form a rectangle of steel. The framework surrounded a rectangular opening in the deck about twenty feet square. They leaned over and peered into a dark shaft. They could hear the hollow swish of waves against metal.

'The shaft goes all the way to the bottom,' Zavala observed. 'Wonder what it was for?'

'My guess is that they used it to put something in and take it out. This framework might have supported a crane of some sort.'

The fallen framework was partially obscured by a tangle of thick electrical cable that looked like a pile of black spaghetti. Austin scanned the tumble of steel and cable, looking for some semblance of order. His gaze came to a stop at a metal mesh cone about twenty-five feet long. It lay on its side, tangled in supporting cable and electrical conduits that snaked down through openings in the deck.

The sight of the cone stirred up images in his mind. Tall fins cutting through the water. The bald man with the strange tattoo on his head fiddling with a black box, assuring him everything was going to be okay. The orcas breaking off their attack as suddenly as it had started.

Without thinking, Austin said: 'Spider Barrett.'

Zavala looked up. 'Spider who?'

'Spider Barrett was the guy who pulled me onto his boat when the orcas went crazy in Puget Sound. He had a miniaturized version of that metal cone on his boat.'

'What's it for?'

'You're the team's mechanical expert. Hazard a guess.'

Zavala scratched his head. 'All the cables lead to that big cone. My guess is that it sat over the hole on some sort of framework. It may have been lowered through the hole into the water. I can't figure out any practical shipboard use for a setup like that. If you gave it some juice, you might get an effect like a big spark plug.'

Austin pondered Zavala's assessment for a few seconds, then said, 'Let's pop the hood and see what's down below.'

A wry smile crossed Zavala's face. 'Who in his right mind could resist an opportunity to crawl into the innards of a ship that could roll over with a sneeze?'

'I thought you were worried about a seagull.'

'How about a sneezing seagull?'

'Look at it this way. Where would you rather be, behind your desk at NUMA or a place like this, where you've got a great ocean view?'

'I'd like to be behind the wheel of my Corvette with a view of a lovely blonde.'

'I'll take that as a yes,' Austin said. 'I think I see a way in.'

Despite their playful badinage, both men were well aware of the chance they would take going belowdecks. But Zavala trusted Austin's judgment and instincts implicitly, and would have followed him into the gates of Hell without hesitation. Austin made his way to a deck hatch, about three feet square, that his sharp eyes had picked out.

He unlatched the cover, braced his feet and pulled back. The cover banged against its hinges, and a foul exhalation flowed from the opening and rocked them back on their heels. Austin undid the halogen flashlight clipped to his belt and pointed it into the opening. The intense beam reflected off the rungs of a metal ladder.

They slipped off their flotation vests. The vests would only get in the way, and would be useless if the ship rolled over while they were belowdecks. Austin was the first down the ladder, which was sharply angled because of the ship's list. He descended twenty feet and felt a solid surface under his feet. The deck slanted sharply, and he held onto the ladder to steady himself.

Zavala was right behind him. He glanced around and said, 'It looks like a fun house.'

'Let's go have some fun,' Austin said.

Bracing himself against the lower wall, he made his way along a narrow passageway. After walking for about fifty feet, they came to a stairwell leading below. The prospect of descending deeper into the stricken ship was not an appetizing one, especially when they felt the deck list another few degrees. Both men knew that if the vessel capsized, they were dead. There would be no time to get out. But Austin was determined to pry out the secrets the ship held.

'Feeling lucky today?' he said, his voice echoing off the walls of the passageway.

Zavala smiled. 'We just tangled with a giant whirlpool and won. I'm betting our luck is still holding.'

The stairs led down to another deck that was identical to the first. The passageway ended not in a stairwell but in an unlocked door, which they opened. As they stepped through the doorway, their noses told them there had been a change in their surroundings. Instead of the briny odor that had pervaded the passageways, the air had an electrical smell to it, as if they had stepped into a Radio Shack.

Austin played the light around. They were standing on

a balcony that overlooked a huge, central hold. The space contained four massive, cylindrical objects set in a line.

'Looks like the electrical generating plant inside Hoover Dam,' Austin said.

'There's enough power here for a small city.'

'Or a big spark plug,' Austin said, thinking about the ruined coil they had seen on the deck. He pointed the light upward. Dozens of thick electrical cables snaked down from the ceiling and ran to the generators.

Creak.

The deck beneath their feet tilted at a sharper angle.

'I think that seagull you were worried about must have landed,' Austin said.

Zavala glanced upward. 'Let's hope he doesn't have a cold.'

Austin was intrepid but not foolish. They retraced their steps through the door, up the stairs and along the passageway, until they were out in the open once more. The fresh air felt good after the claustrophobic darkness inside the ship. The vessel was definitely more tilted than it had been. Austin still wasn't satisfied. There was no foundation for a superstructure, but there had to be a control room. While Zavala called the *Throckmorton* with an update on their status, Austin made his way along the cockeyed deck toward the stern.

He came across several more hatchways that provided access into the ship. He figured that any one of them would be a crapshoot, and that he would have to be very lucky to choose the right one. Then he found what he was looking for. Near a hatchway set into the middle of the deck at the aft end of the ship were some round insulators. He guessed that they might have been the bases for radio antennae blasted off in the whirlpool. He opened the hatch, and motioned for Zavala to follow him down the ladder.

As before, the ladder led to a deck and a passageway, but the corridor was only about ten feet long, and it ended in a door. They opened the door and stepped inside.

'I think we just found the crew,' Zavala said.

There were six decomposed corpses in the control room. They were piled in the lower end of the room. Austin was reluctant to violate the crew's tomb, but he knew it was important to learn as much about the ship as possible. With Zavala a step behind, Austin entered the room and glanced at the large control panel. With dozens of gauges and switches, it was far more complicated than any he had ever seen. He made an educated guess that the dynamos below-decks were controlled from this compact space. He was examining the controls when the ship suddenly creaked, then seemed to moan.

Zavala said, 'Kurt!'

Austin knew that if they stayed with the crew a second longer they would be joining the bloated corpses.

'I think we're done here.' He pointed to the door.

With Zavala leading, they pounded down the corridor and practically vaulted up the ladder onto the deck and into the sunlight.

Austin had tried keeping track in his head of the seconds that had elapsed since they heard the noise, but in their rush he had lost count. There was no time to get in the boat, start the motor and cast off. Not stopping to snatch their flotation vests, they ran for the lower side of the ship and launched their bodies off the side.

When they came up, they swam as fast as they could. The ship would create suction as it sank, and they didn't want to get caught in it. They were well away from the vessel when they stopped swimming and looked back.

The lower rail had dropped so that it was entirely under

water. The ship itself was poised at a dangerous angle, with the deck almost perpendicular to the surface of the sea. Zavala's sneezing seagull must have landed, because the ship suddenly reached the tipping point and rolled over. It floated for several minutes, looking like the shiny wet back of a gigantic turtle. As water flowed into the hold, the ship sank lower, until only a small circle of the hull was visible. Then that, too, disappeared, and was replaced by a frothy mound of bubbles.

The sea had taken back its own.

16

'Pleased to meet you, Professor Kurtz,' said Harold Mumford, a professor of zooarchaeology. 'Is Earl Grey tea all right?'

'My favorite,' said the man seated in Mumford's office at the University of Alaska's Fairbanks campus. He had a long face, with a prominent jaw and light blue eyes. His brown hair was going gray.

Mumford poured two cups of tea and handed one to his guest. 'You've had a long journey. Fairbanks is quite a distance from Berlin.'

'Yes, Germany is many miles from here, Dr Mumford. But I've always wanted to come to Alaska. It is the last frontier.'

'That's changing fast,' said Mumford, a portly, middle-aged man who had a face like a friendly walrus. 'Hell, we've even got a Wal-Mart in town. But with very little effort, you can get into some pretty rugged country, full of grizzly bears and moose. I hope you make it to the park at Denali.'

'Oh yes. That's on my agenda. I'm very excited about the prospect.'

'It's an all-day trip but well worth the time. I'm sorry you missed Karla Janos. As I mentioned on the phone, she left on a field trip a few days ago.'

'It was a last-minute decision to come here,' Schroeder said. 'I had some unexpected time to spare, and decided to drop by the university on a whim. It's quite nice of you to see me on such short notice.'

'Not at all. I don't blame you for wanting to meet Karla. She's a brilliant as well as lovely young woman. She worked on the Gerstle River Quarry site about seventy miles from here. That's where we found some carved mammoth tusks. It was very exciting. Her paper on the exploitation of the mammoth by early hunters was one of the best expositions I've seen on the subject. I know she'd be eager to meet someone with your academic background.'

Schroeder had found his academic credentials at a Kinko's printshop in Anchorage. The business cards he had made up identified him as Herman Kurtz, professor of anthropology at Berlin University. He had borrowed the last name from the enigmatic character in Conrad's *Heart of Darkness*.

Throughout his shadowy career, it had never failed to surprise him how powerful words on a sheet of paper were when combined with an air of confidence. The hardest part of the masquerade was faking an Austrian accent after all the years he'd been speaking western 'Merican.

'I read that paper,' Schroeder lied. 'As you say, *very* impressive. I also read the article stating her thesis about the demise of the mammoth.'

'That was typical of Karla. After she concluded that man had only a negligible impact on the mammoth's extinction, she made the great leap to a catastrophic event being the cause. You can imagine the controversy.'

'Yes, it's rather an innovative theory, but I liked the boldness with which she put it forth. Does her extinction theory have anything to do with her field trip?'

'*Everything*. She's hoping to find evidence to support her theory on a remote island in Siberia.'

Schroeder puffed his cheeks out. 'Siberia is a long way from here. How does one go about getting there?'

'In Karla's case, she flew to Wrangel Island, and then

hopped aboard an icebreaker that took her to the New Siberian Islands. The boat will pick her up in two weeks, and she'll be back in Fairbanks a few days after that. Will you still be in Alaska?'

'Unfortunately, no. But I'm quite envious of her adventure. I'd drop everything and follow in her tracks in a minute, if I could.'

Mumford leaned back in his chair and folded his hands behind his head. 'Ivory Island must be the new Cancún,' he said with a grin.

'Pardon?' Schroeder said.

'Ivory Island is where Karla is working. A guy from the Discovery Channel came into my office yesterday and said he was with a crew in Alaska to do a special on Mount McKinley. Guess he heard about Karla's work. He seemed extremely interested when I told him about Ivory Island. Talked about making a side trip. Asked all about the project. I guess nothing's an obstacle when you've got a fat checkbook.'

'What was his name?' Schroeder said. 'Perhaps I've come across him in my travels.'

'Hunter,' he said. 'Scott Hunter. Big, muscular guy.'

Schroeder smiled, but there was contempt in his eyes for the thinly veiled wordplay behind the fake name. 'Can't say I know him. Of course, you informed him of the difficulties of getting to Ivory Island?'

'I sent him to the airport to talk to Joe Harper. He's a former bush pilot who operates a company called PoleStar Air. They run packaged adventure tours into Russia.'

Schroeder gulped down the rest of his tea even though it burned his throat. He thanked Mumford for his hospitality, and drove his rental car to the Fairbanks airport. The airport's location near the Arctic Circle made it a convenient refueling stop for big cargo planes flying the circle route between the Far East and America. Schroeder saw a 747 taking off as he parked. The airport itself was relatively small, and it took only one inquiry to find the office for PoleStar Air.

The receptionist gave Schroeder a pleasant smile and said Mr Harper would be free as soon as he got off the phone. Harper came out after a few minutes. He looked as if he had been picked for the role of a bush pilot by central casting. He was a lean man with alert eyes and a strong set to his mouth, and, judging from his appearance, he was still making the transition from bush pilot to tour operator.

His beard was neatly trimmed, but his hair was shaggy and over the ears. His shirt was new and pressed and tucked into a pair of faded jeans that were at about the stage when they get comfortable. He projected a professional capability, but there was a hint of worry in his eyes. He leaned close to his receptionist's ear and whispered something about a fuel bill, then ushered Schroeder into his office.

The work space was barely big enough for a desk and computer. Any excess space was taken up by stacks of files.

Harper was acutely aware of the disarray. 'Pardon the mess. PoleStar is still a family operation, and I'm doing a lot of the paperwork myself. In fact, I do almost everything with the help of my wife out there.'

'I understand you've been flying a long time,' Schroeder said.

Harper's face brightened. 'I came up here in '84. Had a Cessna, flew that for years. Expanded into a fleet of puddle jumpers. I sold them all to buy the little corporate jet you see out on the tarmac. It's the blue one with the stars all over it. The high-end clients like their adventure tours fast and first-class.'

'How's it going?'

'Business is coming along okay, I guess. Can't say the same for myself.' Harper picked up a pile of papers and dropped it back on his desk. 'I'm stuck doing this stuff until we get big enough to hire someone. But that's my problem. What's yours?'

'I talked to Dr Mumford at the university a little while ago. He told me that you're taking a television crew to an island in Siberia.'

'Oh yeah, the Discovery people. They're taking a plane that will hook up with a fishing boat at Wrangel.'

Schroeder handed Harper one of his newly minted business cards. 'I'd like to get to the New Siberian Islands. You don't suppose I could hitch a ride with them?'

'Okay by me. There's plenty of room on the plane. All you'd need is the price of admission. Unfortunately, they've reserved all the seats on the plane and boat.'

Schroeder pondered his answer. 'Maybe I can talk your clients into letting me tag along.'

'You're welcome to try. They're staying at the Westmark Hotel.'

'What is your estimated time of departure?'

He checked his watch. 'Two hours and twenty-one minutes from now.'

'I'll go talk to them.'

Schroeder got directions to the hotel, and inquired at the desk about the Discovery crew. The desk clerk said he had seen them go into the bar a few minutes earlier. Schroeder thanked him and went to the lounge, which was only half full, mostly singles and couples. The only group sat at a corner table, talking with their heads close together. There were four of them.

Schroeder bought a newspaper in the lobby, took a

nearby table in the lounge and ordered a club soda with lime. A couple of the men glanced briefly in his direction and went back to their conversation. One advantage to getting old is invisibility, he mused. Younger people simply stop seeing you.

He decided to put his suspicions to the test. He watched one of the men leave his table to go to the restroom. Timing it just right, he rose from his table and deliberately bumped into the man on his way back. Schroeder apologized profusely, but the man only swore, and cut him dead with a fierce glance.

The encounter told him two things. That his new appearance, with his shaved beard and dyed hair, was working, and that the television man was carrying a gun in a shoulder holster. He decided to press the matter further.

After emerging from the restroom, he approached the group's table. 'Hello,' he said in his western accent. 'I understand you folks are from the Discovery Channel. Mr Hunter?'

A large man who seemed to be the leader examined him through narrowed eyes. 'Yeah. I'm Hunter. How'd you know my name?'

'It's all over the hotel. We don't often get celebrities here,' Schroeder said, provoking grins around the table. 'I just wanted to say how much I enjoyed the show you did on the ancient Hittites several months ago.'

A puzzled expression crossed the big man's face. 'Thanks,' he said, regarding Schroeder with hard eyes. 'We've got some business to take care of, so if you'll excuse us.'

Schroeder apologized for taking their time and went back to his table. He could hear the men laughing. He had made up the Hittite reference as a test. He watched the Discovery Channel constantly. There had never been any program on that subject in the last six months. The crew was phony.

He pondered a course of action while he finished his club soda and decided to take the most direct route. He went out to his car, and from under the seat retrieved a pistol with a sound suppressor attached to the barrel.

He was relieved to see that the men were still in the bar when he returned to the hotel. He was just in time. They had paid their bill and risen from the table. He followed them to the elevator. He rode up with them to the third floor, chatting like an old fool, enduring the smirks and hard looks. He got off on the same floor, mumbled something about a coincidence. He ambled down the hallway, acting confused, as if he had forgotten where he was, but when the group broke up and went into their rooms he noted the room numbers.

He waited a minute, then went over to one room. Holding the pistol behind his back, he glanced up and down the hallway to make sure he was alone, then knocked. The door opened a moment later. The man scowled when he saw Schroeder standing there. It was the man he had jostled. He had taken off his jacket, and, as Schroeder had suspected, he was wearing a shoulder holster with a handgun in it.

'What the hell do *you* want?'

'I seem to have lost my room key. I was wondering if I could use your phone.'

'I'm busy.' He put his hand on the holster. 'Go bother someone else.'

The man started to close the door. Schroeder quickly brought the pistol around and snapped off a shot between the eyes. The man crumpled to the floor with a look of abject surprise on his otherwise unmarked face. Glancing up and down the corridor, Schroeder stepped over the body and dragged it just inside the room.

Schroeder followed the same routine, with slight variations but similar results. In one case, he rushed his first shot and had to fire twice. In another, he heard the elevator door open just as he pulled the body into the room. But when it was over, he had killed four men in less than five minutes.

He felt no remorse, dispatching them with the cold, murderous efficiency of his old days. They were simply violent thugs, no different from many he had encountered, even worked with. Worse, they were sloppy and careless. The team must have been assembled in a hurry. They were not the first men he had killed. Nor were they likely the last.

He hung DO NOT DISTURB signs on each door. A few minutes later, he was back in his rental car headed for the airport. Harper was still in his office, burrowing through his paperwork like an overgrown mole.

'I talked to the TV crew,' Schroeder said. 'They've changed their minds. They've decided to head down to Kodiak Island to shoot a feature on bears.'

'*Shit!* Why didn't they tell me?'

'You can call them and ask. But they were on their way out when I called them.'

Harper snatched up the phone and called the hotel. He asked to be connected to the TV crew's rooms. When no one answered, he slammed the phone down on its cradle. He rubbed his eyes, and seemed on the verge of breaking into tears.

'That's it,' he said. 'I was counting on a check from this run to make the monthly payment on the big bird. I'm ruined.'

'You don't have any other charters scheduled?'

'It's not that easy. It takes days, sometimes weeks, to put together a deal.'

'Then the plane and boat are free for charter?'

'Yeah, they're free. You know anyone interested in chartering them?'

'As a matter of fact, I do.' Schroeder reached into his jacket pocket and pulled out a thick packet of bills, which he tossed onto a pile of papers. 'This is for the trip out and the boat. I'll pay you an equal amount for the return flight. My only condition is that you stand by for a few days until I'm ready to leave.'

Harper picked the packet up and riffled the edges. They were all hundred-dollar bills. 'I can practically buy a new plane for this.' He frowned. 'This isn't something illegal, is it?'

'Nothing illegal at all. You'll be carrying no cargo. Only me.'

'You got papers?'

'Passport and visa are all up-to-date and in order.' They *should* be, for the money he paid for them, Schroeder thought. He had stopped in Seattle and waited impatiently while his favorite ID forger had cooked up a set of papers for Professor Kurtz.

Harper extended his hand. 'You've got yourself a deal.'

'Good. When can we leave?'

'Any time you're ready.'

'I'm ready.'

The plane took off an hour later. Schroeder sat back in his seat, enjoying the solitude that came from being the only passenger on the plane, and sipped on a glass of Scotch that Harper had thoughtfully provided. Harper was at the controls. As Fairbanks faded in the distance and the plane struck off toward the west, he took a deep breath. He was aware that he was an old man trying to do a young man's job. Schroeder had asked not to be bothered for a while. He was tired and needed some sleep.

He would need deadly clarity for the task ahead. He cleared his mind of all emotion and closed his eyes.

17

The NOAA ship *Benjamin Franklin* limped along like a sailor who'd been in a bar brawl. The tug-of-war with the whirlpool had taken its toll on the ship's engines, which had to be babied so they wouldn't break down completely. The *Throckmorton* trailed several hundred yards behind in case the NOAA vessel ran into trouble.

As the two ships slowly made their way toward Norfolk, a turquoise-colored utility helicopter with the letters NUMA visible on the fuselage appeared in the western sky. It hovered over the *Benjamin Franklin* like a hummingbird before touching down on the deck. Four people scrambled out, carrying medical supplies and equipment.

Crewmen directed the medical team to the ship's sick bay. None of the injuries sustained when the ship nearly went vertical in the whirlpool were life-threatening. The captain had requested the team to help the ship's paramedic, who had been overwhelmed with the sheer volume of bruises and concussions.

The helicopter was refueled, and two crewmen who had suffered broken arms were loaded aboard. Austin thanked the captain for his hospitality. Then he, along with the Trouts, Zavala and Professor Adler, climbed into the helicopter. Minutes later, they were airborne.

The helicopter touched down at National Airport less than two hours later. The injured were unloaded into waiting ambulances. The Trouts caught a taxi to their Georgetown town house, taking Adler with them as their guest, and Zavala drove Austin to his house on the Potomac River in Fairfax, Virginia, less than a mile from the Central Intelligence Agency headquarters in Langley. They all agreed to meet at eight the next morning after a good night's rest.

Austin lived in a converted Victorian boathouse overlooking the river. He had acquired the turreted building when he worked for the CIA. The mansard-roofed structure was part of an old estate, and the previous owners had let it run down. It had become a waterfront condominium for countless families of mice by the time Austin gutted and redid the interior and restored the exterior to its former glory. The space under the living quarters housed his racing scull and small, outboard hydroplane.

He dropped his bag in the hall and walked into a spacious living room. His house was an eclectic combination of the old and the new. The authentic, dark wooden, colonial furniture contrasted with the whitewashed walls hung with contemporary originals and painterly primitives and charts. Floor-to-ceiling bookcases held the leather-bound sea adventures of Conrad and Melville and the well-worn volumes of the great philosophers he liked to study. Glass cases displayed some of the rare dueling pistols he collected. His extensive collection of music, with a preference for progressive jazz, mirrored his steely coolness, his energy and drive, and his talent for improvisation.

He checked his phone for messages. There was a pile of calls, but nothing that couldn't wait. He flicked the stereo on, and Oscar Peterson's frenetic piano fingering filled the room. He poured a drink for himself of his best *aniejo* tequila, opened the sliding glass door and went out onto the deck with the ice tinkling pleasantly in his glass. He listened to the soft, rippling sounds, and breathed into his lungs the misty, flower-scented river air that was so different from the briny scent of the ocean where he spent much of his working days.

After a few minutes, he went back into the house, pulled a book on ancient Greek philosophers from a shelf and opened it to Plato's 'Allegory of the Cave'. In Plato's parable, prisoners chained in a cave can see only the shadows cast by puppets on the wall and can hear the puppeteers moving behind their backs. On that slim evidence, the prisoners must decide what is shadow and what is reality. Similarly, Austin's brain was sorting the strange events of the last few days, trying to impose order on his mental chaos. He kept coming back to the one thing he could grasp. The mysterious ship.

He went over to a rolltop desk and powered up his laptop computer. Using the Web site information from Dr Adler, he called up the satellite picture of the giant wave area. The image showed that all was quiet. He backed up through the image archives to the date of the *Southern Belle*'s sinking. The two giant waves that had startled Adler were clearly displayed on the date the ship had disappeared. The ship itself was shown as a small blip that was there one minute, gone the next.

He zoomed the picture out so that it showed a greater area of ocean and saw something he hadn't noticed before. Four ships were clustered around the area of the sinking. There was one at each point of the compass, equidistant from one another. He stared at the image for a moment, then backed up a few days. The ships were not there. He jumped ahead to shortly after the sinking. There were only *three* ships. When he went to a day after the *Belle* went down, no blips were visible.

He was like one of Plato's prisoners in the cave, trying to

separate reality from appearance, but he had one advantage they didn't. He could call out for help. He picked up the thick NUMA directory next to the phone, scanned the listings and punched in a number on the phone. A man answered.

'Hello, Alan. This is Kurt Austin. I just got in from a cruise. Hope I didn't wake you.'

'Not at all, Kurt. Nice to hear from you. What can I do for you?'

'Can you make a meeting at my place tomorrow morning around eight? It's quite important.'

'Of *course*.' There was a pause. 'You know what I do?'

Alan Hibbet was one of the dozens of innocuous NUMA scientists who toiled anonymously in the heart of the great oceanographic organization, content to do research of vital importance in exotic subjects with little fanfare. A few months earlier, Austin had heard Hibbet speak at a NUMA symposium on at-sea communication and environmental monitoring. He'd been impressed with the breadth of the man's knowledge.

'I know very well what you do. You're a specialist in applied electromagnetism, with expertise in antennae. You're responsible for designing the electronic eyes and ears NUMA uses to probe the deep and maintain communications among its far-flung operations. I read your paper on the effect of ground plane size on the radiation patterns produced by reduced surface antennae.'

'You *did*? I'm flattered. I'm basically a tinkerer. I think of the Special Assignments Team as swashbucklers.' Austin and his team were legends around NUMA, and Hibbet was stunned at being asked to help.

Austin laughed ruefully. His arm muscles were still sore from rescuing Paul Trout and he was dog-tired. 'I think there's more buckle than swash in the team these days. We could really use your expertise.'

'I'll be glad to help in any way I can,' Hibbet said.

Austin gave Hibbet directions to the boathouse, and said he looked forward to seeing him in the morning. He made some notes in a yellow legal pad while the thoughts were fresh in his head. Then he prepared a full pot of Kenyan coffee, put the coffeemaker on automatic and went upstairs to his turret bedroom. He undressed, slid between the cool sheets and quickly fell asleep. It seemed only minutes before he was awakened by the bright morning sunlight streaming into his bedroom window.

He showered and shaved, got dressed comfortably in T-shirt and shorts, and whipped together an order of scrambled eggs and Virginia ham, which he ate on the deck. He had just finished clearing away the dishes when Zavala knocked on the door. The Trouts showed up a few minutes later with Professor Adler. Al Hibbet arrived at the same time. Hibbet was a tall, thin man with a shock of white hair. He was almost painfully shy, and his skin was as pale as marble, both consequences of spending most of his days in a laboratory away from human contact and sunlight.

Austin handed each person a mug of coffee and herded them to a round, teakwood table on the deck. Austin could have called the meeting at his office in the green-tinted tower in Arlington that was the center of NUMA's operations. But he wasn't ready to answer questions or share his thoughts with anyone outside his innermost circle until he had gathered more facts. He pulled up a chair and gazed longingly at the sun-sparkled river where he usually spent his morning rowing for exercise, then glanced around the table and thanked everyone for coming. He felt like Van Helsing calling together a strategy meeting to battle Dracula, and was tempted to ask if anyone had brought the garlic.

Instead, he got right to the point. 'Something very odd has been going on in the Atlantic and Pacific Oceans,' he began. 'The sea is being stirred up like eggs in a bowl. These disturbances have sunk one ship, and possibly two, that we know of, nearly sank another, and have scared a year's growth off some of the people seated around this table, including yours truly.' He turned to Adler. 'Professor, would you be kind enough to describe the phenomena we've witnessed, and hold forth with some of your theories?'

'I'd be glad to,' Adler said. He recounted the disappearance of the 'unsinkable' *Southern Belle* and the successful search for the lost ship. He described the satellite evidence confirming the existence of giant waves in the ship's vicinity. Last, and with slightly less enthusiasm, he talked about his theory that the disturbances may not have been of natural origin. As he explained his thoughts, he looked from face to face as if he were searching for a hint of doubt. To his relief, he saw only seriousness and interest.

'Normally, we might attribute all this strange ocean activity to King Neptune kicking up his heels, but for a couple of things,' he said. 'Satellite imagery suggests that other areas of the oceans have been similarly disturbed, and that there is an unusual symmetry to the disturbances.' Using Austin's laptop, he showed the satellite images of the killer wave concentrations.

Austin asked the Trouts to describe their descent into the maelstrom. Again, there was silence as Gamay and Paul took turns telling about being sucked into the vortex and their last-minute rescue.

'You say there was lightning at the time this whirlpool first materialized?' Hibbet said.

Gamay and Paul nodded.

Hibbet's reply was succinct. He only said, 'Ah.'

Zavala picked up the story thread, and told the group about boarding the resurrected ship. Hibbet was keenly interested in his description of the power plant and the damaged electrical framework on deck.

'I wish I could have been there to see it,' he said.

'I can do the next best thing,' Zavala said. Moments later, the digital photos he had taken of the mystery ship were displayed on the computer screen.

Austin asked Hibbet what he made of the images. The NUMA scientist stared at the screen with a furrowed brow, and asked for a second run-through of the photos.

'It's fairly obvious that a great deal of electrical power is being fed into a central point.' He pointed to the cone-shaped framework. 'It's hard to know what this apparatus is for in its present state.'

'Joe described it as a giant spark plug,' Austin said.

Hibbet scratched his head. 'Probably not. More like a giant Tesla coil. Many of the circuits that make this thing tick are not visible. Where is the ship now?'

'It sank to the bottom of the sea again,' Zavala said.

Hibbet's reaction wasn't what Austin expected. There was excitement in his gray eyes as he rubbed his palms together. 'This beats fiddling around with antennae any day.' He clicked through the computer pictures again, then he glanced around the table. 'Anyone here familiar with the work of Nikola Tesla?'

'I'm the only one who reads *Popular Science* on a regular basis,' Zavala said. 'Tesla invented alternating current.'

Tibbet nodded. 'He was a Serbian American electrical engineer. He discovered that you could rotate a magnetic field if you took two coils at right angles and juiced them with AC current out of phase.'

189

'I wonder if you might put that in English,' Adler said politely.

Hibbet laughed. 'I'll put it in a historic context. Tesla moved to the United States and worked for Thomas Edison. They became rivals. Edison advocated direct current, and there was a fierce battle. Tesla got the edge when he was commissioned to design the AC generators at Niagara Falls. He sold the patents to his induction motor to George Westinghouse, whose power system was the basis for what we use today. Edison had to be content with the electric lightbulb and the phonograph.'

'Tesla filed a bunch of wild patents, as I recall,' Zavala said.

'That's right. He was an eccentric genius. He filed a patent for an unmanned electrically propelled aircraft that could fly at eighteen thousand miles per hour and could be used as a weapon. He came up with something called "teleforce", which was a death ray that could melt airplane engines at a distance of two hundred and fifty miles. He did a lot of work on wireless transmission of electricity. He was fascinated by the possibility of focusing electrical force and amplifying its effect. He even claimed to have once produced an earthquake from his lab.'

'Tesla may have simply been ahead of his time, with ballistics missiles and lasers,' Austin said.

'His concepts were sound. But the execution never lived up to the expectations. He's become something of a cult figure in recent years. The conspiracy-minded suspect that various governments, including our own, have been experimenting with the more destructive aspects of Tesla's work.'

'What do *you* think?' Austin said.

'The conspiracy theorists are missing the boat. Tesla

attracted a lot of attention because he was such a flamboyant figure. The work of Lazlo Kovacs had far more potential for destruction, in my opinion. Like Tesla, he was a brilliant electrical engineer. He was from Budapest, where Tesla worked in the late eighteen hundreds, and picked up on his work in the nineteen-thirties, concentrating on extra-low-frequency electromagnetic transmission. He became worried about the possibility of electromagnetic warfare. He said that certain transmissions could be used to disrupt the atmosphere, and produce severe weather, earthquakes and all sorts of unpleasant results. He took Tesla to the next level.'

'In what way?'

'Kovacs actually developed a set of frequencies whereby electromagnetic resonance could be focused and thus amplified by the material surrounding it. They were called the Kovacs Theorems. He published his findings in a scientific journal, but he refused to make public the complete set of frequencies that would allow the device he described to be built. Other scientists were skeptical of his findings without proof.'

'It's lucky no one believed him,' Professor Adler said. 'The world has enough trouble controlling the types of warfare we have already.'

'*Some* people believed him. The Nazis were very open to ideas of mysticism, the occult and pseudoscience. Those stories about Nazi archaeologists searching for the Holy Grail are true. They pounced on Kovacs and kidnapped him and his family. After the war ended, it was disclosed that they had put him to work in a secret lab on a project to develop a superweapon that would win the war.'

'They lost the war,' Austin said. 'Tesla wasn't the only one with a credibility problem. Kovacs apparently failed too.'

Hibbet shook his head. 'It's more complicated than that,

Kurt. Papers uncovered after the war suggested that he was on the verge of an electromagnetic warfare breakthrough. Luckily, it never happened.'

'Why not?'

'The Russians overran the lab in East Prussia, where he was said to be working. But Kovacs had already disappeared. After the war, the Soviets carried out research based on the Kovacs Theorems. The United States was aware of their work, and would have loved to talk to Kovacs. The significance of electromagnetic radiation was not lost on our military. There was a big conference years ago at the Los Alamos lab to talk about applied weapons technology based on his work.'

'Home of the Manhattan Project? That was fitting,' Austin said.

'In more ways than one. The manipulation of electromagnetic rays could be more devastating in its own way than a nuclear device. The military took Kovacs very seriously. Electromagnetic pulse weapons were tested during the first Gulf War. Some people claim that those experiments and similar ones conducted by the Soviets caused earthquakes, volcanic eruptions and weather disturbances. That's why I was interested in the bright light flashes in the sky.'

'What's so significant about the bursts of light?' Austin asked.

'Many of the cases reported by witnesses to the Soviet and American experiments said they saw an aurora borealis, or a great burst of light caused by electromagnetic transmissions,' Hibbet said.

'Tell us more about these experiments,' Austin said.

'There's a great deal of controversy over a project called HAARP, short for the High Frequency Active Aural Research Program, being carried out by this country. The idea is to shoot a focused electromagnetic beam into the ionosphere. It's been billed as an academic program to improve worldwide communications. Some people speculate that it's mainly a military project aimed at a wide range of goals, from "Star Wars" defense to mind control. I don't know what to believe, but the project has its roots in the Kovacs Theorems.'

'You said something about a Tesla coil,' said Austin. 'What did you mean?'

'It was a simple type of resonant transformer made up of two coils, actually. Pulses of energy are transferred from one to the other to produce a lightninglike discharge. You've probably seen them in the movies, where they seem to be a common fixture in the lab of the mad scientist.'

Gamay had been listening intently to the discussion. She leaned forward. 'We've talked about the transmission of these waves into solid ground or the atmosphere,' she said. 'What would happen if you sent them into the bottom of the sea?'

Hibbet spread his palms wide apart. 'I don't have a clue. Ocean geology isn't my area of expertise.'

'But it is mine,' Paul Trout said. 'Let me ask you a question, Al. Could amplified electromagnetic waves penetrate deep into the earth's crust?'

'Without question.'

'In that case, it's possible that the transmissions could cause some anomalies in the earth's mantle in roughly the same way the HAARP program you talked about disturbed the atmosphere.'

'What sort of anomalies?' Adler asked.

'Whirlpools and eddies, possibly.'

'Could these create disturbances in the sea?' Austin asked.

Hibbet pinched his chin. 'The swirling molten layer under

the crust is what creates the magnetic field that surrounds the earth. Any disruption of the field has the potential to cause all sorts of disturbances.'

Professor Adler pounded his fist on the table. 'I *knew* I was right! Someone has been monkeying around with my ocean.'

'But we're talking about vast distances and miles of surface material,' Trout said, temporarily squelching Adler's exuberance. 'My sense of this discussion is that it's going back to Joe's big spark plug. Or Al's coil. Even if the device turned out enormous power, it would still be puny compared to the mass of the earth.'

Austin broke the brief silence that followed Trout's evaluation. 'What if there were *more* than one device?'

He pushed the laptop to the center of the table and slowly spun it around so everyone could see the blips surrounding the disturbed area.

Trout grasped the significance right away. '*Four* ships, each concentrating its power on a small area. That might work.'

Austin nodded. 'I'll show you something else that's interesting.' He called up the image taken shortly after the *Belle* sank. 'My guess is that one of these ships became a victim of the sea disturbances it created.'

There was a murmur of agreement around the table.

'That might explain *how*,' Zavala said. 'What I can't figure is *why*?'

'Before we answer that question,' Austin said, 'maybe we should concentrate on *who*. This isn't a case of someone making waves in a bathtub. Nameless and faceless people have gone to a great deal of trouble and expense to stir up the ocean. They have killed the crews of two ships, that we know of, and caused the loss of millions of dollars in property, in their quest for some nameless goal.' He looked around the table. 'Are we all ready to get down to work?'

Hibbet started to rise.

'I hope you're going to get more coffee?' Austin said with a grin.

Hibbet looked embarrassed. 'No, actually, I was about to head into my office at NUMA. I assumed that you had all you need.'

'Joe, tell Al about our "Hotel California" rule.'

'Glad to. It's like the old Eagles song, Al. Once you've been recruited into the Special Assignments Team, you can check out but you can never leave.'

'We need your expertise in electromagnetism,' Austin said. 'It would be a great help if you could see from a technical point of view if these pipe dreams have any basis in reality. Where can we learn more about the Kovacs Theorems?'

'My best advice is to go right to the source. The research in this country was done in Los Alamos. There's even a Kovacs Society out there that's a repository for his work and documents. I've contacted them from time to time with questions.'

Austin turned to Adler. 'Could you work with Al and come up with a paper? Joe, building a fleet of floating power plants is a pretty big deal. Those dynamos were probably commercially built.'

'I'll see if I can come up with a point of origin,' Zavala said.

'We could be in New Mexico this afternoon and back here tomorrow,' Gamay said.

Austin nodded. 'Find out how far those experiments went and if they're still going on. We'll work up everything ever written about Kovacs. Maybe we'll find a nugget that will make it worth our while.'

He thanked everyone for coming, and suggested they meet the same time the next day. He and Zavala would get together in a few hours at NUMA headquarters. On his way back into the house, Austin passed his bookcase and noticed the volume on Plato.

Shadows and echoes. Echoes and shadows.

He wondered what Plato would have made of this new enigma.

18

Karla lay in her sleeping bag and listened to the wail of the wind around the old fur-trappers' shed. She was thinking about her reaction at seeing the baby mammoth. To say she was astonished would have been an understatement. She felt as if she had been hit by a bolt of lightning. She had forced herself to take long, even breaths. Her training had eventually kicked in, and she began to subject the specimen on the table to scientific analysis.

Measuring the creature with her eye, she guessed that it was about forty-five inches long and forty inches high. Weight was probably around two hundred pounds. The mammoth had all the characteristics that Stone Age artists had captured in their cave drawings, including the high-peaked head crowned with its hair-covered knob and the high shoulder hump.

The tusks were starting to curve, making it likely that the animal was a male. In an adult, they could be sixteen feet long. The ears were small and the trunk was stubby compared to the body. Even at full maturity, the trunk would be shorter than that of a modern-day elephant. The body was covered with chestnut-colored hair. From its size, she estimated the mammoth at seven or eight months of age.

Karla thought this could be the most perfectly pre-served example of *Mammuthus primigenius* that had ever been discovered. Most mammoth remains consisted of chunks of meat and bone. This was a whole animal, and in far better condition than Effie, the partial carcass discovered at Fairbanks Creek, and the Russian specimens, *Dima* and *Zharkov*, or, the most famous one of all, the quick-frozen *Beresovka* carcass, whose flesh was still edible. The animal's stomach contained the buttercups it had eaten a short time before its death. Karla turned to the other scientists.

'It's marvelous,' she said. 'Where did you find it?'

'Babar was in the bank of an old riverbed,' Maria said.

'*Babar?*'

'We had to name the poor little thing *some*thing,' Maria said. 'I once had a book about Babar, who was king of the elephants.'

'I think it's a wonderful name. Congratulations to all of you,' Karla said with a smile. 'This must be the scientific find of the century.'

'Thank you,' Maria said. 'Unfortunately, this discovery presents something of a problem for our expedition.'

'I don't understand.'

'It's almost dinnertime,' Arbatov said. 'Let's discuss this around the table.'

From the size of the belly hanging over Arbatov's belt, it was apparent that he didn't miss many dinners. They moved to the big tent. In the convivial surroundings, it was hard to believe they were on a remote Arctic island. The folding table was covered with a flowered, plastic tablecloth. The soft glow of lanterns contributed to the atmosphere with a warm, yellow glow. Gas heaters kept the interior of the tent warm and cozy, even though the fabric slapped from the cool breeze that had come up off the water.

The meal started with Ukrainian borscht, moved on to a hearty beef goulash, with *ponchiki* cookies for dessert. All washed down with tea, and followed with high-octane vodka that took the edge off the late-afternoon coolness. After sampling Maria's cooking, Karla understood that Sergei's girth may not have been all his own fault.

Karla downed her last cookie. 'I'm amazed that you can turn out such great food under relatively primitive conditions.'

'There is no need to starve, or eat freeze-dried food like the Americans like to do,' Maria said. 'As long as I have fire, a pot and the right ingredients, I can cook as well as the finest Moscow restaurant.'

Karla raised her glass of vodka. 'I want to congratulate you again on your find. You must be very happy.'

Dr Sato's Japanese ear for subtlety picked up on Karla's oblique attempt to introduce a touchy subject into the dinner conversation.

'Thank you,' he said. 'As we indicated earlier, it is a bit of a problem.' He glanced at Arbatov.

The Russian nodded. 'You know what we are trying to do with this expedition?'

'Yes,' Karla said. 'You are trying to find the remains of a mammoth that will lend itself to cloning.'

'Correct,' Arbatov said. 'The seeds for this project were planted in 1999, when a multinational expedition unearthed some promising remains in a block of frozen mud.'

'The *Zharkov* mammoth,' Karla said. The remains had been named after the Siberian family that owned the land where they were found.

'That's right. There was a great deal of interest in the beast from a number of genetic research facilities from all parts of the world. They said that if DNA could be extracted from the soft tissues it might be used to clone a woolly mammoth.'

'The mud yielded only bones and no soft tissue, as I recall.'

'With no soft tissue, the cloning attempt died, but not the

interest. Experiments continued,' Arbatov said. 'A group of Japanese and Chinese researchers cloned two cows, using skin cells from a dead cow embryo that was kept frozen at the same temperature as the Russian permafrost. Since then, expeditions have continued to search for suitable remains in Siberia. My wife and I work for a Siberian wildlife park that plans to impregnate a female Indian elephant as a surrogate to produce a partial-mammoth offspring, then repeat with its offspring as well. They hope to have a creature that is eighty-eight percent woolly mammoth in fifty years.'

'This is a joint venture with the Japanese,' Dr Sato said, picking up the thread of the explanation. 'Students from Kinki University and veterinary experts from Kagoshima, where Dr Ito is from, have been looking in Siberia for DNA samples since 1997. There are estimated to be ten million mammoths buried beneath the Siberian permafrost, so we came here hoping to find what we need.'

'How would the cloning be done?' Karla said.

'It's extremely complicated. Every step has to work perfectly,' said Ito, the veterinary expert. 'We would extract a complete DNA strand from soft tissue, remove an egg from a female elephant, which would be irradiated to destroy its DNA. We would replace it with mammoth DNA and insert it in the elephant. The elephant's normal gestation period is twenty-two months, but we have no idea what it would be for this creature. Nor do we know how to care for the baby hybrid.'

'Any one of those obstacles would be formidable by itself,' Karla said.

'Finding the soft tissue has been the most difficult obstacle to overcome,' Maria said.

'Up to now,' Karla said.

'Ideally, we would like to have found a pregnant mammoth,' Maria said, 'but this may do very nicely.'

'I'm puzzled,' Karla said. 'It seems to me that you have a surplus of riches locked in the body of the young animal in the shed.'

The exchange of glances among the four scientists was almost comical.

Dr Sato said, 'There is a jurisdictional dispute. Like two parents fighting over the custody of a child.'

'You don't need possession of the whole body. A sample of DNA should be sufficient.'

'Yes,' Sato said. 'But you know how competitive the scientific world is. Whoever brings the specimen home will get a major boost to his or her career and wealth.'

'Who found it?'

Arbatov shrugged. 'Sato and Ito, but we claimed ownership because we helped remove it to the shed and it's on Russian soil.'

'Wasn't there an agreement to govern this sort of thing?'

'Yes, but no one thought we'd ever find a specimen so perfect,' Maria said.

'We're all rational people,' Arbatov said. 'Maria was instrumental in helping us curb our male tempers. We've had some spirited discussions, and talked at great length about whether we should even tell you. We decided that it would be impractical to hide it from you, as well as intellectually dishonest. We are still at a loss at what to do.'

'You're right. You *do* have a problem,' Karla said.

Four heads nodded in agreement.

'But it's not an unsolvable problem,' she added, and the heads froze in mid-nod.

'Please, don't tell us to play Solomon and split the baby down the middle,' Arbatov said.

'Not at all. The answer seems fairly obvious. Go out and find another specimen. There may be others like this in the same vicinity. I'll help you. I've done extensive topographical studies of Ivory Island going back to the Pleistocene period, when the steppes here teemed with the creatures. I think I can place you at the areas of greatest concentration and environmental conditions, increasing the odds in your favor.'

Dr Sato said, 'In our country, we value consensus over confrontation. I propose that we look for a second specimen. If we have not found it when the ship returns, we will tell our respective sponsors about the situation and let them fight it out in court.'

Maria diplomatically deferred to her husband. 'Sergei? As project director, what do you think?'

'I think that Ms Janos has offered a solution that we can all live with.'

'There's a quid pro quo,' she said. 'Maybe you can help me with *my* project.'

'My apologies,' Dr Sato said. 'We've been so self-absorbed with our own issues that we've become impolite. What exactly do you hope to find here?'

'An answer to the riddle of the mammoth.'

'The Pleistocene extinction?' Maria said.

Karla nodded. 'Picture this island twenty thousand years ago. The land outside our tent was green with vegetation. The earth shook with the thunder made by the feet of vast herds of *Mammuthus*. These creatures stood up to fourteen feet tall, making them the largest of all the elephants. Their great herds roamed the ancient world, going back more than three million years. They were in North America, from North Carolina to Alaska, in most of Russia and Europe, and even in Britain and Ireland. But by eight thousand BC, they were nearly gone, except for remnants here and there. The herds of mammoths vanished, along with hundreds of other species, leaving their frozen bones to puzzle scientists like us.'

'The extinction is one of the greatest mysteries in the world,' Maria said. 'Mammoths, mastodons, saber-toothed tigers – all disappeared from the face of the earth ten to twelve thousand years ago, along with nearly two hundred other species of large mammals. Millions of animals died on a global scale. What do you hope to find here?'

'I'm not sure,' Karla said. 'As you know, there are three theories explaining the extinction. The first is that the Clovis people hunted them to extinction.'

'The main problem with that theory is that it doesn't explain the extinction in the rest of the world,' Arbatov said.

'There is also no fossil evidence to support this idea, so we move on to theory two, that a killer virus swept through the mammal populations of the world.'

'So you think the virus theory is the most plausible?' Dr Sato said.

'Yes and no. I'll get back to it after we discuss the third theory, drastic climate change. Near the end of the period, the weather changed suddenly. But that theory has a big hole in it. Creatures on a number of islands survived. They would have died out if the extinction were weather-related.'

'So if it wasn't overhunting, or a virus or climate change, what was it?' Sergei said.

'The argument has always boiled down to two schools of thought. Catastrophism, which says that a single event or a series of events caused the extinction. And uniformism, which maintains that extinction happened over a long period of time, from a number of causes.'

'Which are you, a catastrophist or a uniformist?' Arbatov said.

'Neither. No single theory fits all the facts. I think it is all of the above, with the extinction set in motion by a cataclysm or series of cataclysms. Tsunamis. Volcanic eruptions that produced killing clouds and gas, altering the pattern of vegetation.'

'There's a hole in that theory too,' Arbatov said. 'The evidence suggests that extinction occurred over a period of hundreds or thousands of years.'

'That wouldn't be a problem. My theory takes into account the discovery of vast numbers of mammoths found tumbled in a common grave, and explains why some of the creatures survived long after that. Evidence demonstrates that many were killed by sudden violence. But we also know that a few mammoth species were around when the Egyptians were building the Pyramids. The cataclysm weakened the mammoth herds to a point where disease and hunters could polish them off. The extinction of certain species had a ripple effect. The predators that preyed on the mammoths and other creatures would lose their food source.'

'I think you're onto something, but you're saying that this worldwide cataclysm occurred suddenly. One minute, the mammoths were peacefully chewing on grass. The next, they were on their way to extinction. Isn't that far-fetched?'

'Not at all. But I would be the first to admit that the theory of polar shift is controversial.'

'Polar shift?'

'A realignment of the poles.'

'None of us is a geologist,' Arbatov said. 'Please explain.'

'I'd be glad to. There are two types of polar shift. A "magnetic polar shift" would involve a reversal of the magnetic poles, causing all sorts of unpleasantness but nothing we couldn't survive. A "geologic polar shift" would mean actual movement of the earth's crust over its molten core. Something like that could create a cataclysm like the one I believe killed the mammoths as a species.'

Arbatov was unconvinced. 'You're basing your extinction theory on the theoretical shifting of the poles? You'll have to admit that it's unlikely that such a disruption could occur.'

'On the contrary. It has happened, and could happen again.'

Arbatov made a show of taking Karla's glass. 'Our guest has had a little too much vodka.'

'I'll be glad to let you read my paper setting forth my theory, Dr Arbatov. I think you'll find it enlightening. Especially the equations showing how a disruption in the electromagnetic field of the earth could precipitate a polar reversal.'

An argument broke out around the table between those who agreed with her theory and those who didn't. Despite their civilized veneer, it was evident that some tension remained among the group. She wasn't surprised. Scientists were no different from anyone else, except they were possibly more vain and petty. Maria's forcefully pleasant personality broke up the verbal brawl.

'My apologies for being so rude to a guest,' she said, shooting dagger eyes at her husband. 'What are your plans for tomorrow?'

With Arbatov neutralized, the argument ended as quickly as it started.

'Maybe someone could show me where you found Babar.'

She was told that it would not be a problem. Everyone

helped Maria clean up. A short while later, Karla was in her sleeping bag. The old building was remarkably tight and warm, and, except for the scurrying of tiny animals, she felt quite comfortable. In her excitement over the baby mammoth, she found it hard to sleep.

She remembered a good-night poem her grandfather used to recite to her when she went to live with him after her parents died.

She hardly got past the first line before she fell fast asleep.

19

The Trouts flew into Albuquerque late in the afternoon and drove to Santa Fe, where they stayed the night. Early the next morning, they got into their rental car and headed toward Los Alamos, which was located on a natural citadel atop the three mesas that extended from the Panaretos Plateau.

Trout noticed a change in his wife during the twenty-five-mile drive. She had been chatting about the scenery, wishing they had time to stop at an Indian pueblo, when she became uncharacteristically silent.

'A penny for your thoughts,' he said. 'Adjusted for inflation, of course.'

'I was just looking at this peaceful landscape, thinking about the work here with the Manhattan Project and the terrible forces it unleashed.'

'Someone was bound to do it. Just be glad that we were the first.'

'I know that, but it still depresses me to think that we still haven't learned how to control the genie that we let out of the bottle.'

'Cheer up. Nuclear power may be old hat compared to whirlpools and waves on steroids.'

Gamay gave him a sour look. 'Thanks for pointing out the bright side.'

Los Alamos had changed a great deal from the day when Robert Oppenheimer and his team of geniuses figured out how to put the power of the atom into a metal, finned cylinder. It was a bustling southwest town with malls, schools, parks, a symphony orchestra and theater, but it has never been able to – or wanted to – escape its dark past. Although the Los Alamos National Laboratory is engaged these days in a number of peaceful scientific explorations, the ghost of the Manhattan Project lingers still.

Lab buildings where research is conducted into the maintenance of nuclear weapons are still off-limits to the public, hinting that the town is still very much in the business of nuclear war. Tourists who drop into the laboratory's museum can touch replicas of 'Fat Man' and 'Little Boy,' the first A-bombs, view various types of warheads and cozy up to life-size statues of Robert Oppenheimer and General Groves, the binary stars of the ultrasecret alliance of military and science that created the bombs dropped on Hiroshima and Nagasaki.

The Trouts stopped at the national laboratory's research library and talked to a research assistant they had contacted earlier. She had prepared a folder with information about Lazlo Kovacs, but most of it was biographical and offered nothing beyond what they already knew about the scientist. Kovacs, it seemed, was pretty much a footnote. Like Tesla, about whom more was known, Kovacs had become a cult figure, the assistant explained, and his theories belonged more in the area of science fiction than science.

'Maybe we'll learn more at the Kovacs Society,' Gamay said.

The assistant gave the Trouts a blank look, and then she burst into laughter.

'What's wrong?' Gamay said.

The assistant blushed and said, 'I'm sorry. It's just that – well, you'll see.'

She was still laughing when she ushered them to the door.

The contact at the Kovacs Society was an ebullient-sounding man whose name was Ed Frobisher. When they called Frobisher, he said he'd be out and about doing errands and suggested that they meet him at a surplus store called the Black Hole.

The shop was on the edge of town next to an A-frame with a sign out front designating it as the OMEGA PEACE INSTITUTE, FIRST CHURCH OF HIGH TECHNOLOGY. The church and the Black Hole were owned by a local named Ed Grothus, who had bought up decades of lab surplus that went back to the Manhattan Project days. He called it 'nuclear waste', and advertised his wares for mad scientists, artists and pack rats.

The yard around the store was cluttered with empty bomb casings, turrets, office furniture and electronic gear. Inside the big warehouse there was aisle after aisle of shelves, all piled high with obsolete electronic gear, such as Geiger counters, oscilloscopes and circuit boards. The Trouts asked the cashier if he knew Frobisher. He led them to an aisle where a man was talking to himself as he rummaged through a stack of control panels.

'Look at this stuff,' Frobisher said after they had introduced themselves. 'This board probably cost a month's wages of the average taxpayer back in the fifties. Now it's junk, except to a few tech nuts like me.'

Frobisher was a big man, over six feet tall, with a barrel chest that flowed into a belly that hung over his wide, military belt. He wore a yellow plaid shirt that would have hurt the eyes even if it hadn't clashed with the red suspenders that struggled to hold his pants up under the weight of his belly. The pants were tucked into knee-high, rubber fisherman's boots, although the day was desert dry. His thick, pure white hair was cut in bangs that hung over rectangular, horn-rimmed glasses.

Frobisher paid for the control board, and led the way out of the store to a dusty and dented Chrysler K-car. He told the Trouts to call him 'Froby,' and suggested that they follow him to his house where the Kovacs Society had its headquarters. As the vehicles headed out of town, Gamay turned to Paul, who was at the wheel.

'Does our new friend Froby remind you of anyone?'

Trout nodded. 'A tall and loud Captain Kangaroo.'

'Kurt is going to owe us after this one,' Gamay said with a sigh. 'I'd rather get sucked down into a whirlpool.'

The road went higher, winding through the hills above the town. Houses became fewer and farther between. The sedan turned up a short gravel drive, bouncing like a rubber ball on its worn-out shock absorbers, and parked in front of a doll-sized adobe house. The yard was filled with electronic junk, resembling a smaller version of the Black Hole.

As they walked the path between piles of rusting rocket casings and electronic housings, Froby waved his arm expansively.

'The labs have an auction every month to sell off their stuff. Guess I don't have to tell you that I'm at every sale,' Froby said.

'Guess you don't,' Gamay said with an indulgent smile.

They went into the house, which was surprisingly well ordered in contrast to the haphazard nature of its surplus landscaping. Frobisher ushered them into a compact living room furnished with institutional leather-and-chrome office furniture. A metal desk and two metal filing cabinets were pushed against a wall.

'Everything in this house comes from the national lab,' Frobisher bragged. He noticed Trout looking at a

RADIOACTIVE warning sign on the wall and gave him a horsy grin. 'Don't worry. That's there to cover a hole in the wall. As president of the Lazlo Kovacs Society, I'd like to welcome you to the world headquarters. Meet our founder.' He pointed to an old photograph that hung on the wall next to the sign. It showed a fine-featured man in his forties with dark hair and intense eyes.

'How many members does the society have?' Gamay said.

'*One.* You're looking at him. As you can see, it's a very exclusive organization.'

'I noticed,' Gamay said with a sweet smile.

Trout gave his wife a look that said he was bolting for the door at the first opportunity. She was busy scanning the floor-to-ceiling bookshelves that filled a good percentage of the wall space. Her female eye for detail had seen what Trout had not: judging from their titles, the books were on highly technical and arcane subjects. If Froby understood even a fraction of his reading material, he was a very intelligent human being.

'Please have a seat,' Frobisher said. He sat in the desk chair and swiveled around to face his guests.

Trout sat down next to Gamay. He had already decided that the best way to end the conversation was to begin it. 'Thank you for seeing us,' he said as a prelude to saying good-bye.

'My pleasure,' Froby beamed. 'To be honest, I don't encounter much interest in the Kovacs Society these days. This is a big deal. Where are you folks from?'

'Washington,' Trout said.

His baby blue eyes lit up. 'An even *bigger* deal! You'll have to sign my guest book. Now, tell me, how did you come to be interested in Lazlo Kovacs?'

'We're both scientists with the National Underwater and

Marine Agency,' Gamay said. 'A colleague of ours at NUMA told us about Kovacs's work, and said there was a society here in Los Alamos that had the most complete files on the subject. The national lab's library has very little on Kovacs.'

'That bunch over there thinks he was a quack,' Frobisher said with disgust.

'We got that impression,' Gamay said.

'Let me tell you about the society. I used to work as a physicist with the national laboratory. I played cards with a bunch of my fellow scientists, and invariably the work of Nikola Tesla came up. Some of us used to argue that Kovacs was overshadowed by Tesla's flamboyant style and deserved more credit for his discoveries than he had been given. We named our poker group the Kovacs Society.'

Trout smiled, but he was groaning inwardly as he thought about the time being wasted. He cleared his throat.

'Your society was named after a *poker* group?'

'Yes. We thought about calling it Poker Flats. But some of the fellows were married and thought a discussion group would be good cover to put their wives off.'

'So you never did discuss the Kovacs Theorems?' Gamay said.

'Yes, of *course* we did. We were bad poker players but good scientists.' He reached over to a shelf on his desk and pulled out two booklets, which he handed to the Trouts. 'We ran off these copies of the original article in which Kovacs discussed his revolutionary theories. This is an abstract of a conference on his work held here about twenty years ago. It was mostly a dump-on-Kovacs affair. They're on sale for $4.95 apiece. We've got biographies you can buy for a little more, to cover the cost of printing.'

Paul and Gamay perused one of the booklets. The dense

text was written in Hungarian, and was heavy on long, incomprehensible mathematical equations. Trout gave his wife a 'That's it' grin and leaned forward, preparing to launch his tall body from the chair and out the door. Sensing his impatience, Gamay touched his arm.

'The books I see on the shelves are highly technical, and you said you were a physicist with the lab, so we'd value your opinion. I hope you don't take this the wrong way, but you must know that there has been a great deal of controversy over Kovacs and his theories. Was Kovacs nothing but a brilliant quack? Or did he have something?'

'He *definitely* had something.'

'But he never proved it by experiment, and refused to release details of his findings to the public.'

'That's because he knew the information was too dangerous.'

Gamay smiled. 'Forgive me, but that sounds like an excuse to hide his failure.'

'Not at all. It was a respect for mankind.'

Trout sensed that Gamay had a plan, and went along with it.

'If he cared about mankind, why did he work for the Nazis?' Trout said.

'He *had* to work for the Nazis. They threatened to kill his family.'

'I understand that's exactly what happened,' Gamay said. 'It's all such a shame, don't you think? The man's wife and children died for *this*.' She slapped her knee with the brochure. 'An empty theory about deadly extra-low-frequency electromagnetic waves.'

Frobisher's pale cheeks turned the color of boiled lobster. After a moment, the frown on his face dissolved into his big-toothed smile.

'That was a skillful job of baiting me.' He looked from face to face. 'Now, please tell me who you *really* are.'

Gamay glanced at Paul, who nodded his head.

'We're with NUMA's Special Assignments Team,' she said. 'Would you like to see some ID?'

'I believe you. What are a couple of people from the world's largest ocean studies organization doing in Los Alamos, far from the Atlantic and the Pacific?'

'We think that the key that will unlock the mystery of some unusual ocean disturbances can be found here in New Mexico.'

He furrowed his brow. 'What *sort* of disturbances?'

'Whirlpools and giant waves big enough to sink ships.'

'Please excuse me, but I still don't know what you're talking about.'

'One of the NUMA scientists we talked to suggested that the disturbances could have been caused by disruptions in the earth's electromagnetic flow. He brought up the Kovacs Theorems.'

'Go on,' Frobisher said.

Taking turns, they told him about the ocean disturbances, and the speculation that they were man-made.

'Dear God,' Frobisher said, his voice hoarse. 'It's happening.'

'What's happening?' Trout said.

'NUMA or not, you've blundered into something much larger than anything you could imagine.'

'We do that a lot,' Trout said. 'It's part of the NUMA job description.'

Frobisher stared at Trout and Gamay. Their calm expressions brought him back to earth, and he got a grip on himself. He went into the kitchen and returned with three cold bottles of beer, which he offered around.

'We've told you who we are,' Gamay said with her beguiling smile. 'Now perhaps you'd tell us who *you* are.'

'Fair enough.' He gulped down half his beer. 'Let me start with a little history. Most everyone knows about the letter Einstein wrote President Roosevelt.'

Trout nodded. 'Einstein said that with a controlled chain reaction a reality, an atomic bomb was possible. He suggested that the United State develop such a weapon before the Germans did.'

'That's right,' Frobisher said. 'The president appointed a committee to look into it, and the result was the work here at Los Alamos. Few people know that near the end of the war, Einstein wrote a second letter that has never been published. In it, he warned of the dangers of electromagnetic war, based on the theorems. But unlike Kovacs, who was considered by some to be a bit of a quack, Einstein's opinion had weight. Truman was president by then. He appointed a committee to look into Einstein's suggestion, and out of that came a research effort similar to the Manhattan Project.'

'We've heard that the Russians were pursuing the same line of research,' Gamay said.

'That's right. By the mid-sixties, we were neck and neck with the Russians.'

'How far did the research go?'

'*Far.* They concentrated on the land rather than the sky, and created some earthquakes. After the big Alaskan quake, this country retaliated. We caused some nifty floods and droughts in Russia. That was all small potatoes.'

'Floods and quakes hardly seem minor occurrences,' Gamay said.

'That was only the warm-up. Scientists from both countries discovered about the same time that the combined force from their experiments could cause major changes in the earth's electromagnetic field. A top secret meeting between the two countries was held on a remote island in the Bering Sea. Scientists and government officials attended. Both countries were presented with evidence showing the serious consequences of further experimentation using the Kovacs Theorems.'

'How do you know all this if it was so secret?' Gamay said.

'Simple. I was one of the participants. We agreed to end research and get back to lesser evils, such as nuclear warfare.'

'It's hard to believe there is something worse than a nuclear holocaust,' Gamay said, raising an eyebrow.

'*Believe* it.' Frobisher leaned forward in his chair and lowered his voice from habit, as if he thought that the room was bugged. 'Keeping the secret was considered of such consequence that a security apparatus was set up in each country. Anyone who became too inquisitive or knowledge-able about Kovacs and his work was discouraged or, if necessary, eliminated.'

'Then the Kovacs Society wasn't formed as a cover for a poker game?' Trout said.

Frobisher smiled. 'That story usually turns most people off. No, the Kovacs Society was formed here as part of the setup. The reasoning was that it would be a first stop for someone interested in his work. If you had wandered in here a few years ago asking questions that crossed a certain threshold, I would have made a telephone call and you would have disappeared. You're lucky the unit was dis-banded a few years ago.'

'What happened?' Trout said.

'Budget cuts,' Frobisher said with a smirk. 'Loss of institutional memory. The few people who were acquainted with the agreement died, taking the secret to the grave. No one was around to support the budget item, so it was cut. As time went on, Kovacs and his work faded into the woodwork. Like Nikola Tesla, Kovacs has become a cult figure of the conspiracy nuts, only lesser known. Most of the people who stop by here are crazies, like one guy who had a spider tattooed on his scalp. The more serious-minded are put off by my Froby act.'

'It's a very good act,' Gamay said.

'Thanks. I was beginning to believe it myself. I've been a one-man gatekeeper, fending people off when they get too nosy.'

'You talked about worldwide consequences from the electromagnetic manipulation,' Trout said.

Frobisher nodded. 'What scared everyone was the possibility that the electromagnetic manipulation would cause a shift of the earth's poles.'

'Is that possible?' Gamay said.

'Oh yes. Let me explain. The earth's electromagnetic field is created by the spinning of the outer crust around the solid part of the inner core. Scientists at Leipzig University developed a model that showed the earth as a gigantic dynamo. The heavy metals and liquid magma of the inner-core electromagnet are the clutch. The lighter metals at the crust are the windings. The planet's poles are determined by the electromagnetic charge. The magnetic poles are the result of vortices deep in the molten core. The magnetic poles tend to wander. Navigators take this phenomenon into account all the time. If one pole declines in strength, you might see an actual reversal of the magnetic north and south poles.'

'What would be the effect of a magnetic pole shift?' Gamay said.

'Disruptive, but short of catastrophic. Power grids would be knocked out. Satellites rendered useless. Compasses confused. Atmospheric holes might be punched in the ozone, causing long-term health problems from solar radiation bursts. You'd see the aurora borealis farther south. Migrating birds and animals would be disoriented.'

'You're right about a polar shift being disruptive,' Gamay said.

'Yes, but it would be nothing compared to the effects of a *geological* polar shift.'

As a deep-ocean geologist, Trout knew exactly what Frobisher was talking about. 'You're talking about actual movement of the crust over the inner core rather than a change in the earth's electromagnetic field.'

'Precisely. The solid part of the earth moves over the liquid part. There's evidence that it has happened before, caused by a natural event like a passing comet.'

'I'm a deep-ocean geologist,' Trout said. 'A comet is one thing. I find it hard to envision that man-made machinations could cause major physical changes.'

'This is why the work of Kovacs was so important.'

'In what way?'

Frobisher rose and paced back and forth a couple of times in the small room to gather his thoughts, then stopped and made a rotating motion with his forefinger.

'This is different. Electromagnetism runs the whole universe. The earth is charged up like a huge electromagnet. Changes in the field can cause a shift in polarity, as we discussed a few minutes ago. But there's another effect, which Kovacs homed in on in his research. Matter oscillates between the stages of matter and energy.'

Trout nodded in understanding. 'What you're saying is that by changing the electromagnetic field of the planet, it is possible to change the location of matter on the earth's surface.'

'That might explain the ocean disturbances,' Gamay added.

Frobisher snapped his fingers and smiled in triumph. 'Give that man and woman a cigar each.'

'What would happen with a land shift?' Gamay said.

Frobisher's smile vanished. 'The forces of inertia would react to the shift of matter. The waters in the world's oceans and lakes would be jerked in a different direction, pounding the coastline, causing massive floods. All electrical devices would fail. We'd have hurricanes and tornadoes of unheard-of force. The earth's crust would break open, causing huge earthquakes and volcanic eruptions and massive lava flows. Climate changes would be drastic and long-lived. Radiation sickness from solar rays penetrating the earth's magnetic field would kill millions.'

'You're talking a catastrophe of major proportions,' Gamay said.

'No,' Frobisher said, his voice almost a whisper. 'I'm talking about nothing less than the end of all living matter. The end of the world.'

On the drive back to Albuquerque to catch their flight home, it was Trout's turn to be silent.

'A penny for your thoughts,' Gamay said. 'Adjusted for inflation, of course.'

Trout came out of his trance. 'I was just thinking about Roswell, New Mexico, where the UFO supposedly crashed.'

'Maybe we can go there another time. My head is still spinning with conspiracy theories after listening to our friend Froby.'

'What was your take on him?'

'He was either entertainingly eccentric or frighteningly sane.'

'That was my opinion as well, which was what got me thinking about Roswell. Some of the UFO enthusiasts say that after the incident, the president appointed a high-ranking board of scientists and government officials to look into the matter and cover it up. The group was called MJ12.'

'Sounds familiar. Are you thinking that the parallels with what we heard might be too close?'

'Maybe, but there's one way to confirm what he said one way or the other.'

'How is that?'

A plain-bound pamphlet was lying on the car's console between the two seats. Frobisher had given it to them, explaining that Kovacs had printed this single copy of the mathematical underpinnings of his controversial theorems. The booklet contained page after yellowed page of equations. Trout picked the publication up off the console and said, 'Lazlo Kovacs couldn't test his theorems. But we can.'

20

Austin stood on his deck and gazed out at the sparkling ribbon that flowed behind his house. The morning mists had burned away. The Potomac gave off a fragrance of sun-baked mud and wildflowers. Sometimes he imagined that the river had its own Lorelei, a sultry-eyed, Southern version of the Germanic siren whose singing lured Rhine rivermen to their deaths.

Heeding her irresistible call, he hauled his twenty-one-foot-long Maas racing scull from under the boathouse and eased it down the ramp to the water's edge. He slipped into the open cockpit, tucked his feet under the clogs bolted to the footrests, pushed his sliding seat back and forth a few times to limber up his abdominal muscles and adjusted the outrigger oarlocks for maximum efficiency.

Then he pushed off into the river, dipped his Concept 2 composite oars into the water, leaned forward and pulled the handles back, using the weight of his body. The nine-foot oars sent the needle-sharp scull flying through the water. He increased his rowing rate until the dial of the StrokeCoach told him he was doing his usual cruising speed of twenty-eight strokes per minute.

Rowing was a daily ritual and his main form of exercise. It emphasized technique over power, and the melding of mind and body necessary to send the light craft skimming over the water was a way to exclude the chatter of the outside world and to bring his concentration into sharp focus.

As he glided past stately old mansions, he tried to make

sense out of the events that whirled around in his head like the whirlpool currents that had nearly drawn the Trouts to their deaths. One fact seemed indisputable. Someone had found a way to stir up the oceans. But to what end? What profit was there in producing killer waves and huge maelstroms capable of gulping down whole ships? And who was capable of wielding such immense and godlike power?

Austin saw movement out of the corner of his eye, cutting his meditation short. Another scull was pulling alongside his. Austin shipped his oars and coasted to a stop. The other rower did the same. They stared at each other. His newfound companion didn't fit the mold of the clean-cut, athletic types he often encountered on his morning rows. To begin with, long Rastafarian dreadlocks hung down from under the tan baseball cap. He wore sunglasses with blue lenses.

'Good morning,' Austin said.

The man removed his cap with the attached dreadlocks and took his sunglasses off. 'Damn, this thing is hot!' he said. He grinned at Austin. 'Been to any good kayak races lately?'

The sun gleamed off the bizarre tattoo on the sweaty scalp.

Austin leaned on his oars. 'Hello, Spider,' he said.

'You know who I am?'

Austin nodded. 'The Bob Marley disguise had me fooled for a second.'

Barrett shrugged. 'It was the best I could do on short notice. A guy was selling them at a souvenir booth near the boat rental place. It was either this or Elvis.'

'Good choice. I can't see you singing "Hound Dog",' Austin said. 'Why the need to go incognito?'

Barrett pointed to a bandage that was wrapped around his head. 'Someone is trying to kill me.'

'Why?'

'Long story, Kurt.'

Austin decided to take a stab in the dark. 'Does this have anything to do with extra-low-level electromagnetic transmissions?'

It was obvious from the look of astonishment on Barrett's face that the comment had struck home. 'How'd you know about that?'

'That's about all I *do* know.'

Barrett squinted at the sparkle on the river. 'Pretty.'

'I think so, but you didn't come here for the scenery.'

'You're right. I came by because I need a friend.'

Austin swept his arm around. 'You're in friendly waters here. If it hadn't been for you and your boat, I would have been killer whale bait. Come back to my house and let's talk about it.'

'That's not a good idea,' Barrett said with a furtive glance over his shoulder. He reached into his shirt pocket and produced a black box about the size of a pack of cigarettes. 'This will tell us if there's any electronic surveillance in the area. Okay, it's clear right now, but I'd rather not take any chances. Mind if we row? I'm enjoying myself.'

'There's a place we can pull off not far from here,' Austin said. 'Follow me.'

They rowed another eighth of a mile and pulled the sculls up onto a low bank. A kind soul had placed a picnic bench in the shade of the trees for the benefit of passing boaters. Austin shared his water bottle with Barrett.

'Thanks,' he said after gulping down a couple of swallows. 'I'm way out of shape.'

'Not from what I saw. I was flying right along when you caught up with me.'

'I was on the rowing team at MIT. Rowed practically

every good day on the Charles River. It's been a long time,' he said, smiling at the memory.

'What was your major at MIT?'

'Quantum physics, specializing in computer logic.'

'You wouldn't know it from the biker look.'

Barrett laughed. 'That's for show. I was always a computer geek. I grew up in California, where my parents were both university professors. I went to Caltech to study computer sciences, then on to MIT for my grad work. That's where I met Tris Margrave. We put our heads together and came up with the Bargrave software system. Made a zillion bucks on it. We were doing fine, enjoying ourselves, before Tris got involved with Lucifer.'

'Lucifer? As in the Devil?'

'*Lucifer* was an anarchist newspaper published in Kansas back in the eighteen hundreds. It's what they used to call "matches" years ago. It's also the name of a small group of neo-anarchists Tris has been involved with. They want to topple what they call the "Elites," the unelected people who control most of the world's wealth and power.'

'Where do you fit in?'

'I'm part of Lucifer. That is, I was.'

Austin eyed Barrett's head tattoo. 'You don't strike me as a conventional person, Spider, but don't you and your partner control a considerable amount of the world's wealth?'

'*Absolutely.* That's why we're the ones to carry on the fight. Tris says men of wealth and education – those that had the most to lose – started the American Revolution. Guys like Hancock, Washington and Jefferson were well-off.'

'What's Margrave's role in Lucifer?'

'Tris refers to himself as Lucifer's driving force. Anarchists don't like the idea of following a leader. It's a loosely organized group of a hundred or so like-minded people affiliated with some of the more active neo-anarchist groups. A couple of dozen of the more violence-prone guys call themselves "Lucifer's Legion". I was more involved in the technical than the political side of the project.'

'What makes Margrave so driven?'

'Tris is brilliant and ruthless. He is guilty about the way his family made its fortune off of slavery and rum-running, but I think he is driven mainly by an obsession with power. He got me into the Lucifer scheme.'

'Which is?'

'We were going to mess up the Elites' empire, so they'd cave in to our wishes and relinquish some of their power.'

'That's a pretty tall order,' Austin said.

'*Tell* me about it. We gave them a taste of what would happen a couple of weeks ago in New York. We shut down the city for a time during a big economic conference, hoping to get them to deal, but it was like an elephant being stung by a bee.'

Austin raised an eyebrow. 'I heard about the blackout. You were responsible for that?'

Barrett nodded. 'It was just a sample to show them we could cause chaos. Our long-range plan is to cause massive communications and economic disruption around the world.'

'How were you going to do that?'

'By using a set of scientific principles to temporarily foul up their communications and transportation systems and cause general economic chaos.'

'The Kovacs Theorems.'

Barrett stared at Austin as if he had just sprouted a second head. 'You've been doing your homework. What do you know about the theorems?'

'Not much. I know that Kovacs was a genius who came up with a way to use extra-low-frequency electromagnetic transmissions to disrupt the natural order of things. He was worried that, in the wrong hands, his theorems could be used to alter weather, cause earthquakes and other sorts of mischief. From what you've told me about your Lucifer pals, his fears seem to have been borne out.'

Barrett winced at the mention of 'pals', but he nodded in agreement. 'That's about right, as far as it goes.'

'How far *does* it go?'

'We were trying to cause a polar reversal.'

'A shifting of the north and south poles?'

'The *magnetic* poles. We wanted to knock out communications satellites. Mess up commerce, and throw a scare into the Elites. Strictly low-end stuff.'

Austin's jaw hardened. 'Since when are killer waves, ship-swallowing whirlpools and the loss of a cargo ship and crew considered low-end?'

Barrett seemed to draw into himself. Austin feared his sharp comment may have shut off further communication. But then Barrett nodded in agreement.

'You're right, of course. We didn't think of the consequences, only the means.'

'What were the means?'

'We built a fleet of four ships, each carrying a device modeled on the Kovacs Theorems. We concentrated the beam at an oblique angle into a vulnerable spot on the ocean floor. The power in each ship is enough to light a small city, but it's feeble when compared to the great mass of the earth. That's where the theorems come in. Kovacs said that at the proper frequency, the transmissions would be amplified by the very mass they were trying to penetrate, in the way a tuba amplifies the sound of air being blown through pursed lips.'

'I saw the giant whirlpool you created. That was more than a set of pursed lips.'

'A *whirlpool*!'

Austin gave him a condensed version of the maelstrom and the disaster it nearly caused.

Barrett whistled. 'I knew about the giant waves we created with one of our field tests. The kickback sunk a cargo ship and one of our transmitter vessels.'

'Sometimes the sea gives back what it takes. The whirlpool churned up your transmitter ship. I managed to board her before she sank.'

Barrett looked stunned at the revelation.

'What's going on, Spider?'

The question shocked Barrett out of his daze.

'We didn't consider the violent ocean disruptions that would be caused by the anomalies we created in the earth's electromagnetic field. From what you told me, the disruptions continued even after we stopped transmitting and moved the ships off. The magma under the earth's crust must continue to move even after the initial stimulus. It's like the secondary ripples that bounce around a pond when you throw a rock into the water. That's the dangerous part of the theorems. It's what worried Kovacs. The unpredictability of the whole thing.'

'What were you doing the day I saw you in Puget Sound?'

'After the *Southern Belle* sank, I went back to the drawing board. I was conducting a test, using a miniaturized version of the setup on the transmitter.'

'That's what drove the orcas into a frenzy?'

He nodded.

'What was the problem?'

'The waves were bouncing all over the place. We had

made an educated guess, but even if it were off by a nano-second the transmissions can go haywire.'

'So Kovacs was wrong?'

Barrett threw his arms wide apart. 'He published his general theory as a warning to the world, but he withheld the information that would make it work. Look, it's like an atomic bomb. You can find plans for an A-bomb on the Internet, and you can even acquire the materials to put one together. But unless you have specific knowledge about the way things act, it's going to fail, and the best you can get is a dirty, radioactive bomb. That's what we've got here: the electromagnetic equivalent of a dirty bomb.'

'The loss of your ship must have stopped the project in its tracks,' Austin said.

'It only delayed it. We had a ship in reserve. It's being moved onto station for the big, major zapping.'

'Where is that going to be?'

'Tris never told me. There were a number of possible locations. The final choice is all in his head.'

'How did you get into this insanity?'

'In a very routine way. I first brought the Kovacs Theorems to Tris's attention. I thought there might be something there for our company, but he saw it as a way to advance his anarchist cause. He asked me to develop a system that would cause a temporary magnetic shift. I saw it as a technical challenge. Using Kovacs's work as a basis, I filled in the gaps.'

'Tell me about the attempt on your life.'

Barrett gingerly touched the side of his head. 'I was visit-ing Tris on his island in Maine. Mickey Doyle, who flies Tris's private plane, tried to kill me. He faked engine trouble and landed on a lake. His bullet grazed my head and caused a lot of blood. I was rescued by a couple of fishermen from

Boston. One of them happened to be a doctor. I gave him a fake name, and took off as soon as I got the chance. That's why I was doing the Rasta thing. I don't want anyone to find out I'm still alive or I *will* be dead!'

'Was Doyle acting on Margrave's orders?'

'I don't think Tris was behind it. He's gone ultraweird on me. He's become a megalomaniac. He's hired his own army, guys he says are around for security. But when I told Tris I was pulling out of the project after the *Southern Belle* sank and the orcas went crazy, he said he would put things off until I had a chance to go through some new material he'd come across. Just before he shot me, I asked Mickey if Tris was behind it. He said he was working for someone else. I don't think he was lying.'

'That begs the question: who would want to take you out?'

'Mickey was trying to warn me against going public. When I refused, he tried to kill me. Whoever he was working for didn't want the project stopped.'

'Wouldn't the project screech to a halt if you were dead?'

'Not anymore,' Barrett said with a sad smile. 'The way I've got this thing set up, Tris can direct the ships and unleash their power with a minimum of personnel and equipment.'

'Who else has an interest in seeing this scheme succeed?'

'There's only one other person I know who's got the inside track. Jordan Gant. He runs Global Interests Network. GIN for short. It's a foundation out of Washington that lobbies for many of the same causes as Lucifer. Abuse of corporate power. Tariff policies that hurt the environment. Arms buildups in developing countries. Tris says Gant's foundation is like Sinn Fein, the political wing of the Irish Republican Party. They can keep their hands clean, more or less, while the IRA is the secret organization that uses the muscle.'

'Then a threat to Tris's project would be a threat to Gant's goals as well.'

'That's a logical conclusion.'

'What's Gant's background?'

'He's an apostate from the corporate world. He was working for some of the same groups we're fighting until he saw the light. He's pretty much a front man. Smooth talker. Lots of oily charm. I can't picture him behind a murder plot, but you never know.'

'It's a trail worth following. You say Margrave gave you some material, hoping it would change you mind.'

'He said that Kovacs had come up with a way to stop a polar reversal even after it had been started. I said I wouldn't pull out if he could come up with a fail-safe plan.'

'Where would he begin to find something like that?'

'There's evidence that Kovacs survived after the war, and that he moved to the US, where he remarried. I think his granddaughter knows about the antidote to a polar shift. Her name is Karla Janos.'

'Does Gant know this?'

'He would if we're right about Doyle.'

Austin pondered the implication of the answer. 'Ms Janos could have a bull's-eye on her back. She should know that she may be a target. Do you know where she lives?'

'In Alaska. She's doing some work at the University of Alaska at Fairbanks. But Tris said she's on an expedition to Siberia. She may be cold, but she should be safe there.'

'From what you've told me, Margrave and Gant have a long reach.'

'You're right. What should we do?'

'We've got to warn her. The safest course for you is

to stay "dead". Do you have a place to stay? Someplace Margrave or Gant don't know about?'

'I've got a sleeping bag on my Harley and a pocket full of cash, so I don't have to use credit cards that can be traced. My cell phone calls are laundered through half a dozen remote stations, so they're practically impossible to trace.' He pulled the little black box out of his pocket. 'I put this together for fun. I can route phone calls to the moon if I want to.'

'I'd suggest that you stay on the move. Call me this time tomorrow and we'll have a plan in place by then.'

They shook hands and went back to their boats. Austin waved good-bye and pulled off at his house, while Barrett rowed his scull back to the boat rental place half a mile farther along the river. Austin put his boat up in its rack. In the few seconds it took to climb the stairs to the living room, he had put together a plan.

21

Ten thousand years after the last woolly mammoth shook the earth beneath its feet, its bones and tusks are providing the fuel for a booming international trade. The center of that trade is the city of Yakutsk in East Siberia, about six hours by plane from Moscow.

It is an old city, founded in the 1600s by a band of Cossacks, and was long considered the last outpost of civilization for explorers. It gained later fame, or notoriety, as one of the islands in the Gulag system, where enemies of the Soviet state found ready employment as slave laborers in the gold and diamond mines. Since the nineteenth century, it has been the world capital for the woolly mammoth ivory trade.

The Ivory Cooperative is one of the prime distributors in the ivory trade. The cooperative is housed in a dark and dusty warehouse, surrounded by crumbling apartment buildings that go back to the time of Khrushchev. Behind the nondescript, concrete walls and steel door are thousands of pounds of mammoth ivory worth millions of dollars, waiting to be shipped out to China and Burma, where they will be carved into trinkets for the thriving Asian tourist market. The white treasure is contained in crates that are stacked on shelves running from one end of the warehouse to the other.

Three men were standing in one of the aisles. They were Vladimir Bulgarin, the owner of the ivory business, and two helpers, who were holding each end of a huge mammoth tusk.

'This is beautiful,' Bulgarin was saying. 'What's its weight?'

'One hundred kilos,' one of his helpers said with a grunt. 'Very heavy.'

'Wonderful,' Bulgarin said. Prime ivory was going at one hundred dollars a kilo.

A third helper was hustling down the aisle. 'Your partner is here,' he said.

Bulgarin looked as if he had bit into a lemon. He instructed his helpers to load the tusk into a sawdust-filled crate and to set it aside. He might have the tusk carved into little ivory mammoths or earrings rather than send it out as raw ivory, increasing the value even more.

As he headed back to his office, he had a frown on his fleshy face. His so-called partner was what they called a 'bagman' in the United States. He was a Mafia thug who showed up once a month from Moscow to collect a percentage of the take, accuse Bulgarin of holding out and threaten to break his legs if he was.

It was inevitable that the Russian Mafia would find a way to get its sticky fingers into the profitable mammoth tusk trade. Business was booming, thanks to the international ban against the sale of ivory from the African elephant herds that had been decimated by hunters. Inhabitants of Yakutsk had a history in the mammoth trade going back hundreds of years, and, with an estimated ten million mammoths buried under the Siberian permafrost, a vast source of material.

Political change had boosted the ivory trade as well. Moscow had always regulated commerce in Yakutsk, and still controlled the diamond and gold business, but the local inhabitants had been trading with the Chinese for two thousand years, and they knew better than anyone how to make money off the bones of ancient, dead giants. The ivory first had to be worked in order to be exported legally but some distributors, like Bulgarin, ignored the law and sent raw ivory directly to the buyers.

When Moscow stepped out, the Mafia stepped in. The previous year, the cooperative received an unannounced visit from a group of the most frightening men Bulgarin had ever met. They wore black turtlenecks and black leather jackets, and they spoke softly when they said they were becoming partners in the business. Bulgarin was a petty thief, and he rubbed elbows with the more violent elements of the Russian underworld. When these hard men said he and his family needed protection, he knew exactly what they meant. He agreed to the arrangement, and the people from Moscow installed the two guards with machine guns at the door to protect their investment.

Bulgarin was puzzled as well as annoyed at the timing of the visit. As regular as clockwork, his partner showed up on the fourth Thursday of every month. This was the second Wednesday. Despite his annoyance, when he entered his tiny, cluttered office near the entrance to the warehouse he wreathed his face in a broad smile, expecting to see Karpov, the usual representative from Moscow. But the man dressed in the black suit and turtleneck was younger, and, in contrast to Karpov, who stole money with a tough-guy affability, his expression was as cold as Yakutsk on a winter night.

He glared at Bulgarin. 'I don't like to be kept waiting.'

'I'm very sorry,' Bulgarin said, maintaining his smile. 'I was at the far end of the warehouse. Is Karpov ill?'

'Karpov is only a money collector. We have serious business. I want you to get in touch with the men on Ivory Island.'

'It's not easy.'

'Just do it.'

Several days before, Moscow had called, and told him

to assemble a team of his most hardened ivory hunters and send them to the island. They would find a scientific party working there, and were instructed to hold a woman scientist named Karla Janos. They were to hand her over to a team coming in from Alaska.

'I can try,' Karpov said. 'The weather –'

'I want you to change their orders. Tell them to take the girl and transport her off the island.'

'What about the Americans?'

'Their people are unable to come. They were willing to pay a great deal of money for the job, so she is evidently of some value. We will talk to her, to see what she has to say, and hold her for ransom.'

Karpov shrugged. It was typical of the Moscow Mafia. Double cross. Crude and direct.

'What about the other scientists?'

'Tell your men, no witnesses.'

A chill ran down Karpov's spine. He was no angel, and had broken a few heads as a young smuggler. Ivory hunting was a cutthroat business. After the Mafia got into ivory hunting, they had recruited men who could be charitably called 'scum of the earth'. Some of his competitors had conveniently vanished.

At the same time, he was smart enough to know that, as a witness, he too would be in line to be eliminated. He would do as the man said, but his mind was already working on ways to fold his business and leave Yakutsk. He nodded, his mouth dry, and opened a cabinet that housed a state-of-the-art radio.

Within minutes, he had contacted the ivory hunters. Using a carefully crafted code in case someone was listening, he called the leader of his team, a violent man named Grisha, who was a Sakha descendant of the Mongols that had lived as ivory hunters going back hundreds of years. He relayed the instructions. Grisha asked only for clarification to make sure he had heard the order correctly, but otherwise had no questions.

'It's done,' he said, replacing the microphone.

The Mafia man nodded. 'I will come back tomorrow to make sure.'

Karpov wiped the sweat off his brow after the man left. He didn't know which was worse, dealing with the cutthroats from Moscow or the cutthroats who worked for him. What he did know was that his days in Yakutsk were numbered. He would be safe until they brought someone in to replace him, but, in the meantime, he would activate plans made long ago. He had millions of dollars in Swiss bank accounts.

Geneva would be nice. Or Paris or London. The gem business would be profitable.

Anything would be preferable to a Siberian winter.

He smiled. The Mafia may have done him a great favor.

22

Petrov was leaving his office in the drab Moscow government building when his secretary told him he had a telephone call. He was in a foul mood. He had been unable to
extricate himself from a diplomatic party at the Norwegian
embassy. Norway, for God's sake! Nothing but smoked fish
to eat. He planned to get tanked up on vodka and disgrace
himself. Maybe they wouldn't invite him back.

'Take a message,' he had growled. As he was going out
the door, he turned. 'Who's on the line?'

'An American,' his secretary said. 'He says his name is
John Doe.'

Petrov looked dumbstruck. 'You're sure?'

Petrov brushed by his astonished secretary and returned
to his office, where he snatched the phone off the desk and
stuck it to his ear. 'Petrov here,' he said.

'Hello, Ivan. I remember when you answered the phone
yourself,' said the voice on the other end of the line.

'And *I* remember when you were still named Kurt Austin,'
Petrov said. His snarl didn't match the gleam of amusement
in his eyes.

'Touché, old pal. Still the same old, sharp-tongued KGB
apparatchik. How are you, Ivan?'

'I'm fine. How long has it been since the Razov affair?'

'A couple of years, anyway. You said to call if I ever need
a favor.'

Austin and Petrov had worked together to torpedo the
plans of Mikhail Razov, a Russian demagogue who was

behind a plot to launch a tsunami against the East Coast by using volatile methane hydrate ocean deposits.

'You're lucky to catch me. I was on my way to a *thrilling* party at the Norwegian embassy. What can I do for you?'

'Zavala and I need to get to the New Siberian Islands as soon as possible.'

'*Siberia!*' Petrov chuckled. 'Stalin is *dead*, Austin. They don't send people to the Gulag anymore.' He glanced around him. 'Those who offend their superiors are given a promotion, a title and a large office decorated in atrocious taste, where they are bored to death.'

'You've been a bad boy again, Ivan.'

'The term doesn't translate into Russian. Suffice it to say that it's never wise to offend one's superior.'

'Next time I talk to Putin, I'll put in a good word for you.'

'I would appreciate it if you didn't. President Putin is the superior I offended. I exposed a close friend of his who had been embezzling money from an oil company that the government had taken over after arresting its owner. The usual Kremlin follies. I was removed from my intelligence position. I have too many friends in high places, so I couldn't be punished overtly, and instead was placed in this velvet cage. Why Siberia, if I may ask?'

'I can't go into details now. I can only tell you it's a matter of great urgency.'

Petrov smiled. 'When is it *not* urgent with you? When do you want to go?'

Austin had called Petrov after trying to trace Karla Janos at the University of Alaska. The department head he spoke to said Karla was on an expedition to the New Siberian Islands. Austin knew he had to act fast when the department head mentioned that this was the third time that week people had inquired about the Ivory Island expedition.

'Immediately,' he told Petrov. 'Sooner, if you can pull it off.'

'You *are* in a hurry. I'll call the embassy in Washington and have a courier deliver the paperwork to you. There is a price for my help, though. You must allow me to buy you a drink, so we can talk over old times.'

'You've got a deal.'

'Will you need support once you get here?'

Austin thought about it. From past experience, he knew that Petrov's idea of support would be a tough, special ops team armed to the teeth and spoiling for a fight.

'Maybe later. This situation may require a more surgical touch at the outset.'

'In that case, I will have my medical team ready in case you need surgery. I may join them myself.'

'You weren't kidding about being bored,' Austin said.

'It's a far cry from the old days,' Petrov said with nostalgia in his voice.

'We'll reminisce over our drinks,' Austin said. 'Sorry to cut you off, but I've got to make some calls. I'll call you with my final travel details.'

Petrov said he understood, and told Austin to be in touch. He hung up, and told his secretary to cancel the car that was supposed to take him to the Norwegian embassy. He called the Russian embassy in Washington. No one there knew about his bureaucratic exile, and he was able to authorize papers that would get Austin and Zavala into Russia for a NUMA scientific expedition. After he had been assured that the paperwork would be delivered within the hour, he sat back in his chair and lit up one of the slim Havana cigars he favored, and thought about his encounters with the brash and daring American from NUMA.

Petrov was in his forties, with a broad forehead and high

cheekbones. He would have been handsome, if not for the massive scar that defaced his right cheek. The scar was a gift from Austin, but he bore the American no ill will. He and Austin had clashed several times when they were working for specialized naval intelligence units in their respective countries during the Cold War. Things got hot when their paths crossed during a Soviet attempt to capture a sunken American spy submarine and its crew.

Austin had rescued the crew, and warned Petrov that he had placed a timed explosive charge on the sub. Angry at being bested, Petrov dove in his minisub and was caught in the explosion. He had not held the incident or the resulting scar against Austin, and, in fact, took it as a lesson not to let his temper guide his actions. Later, when they found themselves working together on the Razov affair, they proved a formidable team. If Austin thought he was going to cut him out of some fun in his own country, he was greatly mistaken, Petrov ruminated. He picked up the phone to start things rolling.

Austin was on the phone to Zavala. 'I was on my way out the door,' Zavala said. 'See you at NUMA.'

'There's been a change of plans,' Austin said. 'We're going to Siberia.'

'Siberia!' Zavala said with a distinct lack of enthusiasm. 'I'm Mexican American. We don't do well in the cold.'

'Just remember to pack your fur-lined jock and you'll be fine. I'm bringing along my blunderbuss,' he said, using Zavala's nickname for his large-caliber Bowen revolver. 'You might want to pack some insurance as well.'

He arranged to meet Zavala at the airport, and went to dig out clothes that would be fit for Arctic conditions.

*

Thousands of miles away, Schroeder was in his cramped cabin, taking one more look at the topographical map before he set foot on the island.

Schroeder had learned long ago of the need to know the theater of operations one expected to operate in, whether it was a hundred square miles of countryside or a few blocks of city alleyways.

He had studied the map a number of times and felt that he knew Ivory Island as well as if he had been there. The island was about ten miles wide and twenty miles long, elongated in shape. The sea had eroded the permafrost, so that the coast was as jagged as a pottery shard. On the south shore, a half-moon indentation in the shoreline offered a sheltering harbor, near where a river emptied into the sea.

Ancient rivers, some dry and some still active, had created a mazelike warren of winding, natural corridors through the rolling tundra. A long-dormant volcano rose from the permafrost like a huge, black carbuncle.

He put the chart aside and thumbed through a well-worn Russian travel guide he had picked up in a secondhand bookstore while he was trying to arrange transportation to the island. He was glad to see that his command of Russian was still serviceable. Ivory Island was discovered in the late 1700s by Russian fur traders. They found the huge piles of animal bones and mammoth tusks that lent the island its name. The bones were piled everywhere, lying on the open ground or forming hills cemented together by the cold.

The fur-trading business was wiped out in an orgy of murder, and the ivory hunters started coming in. Fine ivory found a ready market in the master carvers of China and other parts of the world. Recognizing the white bonanza, the Russian government awarded franchises to entrepreneurs.

One businessman hired an agent named Sannikoff, who explored all the Arctic islands.

Ivory Island held the richest trove, but because of its remoteness it was left relatively unscathed in favor of more accessible sources to the south. A few intrepid ivory hunters established a settlement at the mouth of the river, which they called Ivorytown, the book said, but the island had been largely abandoned in favor of more hospitable locations.

The knock on the cabin door interrupted his research. It was the captain, a round-faced man who was half Russian, half Eskimo.

'The boat is ready to take you ashore,' the captain said.

Grabbing his duffel bag, Schroeder followed the captain to the port rail of the trawler and climbed down a ladder to a rowboat. While a crewman pulled at the oars, Schroeder used a long-handled gaff to fend off hunks of ice that floated in the still, cold water. Minutes later, the bottom of the boat scraped onto the gravelly beach. Schroeder tossed his bag onto the beach, got out of the boat and helped push it off.

He watched the skiff disappear into the mists. Although the fishing boat was only a few hundred yards offshore, it was barely visible behind the damp, vaporous curtain of mist. The agreement was for the boat to wait twenty-four hours. Schroeder would stand on the beach and signal for a pickup. He hoped he would have Karla with him. It hadn't occurred to him before whether she would be persuaded enough by his warning of danger to leave the island. He would deal with that problem later. His immediate task was to find her. He hoped it was not too late. He was in good shape for his age, but his body couldn't deny the fact that it had nearly eight hard decades behind it and was starting to fray around the edges. His muscles and joints ached, and he had developed a limp in one leg.

Schroeder heard the grumble of the fishing boat's engine. The boat was moving off. The captain must have decided that he would rather leave with only half the money than wait for Schroeder to return, as they had agreed, before he was paid the entire fee. Schroeder shrugged. He had the captain pegged as a pirate from the beginning. There was no going back now.

He studied what he could see of the island. The beach rose gradually to a low banking, which wouldn't be difficult to climb. He shouldered his duffel bag, moved closer and saw that there were boot prints in the sand. This must be the main route to Ivorytown.

He hiked along the river for around ten minutes and laughed out loud when he set eyes on the pitiful encampment of sorry-looking buildings that had been labeled a town. The large, colorful tents erected next to the old structures told him he had found the expedition's campsite.

As he approached the camp, he was surprised to see that the structures, which he had assumed to be of stone, were actually built of thousands of large bones. He poked his head into a couple of buildings and saw some sleeping bags. A third building was locked for some inexplicable reason. He explored the tents and discovered one of them had been set up as a kitchen and mess hall. Schroeder walked around the perimeter of the encampment and called out several times, but there was no reply. He looked off toward the brooding, old volcano and scanned the island but saw no movement. He was not surprised; an army could have hidden in the maze of ravines that laced the island.

He trekked back to the river and saw boot prints along the edge leading into the interior. His practiced eye picked out five different sets of boot prints, including two smaller, less deep ones that looked as if they belonged to women. He felt less tired, energized by the prospect of a reunion with his goddaughter, and began to pick up his pace. Some time later, Schroeder's elation changed to alarm.

Heavy boot tracks obliterated the others. Karla and her party were being stalked.

23

From the top of the knoll she had climbed, Karla could see that Ivory Island was not the Arctic desert she had first assumed it to be. The tundra was treeless, but it was thick with low-lying, dwarf shrubs, grasses, mosses and sedges that formed a muted carpet. Dandelions, buttercups and fireweed created vibrant splashes of color. The morning sunlight glittered on distant lakes and rivers. Noisy seabirds wheeled overhead.

In her mind's eye, she pictured the rugged landscape as verdant grassland, the steppes teeming with vast herds of woolly mammoth. There would have been bison and woolly rhinos, giant ground sloths, all stalked by predators like the scimitar or saber-toothed cats. She could almost smell the musky animal odor and feel the ground shake from the passage of thousands of huge animals.

Somehow, as if an evil sorcerer had waved a magic wand, the mammoths and the other creatures had became extinct. The question of extinction had intrigued her as far back as she could remember. Like many children, she had been fascinated by dinosaurs and the great mammals that succeeded them as the earth's masters.

Her grandfather was the only scientist she knew, so of course she went to him and asked what had caused these magnificent creatures to die. She had listened wide-eyed as he explained how the world had shifted, and asked him if it could happen again. He had said yes, and she had been unable to sleep. Seeing her fear, a few nights later he had taught her a nursery rhyme that would make the topsy-turvy world right again. She was trying to dig the rhyme from her memory when she heard someone shout.

'*Karla!*'

Maria Arbatov was waving her arms at Karla. The expedition was ready to get moving again. Karla started walking back to rejoin the others. It was time to return to the task at hand. She knew it would not be easy. The discovery of the baby mammoth carcass had been an astounding stroke of luck. But Ivory Island was a rich trove of the ancient past. If she couldn't find what she wanted here, she should forsake field trips forever and stick to cataloging museum specimens.

Fortified by a hearty breakfast, the expedition got off to an early start that morning. Ito and Sato were ready before anyone else. They were dressed identically in warm-weather clothes, from their boots to their hats. Sergei was grumpier than usual, and even Maria's lovely smile couldn't dispel his sour mood, so she just ignored him.

They had shouldered their packs and headed into the interior of the island, using the river as a guide. They made good time across the flat tundra. By midmorning, when they had taken their first break, near Karla's knoll, they had trudged several miles.

As she hoisted her pack to resume the trek, Karla said: 'I've been wondering. How did you transport the specimen all the way back to the camp? It must weigh hundreds of pounds.'

Ito smiled and pointed to the packs he and Sato were carrying. 'Inflatable rafts. We got the specimen to the river and floated all the way back to camp.'

Ito smiled and bowed politely when Karla congratulated them on their ingenuity.

Sergei took up the lead, followed by the two women with the Japanese men taking up the rear. They struck off inland, away from the river. The topography changed from flat tundra to rolling hills and valleys, and eventually they were on the edge of the rolling foothills that ringed the base of the volcano. As they drew closer to it, the black, truncated mountain that they had seen in the distance began to loom above their head like an altar to Vulcan, the lord of the underworld.

They hiked along the shores of several small lakes and made their way around tussocks of cotton grass that marked boggy areas teeming with migrating birds. The temperature rose to around thirty degrees, but a breeze coming off the Arctic Ocean created a windchill factor that halved that, and Karla was glad that she was wearing her down parka.

The cold wind was no longer a problem, once they had descended into a ravine about thirty feet wide. Twenty-foot banks hemmed them in on both sides. A narrow stream a couple of feet deep ran down the middle, with plenty of room for walking on either side. They traveled along the winding gorge for two hours, and the composition of the banks began to change. Soon it became apparent that the ravine was an ancient mortuary. The river that had created the ravine had cut through layers of time to reveal scores of bones that protruded from the sand under their feet.

Karla stopped and picked up a bison leg bone that fitted perfectly into the socket of another bone she found a few feet away. The other scientists were not impressed. They barely gave the find a second look, and she had to drop the bones and hurry to catch up.

She was annoyed and frustrated at their indifference, but the reason for their casual attitude soon became apparent. As they rounded a bend, she saw that the low cliffs were composed almost entirely of bones of every size and species cemented together by the permafrost. She quickly identified pygmy horse and ancient reindeer fossils, ribs and femurs, along with massive mammoth bones and tusks. The graveyard went on for at least two hundred yards.

With great fanfare, Sergei announced that they had reached their destination. He dropped his rucksack on the ground next to the blackened ashes of a fire. 'This is our base camp,' he said.

The others left their bags as well, and continued along the ravine carrying only camera equipment and a few hand tools. As they trekked along, Karla thought about the baby mammoth back at the base camp. She was dying to test it. From its tissue and cartilage, they could perform radiocarbon tests to determine when it lived and died. The tusks would provide growth lines, like those in a tree, that would reveal seasonal differences and metabolic rate and migratory patterns. Seeds and pollen in the stomach contents would tell much about the biological world that existed thousands of years ago.

After hiking along the ravine for another ten minutes, they came to a section where there was a shallow cave in the wall of the gorge.

'This is where we found our little baby,' Sergei said.

The ragged cavity was several feet across and about a yard deep.

'How did you get it out of the permafrost?' Karla said.

'Unfortunately, we had no water hose to melt the permafrost,' Maria said. 'We relied on hammer and chisel to extract the specimen.'

'Then it was partly exposed?'

'Yes,' Maria said. 'We had to chop a little around the edge of the carcass before we could pry it out.' She explained that they had rigged up a crude travois from mammoth tusks and dragged the frozen specimen to the river. It was floated back to the base camp and moved into the shed, where the temperature was below freezing even in the daytime.

Karla examined the hole. 'There's something strange here,' she said.

The other scientists clustered around her.

'I don't see anything,' Sergei said.

'Look. There are other bones much deeper in the perma-frost. They are evidently thousands of years old.' She reached into the hole and scraped out some decayed vege-tation and showed it to her colleagues. 'This stuff is not very old. Your little elephant came into the hole more recently.'

'Perhaps it is my poor English, but I'm not sure if I understand what you're saying,' Sato said politely.

'Yes, what *are* you saying?' Sergei said with no attempt to hide his impatience. 'That the mammoth is not part of its surroundings?'

'I don't know what I'm saying. Only that it is odd that the flesh is not rotting.'

Sergei crossed his arms and looked around at the others with a triumphant grin on his face.

'I understand,' Maria said. 'I'm surprised we didn't see it before. This ravine still floods from time to time. It's possible that a flash flood washed the specimen away from a wall farther along and that the baby floated here, where it lodged in the hole and froze again.'

Sergei saw that he was losing his conversational edge. 'We're not here to look at holes,' he said brusquely. He led the way about a hundred feet from the discovery site to where the ravine branched off. 'You go with Maria down there,' he said, pointing to the left-hand branch. 'We'll examine the other ravine.'

'We've already been down this one,' Maria protested.

'Look again. Maybe you'll find some more of your floating mammoths.'

Maria's eyes flashed. Sato saw that a salvo was coming and intervened. 'We had better make sure our hand radios are tuned to the same channel,' he said.

With a verbal brawl averted, they all checked their walkie-talkies and made sure the batteries were good. Then they split up into two groups, with the three men going one way and the women the other.

'What's wrong with Sergei today?' Karla asked.

'We got into an argument over your theory last night. He said it was all wrong. I said he wasn't giving you credit because you were a woman. He's such a male chauvinist, my husband.'

'Maybe he just needs a little time to cool off.'

'The old goat will be sleeping with an iceberg tonight. Maybe that will cool him off.'

They both burst into laughter that echoed off the walls of the ravine. After walking several minutes, Karla saw why Maria had been so angry about being ordered to the left-hand branch. There were few bones to be found. Maria confirmed that the expedition had partially explored the other gorge and found it far richer in bones than the one they were in.

As they scanned the walls of the gorge, Maria's hand radio crackled. Ito's voice came on.

'Maria and Karla. Please return immediately to the point where the party split up.'

Minutes later, they were back at the place the ravine forked. Ito was waiting for them. He said he had something to show them, and led the way along the tributary to where the other two men were waiting in front of a section of banking that looked as if it had been blasted open with dynamite.

'Somebody has been digging here,' Sergei said, stating the obvious.

'Who could have done such a thing?' Sato said.

'Is there anyone else on the island?' Karla asked.

'We didn't think so,' Ito said. 'I thought I saw a light a few nights ago, but I couldn't be sure.'

'It appears that your eyesight was working very well,' Sato said. 'We are not alone on the island.'

'Ivory hunters,' Sergei pronounced. He picked up a splint of bone from the hundreds of broken pieces that littered the ground. 'I had no idea they had found this place. It's a sin. There's no science here. It looks as if someone has taken a hammer and chisel to it.'

'Actually, we use a portable jackhammer.'

The words came from thickset man who stood looking down on them from the top of the bluff. His broad face, his narrow, hooded eyes and high cheekbones advertised his Mongol ancestry. A thin mustache drooped down on either side of his mouth, which was wide in a thin-lipped grin. Karla had studied Russian while she was in Fairbanks and got the gist of what he was saying. The assault rifle cradled in his arms spoke louder than any words.

He whistled and a second later four more men appeared in the gorge, two from each side, all armed with similar weapons. They had tough-looking, unshaven faces, with sneering mouths and hard eyes.

Sergei may have been vain and disagreeable, but he displayed an unexpected courage born of scientific anger. He pointed to the broken bones. 'You did this?'

The man shrugged.

'Who are you?' Sergei said.

The Mongol ignored the question and looked past Sergei. 'We are looking for the woman named Karla Janos.'

The man was staring at Karla, but she was startled to hear her name from the stranger's lips. Sergei glanced at her in reflex, then thought better of it.

'There is no one here by that name.'

The Mongol issued a curt order, and the man nearest to Karla grabbed her roughly by the arm with his dirt-encrusted fingers and pulled her away from the others.

She resisted. He squeezed her arm so hard it bruised. He smiled when she grimaced in pain, and he put his face close to hers. She almost gagged on the odor of his unwashed body and his foul breath.

She glanced over her shoulder. The other scientists were being herded along another ravine. The man at the top of the banking had disappeared. As she was hustled out of sight, she heard Maria scream, then male voices shouting.

Shots rang out, the noise echoing off the walls of the gully. She tried to run back to her colleagues, but the man grabbed her by the hair and jerked her back. First came excruciating pain, then anger. She whirled around and tried to claw his eyes out. He pulled his head back, and her finger-nails scraped harmlessly against the stubble of his scruffy beard.

He lashed out with the back of his hand. Karla was stunned by the blow, and offered little resistance when he put his foot behind her legs and pushed her down. The back of her head hit the ground and galaxies whirled before her eyes. Her vision cleared, and she saw the man staring down at her with amusement, then lust, in his piglike eyes.

He had decided to have some fun with his lovely captive. He put his gun safely out of reach and began to unbutton his fly. Karla tried to crawl out of his way. He laughed, and put his boot on her neck. She pounded at his ankle and struggled to escape. She could barely breathe.

The man coughed suddenly, and the grin on his face changed into a mask of shock. A trickle of blood appeared at the corner of his mouth. He pivoted in slow motion, his boot slipped off Karla's neck and she saw the hilt of a hunting knife protruding from between his shoulder blades. Then his legs turned to rubber and he collapsed.

Karla rolled over to keep from being crushed by the falling body. Her elation was cut short. Another man was coming toward her.

He was tall, and limped when he walked. The sun slanting into the ravine was behind him and his face was obscured in shadow. She wanted to get up, but she was still dizzy and disoriented from hitting the ground.

The man called her by her first name. It was a voice she hadn't heard in many years.

Then she fainted.

When she came to, the man was bending over her, holding her head in his hands, soothing her bruised lips with water from a canteen. She recognized the long jaw and the pale blue eyes that were filled with concern. She smiled even though it hurt her cracked lips.

'Uncle Karl?' she asked as if in a dream.

Schroeder placed his fox-fur hat under her head as a pillow, then went over to retrieve his knife, wiping the blade on the man's coat. He picked up the dead man's assault rifle and slung it over his shoulder. Then he took his hat back, placed his arms under her body and lifted her like a fireman carrying a smoke-inhalation victim.

Voices were coming along the ravine.

Pain shot up his leg from his ankle, but Schroeder ignored it. Stepping smartly, he carried Karla in the opposite direction, vanishing around a bend only seconds before the Mongol man and the rest of his gang found their companion. It took them only a second to see that he was dead. Crouching low, they advanced along the wall of the ravine with their weapons cocked.

Schroeder ran for his life. And for Karla's.

24

Less than ten hours after leaving Washington, the turquoise executive NUMA jet descended from the skies over Alaska and touched down at Nome airport. Austin and Zavala exchanged their jet for a two-engine propeller plane operated by Bering Air and took off within an hour, heading toward Providenya on the Russian side of the Bering Strait.

The flight across the strait took less than two hours. Providenya airport was on a scenic bay surrounded by sharp-peaked, gray mountains. The town had been a World War II stopover for lend-lease aircraft being flown to Europe from the United States, but those glory days were in the past. There were only a few charter planes and military helicopters at the airport when the plane taxied up to the combination flight tower and administration building, a tired-looking, two-story structure of corrugated aluminum that looked as if it went back to the time of Peter the Great.

As the only arriving passengers, Austin and Zavala expected to be processed quickly by customs and immigration. But the attractive young immigration agent checking paperwork seemed to read every word on Austin's passport. Then she asked for Zavala's papers as well. She placed the passports and visas side by side.

'Together?' she said, looking from face to face.

Austin nodded. The woman frowned, then she signaled an armed guard who had been standing nearby. 'Follow me,' she barked like a drill sergeant. Gathering their papers, she led the way to a door on the other side of the lobby, with the guard taking up the rear.

'I thought you had friends in high places,' Zavala said.

'They probably just want to give us the key to the city,' Austin replied.

'I think they want to give us a shot,' Zavala said. 'Read the sign over the door.'

Austin glanced at the red letters on the white placard. Written in English and Russian was the word QUARANTINE. They stepped through the door into a small, gray room. The room was bare except for three metal chairs and a table. The guard followed them into the room and posted himself at the door.

The immigration agent slapped the papers down on the table. 'Strip,' she said.

Austin had caught a few hours of sleep on the plane, but he was still bleary-eyed and wasn't sure he had heard her correctly. The woman repeated the order.

Austin smirked. 'Gosh. We hardly know each other.'

'I've heard the Russians were friendly. But I didn't know they were *that* friendly,' Zavala said.

'Strip or you will be made to strip,' the woman said, glancing at the armed guard to emphasize her point.

'I'll be glad to,' Austin said. 'But in our country, ladies go first.'

To his amazement, the woman smiled. 'I was told that you were a hard case, Mr Austin.'

Austin was beginning to smell a rat. He cocked his head. 'Who would have told you something like that?'

The words were barely out of his mouth when the door opened. The guard stood aside and Petrov stepped into the room. His handsome face was wreathed in a wide grin that looked lopsided because of the curved scar on his cheek.

'Welcome to Siberia,' he said. 'I'm glad to see that you are enjoying our hospitality.'

'*Ivan,*' Austin said with a groan. 'I should have known.'

Petrov was carrying a bottle of vodka and three shot glasses, which he placed on the table. He came over and threw his arms around Austin, and then crushed Zavala in a bone-crunching bear hug. 'I see you have met Dimitri and Veronika. They are two of my most trusted agents.'

'Joe and I never expected such a warm welcome in a cold place like Siberia,' Austin said.

Petrov thanked his agents and dismissed them. He pulled up a chair and told the others to do the same. He unscrewed the cap from the bottle of vodka, poured the glasses full and passed them around.

Raising his glass high, he said, 'Here's to old enemies.'

They clinked glasses and downed their drinks. The vodka tasted like liquid fire, but it had more wake-up power than pure caffeine. When Petrov went to pour another round, Austin put his hand over the glass. 'This will have to wait. We have got some serious matters to deal with.'

'I'm pleased you said *we*. I felt excluded after our call.' He poured himself another shot. 'Please explain why you found it necessary to hop onto a plane and fly halfway across the world to this lovely garden spot.'

'It's a long story,' Austin said with a weariness that wasn't all due to the hours on a plane. 'It begins and it ends with a brilliant Hungarian scientist named Kovacs.'

He laid the story out chronologically, going back to Kovacs's escape from Prussia, bringing it to the recent past, with the giant waves and whirlpool and his talk with Barrett.

Petrov listened in silence, and, when Austin was done, he pushed away his untouched glass of vodka.

'This is a fantastic story. Do you truly believe that these

people have the capacity to create this polar reversal?'

'You know everything we know. What do *you* think?'

Petrov pondered the question for a moment. 'Did you ever hear of the Russian "woodpecker" project? It was an effort to control weather for military purposes, using electromagnetic radiation. Your country followed the same line of research for similar purposes.'

'How successful were these projects?'

'Over a period of time, there was a series of unusual weather events in both countries. They ranged from high winds and torrential rains to drought. Even earthquakes. I'm told the research ended with the Cold War.'

'Interesting. That would fit in with what we know.'

A slight smile cracked the ends of Zavala's lips. 'Are we *sure* it ended?'

'What do you mean?'

'Have you looked out the window lately?'

Petrov glanced around the windowless room before he realized that Zavala was speaking metaphorically. He chuckled, and said, 'I have a tendency to take statements literally. It's a Russian thing. I'm well aware that the world has experienced a number of weather extremes.'

Austin nodded. 'Joe makes a good point. I don't have the statistics in front of me, but the empirical evidence seems to be pretty strong. Tsunamis. Floods. Hurricanes. Tornadoes. Quakes. They all seem to be on the rise. Maybe this is a hangover from the early experiments.'

'But from what you say, these electromagnetic efforts are causing disturbances in the ocean. What has changed?'

'I don't think it's that difficult to understand. Whoever is behind this has seen a reason to focus on a specific end with a specific goal in mind.'

'But you don't know what that goal is?'

'You're the former KGB guy. I'm just a simple marine engineer.'

Petrov's hand went to the scar. 'You're far from simple, my friend, but you're right about my conspiratorial twist of mind. While we talked, I remembered something one of your government officials, Zbigniew Brzezinski, said many years ago. He predicted that an elite class would arise, using modern technology to influence public behavior and keep society under close surveillance and control. They would use social crises and the mass media to achieve their ends through secret warfare, including weather modification. These people you talked about, Margrave and Gant. Do they fit this role?'

'I don't know. It seems unlikely. Margrave is a rich neo-anarchist, and Gant runs a foundation that does battle with the multinationals.'

'Maybe you *are* a simple engineer. If you were part of an elite class that had conceived a plot against the world, would you advertise it?'

'I see your point. No, I would lead people to believe that I opposed the elite.'

Petrov clapped his hands. 'You don't know how pleased I am to learn that the latest plot against the world is being hatched by *Americans* rather than a mad Russian nationalist with czarist pretensions.'

'I'm glad to know that this is making you warm and bubbly, but we should get down to business.'

'I'm completely at your service. You obviously have a plan or you wouldn't be here.'

'Since we're not sure of *who*, and don't know *why*, we're stuck with *what*. Polar reversal. We have to stop it.'

'I agree. Tell me more about this so-called antidote you mentioned.'

'Joe's the technical guy on our team. He can explain it better than I can.'

'I'll do my best,' Zavala said. 'From what I understand, the idea is to cause a polar shift using electromagnetic transmissions beamed into the earth's mantle, creating sympathetic vibrations in the inner core. You can compare these transmissions to sound waves. If you're in a hotel and you want to mask loud voices from the next room, you could turn on a fan and the vibrations would neutralize the racket. If you wanted to mask a higher tone, like a hair dryer, you would need a different set of frequencies. It's called white noise, or white sound. You might hear it as a hiss or something like rustling leaves. This antidote is comparable. But it wouldn't work unless you had the exact frequencies.'

'And you think this woman, Karla Janos, knows about these frequencies?'

'She may not know it, but the evidence seems to point that way,' Austin said. 'Aside from the global implications, there is an innocent young woman here who could lose her life.'

Petrov's somber expression remained the same, but his eyes crinkled in amusement. 'That is one of the many reasons I like you, Austin. You are the embodiment of gallantry. A knight in shining armor.'

'Thanks for the compliment, but we don't have much time, Petrov.'

'I agree. Do you have any questions?'

'Yeah,' Zavala said. 'Does Veronika have a phone number?'

'You can ask her yourself,' Petrov said.

He downed the shot of vodka, screwed the cap back on the bottle and tucked it under his arm, then led the way from the room and through the exit. A car and driver were waiting for them.

'We had some special luggage,' Austin said. He pointed to two oversize bags. 'Please give them special attention.'

'Everything has been transferred.'

They got in the car, which drove them to the water side of the airport and onto a wide, sagging dock. A boat about sixty feet long was tied up at the end of the dock. Several men were waiting at the gangway.

Austin got out of the car and asked about the words painted in Cyrillic on the white hull.

'Arctic Tours. It's a real tourist company that takes wealthy Americans into godforsaken places for obscene sums of money. I have chartered the boat for a few days. If anyone asks, we are taking some Boy Scouts on a nature tour.'

As Petrov escorted the two men up the gangway, Austin was glad to see that their luggage had appeared magically on the deck. They were traveling light, with one duffel bag apiece, and the two bags that Austin asked be given special attention.

Petrov led them into the main cabin. Austin had only to take a quick glance around to see that this was no tourist boat. Most of the built-in furniture had been removed, leaving a stationary table in the center and padded benches along the perimeter. Dimitri and Veronika sat on the bench with four men in camouflage uniforms. They were busy cleaning an impressive array of automatic weapons.

'I see your Boy Scouts are preparing for their merit badges in marksmanship. What do you think, Joe?'

'I'm more interested in the Girl Scout,' Zavala said. He went over and struck up a conversation with the young Russian woman.

Austin gave Petrov a questioning look.

'I know you said that a quiet approach was necessary,' Petrov said. 'I am in complete agreement. These people are only here in reserve. Look, there are only six of them. Not a whole army.'

'They're packing more firepower than both sides at the Battle of Gettysburg,' Austin observed.

'We may need it,' Petrov said. 'Come to my cabin and I'll bring you up to date on the situation.'

Petrov led the way to a compact stateroom and picked up a large envelope on the bunk. He extracted a number of photographs from the envelope and handed them to Austin, who held them close to the light streaming in through the porthole. The photos showed various views of a long, grayish island with a doughnut-shaped mountain in the center of the landmass.

'Ivory Island?' he said.

'The views were taken by satellite over the last several days.' Petrov produced a small magnifying glass from his pocket. He pointed to an indentation in the south side of the island. 'This is the natural, deepwater harbor that the icebreaker, which supplies and transports the expedition, uses in coming and going. The ship dropped Karla Janos off here two days ago to join an expedition already in progress.'

'What's the nature of this expedition?'

'Science fiction. Some crazy Russians and Japanese hope to find DNA from a woolly mammoth that can be cloned into a live creature. Look, here on the other side of the island, where the permafrost had been eroded, there are natural inlets.'

Austin saw an elongated shape lying in a cove. 'A boat?'

'Whoever owns it didn't want to be seen or they would

have come into the main harbor. I think the assassins have arrived.'

'How soon can we get there?'

'Ten hours. The boat will do forty knots, but the distances here are vast, and we may be slowed by ice.'

'We don't have that long.'

'I agree. That's why I have made contingency plans.' He glanced at his watch. 'In forty-five minutes, a seaplane will arrive here from the mainland. After it refuels, it will take you and Zavala to a rendezvous with the icebreaker *Kotelny*, which is between Wrangel Island and the polar ice. A trip of about three hours by air. The icebreaker will transport you to Ivory Island.'

'What about you and your friends?'

'We will leave as soon as you do, and, with any luck, we'll arrive sometime tomorrow.'

Austin reached out and gripped Petrov's hand. 'I can't thank you enough, Ivan.'

'I should be the one thanking *you*. Yesterday, I was rotting in my Moscow office. Today, I am rushing to save a damsel in distress.'

'I may have a problem prying Zavala away,' Austin said.

His fears were unfounded, as it turned out. When he returned to the main cabin, Zavala was chatting with one of Petrov's men about his weapon. Veronika and Dimitri were sitting off by themselves engaged in animated conversation.

'Sorry to take you away from your budding romance,' Austin said.

'Don't be. Petrov failed to tell me that Veronika and Dimitri are married. To each other. Where are we going?'

Austin explained Petrov's plans, and they went out on the dock to wait. The seaplane was fifteen minutes early. It taxied up to the fuel pump at the end of the pier. Austin supervised the handling of his luggage while the plane was being refueled, then he and Zavala boarded the plane. Within minutes, it skimmed across the bay, lifted its nose and climbed at a sharp angle over the jagged peaks of the gray mountains that flanked the bay, then headed north into the unknown.

25

Karla's eyelids fluttered open. She saw only blackness, but senses that had been temporarily put on hold stirred to life. She had a coppery taste of old blood in her mouth. Her back felt as if it were resting on a bed of nails. Then she heard a rustling noise close by. She remembered the yellow-toothed attacker. Still only half conscious, she put her arms up and flailed away in the dark, defending herself against an unseen assailant.

'No!' she called out in fear and defiance.

Her thrashing arms struck soft flesh. A big hand with fingers like steel clamped down over her mouth. A light flashed on. Its beam illuminated a disembodied face floating in the darkness.

She stopped fighting. The long-jawed face had aged dramatically since the last time she had seen it. There were more wrinkles, and a general droopiness to skin that was once as taut as a drumhead. The watchful eyes were framed by crow's-feet, pouches and white brows, but the irises were the same piercing blue she remembered. He removed his hand from her mouth.

She smiled. 'Uncle Karl.'

The ends of the thin lips curved up slightly. 'Technically speaking, I am your godfather. But, yes, it is me. Your uncle Karl. How do you feel?'

'I'll be all right.' She forced herself to sit up, even though the effort made her dizzy. As she ran her tongue across her swollen lips, the memory of the attack came flooding back.

'There were four other scientists. They took them away, and then I heard shots.'

A pained look came to the pale eyes. 'I'm afraid they were all killed.'

'Killed. But *why?*'

'The men who killed them didn't want witnesses.'

'Witnesses to *what?*'

'Your murder. Or abduction. I'm not sure what they had in mind, only that it was no good.'

'This doesn't make sense. I just arrived here two days ago. I'm a stranger in this country. I'm simply a bone scientist like the others. What reason would anyone have to murder me?'

Schroeder turned his head slightly as if he were listening for something, then he switched the light off. His mellow voice was cool and soothing in the darkness. 'They think your grandfather had a secret of great importance. They think he passed it on to you, and they want to make sure no one else learns about it.'

'*Grandpa!*' Karla almost laughed through her pain. 'That's ridiculous. I don't know any secret.'

'Nonetheless, they think so, and that's what's important.'

'Then the deaths of those scientists are *my* fault.'

'Not at all. The men who pulled the trigger are responsible.'

He pressed the flashlight into her palm to restore a measure of control to her damaged psyche. She flashed the light around so that the beam illuminated the black rock ceilings and walls.

'Where are we?' she said.

'In a cave. I carried you here. It was sheer luck that I found a low place to climb out of the gorge and immediately came to a natural wall of stone. It was split in many places, and I thought we could hide in a narrow gap in the rocks. I saw an opening at the end of a narrow fissure. I cut some bushes and put them around the mouth of the cave.'

She reached out in the darkness and grabbed onto his big hand. 'Thank you, Uncle Karl. You're like some guardian angel.'

'I promised your grandfather that I would look after you.'

Karla sat in the dark, thinking back to the first time she remembered meeting Schroeder. She was a young girl, living at her grandfather's house after her parents died. He appeared one day, bearing an armful of gifts. He seemed enormously tall and strong, more like a walking tree than a man. Despite the strength that he projected, he seemed almost shy, but her child's eye had detected a kindliness in his manner, and she quickly warmed up to him.

The last time she had seen him was at her grandfather's funeral. He never forgot her birthday, and sent her a card with money in it every year until she graduated from college. She didn't know the details of the bond between Schroeder and her family, but she knew from hearing the story many times that when she was born her grandfather had persuaded her parents to name her after the mysterious uncle.

'I don't know how you found me in this remote spot,' Karla said.

'It wasn't hard. The university told me where you were. Getting here was the difficult part. I hired a boat to bring me in. When I didn't see anyone at your camp, I followed your trail. The next time you go off on an expedition, please make it closer. I'm getting too old for this kind of thing.' He cocked his ear. '*Hush.*'

They sat in the silent darkness, listening. They heard muffled voices, and the scrape of boots against rocks and gravel at the mouth of the cave. Then the darkness was leavened by a yellowish light as the bushes blocking the entrance were moved aside.

'Hey in there,' a man's voice called in Russian.

Schroeder squeezed Karla's hand in a signal to be silent. It was an unnecessary gesture, because she was nearly frozen with fear.

'We know you're in there,' the voice said. 'We can see where someone cut the bushes. It's not polite not to answer when people are talking to you.'

Schroeder crawled forward a few yards, where he had a view of the cave's mouth.

'It's not polite to kill innocent people, either.'

'You killed my man. My friend was innocent.'

'Your friend was *stupid* and deserved to die,' Schroeder said.

Hoarse male laughter greeted his answer.

'Hey, tough guy, my name is Grisha. Who the hell are you?'

'I'm your worst nightmare come true.'

'I heard someone say that in an American movie,' the voice said. 'You're an old man. What do you want with a young girl? I'll make a deal. I'll let you go if you give us the girl.'

'I heard someone say that in a movie too,' Schroeder said. 'Do you think I'm stupid? Let's talk some more. Tell me why you want to kill the girl.'

'We don't want to kill her. She's worth a lot of money to us.'

'Then you won't harm her?'

'No, no. Like I said, she's worth more as a hostage.'

Schroeder paused as if he were seriously considering the offer. 'I have lots of money too. I can give it to you right

268

away and you won't have to wait. How does a million dollars American sound?'

There was a whispered discussion, then the Russian came back. 'My men say it's okay, but they want to see the money first.'

'All right. Come closer to the cave and I'll throw it out to you.'

The conversation had been in Russian and Karla had understood only part of it. Schroeder whispered to Karla to move deeper into the cave and to cover her ears. He reached into his pack and pulled out an object that looked like a small metal pineapple. He knew that his offer would draw the attackers in like jackals, and, with any luck, he could take out all of them. He stood up. Shards of pain shot up his right leg. The run and climb while carrying the young woman had aggravated the ankle injury.

He moved closer to the entrance. He could see shadows moving closer. *Good.* There was a slight bend in the cave, and the entrance was a narrow slit, so his aim and timing would have to be just right.

'Here's your money,' he said, and pulled the pin from the hand grenade.

As he stepped forward to toss it out of the hole, his injured right leg buckled and he fell, slamming his head against the wall of the cave. He almost blacked out. As his eyes were closing, he saw the grenade hit the ground and roll to a stop only a few feet away. He pulled himself back to consciousness and forced himself to hang on. He lunged for the grenade, felt the hard metal in his hand and again tossed it to the entrance.

His aim was better this time, but the grenade glanced off the wall and came to rest in the dead center of the opening.

Schroeder threw himself deeper into the cave and around

the bend, where he gained the shelter of the wall. He clamped his hands over his ears just as the grenade exploded. There was a flash of light and a burst of white-hot metal as the shrapnel peppered the cave in a deadly fusillade. Then came a secondary roar as the entrance collapsed.

The cave was filled with dust. Schroeder lifted his head up and crawled toward the sound of coughing. The light flashed on, but the beam was diffused by the brown curtain of dust that hung in the air.

'What happened?' Karla said after the dust settled.

Schroeder groaned and spat out a mouthful of dirt. 'I told you I'm getting too old for this sort of thing. I was about to toss out the grenade when I tripped and banged my head. Wait.' He took the flashlight and made his way to the entrance. He came back after a minute and said, 'I did a good job. We can't get out, but they can't get in.'

'I don't know about that,' Karla said. 'The leader of those men said they have a portable jackhammer.'

Schroeder considered her comment. 'We'll have to go farther into the cave.'

'This place could go on underground for miles! We could become hopelessly lost.'

'Yes, I know. We will only go as far as we need to set up an ambush. I will try not to be so clumsy next time.'

Karla wondered if she was talking to the same man who had bounced her on his knee so many years ago. He had cleanly dispatched the man who tried to rape her, calmly negotiated with a band of murderers, and then, in a businesslike fashion, tried to kill the gang.

'All right,' she said. 'But this secret you mentioned. What do you know about it?'

Karl fished a candle out of his pack, lit the wick and stuck it onto a ledge using melted wax.

'I met your grandfather for the first time near the end of World War Two. He was a brilliant and courageous man. Many years ago, he came upon a scientific principle that, if used unwisely, could cause great death and destruction. He wrote a paper warning of the possibilities, and the result was not what he expected. The Nazis captured him and forced him to work on a superweapon, using his theories.'

'That's incredible. He never gave any hint that he was anything but an inventor and businessman.'

'It's true. However, I helped him escape from the lab. He had refused to give up his secrets, and his stubbornness cost him his family. Yes, that's right. He was married and had a child before he moved to the United States after World War Two. He took his secret to the grave, but these men, or the ones they work for, think he passed the secret on to you.'

'What makes them think I know anything like that?'

'History repeats itself. You published an article on the extinction of the woolly mammoths.'

'That's right. I said it was due to climate changes caused by a polar shift. I used some of my grandfather's papers and his calculations to back up my theory. Dear God! Is *that* what they want?'

'That and more. They will do anything and kill anyone to get it.'

'But everything I know is in public view. I don't know *anything* about any secret!'

'Your grandfather told the Nazis the same thing. They didn't believe him either.'

'What can I do?'

'For now, you can keep yourself well.' He went back into his pack again and came out with some jerky and water. 'Not exactly cordon bleu, but it will do for now. Maybe we will find some bats that we can cook into a big stew.'

'Now I remember,' Karla said with a smile. 'You were always telling me about the crazy things you were going to cook up for me. Snails. Puppy dogs. Brussels sprouts. Ugh. Disgusting.'

'It was the best I could do. I had limited experience entertaining children.'

They talked about shared memories as they chewed the tough jerky. They were washing their meat down with water when they heard what sounded like a giant woodpecker at the mouth of the cave.

'They've started drilling,' Karla said.

Schroeder gathered up his things. 'Time to get moving.' He handed Karla a light and suggested she use it sparingly, although he always carried plenty of batteries. Then they followed the cave deeper into the ground.

Schroeder had expected the temperature to rise the deeper they went and was heartened that it remained temperate, and that the air was relatively fresh. He remarked on the phenomenon to Karla, and suggested that the cave might eventually lead outdoors. He knew it was a slim hope, especially after the cave floor began to slant downward, but it seemed to give Karla courage.

The cave meandered, going slightly left, then right, but always down. Sometimes the ceiling was high enough to allow them to walk upright. For some stretches, the cave was only about four feet high, and they had to crouch. Schroeder was glad to see that there was only one tunnel, with no branches that would have required a decision and increased the chances of becoming hopelessly lost.

After they had been walking for about an hour, the cave broke open to a larger space. They had no idea how big it was until they started to explore it.

As their flashlight beams bounced off the moisture that

cast a sheen on the high ceilings and far walls, it became apparent that the cavern was as big as the lobby of a grand hotel. The floor was almost flat. At the far end, opposite where they had come in, was the only other opening, which loomed as large as a garage door.

They walked around the perimeter of the chamber, sipping from their water bottles, marveling at the size and shape of the space. Schroeder had been examining it with an eye toward setting up ambush, and had decided, with its nooks and wall crannies, that it would make an ideal killing field. Karla had wandered over to the other entrance, where she swept the interior with her light, then stepped inside.

'Uncle Karl,' she called out, her voice echoing.

He strode over to where she knelt on the cavern floor. Illuminated in the bull's-eye of light from her flashlight was a brownish mass of vegetation.

'What is it?' Schroeder asked.

She didn't answer right away. After a moment, she said, 'It looks like elephant scat.'

Schroeder roared with laughter. 'Do you think the circus passed this way?'

She stood up and touched it with the toe of her boot. A musky, grassy smell arose from the mound. 'I think I need to sit down,' she said.

They found a wall outcropping to sit on and refreshed themselves from their water bottles. Karla told Schroeder about the baby mammoth that had been discovered not far from the cave entrance. 'I couldn't figure out how it could be so well preserved,' she said. 'No one has ever found a specimen like that. It seemed to have died only days or weeks ago.'

'Are you suggesting that there are woolly mammoths living in these caves?'

'No, of course not,' she said with a laugh. 'That would be

impossible. Maybe they once did, though, and the scat is very old. Let me tell you a story. In 1918, a Russian hunter was traveling through the taiga, the great Siberian forest, when he saw huge tracks in the snow. For days, he followed the creatures that made them. They left behind piles of dung and broken tree branches. He described seeing two huge elephants with chestnut hair and massive tusks.'

'An apocryphal hunter's tale, with no evidence, meant to impress?'

'Possibly. But the Eskimos and North American Indians recounted legends of great shaggy creatures. In 1993, the skeletons of dwarf mammoths were found on Wrangel Island, between Siberia and Alaska, not far from here. Their bones were dated between seven thousand and thirty-seven hundred years ago, which means mammoths roamed the earth well past Paleolithic times, when men were building Stonehenge and the Pyramids.'

Schroeder chuckled and said, 'You'd like to explore further, wouldn't you?'

'I wouldn't want to waste an opportunity like this sitting around and twiddling our thumbs. Maybe we'll come across some well-preserved specimens.'

'I don't think preparing to repel a gang of desperate cutthroats qualifies as twiddling our thumbs, but I shouldn't be surprised. Once, when you were a child, I read you *Alice in Wonderland*. Not long after, I found you out in the yard trying to squeeze your head down a rabbit hole. You said you wished you had some tonic that would shrink you, like Alice.'

'It must have been your fault for reading me such stories.'

'Well, now it seems we have little choice,' he said wearily. He picked up his pack and limped toward the opening. 'Down the rabbit hole we go.'

26

The chestnut stallion galloped across the verdant Virginia countryside as if it were racing neck and neck in the Kentucky Derby. Jordan Gant crouched in the saddle like an overgrown jockey and whipped his crop repeatedly on his mount's haunches. The horse had been running a punishing pace. Its eyes rolled, its sleek coat was shiny with sweat and its tongue hung from its mouth. Still Gant showed no mercy. It was not so much cruelty, which would have assumed emotion on his part, but rather the disregard he held for anything that came under his control.

Gant crossed meadows and pastures, and rode along the edge of a driveway bordered by poplar trees until he came to a sprawling country house. He headed to a stable area near the house, and allowed the exhausted animal to come to a trot, then a walk and finally to a halt. Gant slid easily out of the saddle, took a towel from a waiting groom and carelessly tossed him the reins. The horse was limping as it was led away.

Gant strode up a stone walkway toward the front door. He was dressed for polo in a black short-sleeved shirt and jodhpurs. Gant had a muscular, athletic physique, and he would have worn his clothes well even if they weren't custom-tailored. He whipped his knee-high boots of cordovan leather with his crop as he walked, as if his arm had a mind of its own. The massive wooden front door opened at Gant's approach, and he stepped into an enormous foyer with a fountain bubbling in the center. Gant handed his gloves and towel to the cadaverous butler who had opened the door.

The butler said, 'Your guest has arrived, sir. He's waiting in the library.'

'A Bombay Sapphire martini, straight up, and the usual for me.'

The butler bowed and disappeared down a long hallway. Gant went through a door off the foyer into a spacious chamber lined with floor-to-ceiling bookshelves filled with the priceless volumes that he collected. Margrave stood near a set of French doors that overlooked manicured lawns that were as green as the top of a billiard table. He was perusing an antique book bound in red Moroccan leather.

'That's a rare edition of the *Divine Comedy* published in 1507,' Gant said. 'There are only three known copies. I own them all.'

'You've got quite the extensive collection of Dante.'

'Actually, it's the best in the world,' Gant said without pretense.

Margrave smiled and slipped the book back onto the shelf. 'I would expect no less. Did you have a good ride?'

Gant tossed the whip onto a side table. 'I *always* have a good ride. The horse does all the work. The animal that I rode today is new to my stables. It's a stallion that needed to be shown who the boss is. I always take a new horse out for a test-drive. Those that survive are treated like royalty. Those that don't end up in a glue factory.'

'Survival of the fittest?'

'I'm a great believer in Darwin.'

The butler arrived carrying a tray with two drinks. Gant handed one glass to Margrave, and took the sixteen-year-old, double-matured scotch whisky on the rocks for himself.

Margrave sipped his drink. 'Perfect martini,' he said. 'You know exactly what I drink. I'm impressed.'

'You forget that I'm in a business where deals are often lubricated with alcohol,' Gant said. 'Nothing makes a favorable impression like remembering someone's particular poison.' He settled into a comfortable chair, and gestured for Margrave to take a seat. 'What's the latest on our project?'

'On schedule. But I'm worried about Spider. I haven't heard from him since he left the island a few days ago.'

'Barrett is a big boy,' Gant said. 'He can take care of himself.'

'I don't care about his health; it's his *mouth* I'm concerned about. He's had an acute attack of conscience. I don't want to see him on *60 Minutes* telling Mike Wallace about our project.'

'You said he agreed to stay with the project until you made contact with Karla Janos.'

'That's right. He wanted a fail-safe option that could shut the project down in a hurry.'

'Then you have nothing to worry about. Barrett is probably off sulking somewhere. The main question is whether the project can proceed without him.'

'That's not a problem. Spider has already laid the groundwork that made him indispensable. We don't need him anymore. All is proceeding according to plan. I worked up this presentation for you.'

Margrave opened a carrying case and pulled out a portable DVD player, which he set up on a mahogany desk. He pressed the ON button and the schematic profile of a ship appeared on the screen.

'This is one of the transmitter ships as originally designed. Here are the power plants in the hold leading to the electro-magnetic low-frequency antenna, which can be lowered into the sea.' He forwarded the picture. 'This is the new ship that will do the work of our four experimental vessels.'

'A small ocean liner. Ingenious. How soon will it be on-site?'

'The old transmitter vessels have left the Mississippi shipyard and are on their way to the debarkation point in Rio. They can still be useful as decoys for insurance. The name of the liner is the *Polar Adventure*. She'll be in Rio as well, but no one will suspect she is carrying the payload.'

'You've made a final choice of a target site, then.'

Margrave pressed a key on the player. A map of the Southern Hemisphere appeared on the screen. The map showed a reddish patch shaped like a flattened sphere that covered a good portion of the ocean between the coast of Brazil and South Africa.

'The South Atlantic Anomaly.'

Margrave nodded. 'As you know, the anomaly is a region where the earth's geomagnetic field flows the wrong way. Some scientists describe it as a "pothole", or a dip, in the field. There are sections where the field is completely reversed and weakened. Magsat discovered a North Polar region and a spot below South Africa where the magnetism has been growing extremely weak. Exploiting the weakness in the south ocean magnetic field will cause a similar reaction in the North Pole region.'

Gant chuckled. 'That's the beauty of this whole scheme. We're not precipitating the event as much as we're hastening its arrival.'

'True. The north and south magnetic poles have reversed themselves in the past without help, and the earth's electro-magnetic field started collapsing on its own about a hundred and fifty years ago. Some experts say a shift is overdue. The earth's magnetism is already affected by the vortices in the molten layer under its crust. Stir up some additional turbulence and only a nudge will be needed to cause a shift. As you say, we're just helping the process along.'

'Fascinating,' Gant said. 'I take it that there has been no change in our original expectations of the impact of this little flip?'

'The computer models still hold. The main magnetic fields will weaken, and then almost vanish. For three days or so, there will virtually be no magnetic poles. Then they will return with opposite polarity. Compass needles that normally point north will point south. The electromagnetic battering will knock out power grids and satellites, confuse birds and mammals, send polar auroras flashing around the equator and widen ozone holes. That will be the period of optimum danger. The collapse of the field will temporarily eliminate the earth's defense against solar storms. In the longer term, there will be an increase in the number of people who develop skin cancer.'

'Unfortunate collateral damage,' Gant said without sympathy. 'There's an extensive shelter under this house. You've taken similar precautions, I understand.'

'The ship is shielded for radiation to protect us on the return trip. I've got a comfortable shelter under the lighthouse. I could live there in great comfort for a hundred years, although the period of danger should lessen after the initial bursts.'

'Will the other members of Lucifer be keeping you company on the island?'

'Only a select few. Anarchists are good at creating chaos, but they don't have a clue about what to do once they're done smashing windows. The others will have served their purpose by then and are on their own.'

'You're going to abandon Lucifer's Legion to a possibly painful death?' Gant said.

'You can invite them to *your* shelter,' Margrave said with a sardonic smile.

'I need room for my horses,' Gant said.

'Understandable. What are your plans for the period following the big flash?'

'There will be confusion on a massive scale. People will be unable to communicate or navigate. Power will be out temporarily. Once communications are reestablished at great expense, we will broadcast a message to the world's leaders demanding an international conference to dismantle the instruments of globalization. For starters, we will call for immediate steps to disband the World Bank and the WTO.'

'And if they don't do what we ask?'

'I don't think that will be a problem,' Gant said. 'We will point out the fragility of the global infrastructure and suggest that even if they rebuild it will be a simple matter to destroy it again. We can play topsy-turvy with the magnetic poles for as long as they like.'

Margrave grinned. 'How does it feel to be one of the gods on Mount Olympus?'

Gant took a sip of his drink. 'Intoxicating. But even the gods have housecleaning matters they have to deal with. There's the matter of the woman, Karla Janos.'

'The last I heard, we had a team on its way to Siberia to take care of her.'

Gant rose from his chair and went over to the French doors. He gazed at the rolling lawns, lost in thought, then turned to Margrave. 'There's something going on and I'm not sure what it is. The assassination team never got any farther than Fairbanks, Alaska. They were all murdered in their hotel rooms.'

Margrave set his drink aside. 'Murdered?'

'That's right. They were all shot in the head. The killings were done quite professionally. These were crack members of our security company. There was no effort to dispose of the bodies. The executions were bold, even reckless, which makes me think that whoever put the plan together did it in a hurry.'

'Who knew about the team?'

'You. Me. And the Russian Mafia, of course.'

'You think the Russians are responsible?'

'They're capable of anything. But it doesn't fit. They knew a team was on its way, but had no idea who they were or where they were staying. They were passing themselves off as a television production crew and were due to leave for Siberia within hours when they were killed.'

'Do the police have any leads?' Margrave asked.

'One. The charter pilot who was hired to transport the team said he talked to someone who may have been the last one to see them. In fact, he took their place on a charter flight to Siberia. He was an older man, probably in his seventies.'

'Your original contact on Karla Janos, the one who killed two security men, wasn't he an older man as well?'

'Yes,' Gant said. 'My guess is that they are one and the same.'

'Who *is* this guy? We go looking for Karla Janos and we turn up a killer old enough to collect Social Security.'

'When my men broke into his house, they found letters written to Janos on his computer and replies from the woman. He referred to himself as "Uncle Karl".'

Margrave frowned. 'The dossier we compiled on the Kovacs family never said anything about any uncle.'

'I wouldn't worry too much about him. When I let the

Russians know that the team wasn't coming for Ms Janos, they asked what they should do with her. I told them to kill her, and the old man, if they should come across him, as I expect they will.'

Margrave nodded. 'You've been busy.'

'I don't like loose ends, like Kurt Austin, the NUMA man. I think he should be taken out.'

'I thought we were going to watch and wait on Austin to see if he developed into a threat.'

'When Austin first came into the picture, I looked into his background. He's a marine engineer and salvage expert with NUMA who has been involved in some high-profile missions. He saw the apparatus on Barrett's boat. He's in a position to cause us a great deal of trouble.'

'Are you saying that Austin could torpedo our project?' Margrave said.

'Not if he's dead. As Joseph Stalin said, ". . . no man, no problem." Doyle was making plans to take care of Austin. Unfortunately, Mr Austin left his house suddenly for an unknown destination.'

'So what do we do?'

'We keep Austin's house under constant surveillance. When he comes back we solve our problem. In the meantime, I'd suggest that you do everything you can to expedite the technical end of the project.'

'Then I'd better get going,' Margrave said.

Gant walked his guest to his car. They shook hands and agreed to stay in touch. He was on his way back into his house when the groom came up to him.

'How is the new horse?' Gant said.

'He's lame, sir.'

'Shoot him,' Gant said. Then he went back into his house.

27

The rooms and passages of the cavern were like a dream-scape. Mineral curtains of soft orange and yellow draped the walls and stalactites that ranged in size from pencil-thin rods to tall cascading columns as thick as a man's waist hung from the ceiling.

The ethereal beauty of his subterranean surroundings was lost on Schroeder. The bruise on his forehead throbbed like a tom-tom, and walking on the uneven floor of the cave aggravated his swollen ankle. He was struggling up a natural staircase when the exertion triggered a dizzy spell.

His vision swam and he began to see double. The loss of equilibrium made him nauseous. Beads of sweat broke out on his forehead even though the air was cool. He stopped and pressed his head against the cave wall. The cold rock had the soothing effect of an ice pack.

Karla was right behind him. She saw him falter and went to his aid.

'Are you all right?'

'I cracked my head back there at the cave entrance. Probably suffered a slight concussion. At least it takes my mind off my sore ankle.'

'Maybe we should stop and rest,' Karla said.

Schroeder saw a low ledge. He sat down with his back against the wall and closed his eyes. He felt as if he had aged twenty years. The dampness was working on his joints, and he was having a hard time breathing. His ankle was swollen so much that he couldn't even see the bone.

For the first time in his life, he felt like an old man. Hell, he *was* an old man. He glanced at Karla, who sat beside him, and he was awestruck at how the baby he had awkwardly held in his arms on their first meeting had become a lovely and intelligent young woman. How sad he had never allowed himself to have a family. He consoled himself. Karla *was* his family. Even if he had not made a pledge to her grandfather, he would have done everything in his power to keep her from harm.

Their respite was short-lived. Muffled voices could be heard coming from the passageway they had just passed through. Schroeder was on his feet instantly. He whispered to Karla to turn the flashlight off. They stood in the darkness and listened. Distorted by the twists and turns in the cave, the echoes were like the mutterings of some troll-like creature. As the voices grew louder, they became more distinct. Men could be heard speaking in Russian.

Schroeder had hoped that he and Karla would not be pushed deeper under the mountain. He had been worried about finding their way back. Apparently he had underestimated the determination of Grisha and his murderous band of ivory hunters.

Putting his aches and pains aside, he took the lead again. The passageway went down at a shallow angle for a few hundred feet before leveling out. The trek had taken its toll on Schroeder's ankle, and he had to lean against the wall a number of times to keep from falling. They were in danger of losing the race with their pursuers.

Karla was the first to see the cleft in the wall. Schroeder had been so intent on putting distance between them and their pursuers that he had walked by the wrinkle in the limestone where the wall folded in on itself, creating a narrow opening little more than a foot wide and five feet tall.

Schroeder's first instinct was to keep going. The hole could be a death trap. He stuck his head through and saw that the tunnel actually widened after a few feet. He told Karla to wait and he walked for fifty paces or so along the main cave. He placed his flashlight on the floor as if it had been dropped in haste.

The voices got louder. He went back to where Karla was waiting, squeezed his tall body through the cleft, then helped Karla through. They kept moving until they found a place where the cave curved slightly. He slipped the rifle off his shoulder and flattened his back against the wall. The first man through the hole would be dead.

They could see the ghostly glow of lights from the main tunnel. Grisha's harsh voice was clearly identifiable as he urged his men on with threats and jokes. The ivory hunters passed the crevice, and there was an excited yell. They had seen the flashlight. The voices receded.

Schroeder's intention was to slip back into the main tunnel and backtrack, but Grisha was no fool. He must have assumed that the flashlight's placement was too convenient to have been accidental. He and his men turned around and came back to the cleft in the wall.

Schroeder whispered in Karla's ear to get moving. As they hurried through the winding passageway, Schroeder decided their only course of action was to remain on the run. The flashlight beam was growing dimmer, indicating that the batteries were weakening. He would have to pick an ambush spot before they became lost or found themselves deep in the mountain with no light to show the way.

They walked for another ten minutes. The air was musty but it was still breathable, indicating that there was a flow coming in from the outside. The cave narrowed, and Schroeder saw a narrow fissure ahead. He stepped through the breach and his foot came down on thin air. He crashed down onto a slope and rolled several feet.

He crawled over, picked up the light and pointed it at Karla, who was peering from the fissure. The opening was about six feet above the floor. She looked bewildered. One second Schroeder had been there, leading the way. The next, he had dropped out of sight, the flashlight had gone flying, and she had heard a thud.

'I'm all right,' he said. 'Be careful, there's a drop.'

She eased out of the hole and picked her way down the slope. Schroeder tried to stand. The fall had aggravated his injured ankle even more, and shards of pain shot up his leg when he put weight on his foot. He leaned on Karla's shoulder.

'Where *are* we?' she said.

Schroeder explored their surroundings with the flashlight. The tunnel was around thirty feet wide and thirty feet high. A section of the wall collapsed to uncover the hole. The ceiling was vaulted, and, unlike the cave they had come through, the floor was as level as a pancake.

'This isn't a cave,' Schroeder said. 'It's man-made.' He aimed the light at the opposite wall. 'Well, it seems we have company.'

Life-size figures of men and women adorned the wall. They were painted in profile, as they marched along in a procession, carrying flowers, jugs and baskets of food and herding sheep, cows and goats with the aid of large, wolflike dogs.

The women wore long, diaphanous white dresses and sandals. The men were dressed in kilts and loose, short-sleeved shirts. Trees and other greenery made a backdrop for the parade.

The people had medium complexions, high cheekbones

and raven hair worn in a bun by the females, cut short for the men. Their facial expressions were neither solemn nor happy, but somewhere in between; they could have been out for a Sunday stroll. The colors were brilliant, as if the paint had only been applied the day before.

The murals covered both walls. No figure was repeated. Most were young, in their teens and twenties, but there was a scattering of children and old people, including gray-haired men who wore ornate headgear and could have been priests.

'It looks like a religious procession,' Karla said. 'They're carrying gifts for a god or a leader.'

Schroeder leaned on Karla's shoulder as he limped beside her. As they continued through the tunnel, the figures began to number in the hundreds.

'It's good to have company, in any case,' Schroeder said. 'Maybe our new friends here will show us the way out.'

'They're definitely headed somewhere. Look!'

The mural had changed in nature. There were new animals in the mural – large, lumbering creatures that resembled elephants except for the shaggy, grayish-brown fur covering their bodies. Flowers had been twined into their fur. The animals had high-peaked heads, and trunks that were relatively stubby. Some had tusks, almost as long as their bodies, that curved like the runners on an old-fashioned sleigh. Men rode on the animals like Indian mahouts.

'Impossible,' Schroeder said.

Spellbound, Karla stepped closer for a better look. In her eagerness, she forgot that Schroeder was using her for a crutch. He went down on one knee.

'I'm so sorry,' she said, seeing his predicament. She helped him up. 'Do you know what these pictures mean? People of an advanced civilization lived on this island thousands of

287

years before the Egyptians built the Pyramids. Probably back when the island was connected to the mainland. That's astounding enough on its own. But the fact that they had domesticated wild mammoths is just stunning. My paper on man's exploitation of the mammoth is trash! I had primitive man depending on mammoths as a source of food, and utilizing bones and tusks to make tools and weapons. The reality here is that they had learned to use these wild creatures as beasts of burden. This is the scientific discovery of the century. We'll have to rewrite all the textbooks.'

'I share your excitement,' Schroeder said. 'But I think we have to look on the practical side. No one will ever know of this discovery unless we get out of this place.'

'I'm sorry, this is just so . . .' She tore her gaze away from the stunning murals. 'What should we do?'

Schroeder flashed the light along the wall. 'We will let our friends tell us. The pretty young ladies up there are carrying flowers *into* the mountain. I propose that we determine where they came from and see if this tunnel leads outside. As you can see, I'm not ready to run in the Olympics, and our flashlight is dimming.'

Karla cast a longing glance at the figures. 'You're right. Let's go before I change my mind.'

They started back. They had only taken a few steps when they heard men speaking Russian. Grisha and his thugs had found the opening into the main tunnel. Schroeder and Karla had to turn around and go the other way.

Schroeder broke into a loping run. The maneuver put pressure on his swollen ankle, but he gritted his teeth and kept moving. Leaning on Karla helped, but it slowed them down. He suggested that they turn off the flashlight. Its light was so dim now as to be almost useless, but it was bright enough to provide a beacon for their pursuers. Schroeder used his free hand as a guide in the dark, trailing his fingers along the wall. The tunnel seemed to stretch out with no end.

After a few minutes, the voices became louder. Grisha and his band of cutthroats were in full pursuit. Schroeder tried to take bigger steps, but the effort threw him out of synch and actually slowed their progress. He would have to stop soon and tell Karla to go on without him. He was formulating a reply to her expected protests, when Karla said, 'I see light.'

Schroeder blinked the sweat out of his eyes and squinted into the darkness. There was a paleness ahead that was only one shade removed from complete blackness. He was confused. Maybe he had been wrong about their direction and the wall murals had actually led them out of the mountain.

They kept on moving, and the floor sloped down in a long ramp. The tunnel fed into a vast cavern. The space was filled as far as the eye could see with two-story, flat-roofed buildings. The structures were built of material that glowed with a silvery green that cast the scene in a dusky light.

Rough voices came from behind and jerked them out of their trance. With a mixture of awe and apprehension, they began to descend the long ramp into the crystal city.

28

Housed on the tenth floor of NUMA headquarters is the modern-day equivalent of the famed Alexandria Library. The glass-enclosed computer center that takes up the entire level contains a vast digital library that includes every book and article, every scientific fact and record on the world's oceans, all connected to a high-speed computer network with the capacity to transfer enormous amounts of data in a blink of the eye.

The center is the brainchild of NUMA's computer genius, Hiram Yeager, who dubbed the artificial intelligence entity he created 'Max'. It was Yeager's idea to give Max a feminine human face represented by a three-dimensional holographic image with auburn hair, topaz eyes and a soft, feminine voice.

Paul Trout had decided to forgo the flirtatious holographic image. Rather than use Max's central control panel, where Yeager communicated with the computer by voice, Trout had taken over a meeting room in the corner of the data center. He had set up a simple keyboard to tap into Max's vast store of knowledge. The keyboard communicated with an oversize monitor that took up most of one wall. Seated with Trout at a mahogany table where they faced the screen were Gamay; Dr Adler, the wave scientist; and Al Hibbet, the NUMA expert on electromagnetism.

Trout thanked everyone for coming and explained that Austin and Zavala had been called away. Then he tapped the keyboard. A photo of a thin-faced man with dark hair and soulful gray eyes appeared on the screen.

'I'd like you to meet the gentleman whose genius brought us here today,' Trout said. 'Here you see Lazlo Kovacs, the brilliant Hungarian electrical engineer. This photo was taken in the late thirties, about the time he was working on his revolutionary electromagnetism theories. And *this* is what can happen when scientific brilliance is perverted.'

Trout changed the picture to a split screen that displayed two satellite photos. On the left was the photo of the freak waves that sank the *Southern Belle*. The other side showed the giant whirlpool, as viewed from space.

He let the significance of the pictures sink in.

'We in this room have speculated that someone might have used electromagnetic transmissions based on the Kovacs Theorems to cause these disturbances. As you know, Gamay and I went to Los Alamos and talked to an authority on Kovacs's work. He confirmed our suspicions of human interference, and suggested the type of electro-magnetic manipulation we've been seeing could cause a polar reversal.'

'I assume we're talking about a reversal of the magnetic poles,' Adler said.

'I wish that were so,' Gamay interjected. 'However, we may be facing a *geologic* polar reversal where the earth's crust actually moves over its core.'

'I'm not a geologist,' Adler said, 'but that sounds like a recipe for a catastrophe.'

'Actually,' Gamay said with a smile as bleak as it was lovely, 'we may be talking about doomsday.'

A heavy silence followed her pronouncement. Adler cleared his throat. 'I heard the word "may". You seem to be giving yourself some wiggle room.'

'I'd be happy if I could wiggle out of this situation

entirely,' Gamay said. 'But you're right in sensing that we've given ourselves room for doubt. We don't know how reliable our Los Alamos source is, so Paul has come up with a way to test the Kovacs Theorems.'

'How could you do that?' Adler said.

'By using a simulation,' Trout said, 'much the same way you would re-create sea conditions in your lab using a laboratory wave machine or computer model.'

Hibbet said, 'Kovacs only wrote of his theories in a *general* way. He left out some of the specifics.'

'That's true,' Gamay said. 'But Kovacs self-published a more detailed summary of his theorems. He used it as the basis for his published writings. There is only one copy in existence.'

'If only we had it,' Adler said.

Gamay slid the Kovacs folio across the table without comment.

Adler carefully picked the papers off the table and noted the name on the cover: Lazlo Kovacs. He glanced through the yellowed pages. 'This is written in Hungarian,' he said.

'One of our NUMA translators came up with an English copy,' Trout said. 'The math is a universal language, so there was no problem there. Testing was another matter. Then I remembered the work being done at the Los Alamos National Laboratory where scientists have come up with a way to test nuclear bombs from our arsenal without violating international treaty. They test the bomb's components, figuring in factors such as materials deterioration, and they feed the data into a computer which runs a simulation. I propose to do the same.'

'It's certainly worth a try,' Hibbet said.

Trout tapped the keyboard and an image of the earth

appeared on the screen. The globe had a section cut out like a slice of orange to expose the layers of the inner core: liquid iron outer core, the mantle and the crust. 'Maybe you can explain this diagram, Al.'

'Glad to,' Hibbet said. 'The earth is like a big bar magnet. The inner core of solid iron rotates at a different speed from the outer core of molten iron. This movement creates a dynamo effect that generates a magnetic field called the geodynamo.'

The picture changed to depict the intact globe. Lines looped out into space from one pole and curved back into the opposing pole.

'Those are the lines of magnetic force,' Hibbet explained. 'They create a magnetic field that surrounds the earth, and allows us to use compasses. Even more important, the magnetosphere extends out thirty-seven miles. This creates a barrier that protects us from the harmful solar wind radiation and swarms of deadly particles that bombard the earth from space.'

Trout changed the computer image. They were looking at a map of the world. The ocean surface was splotched with blue and gold patches.

'In the 1990s, scientists pulled together everything known about the earth's molten core and fed it into a super-computer,' Trout said. 'They threw all sorts of stuff into the mix. Temperature. Dimensions. Viscosity. They found that the poles reversed themselves every hundred thousand years or so, usually when one started to weaken. It looks like we're in for another cycle.'

'The earth is undergoing a natural polar reversal?' Adler said.

'Apparently,' Trout said. 'The earth's magnetic field started to deteriorate seriously around a hundred and fifty years ago. Its strength has waned by ten to fifteen percent since then, and the deterioration in the field has accelerated. If the trend continues, the main field would weaken and almost vanish, and it would reappear with the opposite polarity.'

'Needles that point north would point south,' Hibbet added.

'That's right,' Trout said. 'A magnetic polar reversal would mean a whole host of disruptive events, but the impact would be minimal. Most of us would be able to adapt and survive. Studies show that the magnetic poles have reversed many times.'

'Herodotus wrote about the sun rising where it normally sets,' Gamay said. 'The Hopi talked about the chaos that comes about when the two twins who hold the earth in place leave their position. These could have been interpretations of ancient polar shifts.'

'While legend is fascinating, and often contains a grain of truth, all of us at this table are versed in the scientific method,' Adler said.

'That's why I didn't mention the clairvoyants and pseudo-scientists who predicted an end of the world,' Gamay said. 'The whole concept of polar shift got mixed up with theories of Atlantis and ancient astronauts.'

'As a wave expert, I deal with huge ocean forces,' Adler said, 'but a shift in the outer surface of an entire world seems unbelievable.'

'Normally, I would agree,' Gamay said. 'But paleo-magnetists who have studied lava flows have shown that the ground has moved in relation to the earth's magnetic north. North America was once deep in the Southern Hemisphere, where it straddled the equator. Einstein theorized that if enough ice accumulated on the polar caps, a shift could result. Scientists have found that there was a major reorganization of the earth's tectonic plates about half a billion years ago. The previous north and south poles relocated to the equator, and points on the equator became the poles we have now.'

'You're talking about a process that takes millions, billions of years,' Adler said.

Trout brought the discussion back to the computer simulation. 'That's why we should look closer at the present. The image on the screen shows the earth's magnetic fields. Those splotches in blue are inward-directed fields. The gold is outward-directed. The British navy kept records of the magnetic and true north for three hundred years, which means we've got a pretty good database. What we see here is an increase in the number of blue islands.'

'Which would indicate magnetic anomalies where the field is flowing the wrong way,' Hibbet said.

'That large patch of color is the South Atlantic Anomaly where the field is *already* flowing the wrong way,' Trout said. 'The anomaly's growth accelerated around the turn of the century. This ties in with Magsat readings that show weak areas in the north polar region and below South Africa. The observations are consistent with computer simulations that show the possible beginnings of a flip.'

'You've made a convincing case that geologic and magnetic polar reversals have occurred,' Adler said. 'But what we're talking about is the possibility of man precipitating such an event. That's a lot of hubris on our part. Man is capable of much, but our puny efforts are not capable of shifting the entire surface of the planet.'

'Seems crazy, doesn't it?' Trout said with a crooked grin. He turned to Hibbet. 'You're our electromagnetism expert. What do you think?'

Hibbet stared at the screen. 'I had no idea the southern ocean anomalies had grown so rapidly.' He paused in thought, then, choosing his words carefully, said, 'What Lazlo Kovacs got into was the nature of matter and energy. He discovered that matter oscillates between the stages of matter and energy. Energy is not subjected to the rules of time and space, so the shift from one phase to another is instantaneous. And matter follows energy's lead. In addressing this question, we have to look at the earth's electromagnetic makeup. If the electromagnetic energy changes in a certain way, matter – in this case the crust of the earth – can change as well.'

'You're saying a geologic polar shift is possible,' Gamay said.

'I'm saying that a man-made magnetic polar shift, with its intense, short-term nature, may precipitate irreversible geologic movement, especially now with a natural shift shaping up. All it needs is a *nudge*. An addition or discharge of electromagnetic energy that changes the field could stir up changes in matter. Cyclonic disruptions of the earth's core or magnetic field may have been responsible for the freak waves and the whirlpool. It wouldn't be the slow shifting of tectonic plates. The structure of the entire planet could change in an instant.'

'With what results?' Gamay said.

'*Catastrophic.* If the crust slips around the molten core, inertial forces would come into play. The shift would create tsunamis that could sweep across continents, and winds more powerful than any hurricane. Earthquakes and volcanic eruptions with massive lava flows would develop. There would be drastic climate changes and radiation storms.' He paused. 'Species extinction is a definite possibility.'

'There's been an increase in violent natural phenomena

over the past few decades,' Gamay said. 'I wonder if those are warning signs.'

'Maybe,' Hibbet said.

'Before we scare ourselves silly, let's get back to the facts,' Trout suggested. 'I've taken the polar shift simulations from Caltech and Los Alamos as a base. I fed in the report Dr Adler compiled on the ocean disturbances and the material Al submitted on the use of electromagnetic low-frequency transmissions. We've also simulated conditions of the molten currents in the core of the earth where the magnetic fields are formed. The Kovacs papers are the final part of the equation. If we're all ready . . .' He tapped the keyboard.

The globe disappeared and a message appeared on the screen:

HELLO, PAUL. HOW'S THE BEST-DRESSED MALE ON THE SPECIAL ASSIGNMENTS TEAM?

Max had picked up on his password. Trout squirmed in his chair, and yearned for the time when computers were simply dumb machines. He typed in:

HELLO, MAX. WE'RE READY FOR THE COMPUTER SIMULATION.

IS THIS AN ACADEMIC EXERCISE, PAUL?

NO.

Max paused for several seconds. It was an unusual response from the high-speed computer.

THIS EVENT CAN'T BE ALLOWED TO HAPPEN.

Trout stared at the words. Was it his imagination, or did Max seem alarmed? He typed a question:

WHY NOT?

IT WILL RESULT IN THE COMPLETE DES-TRUCTION OF THE EARTH.

Trout's Adam's apple bobbed. He typed one word:

297

HOW?

WATCH.

The globe reappeared on the screen, and the gold patches on the oceans began to move. The red patch in the South Atlantic linked up with other patches of the same color until the entire ocean area below South America and South Africa blazed in red. Then the continents began to change their positions. North and South America did a 180-degree shift, so that they were lying on their sides. The points that had once marked the equator became the north and south poles. Violent surface phenomena spread over the globe like a virulent disease.

Trout typed another question, and held his breath:

IS THERE A WAY TO NEUTRALIZE THIS?

YES. DON'T LET IT BEGIN. IT CAN'T BE REVERSED.

IS THERE ANY WAY TO STOP THE REVER-SAL?

I DON'T HAVE SUFFICIENT DATA TO ANSWER THAT QUESTION.

Trout knew he had gone as far as he could. He turned to the others. Adler and Hibbet had the look of men who had just been given tickets for a boat ride on the river Styx.

Gamay was equally stunned, but she had a calm expression on her face and determination in her eyes. 'There's something here that doesn't make sense. Why would anyone do something that could mean the end of the world and of themselves?'

Trout scratched his head. 'Maybe it's the old adage of playing with fire. It could be that they don't *know* the danger of what they're doing.'

Gamay shook her head. 'The capacity of our species for boneheaded actions never ceases to amaze me.'

'Cheer up,' Trout said. 'Pardon the gallows humor, but if this goes through there won't *be* any species.'

29

Most of the Americans Captain Ivanov had encountered were tourists on adventure excursions around the New Siberian Sea. They tended to be affluent and middle-aged, armed with cameras and spotting scopes, and intrepid in their pursuit of one rare bird or another. But the two men who had descended from the sky and boarded his ship as if they owned it were cut from a different mold.

The seaplane carrying Austin and Zavala had caught up with the Russian icebreaker *Kotelny* northwest of Wrangel Island and touched down a few hundred feet from the vessel. Captain Ivanov ordered a boat lowered to fetch the plane's passengers. He was waiting on deck, curious about these Americans who had the political clout to commandeer his ship as their personal ferry.

The first to climb up the boarding ladder was a broad-shouldered man with pale hair and light blue eyes set in a rugged bronzed face. He was followed on deck by a slimmer, dark-complexioned man who moved with the relaxed athleticism that was a holdover from his college boxing days. They waved at the seaplane as it taxied for a takeoff.

The captain stepped forward to introduce himself. Despite his irritation, he strictly adhered to the customs of the sea. Their handshakes were firm, and behind the friendly smiles the captain detected a cool self-assurance that told him these were no bird-watchers.

The blue-eyed man said, 'Thank you for having us aboard, Captain Ivanov. My name is Kurt Austin, and this is my friend and associate Joe Zavala. We're with NUMA, the National Underwater and Marine Agency.'

The captain's stolid features softened. He had run into NUMA scientists a few times during his many years at sea and had been impressed with the agency's ships and the professionalism of its people.

'I'm honored to have you as my guests,' he said.

The captain ordered his first mate to get the ship under way. He invited his guests to his cabin and pulled a bottle of vodka from a cabinet.

'How long before we make landfall?' Austin said.

'We'll be off Ivory Island in about two hours,' the captain said.

'Then we'll pass on the vodka for now. Can we get to the island any sooner?'

The captain's eyes narrowed. NUMA or not, he was still annoyed at the directive to change course and head back to the island. The order from Naval Command had been to accommodate his visitors in whatever way they asked, but he didn't have to be happy about it.

'Yes, of course, if we increase speed,' he said. 'But I am not used to strangers telling me how fast to run my ship.'

Austin couldn't miss the sour note in the captain's tone. 'Maybe we'll take that vodka after all. What do you say, Joe?'

'Sun's over the yardarm somewhere,' Zavala said.

The captain poured three shot glasses full to the brim and passed them around. They clinked glasses, and the NUMA men tossed down their drinks, impressing the captain, who had expected – even hoped – that his guests would gag on the high-octane liquor.

Austin complimented him on his vodka, and then said, 'We apologize for diverting your ship, Captain, but it's important that we get to Ivory Island as soon as humanly possible.'

'But if you are in a hurry, why didn't you just fly there in the seaplane?'

'We'd like to arrive without our presence being detected,' Austin said.

Ivanov responded with a loud guffaw. 'The *Kotelny* is not exactly invisible.'

'A valid point. It's important that the ship stay out of visual range of the island. We'll go the rest of the way on our own.'

'As you wish. Ivory Island is a remote place. The only people you will see are some scientists on a crazy expedition to clone woolly mammoths.'

'We know about the expedition,' Austin said. 'That's the reason we're here. One of the scientists is a young woman named Karla Janos. We think she may be in danger.'

'Miss Janos was a passenger on the *Kotelny*. What sort of danger is she in?'

'We believe there may be people on the island who want to kill her.'

'I don't understand.'

'We don't have many details. We only know that we have to get to the island as soon as possible.'

Captain Ivanov snatched up the ship's phone and ordered the engine room to proceed at full speed. Austin raised an eyebrow. Karla Janos must be a remarkable young woman. She had obviously entranced the weathered old Russian sea dog.

'Another request, if you don't mind,' Austin said. 'I wonder if there is a clear area of the deck where Joe and I can work without interfering with the ship's crew.'

'Yes, of course. There is plenty of room in the stern.'

'We brought two large bags aboard. Could you see that they are brought aft for us?'

'I'll give the order right away.'

'One more thing,' Austin said as they rose.

These Americans seemed to have an endless list of requirements. 'Yes?' he said gruffly.

'Don't put that bottle away,' Austin said with a grin. 'We will want it to toast Ms Janos's safe return.'

The captain's frown turned to a broad grin. He gave Austin and Zavala several bone-cracking back thumps and led the way to the main deck. He rounded up a couple of crewmen, who carried the large bags to an area behind the superstructure.

After the captain left to attend to his duties, the crewmen watched in fascination as Austin and Zavala pulled a circular metal framework from the bags.

The aluminum-tubing backpack unit enclosed a compact, two-stroke engine, a 2.5-gallon fuel tank and a four-blade propeller. They attached the framework to a narrow seat. Then they attached lines from the framework to a canopy made of ripstop nylon, which they spread out on the deck. In a short time, they had assembled the Adventure X-Presso, a French-made paraglider.

Zavala, who had piloted a wide range of aircraft, cast a skeptical eye at the paraglider.

'That thing looks like a marriage between an electric fan and a barber's chair.'

'Sorry,' Austin said. 'I couldn't fit an Apache helicopter into the carry-on.'

Zavala shook his head. 'We'd better pull our gear together.'

Their other luggage had been stowed in a cabin. Austin pulled a holster out of his duffel, checked the load in his

Bowen revolver and stuffed extra ammunition into a fanny pack. For this mission Zavala had chosen a Heckler & Koch .45 model that was developed for the army Special Forces. They carried a GPS, compass, portable radios, a first-aid kit and other emergency items. They wore inflatable flotation belts instead of bulky life vests, and dressed for the damp weather with waterproof outer layers over wool.

A crewman knocked on the door and relayed the captain's invitation to come to the bridge. When they entered the pilothouse, Ivanov beckoned them over to a radar screen and pointed to an elongated blip on the monitor.

'This is Ivory Island. We're about ten kilometers from landfall. How close do you want to go?'

There was a slight haze rising from the ice-flecked green water. The sky was overcast. Visibility was less than a mile. 'Have someone keep watch through binoculars,' Austin said. 'When he sees the island, drop anchor.'

The captain spread out a chart. 'The main harbor is on the south side of the island. There are many smaller coves and inlets around the perimeter.'

After conferring with Zavala, Austin decided to explore the expedition headquarters, then follow the river inland.

'We have enough fuel for roughly two hours in the air, so we'll have to keep our search itinerary tight,' Austin said.

They went over their plans again and had wrapped up the discussion when the lookout said he could see the island.

'Joe and I are grateful for all your help,' Austin told the captain.

'It's nothing,' Ivanov said. 'Ms Janos reminds me of my own daughter. Please, do whatever you can to help her.'

At Austin's request, the ship was positioned with its stern to the wind and a portion of the deck cleared for takeoff. Austin was pleased to see that the wind was no more than ten miles an hour. A stronger wind might push them back-ward. He knew, too, that the wind speed in the air would be higher than on the ground.

They first practiced takeoff without the canopy. The trick in a tandem takeoff was to run with synchronized leg movements and launch gently.

'That wasn't bad,' Austin said after their first clumsy attempt.

Zavala glanced at the crewmen, who had been watching the practice runs with a mixture of amusement and horror. 'I'll bet our Russian friends have never seen a four-legged duck before.'

'We'll do better the next time.'

Austin's confidence was misplaced. They stumbled half-way to takeoff, but the next two practice runs were nearly perfect. They put on their goggles, spread the canopy on the deck, extended the lines and connected them to the backpack. Austin hit the starter button and the engine whirred softly. The prop wash inflated the canopy so that it rose off the deck. Austin squeezed the hand throttle to rev up the engine, and they began their awkward, double-legged run toward the stern and into the wind. The three-hundred-square-foot canopy caught the wind and jerked them into the air.

Austin added power and they began to climb. The paraglider had a climb rate of three hundred feet per second, but its ascent was logy because they were riding tandem. Eventually, though, they reached an altitude of five hundred feet. Austin pulled on the left-hand line, which brought the wingtip down, and the paraglider went into a left-hand turn. They flew toward the island at a speed of twenty-five miles per hour.

As they neared land, Austin pulled both wingtips down

simultaneously and the paraglider went into a gradual descent. They came in over the right-hand spit of land that enclosed the harbor and swung around on a gradual turn that took them over the deserted beach toward the river he had seen in the charts. Austin saw an object near the river, but the mists enshrouding the paraglider made it difficult to see details.

Zavala shouted, 'There's a body down there!'

Austin brought the paraglider lower. The body was in a small, inflatable life raft that had been drawn up on the beach barely out of reach from the river's flow. He saw that the figure had long gray hair. He forced into the wind, stopped the engine and pulled back on both brake handles.

The wing was supposed to act like a parachute and allow for stand-up landings. But they came in too fast and too high. Their knees buckled, and they did a double nose plant in the sand, but at least they were down.

They collapsed the wing, unharnessed the backpack and approached the body of a woman, who was curled up in the raft in a fetal position. Austin squatted next to the raft and felt her pulse. It was weak, but she was alive. He and Zavala gently rolled her over onto her back. Blood stained her jacket near the left shoulder. Austin pulled the first-aid kit from his pack, and Zavala went to open the jacket so they could inspect the wound. The woman groaned and opened her eyes. They filled with fear when she saw the two strangers.

'It's all right,' Zavala reassured her in his soft-spoken voice. 'We're here to help you.'

Austin brought his canteen to the woman's mouth and gave her a drink of water.

'My name is Kurt, and this is my friend Joe,' Austin said when the color came back to her face. 'Can you tell us your name?'

'Maria Arbatov,' she said in a weak voice. 'My husband . . .' Her voice trailed off.

'Are you with the expedition, Maria?'

'Yes.'

'Where are the others?'

'Dead. All dead.'

Austin felt as if someone had kicked him in the stomach. 'What about the young woman? Karla Janos?'

'I don't know what happened to her. They took her away.'

'The same people who shot you?'

'Yes. Ivory hunters. They killed my husband, Sergei, and the two Japanese men.'

'Where did this happen?'

'The old riverbed. I crawled back to the campsite and put the raft in the river.' Her eyes flickered and she passed out.

They inspected the shoulder more closely. The injury wasn't fatal, but Maria had lost a great deal of blood. Zavala cleaned and bandaged the wound. Austin called the *Kotelny* on his hand radio.

'We found an injured woman on the beach,' he told the captain.

'Miss Janos?'

'No. Maria Arbatov, one of the expedition scientists. She needs medical attention.'

'I'll send a boat in immediately with my medical officer.'

Austin and Zavala made Maria as comfortable as possible. The boat arrived with the medical officer and two crewmen. They carefully loaded the woman aboard and headed back to the icebreaker.

Austin and Zavala hooked up the paraglider. The takeoff went much smoother than their icebreaker launch. As soon as they had gained altitude, Austin steered the paraglider along the river. Alerted by Maria, they kept a sharp eye out for the ivory hunters. Minutes later, they made a soft landing in the permafrost near the old sheds. They slipped their side arms from their holsters and cautiously made their way toward the settlement.

While Joe covered him, Austin checked out the main tent. There were broken eggshells in the rubbish bin, evidence of a recent breakfast. They peeked into the smaller tent, then made their way to the sheds. All the buildings were unlocked except one. They pounded the padlock with a boulder. The lock stayed intact, but the nails holding the clasp in the rotting wood gave out. They opened the door and stepped inside. A musky animal smell greeted their nostrils. The shaft of light coming through the open doorway fell on the fur-covered creature stretched out on the table.

'This isn't something you're likely to see at the Washington Zoo,' Zavala said.

Austin bent over the frozen carcass and examined the stubby trunk and undersize tusks. 'Not unless they've opened a prehistoric wing. This is the carcass of what looks like a baby mammoth.'

'The state of preservation is incredible,' Zavala said. 'It looks freeze-dried.'

After inspecting the frozen animal for a few minutes, they went back outside. Austin noticed boot prints in the permafrost leading to a path that ran alongside the river. They set the paraglider up for a takeoff from a low hill and flew along the winding path of the river, reasoning that Maria Arbatov couldn't have been far from the waterway when she was shot. Austin saw three bodies lying near a fork in a narrow canyon. He circled the immediate area but saw no sign of ivory hunters, and set the paraglider down near the edge of the gorge.

They climbed down the side and made their way to the bodies. The three men had been shot. Austin's jaw hardened, and all traces of warmth vanished from his light blue eyes. He thought about Maria Arbatov's harrowing escape down the river and vowed that whoever did this would be made to pay.

Zavala was bending over scuff marks in the gravelly sand. 'These guys didn't care about covering their tracks. The trail should be easy to follow.'

'Let's go pay them our respects,' Austin said.

Moving stealthily with guns in hand, they followed the footprints along the winding canyon. Rounding a corner, they came upon a fourth body.

Zavala knelt by the side of the dead man. 'Knife wound between the shoulder blades. Strange. This gentleman wasn't shot like the other people. I wonder who he is.'

Austin rolled the corpse over and stared at the unshaven features. 'Not the kind of face you'd see at a chamber of commerce meeting.'

The ground around the dead man showed evidence of a scuffle, and prints led away from the body. Austin thought he saw the smaller boot prints of a woman in with the others. Moving even more quietly, they made their way along the gorge and eventually came to a place where the footprints ended and the banking had been broken down.

They climbed from the ravine, and picked up the trail again in the permafrost. Although the countryside was open and they could see for miles, there was no sign of life except for a few wheeling seabirds. The trail led to a shallow valley that brought them to the cave entrance.

'Someone has been doing some mining,' Zavala said.

'Nice call, Sherlock.' Austin picked up a jackhammer,

attached to a portable compressor, that had been lying on the ground near the entrance.

Zavala's sharp eyes examined the charred rubble around the hole. 'Okay, Watson. Someone did a little blasting here too.'

Austin said, 'We've been here less than an hour and I'm already starting to dislike Ivory Island.'

He crawled into the hole and came out a minute later shaking his head. 'Suicide. We don't know how far it goes. We don't even have a flashlight.'

They made their way back to the paraglider, called the icebreaker and asked Ivanov to send in a party to collect the dead and to bring in electric torches. Austin suggested that his men be armed. Knowing the captain's interest, Austin said he was hopeful that Karla was still alive. The captain said Maria Arbatov had been treated and was doing well. They wished each other good luck and clicked off.

Minutes later, the paraglider took off from a low hill with all the grace of a drunken gooney bird. They gained altitude and wheeled high over the island. Austin had thoroughly examined the charts, but still he was surprised at the size of the island. There was a lot of territory to cover with an aircraft that moved with a cruising speed of twenty-six miles per hour.

Austin marked their takeoff point as a center, and then he flew in an expanding spiral that allowed for an overlapping search of a large area. They saw only the featureless permafrost. Austin was about to head back to the beach to rendezvous with the boat party when Zavala shouted in his ear.

Austin followed Zavala's pointing finger and saw a well-defined track leading up the side of the volcano. They flew toward the volcano and saw that the trail was not a natural feature but rather a series of switchbacks cut into the side of the mountain. Austin suspected that man had a hand in the track's creation.

'Looks like a road,' Austin said.

'That's what I thought. Want to take a look?'

The question was unnecessary. Austin had already brought the paraglider around, and they were soaring toward the lip of the caldera.

30

The subterranean city was laid out in a grid pattern under the domed roof of an enormous cavern. The ancient metropolis was cut off from the sun and should have been in complete darkness, but it shimmered in a silvery-green light that emanated from every building and street.

'What makes everything glow so brightly?' Schroeder asked as he limped along a street with Karla at his side.

'I studied light-emitting minerals as part of a geology course,' Karla said. 'Some minerals glow under the influence of ultraviolet rays. Other types emit light from radiation or chemical change. But if we're right, and this is an old volcano, maybe there's a thermoluminescent effect caused by heat.'

'Could this be an old magma chamber?' Schroeder said.

'That's possible. I just don't know. But there's one thing that I'm absolutely sure of.'

'What's that, my dear?'

She gazed with awe at the glimmering edifices that stretched off in every direction. 'We are strangers in a strange land.'

After leaving the mural tunnel that led to the city, they had walked under a huge corbel arch down a broad ramp to an open plaza with a step pyramid built of huge blocks at the center. The processional motif, including the domesticated woolly mammoths, was continued on the exterior levels of the pyramid, although the colors were less bright than in the access tunnel. Karla surmised that it was a temple or platform for priests or speakers to address people gathered in the plaza.

A paved boulevard about fifty feet wide led into the heart of the city. They had strolled along the thoroughfare like a couple of tourists bedazzled by the bright lights of Broadway. The buildings were much smaller than Manhattan's skyscrapers – three stories at the most – yet they were architectural wonders, considering their probable age.

The promenade was lined with pedestals. The statues they once supported lay in unrecognizable heaps of rubble, as if they had been pushed off their perches by vandals.

Schroeder rested his sore ankle, then he and Karla explored a couple of buildings, but they were as empty as if they had been swept clean with a big broom.

'How old do you think this place is?' Schroeder said as they plunged deeper into the city.

'Each time I try to date it, I become tangled in contradictions. The fact that the murals show humans and mammoths coexisting places them in the Pleistocene period. That was a time span that ran from 1.8 million to ten thousand years ago. Even if we go with the most recent date of ten thousand years, the high level of civilization here is astonishing. We've always assumed that mankind didn't evolve from its primitive state until much later. The Egyptians' civilization is only around five thousand years old.'

'Who do you think built this wonderful city?'

'Ancient Siberians. This island was connected to an arctic continental shelf that extended out from the mainland. I didn't see any pictures of boats, indicating that this was pretty much a landlocked society. From the looks of it, this was a rich city.'

'Since it was such a flourishing society, why did it end?'

'Maybe it *didn't* end. Maybe it simply moved somewhere

and became the basis of another society. There is evidence that Europeans as well as Asians populated North America.'

As Schroeder mulled the implications of Karla's analysis, excited voices could be heard shouting from behind them in the direction of the city gate. He squinted back along the boulevard. Pinpoints of light were moving in the area around the plaza. The ivory hunters had also blundered into the city.

'We're sitting ducks out here in the open,' Schroeder said. 'We can lose them easily if we get off this lovely avenue.'

He slipped into an alley that connected with a narrow side street. The buildings were smaller than on the main boulevard; none was taller than one story. They appeared to serve more of a residential function than the grander, more ceremonial structures lining the main drag.

As a former soldier, Schroeder had accurately sized up the defensive situation. The city was a huge maze of hundreds of streets. Even with the omnipresent halo of light that shimmered over the city, as long as they kept alert and on the move through the labyrinth their pursuers would never catch them. At the same time, Schroeder was aware that they could only run for so long. Eventually, they would run out of food and water. Or luck.

His goal was to get to the far side of the city. He had hopes, supported by the relatively good quality of the air, that there might be another way out. The people who built this subterranean metropolis seemed to have done so with logic and reason. Thus it would be logical and reasonable that they had more than one way to get in and out. They were more than halfway across the city when Karla cried out in alarm.

She dug her fingers into Schroeder's arm. He slipped the automatic rifle off his shoulder. 'What is it?' He glanced around at the silent façades as if he expected to see the leering faces of the ivory hunters in the windows.

'Something ran down that alley.'

Schroeder followed her pointing finger with his eyes. Although the buildings produced their own light, they were built close together, and the narrow spaces between them were in deep shadow.

'Something or some*one*?'

'I – I don't know.' She laughed. 'Maybe I've been underground too long.'

Schroeder had always trusted his senses above his analytical skills. 'Wait here,' he said. He approached the alleyway with his finger tight on the trigger. He edged up to the alley, stuck his head around the corner and flicked the flashlight on. After a few seconds, he turned and came back. 'Nothing,' he said.

'Sorry. It must have been my imagination.'

'Come,' he said, and, to Karla's surprise, he headed toward the alley.

'Where are you going?'

'If there is something out there, it's better that we sneak up on it rather than the other way around.'

Karla hesitated. Her first impulse had been to flee in the other direction. But Schroeder seemed to know what he was doing. She hurried to catch up.

The alley led to another street similarly lined with buildings. The street was deserted. There were only the squat little structures with their windows staring like vacant eyes in the strange half-light. Schroeder checked his internal compass, and again started in a direction he hoped would take them to the far side of the city.

After they had walked for a few blocks, Schroeder stopped suddenly and raised his rifle. He lowered the weapon after a second and rubbed his eyes. 'This strange light has me crazy. Now it's *my* turn to start seeing things. I saw something run from one side of the street to the other.'

'No. I saw it too,' Karla said. 'It was large. I don't think it was human.'

Schroeder started off again. 'That's good. We haven't had much luck with humans lately.'

Karla's nostrils picked up a familiar musky odor. The shed housing the baby mammoth had the same smell. Schroeder's nostrils had picked up the scent as well.

'Smells like a barnyard,' he said.

The fragrance of mud, animals and manure became stronger as they made their way through an alley to another street. The street ended in a plaza similar to the public square they had encountered at the entrance to the city. The plaza was rectangular, about two hundred feet to a side. Like the earlier square it was dominated by a step pyramid about fifty feet high. But what caught Karla's eye was the immediate area around the pyramid.

Unlike the first plaza, whose pavement was made of the same glowing stone as the rest of the city, this space looked as if it were covered by a thick dark growth of weeds or grass. Karla's first impression was that she was looking at an untended garden similar to something she might see in a public park. That didn't make sense given the lack of sunlight. Drawn by her natural curiosity, she started toward the pyramid.

The vegetation began to move.

Schroeder's aging vision had trouble seeing details in the half-light, but the movement caught his eye. The training ingrained long ago came into play. He'd been taught that the best insurance when faced with a potential threat was a lead curtain. He stepped in front of Karla, and he brought his rifle to his hip. His finger tightened on the trigger as he prepared to saturate the square with a lethal spray.

'No!' Karla shouted.

She put her hand in front of his chest.

The plaza undulated, and from the moving mass came a sound of snorts and squeaks and heavy bodies starting to stir. The image of vegetation disintegrated, to be replaced by large furry clumps the size of large pigs.

Schroeder stared at the strange creatures milling around the square. They had stubby trunks and upturned tusks, and their hides were covered with fur. The significance of what he was seeing finally dawned on him.

'Baby elephants!'

'No,' Karla said, amazingly calm in spite of her unbounded excitement. 'They're dwarf mammoths.'

'That can't be. Mammoths are extinct.'

'I know, but look closely.' She pointed the flashlight at the animals. A few of them glanced at the light, showing shiny round eyes of an amber hue. 'Elephants don't have fur like that.'

'This is impossible,' Schroeder said as if he were having a hard time convincing himself.

'Not entirely. Traces of dwarf mammoths were found on Wrangel Island as recently as 2000 B.C. That's only a blip in time. But you're right about this being unbelievable. The closest I've come to these creatures has been the fossilized bones of their ancestors.'

Schroeder said, 'Why don't they run away?'

The mammoths seemed to have been sleeping when they were disturbed by the human intruders, but they weren't alarmed. They moved around the square in singles, two-somes or small groups, and showed little or no curiosity at the strangers.

'They don't think we'll hurt them,' Karla said. 'They've probably never seen humans before. My guess is that they evolved from the full-grown animals that we saw in the murals. They've adjusted to the lack of sunlight and food through generations.'

Schroeder gazed at the herd of pigmy mammoths and said, 'Karla, how do they live?'

'There's an air supply. Maybe it seeps down from the ceiling, or through crevasses we don't know about. Maybe they've learned to hibernate to preserve food.'

'Yes, yes, but what do they *eat*?'

She glanced around. 'There must be a source somewhere. Maybe they get out into the open. Wait! Maybe that's what happened to the so-called baby that the expedition found. It was looking for food.'

'We must try to find out where they go,' Schroeder said. He made his way to the pyramid with Karla close behind. The mammoths moved aside to create a path. Some were slow to get out of the way and brushed against the humans, who had to wind their way through piles of manure. They reached the pyramid steps and began to climb. The effort put pressure on Schroeder's weak ankle, and he had to climb on his hands and knees, but he made it slowly to the flat top of the structure.

The elevation offered a total view of the square. The animals were still milling around with no rhyme nor reason to their movements.

Karla was counting the animals and figured there were about two hundred of them. Schroeder had been scanning the disorganized mob with other goals in mind, and, after a few minutes, he saw what he was looking for.

'Look,' he said. 'The mammoths are forming into a loose queue over there near that corner of the plaza.'

Karla looked at where Schroeder was pointing. The herding animals had squeezed into a street as if suddenly inspired by a common purpose. Other mammoths began to follow, and soon the whole group was moving toward the same part of the square. With Karla helping him, Schroeder climbed off the pyramid and hobbled after the departing herd.

By the time they got to the corner, the entire herd had vanished from the square and was moving slowly along a narrow street that led back to the main boulevard. They tried not to startle the animals, although that didn't seem to be a danger. The mammoths seemed to have accepted the newcomers as part of the herd.

After about ten minutes, they began to see a change in the character of the city. Some of the houses on both sides were damaged. Their walls were knocked in as if hit by a rogue bulldozer. Eventually, they came to an area that looked as if it had been bombed. There were no freestanding buildings, only glowing piles of rubble intermingled with huge boulders made of a different, nonluminous mineral.

The sight revived unpleasant memories for Schroeder. He stopped to give his ankle a rest and looked around at the ruined landscape. 'This reminds me of Berlin at the end of World War Two. Come. We must hurry or we'll lose them.'

Karla dodged a pile of manure. 'I don't think we'll have to worry about that with the trail they're leaving.'

Schroeder's deep laughter echoed off the walls of rubble that now arose high on both sides. Karla joined in despite her weariness and fears, but they picked up the pace more in eagerness to find a way out than concern at losing the herd.

More of the rock they were seeing was composed of nonglowing material. Then all trace of the luminescent rock disappeared and the path in front of them darkened. Karla turned the flashlight on, and its dim beam caught the tails of the mammoths. The creatures had no trouble navigating the darkness. Karla guessed that their eyes must have adjusted to the lack of light in the same way their bodies had shrunk to accommodate a diminishing supply of food.

Then the flashlight went dead. They followed the herd by listening to the scuffle of the many feet, and the chorus of grunts and snorts. The complete blackness assumed a bluer cast that slowly changed to dark gray. They could see the furry rumps about fifty feet ahead. The animals seemed to have picked up their pace. The grayness turned to white. The path made a right, then a left-hand turn, and they were out in the open, blinking their eyes against the sunlight.

The mammoths rambled ahead, but the two humans stopped and shielded their eyes with their hands. As their vision acclimated to the change in light, they looked at their surroundings through narrowed eyes. They had emerged from a gap in a low bluff and were at the edge of a natural bowl several hundred yards across. The mammoths hungrily grazed the short grassy vegetation that covered the bowl's floor.

'This is quite amazing,' Karla said. 'These creatures have adjusted to two worlds: one of darkness, the other of light. They are miracles of adaptation as well as anachronisms.'

'Yes, very interesting,' Schroeder said in a disinterested voice. He wasn't being rude, only practical. He realized that they were far from safe. Their pursuers could be on their heels. He scanned the wall of massive, blackened boulders surrounding the natural basin and suggested that they make their way to the perimeter to look for a way out.

Karla was reluctant to leave the herd of mammoths, but she climbed with Schroeder up a gradually ascending hill to the edge of the boulder field. The rocks ranged in size from some as big as cars to others nearly as big as a house. They were tumbled in heaps more than a hundred feet high, in some cases. Some of the massive rocks were piled so tightly together that it would have been impossible to slip a knife blade between them.

There were openings in the rocky ramparts, but the breaks only went in a few feet or yards. As they made their way along the impenetrable wall, Karla became discouraged. They had escaped the fire only to wind up in a very large frying pan. Schroeder, on the other hand, seemed to have been revived by the fresh air. He ignored the pain in his ankle, his eyes darting along the face of the wall. He disappeared into a gap, and after a few minutes let out a yell of triumph.

Schroeder emerged from the opening and announced that he had found a way through the barrier. He grabbed Karla's hand as if he were leading a child, and they plunged into the mass of monoliths. They had only gone along the path a few steps when a man stepped out from behind a boulder. It was Grisha, the leader of the murderous ivory hunters.

31

Austin looked down into the yawning caldera as the paraglider soared like a condor through the notch in the rim. The road they had been following up the side of the volcano went through the low spot and descended a gradual slope to the midpoint of the caldera, where it ended in a low bluff. On the opposite side of the crater, the rim dropped almost vertically to a boulder field at the bottom. A patch of green roughly shaped in a circle was sandwiched between the bottom of the slope and the field of black boulders.

Austin put the glider into a lazy spiral into the crater and looked for a good landing site.

'What's that down there?' Zavala pointed to the base of the slope where the road ended. 'Looks like a herd of cows.'

Austin squinted through the lens of his goggles. 'Too furry to be cows. Maybe they're yaks.'

'I could use a few yaks after all we've been through.'

Austin cringed at the pun, but his mental pain was short-lived. Zavala called his attention to another section of the green area.

'I'll be damned,' Austin said. '*People!*'

The group stood near the edge of the boulder field. As the paraglider drifted lower, Austin saw someone club another person to the ground. A third figure rushed to the aid of the fallen figure but was jerked away. The paraglider was low enough for Austin to see a flash of blond hair.

'I think we just found Karla Janos,' Austin said.

*

Grisha's thin lips were peeled back in a grin that revealed his bad teeth. He spoke in Russian, and his murderous cohorts appeared from behind the rocks where they had been hiding.

Schroeder quickly sized up the situation. While he and Karla pursued a zigzag path through the city, Grisha and his men could have come straight through the central boulevard and stumbled on the way out.

Grisha motioned for his prisoners to go back the way they had come. As the Russians and their captives broke out of the rocks into the open, Grisha saw the woolly mammoths.

'What are those?' he said. 'Sheep?'

'No,' Schroeder said. 'They're butterflies.'

He was unprepared for the fury of Grisha's response. The Russian didn't like being humiliated in front of his men. He let out a feral snarl, raised his gun like a club and slashed Schroeder across the face with the barrel. As Schroeder crumpled to the ground, the last thing he heard was Karla's scream.

Zavala had been watching the drama unfold below. 'Looks like she's in bad company. How do you want to handle this? Hawk on a mouse or OK Corral?'

Zavala was asking Austin whether they should make a stealth approach or go in with guns blazing.

'How about Butch Cassidy and the Sundance Kid?'

'That's a new one, but anything works for me.'

'Hand me your gun and take over the controls. We'll come in from behind. The sun will be in their eyes.'

'Wyatt Earp could have used one of these rigs against the Clanton boys.'

'As I recall, he did pretty well without it.'

Zavala slipped his Heckler & Koch from its holster. Handling the weapon with great care, he passed it to Austin, and placed his hands on the controls. They were descending rapidly. Austin positioned himself like a gunfighter, with a weapon in each hand.

Grisha had one arm around Karla's neck, his fingers entwined in her hair. The palm of his other hand was pressed against her face so that she could hardly breathe. With a simple twist, he could have broken her neck. He was angry enough to kill her, but his greed was stronger than his more violent tendencies. She was worth more alive than dead.

But that didn't mean he and his men couldn't have some fun with the beautiful young woman. He removed his hand from her face and pulled down the zipper of her jacket. Frustrated by the layers of cold-weather clothing underneath, he cursed and knocked her to the ground. One of his men shouted.

Grisha glimpsed a shadow moving on the ground and he looked up.

His mouth dropped in amazement.

A two-headed man was swooping down on him from out of the sky.

When the distance narrowed to a couple of hundred feet, Austin started blazing away with both handguns. He aimed off to the side to avoid hitting Karla. Her captors ran for their lives.

With Karla out of the way, Austin was free to aim at his fleeing targets, but it was difficult to get a clear shot while he was moving. Zavala yelled at Austin to get ready to land. He tucked one gun into its holster, the other in his belt.

They attempted to land on their feet, but they had come in too fast. They hit the ground and lurched forward onto their hands and knees. Luckily, the vegetation cushioned the impact. They quickly unstrapped the power unit. While Zavala rolled up the lines to the sail, Austin went over to the blond woman who was kneeling beside an older man.

'Miss Janos?' Austin said.

She glanced up at Austin with her striking gray eyes. 'Who are you?'

'Kurt Austin. My friend Joe and I have been looking for you. Are you all right?'

'Yes, I'm fine,' she said. 'My uncle needs help.'

Austin dug a first-aid kit out of his pack. The man was still conscious. He lay on his back with his eyes open. He could have been anywhere from sixty-five to seventy-five years old, but it was hard to tell because his long-jawed face was covered with blood that flowed from lacerations on the cheek and brow.

Austin knelt by his side, cleaned the wound and applied antiseptic on the raw flesh. His ministrations must have been painful, but the man didn't flinch. His arctic blue eyes watched every move Austin made.

Austin had barely started his first aid when the man said, 'That's enough. Help me up.' With Austin's aid, Schroeder struggled to stand. He was a tall man, several inches over Austin's six foot one.

Karla put her arm around her uncle's waist. 'Are you all right?'

'I'm a tough old lizard,' he said. 'It's you I'm worried about.'

'I'm okay, thanks to these two men.'

Austin noticed the evident bond between the older man and the young woman. He introduced himself and Zavala.

'My name is Schroeder,' the man said. 'Thank you for your help. How did you find us?'

'We talked to a woman named Maria Arbatov.'

'*Maria.* How is she?' Karla said.

'She's going to be fine, but her husband and two other men were murdered. I assume they were your fellow scientists. There was another man we couldn't identify.'

Karla glanced at Schroeder, who said, 'He attacked Karla. I had to stop him.' He squinted toward the boulder field. 'This is a dangerous place. They'll be back. They have automatic weapons, and we're totally exposed out here.'

'This is your neighborhood,' Austin said. 'Where can we find cover?'

Schroeder pointed to the base of the slope that came down from the rim of the caldera.

'Down there in the city.'

Austin wondered if the man was delirious from his injuries.

'Did you say "city"?' He saw only the low bluffs at the base of the slope.

'That's right,' Karla said. 'Oh no, the dwarves are gone. The gunfire must have scared them.'

It was Zavala's turn to wonder if he was hearing things. 'Dwarves?'

'Yes,' Karla said. 'Dwarf woolly mammoths.'

Austin and Zavala exchanged glances.

'Enough talk. We've got to get moving,' Schroeder said.

Clutching Karla by the arm, he limped toward the edge of the bowl. Austin and Zavala took up the rear. Schroeder's insistence that they start moving proved to be sound advice. The group had almost reached the edge of the green area when Grisha and his men suddenly broke from their rocky cover and began firing their guns.

Fountains of dirt erupted in the grass about a dozen feet behind the fleeing group.

It would take only a second for Grisha and his men to get the range. Austin yelled at the others to keep going. He turned and threw himself belly-down on the ground and took careful aim with his Bowen at the nearest Russian.

He cracked off a couple of shots that fell short. Grisha and his men were taking no chances. When Austin fired, they stopped shooting and went belly-down as well.

Austin turned and saw that the others were nearly at the face of the bluff. He scrambled to his feet and sprinted after them. Grisha's men started shooting again. The bullets were practically hitting the ground at his heels as he ducked with the others into an opening in the face of the cliff.

Karla shook her flashlight, and the batteries apparently still had a little juice left in them because the bulb glowed dimly. They picked their way through the winding path. When the flashlight finally sputtered and died, they had entered the area where some buildings still stood among the rubble and were beginning to see the glow from the underground city. They followed the beckoning light like moths toward a flame and soon came upon the subterranean metropolis.

Austin gazed at the shimmering streets and buildings.

'What *is* this place, the land of Oz?' he said.

Karla laughed. 'It's an underground city built of some sort of light-producing mineral,' Karla said. 'We don't know who built it, but these are only the suburbs. It's quite extensive.'

Schroeder hushed Karla and said they could talk about it later, and then he led the way through the maze of streets until they were back at the plaza where they had first come upon the mammoths.

The dwarf mammoths had returned to the plaza and were huddled around the pyramid. They seemed restive, snorting frequently as they milled around the square.

Karla saw Austin reach for his gun. She put her hand on his arm. 'It's all right. They won't hurt you. They must have been spooked by the noise.'

Austin had seen many strange sights on missions that took him to remote places around the world and under the oceans. But nothing like the creatures moving around the plaza. He was looking at smaller versions, from the tips of their tails to their curved tusks, of the ancient behemoths he had seen pictured in textbooks.

Zavala was equally dumbfounded. 'I thought these things were extinct.'

'They *are* extinct,' Karla said. 'Rather, they *were*. These animals are the descendants of full-size mammoths that once lived on the island.'

'Karla,' Schroeder said. 'We should be talking about how to get away from those murderers.'

'He's right,' Austin said. 'Is there another way out of here?'

'Yes, but it's long and treacherous,' Karla said.

'I can't make it, but that's no reason for you not to try,' Schroeder said. 'If I can borrow a gun, I'll pin them down here while you and our new friends escape through the cave.'

Austin grinned. 'Nice try, Uncle Karl. Martyrdom went out of style in the Middle Ages. We're sticking together.'

'I'm just starting to like this place,' Joe said. 'Warm. Romantic lighting. A unique, uh, fragrance in the air.'

Schroeder smiled. He didn't know who these men were, but he was glad for Karla's sake that he had them by his side. 'If you are going to be foolish, we'd better get ready.'

At Austin's suggestion, Zavala went to stand watch where the street entered the plaza.

Austin turned to Schroeder. 'Any suggestions?'

'It's useless to run. We can take positions in the square and try to get them in a cross fire.'

Austin was glad Schroeder wanted to go on the offensive. The city provided a protective maze that offered dozens of places to hide, but, like Schroeder, he knew that the constant movement would eventually take its toll.

'I don't know how much firing I'll be doing,' Austin said. 'We brought extra ammunition, but we didn't expect the Little Bighorn.'

'They only have to wait until we run out of ammunition and they can pick us off one by one. Too bad I used my hand grenade.'

Austin gave Schroeder an odd look. The old man didn't look like the type who walked around with a grenade in his pocket. Austin was reminded that looks were deceiving. Schroeder was old enough for Medicare, but he talked as if he were part of a SWAT team.

Zavala trotted over from his lookout post. 'Showtime. Our pals are coming down the street.'

Austin took a quick look around the plaza. 'I've got a crazy idea,' he said. He quickly outlined his scheme.

'It might work,' Schroeder said with excitement in his voice. 'Yes, it might work.'

'It *better* work,' Austin said.

'Isn't there another way?' Karla said. 'They're such beautiful creatures.'

'I'm afraid not. If we do this right, they won't be hurt.'

Karla sighed, but she knew they had little choice. At Austin's direction, Karla and the others moved quietly around the perimeter of the plaza, leaving the side nearest the street open. Then they waited.

The mammoths had picked up their heads when they saw the humans on the move, and became more nervous at the harsh voices of Grisha and his men. The ivory hunters were making no effort to keep the noise down. They may have done it deliberately to frighten their prey, or were just plain stupid. But whatever the reason, their arrival was making the mammoths even more restless.

The herd moved away from the plaza and stopped when the mammoths saw the humans standing around the edge of the square. Those in the front ranks turned and collided with the others in the herd. The snorts and squeaks grew louder.

There was a flicker of movement at the entrance to the street. Grisha stuck his head around the corner. The sight and smell of another unpleasant, two-legged creature spooked the animals closest to him. In their eagerness to escape, they bumped against the other mammoths.

Emboldened at the lack of a challenge, Grisha stepped into the open, followed by the other thugs. They stood at the edge of the square, spellbound at the sight of the animals they had glimpsed only at a distance.

The herd had reached critical mass. Austin set off the chain reaction. He fired his gun in the air. Zavala began firing too. Schroeder and Karla yelled and clapped their hands. The herd was transformed in an instant from an uneasy group of placid animals to a full-blown stampede. Trumpeting in fear, the moving mass of heavy bodies and sharp tusks flowed toward the only avenue of escape, the narrow street that would lead them to safety outside the cave.

Unfortunately for Grisha, he and his men stood between the rampaging herd of mammoths and their goal of freedom.

The Russians raised their guns to fire at the crazed animals, but the herd was almost on top of them. They turned and ran. They got only a few steps before they were knocked to the ground and trampled underfoot by tons of mammoth flesh. Grisha had sprinted past the others, his eyes frantically darting from side to side as he looked for an escape route, but he slipped and fell under the furred onslaught.

Austin and the others took no chances that the herd would turn back. They continued to make as much racket as they could.

It was all over in a few seconds.

The plaza was empty. The rumble of the stampeding herd echoed in the distance. Austin and Zavala cautiously advanced along the street. Zavala looked down at the bloodied mounds of clothing that once had been men. They found a flashlight that had been undamaged by the stampede. Austin yelled at Schroeder and Karla that it was safe to come out.

'They don't look human,' Karla said as they made their way around the mangled bodies.

Austin remembered the dead scientists lying in the ravine. 'Who's to say they ever were.'

Schroeder let forth with a deep laugh.

'I learned long ago that in the right hands anything can be used as a weapon,' he said. 'But there was nothing in the textbook about little furry elephants.'

Austin wondered what book Schroeder was referring to and what school he had gone to. He put his thoughts aside. They weren't out of trouble yet. They made their way through the ruined city and the rubble. The sunlight slanting in through the gap in the rocks gave them renewed energy. They went to retrieve the paraglider, and discovered that

Grisha and his men had smashed the power unit and slashed the canopy.

Using sections of aluminum tubing and pieces of the canopy, they fashioned a rough splint for Schroeder. They climbed the low bluff at the bottom of the slope and ascended the road to the rim of the caldera. The switchbacks cut the steepness of the climb but made it much longer. They stopped frequently for Schroeder's sake, but he only allowed the rest stops to last a few minutes before urging the party to push on.

Hours later, they stood on the rim and looked down on the other side of the volcano. Mist obscured most of the island. After a last, wondering glance back into the caldera, they started down the outside of the volcano. The descent was as difficult as the climb. The road was a glorified mountain trail, the uneven surface covered with rocks and boulders that would have made walking hard even under ideal circumstances.

About two-thirds of the way down the outside of the mountain, they discovered they were not alone. Antlike figures were making their way up the trail. Austin's party kept on moving. They had been seen, so there was no use hiding, but they kept their weapons ready. Austin counted six people in the unknown group. As the newcomers neared, the man leading the procession waved his arm. A few moments later, Austin was close enough to see Petrov's grinning face.

The Russian was accompanied by members of his special ops team, including Veronika and her husband. Petrov sprinted the last few steps up the path.

He was grinning. 'Good afternoon, Austin,' he puffed. 'You and Joe have added mountain climbing to your many accomplishments. You never cease to amaze me.' He turned to Karla. 'And this must be Mademoiselle Janos. Very pleased to meet you. I don't know this gentleman,' he said to Schroeder.

'I'm just an old man who should be home in his rocking chair,' Schroeder said with a weary grin.

'How did you find us?' Austin said.

'We talked to the captain of the icebreaker. He said you were striking off to explore the volcano in some sort of aircraft.'

'We had a paraglider.'

'I remember now. The two large bags you brought with you.'

Austin nodded. 'You missed all the fun.'

'On the contrary,' Petrov said in a cheerful tone. 'We have had a great deal of fun. We encountered a group of armed men coming in on a boat. They gave us a warm welcome, but our thank-you was even warmer. The survivor said they had been sent in to help some men who were already here.' He looked over Austin's shoulder as if he expected to see someone following him.

'Those men are no longer with us,' Schroeder said.

'Yes,' Austin said. 'They were trampled by a herd of woolly mammoths.'

'*Dwarf* mammoths,' Zavala corrected.

Petrov shook his head. 'I studied American culture for years, but I'll never understand your strange humor.'

'That's all right,' Austin said. 'Even *we* don't understand it. Do you think you can give us a hand the rest of the way down the mountain?'

'Of course,' Petrov said with a grin. He reached into his backpack and produced a bottle of vodka. 'But *first* we will have our drink together.'

32

Austin was having a weird dream in which a procession of pygmy mammoths paraded along the streets of a crystal city to the tune of 'St Louis Blues'. His eyes snapped open. The mammoths and the city had vanished, but the blues were still playing. The music came from his phone.

Vowing to stay away from crazy Russians who drank vodka like water, he dug the phone out of his pack and managed a fuzzy, 'Austin.'

Trout's voice said, 'We've been trying to get you and Joe for days. Have you been down in a mine?'

'More like a cave,' Austin said. 'We found Karla Janos, and we're on a Russian icebreaker headed for the Siberian mainland.'

'Glad to hear she's okay. She may be our only hope.'

Austin was struck by the seriousness in Trout's voice. He sat up on the edge of the bunk.

'Our only hope for what, Paul?'

'Gamay and I found a copy of the Kovacs Theorems in Los Alamos. I did a computer simulation based on the Kovacs stuff and existing material on polar reversal. The situation doesn't look good.'

'I'm listening.' Austin was fully awake now.

Trout paused. 'The simulation showed that the magnetic polar reversal is not as elastic as some people think. A shock that's strong enough to cause a magnetic polar reversal will trigger a geologic shift of the earth's crust.'

'Are you saying that a polar shift, once begun, is irreversible?'

'That's the way it looks.'

'Is there any margin for error in the simulation?'

'It's so slim as to be negligible.'

Austin felt as if a wall had fallen on him. 'We're talking about a catastrophe.'

'Worse,' Trout said. 'This is a doomsday scenario. The worldwide destruction if this thing is unleashed is beyond anything that can be imagined or previously experienced.'

'How long do we have?'

'The reaction would be immediate. The timing depends on when the people who've been causing the whirlpools and giant waves decide to pull the switch.'

'I may be able to offer a ray of hope.' He told Trout about his encounter with Barrett, and the possibility of an antidote for a polar shift.

'Encouraging. When will you get back to Washington?'

'We'll make landfall tomorrow. We've got a plane waiting. I'll call when we're in the air to give you an ETA.'

'I'll be standing by.'

After hanging up, Austin sat in his darkened stateroom listening to the grumble of the ship's engines and cursing the slowness of ocean travel. He had been unaware of the urgency of the situation when Captain Ivanov invited him to sail on the icebreaker. Austin could have gone back with Petrov, but he politely refused the offer, saying it was important for him to talk to Karla Janos. Petrov had given him a knowing smile, and told Austin to call on him anytime.

Since coming aboard Austin had spent very little time with Karla. After she and Maria had a tearful reunion, and Uncle Karl got patched up, everyone retired to their respected staterooms to catch up on badly needed sleep.

Austin got dressed and went out on the deck, which was bathed in the subdued arctic light. The *Kotelny* was plowing through the ocean at a steady clip. The cold air hit his lungs like the blast from an open refrigerator. Fully awake now, he made his way to the mess hall and poured himself a mug of coffee. The place was deserted except for a couple of crewmen who were coming on to a shift. He found a corner table, slipped the phone from his pocket and called the number Barrett had given him. After a few seconds, a woman answered and said hello.

'I'd like to speak to Barrett,' Austin said.

'This *is* Barrett. I programmed a woman's voice to take the place of mine.'

'Aren't you taking this electronic cloak-and-dagger stuff a bit too far?'

'Hell, Kurt, *you*'re not the one who got shot,' Barrett said. 'You don't know the kind of people you're dealing with.'

'That's why I called. Do you think Gant and Margrave are open to reason?'

'Gant is about as reasonable as a rattlesnake. Tris could be reached, maybe, but he's so damned convinced of his righteous cause he doesn't care who he hurts. Why do you ask?'

Austin conveyed the gist of his conversation with Trout.

When Barrett's voice came back on, it had assumed its masculine mode. 'I was afraid of something like this. Ohmigod. I'm responsible for the end of the world. I'm going to kill myself.'

'If the world ends you won't have to,' Austin said.

Barrett calmed down. 'That's the most twisted logic I've ever heard.'

'Thanks. Back to my original question. Do you think

Gant or Margrave would react with the same alarm if I laid out the facts for them?'

'The difference is that I *believe* you. They'll think you're trying to throw a monkey wrench in their plans.'

'It might be worth taking the chance. How do I get to them?'

'Gant's foundation has an office in Washington.'

'I was thinking of something more casual.'

'Let me think. I saw something in the paper. Gant is having some sort of private, charitable horsey thing on his estate. Maybe you can get into that. I may be able to help.'

'That's a start. What about Margrave?'

'He rarely comes off of his island in Maine. He's developed a citadel mentality. He's got security people guarding the place, but I might have some ideas on how to get to him.'

'It's worth a try. I'm going to do all I can to try to stop this before it gets to the trigger point. Are you still on the move?'

'Still living out of my sleeping bag. Call me when you get home.'

Austin hung up, finished his coffee and was about to return to his cabin when Karla came into the mess hall. She seemed as surprised to see him as he was to see her. He beckoned her to his table.

She sat down and said, 'I couldn't sleep.'

'I can understand that. You've been through a lot in the last few days.'

'Uncle Karl said that the men who murdered the expedition were after me. Something about a secret I supposedly know. I don't know what's going on, but I feel responsible for much of what has happened.'

'It's not your fault. They think the secret was passed

down from your grandfather, an electrical engineer named Lazlo Kovacs.'

'You're mistaken. My grandfather's name was Janos, like mine.'

Austin shook his head. 'That was the name Kovacs assumed after he escaped from Germany at the end of World War Two.'

'I don't understand.'

'Your grandfather was being forced to work for the Nazis on electromagnetic weapons. He escaped from a secret lab shortly before the Russians overran East Prussia. He was apparently helped by a young member of the German resistance. The German's name was Karl.'

'*Uncle* Karl! I always wondered what his connection was to my grandfather. They seemed so different yet so bound together.'

'Now you know.'

'This is insane! My grandfather never gave me any secret formula for a death ray or whatever it is they're looking for.'

'You may know more than you know. Your paper on the extinction of the woolly mammoth hinted at deeper knowledge of his work.'

'After the discovery of those creatures on the island, my paper is a joke. I can't wait to get back there to do some research.'

'Petrov has vowed to work through academic rather than governmental circles to protect your furry friends. He's had some political trouble, and he thinks this will help his cause.'

'I'm glad to hear that. But getting back to my grandfather, I went to him when I was in college with my theory of a cataclysmic extinction because he was the only scientist I knew. There was skepticism about a polar shift being possible. He said that it could happen, and *had* happened.

That it could be caused by natural phenomena, or man-made, in the future, when the technology became available. He showed me some equations having to do with electro-magnetism that he said proved his point. That's all. Later, when I was working on my thesis after his death, I incorporated his work into the paper.'

'That's all he said on the subject?'

'Yes. We never really talked much about science. When my parents died, he became a father and mother to me. I remember him making up bedtime poems to get me to sleep.' She sipped her coffee. 'How did you and Joe happen to come to our rescue?'

'I heard from a reliable source that your life might be in danger because of your family connection.'

'You rushed all the way from the other side of the world for that?'

'If I had known Uncle Karl had the situation pretty much in hand, I wouldn't have worried as much.'

'Uncle Karl saved my life, but I'm afraid we were both on our last legs when you and Joe dropped down out of the sky. I'm puzzled. I thought NUMA studies the oceans.'

'That's exactly why I'm here. There have been some strange disturbances in the sea that could have something to do with something your grandfather published. It was a set of equations called the Kovacs Theorems.'

'I don't understand.'

'You said Lazlo Kovacs theorized that electromagnetic transmissions could be used to trigger a polar shift. In the future.'

'Yes, that's right.'

'Well, the future is now.'

'Who would want to do something like that? And why?'

Austin spread his hands. 'I'm not sure. When we get back

to Washington, I have someone I'd like you to talk to. Maybe you can sort things out.'

'I was hoping to stop in Fairbanks first.'

'I'm afraid there isn't time for that. There may be a great deal at stake here.'

'I understand. Even if I'm not responsible for what is going on, my family has had a hand in it, according to what you've told me. I'll do everything I can to set things right.'

'I knew you'd say that. We'll make landfall tomorrow. A NUMA plane will take us back to Washington. My colleagues Gamay and Paul Trout have a town house in Georgetown, and I'm sure they'd be very happy to put you up. NUMA will foot the bill for any clothes you need.'

Karla did an unexpected thing. She leaned across the table and kissed Austin lightly on the lips. 'Thank you for all you've done for me and for Uncle Karl. I don't know how I can repay you.'

Austin would normally have responded to an opening from a beautiful and intelligent woman like Karla with an invitation to dinner. But the move so surprised him that the best he could manage was a polite 'You're welcome' and a suggestion that they get some sleep.

Karla told him that she wanted to stay up a few minutes longer, and that she'd see him in the morning. They shook hands and said good-night. As he left the mess hall, Austin looked back. Karla was resting her chin on her hands, apparently deep in thought. For all his philosophical reading, Austin was at a loss when it came to the working of fate. The gods must be laughing themselves to tears at their latest practical joke. They had locked the secret that could save the world in the finely sculpted head of a lovely young woman.

33

Gant considered the final moments of the foxhunt as the most sublime. The riotous red jackets, the horn blowing, the raucous tallyhos and the thundering hooves were merely a prelude to the moment of truth that came when the baying hounds caught the terrified animal and tore it to bloody shreds.

The prey had been unusually resourceful. The wily animal splashed up a stream, ran along the top of a fallen tree and doubled back in an attempt to throw off its pursuers. But, in the end, the pack cornered the doomed animal against a thick privet hedge Gant had had planted to funnel hunted foxes to a dead end against a stone wall. Even then, the fox had attempted to defend itself before being ripped to pieces.

Gant had sent the other hunters back to his house to celebrate the satisfying conclusion. He dismounted near the hedge, and relived the fox's final moments. The hunt was a savage practice, but he considered it a metaphor for what life was all about. The life-and-death struggle between the strong and the weak.

A horse whinnied. Gant looked up at a low hill and he scowled. A horseman was silhouetted against the blue sky. No one was supposed to be riding in his fields and meadows except the foxhunters. He remounted, dug his heels in and galloped up the hill.

The man watched Gant's approach from the saddle of a chestnut-colored Arabian. Unlike the red-jacketed foxhunters, he was dressed simply in faded jeans and turquoise polo shirt. A black baseball cap with a Harley-Davidson emblem on the crown covered his platinum-silver hair.

Gant brought his mount to a wheeling stop. 'You're trespassing,' he snapped. 'This is private property.'

The man appeared unruffled, and his light blue eyes barely flickered.

'Do tell,' he said.

'I could have you arrested for breaking the law,' Gant said, upping the ante.

The man's lips parted in a humorless smile. 'And I could have you arrested for foxhunting. Even the Brits have banned it.'

Gant wasn't used to being challenged. He stood in his stirrups. 'I own more than two hundred acres of land and every living thing on it. I'll do whatever I want to do with my property.' His hand went to a portable radio clipped to his jacket. 'Will you leave on your own or do I have to call my security people?'

'No need to call in the cavalry. I know the way out. The animal rights people won't be happy when they hear that you've had your mutts chewing up the local wildlife.'

'They're not *mutts*. They are purebred foxhounds. I paid a great deal of money to have them brought in from England.'

The stranger nodded, and picked up his reins.

'Wait,' Gant said. 'Who are you?'

'Kurt Austin. I'm with the National Underwater and Marine Agency.'

Gant almost fell off his horse with surprise. He recovered nicely, and pasted a fake smile on his lips.

'I always thought of NUMA in terms of *sea* horses, not Arabian mares, Mr Austin.'

'There's a lot you don't know about us, Mr Gant.'

Gant let a momentary flash of irritation show on his face. 'You know my name.'

'Of course. I came here to talk to you.'

Gant laughed. 'It wasn't necessary to trespass in order to see me. All you had to do was call my office for an appointment.'

'Thanks. I'll do that. And when your secretary asks what I want to see you about, I'll say I'd like to talk to you about your plans to trigger a polar shift.'

Austin had to hand it to Gant. The man was incredibly controlled. A slight tightening of his lips was his only reaction to Austin's bombshell.

'I'm afraid I would have to tell you that I wouldn't know what you were talking about.'

'Maybe the *Southern Belle* might refresh your memory.'

He shook his head. 'A Mississippi riverboat, no doubt?'

'The *Belle* was a giant cargo ship. She was sunk by a couple of giant waves on a voyage to Europe.'

'I'm the director of a foundation dedicated to fighting the global influence of multinational corporations. That's the closest I come to transoceanic commerce.'

'Sorry for wasting your time,' Austin said. 'Maybe I should talk to Tris Margrave about this.'

He rode off at a trot.

'Wait.' Gant spurred his mount and caught up with him. 'Where are you going?'

The Arabian halted, and Austin pivoted in the saddle. 'I thought you wanted me off the property.'

'I'm being very rude. I'd like to invite you back to the house for a drink.'

Austin pondered the invitation. 'It's a little early for a drink, but I'd settle for a glass of water.'

'Splendid,' Gant said. 'Follow me.'

He led Austin off the hill, and they rode through the meadows where horses grazed until they came to a tree-lined driveway that led to Gant's house. Austin had expected a mansion, but he was unprepared for the Tudor-style architectural monstrosity that loomed out of the Virginia countryside.

'Quite the shack,' he said. 'The foundation must pay you well, Mr Gant.'

'I was a successful international businessman before I saw the error of my ways and organized the Global Interests Network.'

'Nice to have a hobby.'

Gant replied with a white-toothed smile.

'It's no hobby, Mr Austin. I'm quite dedicated to my work.'

They dismounted and handed the reins to the grooms, who led the horses to an area where a number of horse trailers were clustered.

Gant noticed Austin watching his horse being led away. 'They'll take good care of your mount. Nice-looking animal, by the way.'

'Thanks. I borrowed her for a few hours to take a ride over here.'

'I was wondering about that,' Gant said. 'How did you get past my security fence? I've got cameras and alarms all over the place.'

'Just lucky, I guess,' Austin said with a straight face.

Gant suspected that Austin made his own luck, but he didn't press the matter. He'd take it up with Doyle. His security chief was making his way toward them. He glanced at Austin, the only person not dressed for the foxhunt. 'Is there a problem, Mr Gant?'

'Not at all. This is Kurt Austin. He's my guest. Remember

his face so you'll recognize him the next time you see him.'

Doyle smiled, but the eyes that studied Austin's face were as pitiless as a viper's.

Gant led Austin to a spacious patio where a crowd of red jackets had gathered. The intrepid hunters were drinking from champagne flutes and laughing as they relived the morning's kill. The gathering was exclusively male and high-powered. Austin didn't spend a lot of time in Washington, but he recognized the faces of a number of politicians, government officials and lobbyists. Gant was apparently well plugged in to the Beltway establishment.

Gant ushered him along a gravel path to a polished marble table set off by itself in the corner of an English garden. He ordered a servant to bring them a pitcher of ice water, and invited Austin to take a seat.

Austin sat down, placed his cap on the table and looked around. 'I didn't know there were any private foxhunting clubs left in Virginia.'

'There are no hunt clubs, at least not officially. We're simply a bunch of old friends trying to keep alive a dying old English custom.'

'That's commendable. I've always felt sad that the English custom of public drawing and quartering went by the boards as well.'

Gant chuckled. 'We're both busy men, so let's not waste time on ancient history. What can I do for you?'

'Cancel your plans for a polar reversal.'

'I'll humor you and pretend that I know what you're talking about, Mr Austin. Why would I want to cancel this so-called reversal?'

'Because if you don't, you could be putting the entire world in jeopardy.'

'How's that?'

'I don't know why you're interested in creating a shift of the magnetic poles. Maybe you're just getting bored with slaughtering innocent animals. But what you don't know is that a magnetic shift will trigger a geologic movement of the earth's crust. The impact will be catastrophic.'

Gant stared at Austin for a moment. Then he laughed until his eyes brimmed with tears. 'That's quite the science fiction plot, Mr Austin. The end of the world?'

'Or close to it,' Austin said in a voice that left no doubt as to his seriousness. 'The ocean disturbances that sunk the *Southern Belle* and one of your own transmitter ships were minor harbingers of the damage to come. I was hoping you would see reason and halt your plans.'

Gant's jovial expression disappeared, to be replaced by a sardonic smile and a raised eyebrow. Pinioning Austin in a level gaze, he said, 'Here's what I see, Mr Austin. I see someone who has concocted a tall tale for reasons that escape me.'

'Then my warnings haven't made a dent in your plans.' Austin's question came out as a statement.

The servant arrived with a pitcher and two glasses.

'I'm curious, Mr Austin, what made you think I was involved in some bizarre plot?'

'I heard it from the Spider's mouth.'

'Pardon?'

'Spider Barrett, the man who developed the polar shift mechanism.'

'This Barrett person has been telling you tales as strange as his name.'

'I don't think so. He and his partner, Margrave, are geniuses who have the money and talent to prove it. I'm not sure where you fit in.'

'You can be sure of one thing, Austin. You made a mistake coming here.'

'I was thinking the same thing.' Austin picked up his cap and put it on his lap. 'You're obviously not interested in anything I have to say. I'll be on my way. Thanks for the water.'

He stood and plunked the cap on his head. Gant rose and said, 'I'll have someone get your horse.'

Oiled by large amounts of alcohol, the boisterous conversation on the patio was becoming even louder. Gant signaled a groom and told him to bring the Arabian to Austin, who pulled himself up on the saddle. Doyle saw him preparing to leave and came over. He held on to the reins as if he were helping.

'I can find my own way out, Mr Gant. Thanks for your hospitality.'

'You'll have to come back when you can spend more time.'

'I'll do that.'

He nudged the horse with his knees, and it shouldered Doyle out of the way. Doyle was a city boy, and the only horses he had been close to before coming to work for Gant were the ones ridden by Boston's mounted police. He released the reins and stepped back so he wouldn't be stepped on. Austin caught the fear in Doyle's face and he smiled. He flipped the reins and galloped away from the house.

Doyle watched Austin ride away. His features were as hard as granite. 'Do you want me to take care of him?'

'Not here. Not now. Have someone follow him. I'd like to find out how he got onto the property.'

'I'll do that.'

'When you're through I have another job for you. Meet me in the garden in fifteen minutes.'

While Gant went off to hobnob with his guests, Doyle

slipped a hand radio out of his pocket and barked an order to two guards who were sitting in a jeep off the main access road to the house. The driver had just finished acknowledging the order when an Arabian mare galloped by with the rider low in the saddle. The driver started the jeep's engine, jammed the stick shift into first and punched the accelerator.

The jeep was going nearly sixty miles an hour when it flew by the copse of elm trees where Austin was hiding. He watched it speed by, consulted a handheld GPS unit and set off across the meadows and fields until he came to woods bordering the property. A horse and rider emerged from the trees and rode up to meet Austin.

'Nice day for a ride in the country, old chap,' Zavala said with a lame attempt at an upper-crust English accent.

'Tallyho, bangers and mash and the rest of it,' Austin said.

Taking their time, they brought their horses to a trot and came out on the other side of the woods where the trees had been cleared for a road allowed by the security patrol. There was no fence, only a number of NO TRESPASSING signs facing outward, each with its own motion-activated cameras.

Zavala took a small black box from his pocket and pushed a button. When a light glowed green, they rode between two of the signs across open land, then onto a public road. A big pickup truck with a horse trailer attached was pulled off the side of the road.

Spider Barrett got out of the truck's cab as the two men rode up. After the horses were led into the trailer and the door locked, Zavala handed the black box to Barrett. 'Worked like a charm,' he said.

'It's a pretty simple concept,' Barrett said. 'This gadget

doesn't interrupt the transmission, which they'd pick up immediately. It just delays it for a couple of hours. They'll eventually get a speeded-up picture of you two guys, but it will be too late, and they won't be able to make much sense out of it. Let me show you something even more exciting.'

He opened the truck door and removed a small television screen from the cab. It was plugged into the cigarette lighter outlet. He switched the set on and Gant's image appeared on the small screen, saying, 'This is private property,' followed by Austin's laconic 'Do tell.'

'Did anyone ever tell you that you were a wiseass?' Zavala said.

'Constantly.'

Barrett fast-forwarded to a picture of Doyle. 'This is the sonofabitch who tried to kill me,' he said.

Austin removed the baseball hat and examined the tiny camera lens hiding in the Harley-Davidson logo on the crown. 'Mr Doyle would have been very surprised if he knew that your beady eyes were watching him from the grave.'

Barrett laughed. 'What was your impression of Gant?'

'Brilliant. Arrogant. Psychopath. I was watching him after the foxhunt. He was gazing at the killing ground as if it were a shrine.'

'Gant always gave me the creeps. I could never figure out why Tris hooked up with him.'

'Evil doings make strange bedfellows, I guess. I didn't think he would go for my appeal to reason, but it gave me a chance to size him up, and plant a bug under the garden table before I left.'

'It's working fine, but hasn't picked up anything yet.'

'Do you think the Trouts will have any better luck with Margrave?' Austin said.

'I hope so, but I'm not very optimistic.'

Austin thought about his encounter with Gant. 'Neither am I,' he said.

Here's to Arthur C. Clarke,' Gant said, raising his glass high.

He was sitting in his study with three other foxhunters dressed in regulation red. One of them, a thickset man with a face like a bull, said, 'Who's Clarke?'

Gant's oily smile veiled his contempt. 'He is the British science fiction writer who first suggested back in 1945 putting three manned satellites in twenty-four-hour orbits over major landmasses to broadcast television signals. His vision is what brings us here today.'

'I'll drink to that,' said the thickset man in an English accent.

He raised his glass, and Gant and two other men in the study followed suit. One man was as gaunt as the bull-faced man was thick. The fourth man in the room was in his eighties. He had tried to stave off the inevitable advance of age and his decadent lifestyle through plastic surgery, chemicals and transplants. The effect was a hideous face that was more like the corpse of a young man.

Even Gant would admit that none of his partners would have won a competition on character, but they were incredibly shrewd and ruthless men who had become wealthy beyond belief with their multinational companies. And they would suit his needs. For now.

'I asked you to join me so I can bring you up to date on our project,' Gant said. 'Things are going well.'

'Hear! Hear!' said the other three men in chorus.

'As you know, the satellite business has grown incredibly fast in the last thirty years. There are dozens of satellites operated by many companies, used for television, communications, military, weather and telephone, with more service on the horizon. These satellites generate billions of dollars.' He paused. 'Soon, all this will be ours.'

'Are you sure there can be no foul-up?' said the old man.

'None at all. The polar shift will be a temporary disruption, but the satellite networks will all be exposed to an electronic mauling.'

'Except for ours,' the gaunt man said.

Gant nodded. 'Our lead-shielded satellites will be the only ones still operating. Our consortium will be in a position to dominate world communications, a position that we will solidify when we absorb existing networks and launch more of our own satellites.'

'Thus generating billions more,' the old man said.

'Yes,' Gant said. 'And the delicious irony is that we will use the anarchist forces to accomplish our goal. They're the ones who will readily take credit for causing the shift. And when the wrath of the world is unleashed against them, Margrave and his people will be destroyed.'

'All well and good,' the old man said. 'But remember, our main goal is the money.'

'And there will be plenty of that,' Gant said, although money was the least important thing to him. More important was the political power that would come when he had total control over the world's communications. No one would be able to make a move without his knowing about it. Millions of conversations would be monitored. Access to any records would give him ample tools for political blackmail. No army could move without his knowing about it. His television stations would channel public opinions. He would have the power to create riots and to quell them.

'Here's to that British chap,' the bull-faced man said. 'What was his bloody name?'

Gant told him. Then he raised his glass for another toast.

34

Trout reeled his fishing line in and examined the empty hook. 'The fish aren't biting today,' he said with disgust.

Gamay lowered the binoculars she had been using to study Margrave's lighthouse island. 'Someone who grew up in a fisherman's family should know that fishhooks usually work much better if you stick a worm on them.'

'Catching a fish would defeat the whole purpose of this seagoing, theatrical production, which is simply to *appear* to be fishing,' Trout said.

Gamay glanced at her watch and looked up at the peppermint, red-and-white-striped lighthouse high on its bluff. 'We've been here for two hours. The folks who have been watching us from the island should be convinced by now that we're harmless. That little "bow babe" show I did a while ago must have convinced them that we're but simple fisherfolk.'

'I was thinking that they'd been sucked in by my fisherman's outfit.'

Gamay eyed the miniature Budweiser can on the brim of Trout's rumpled hat and dropped her gaze to study the girly print on the cheap Hawaiian shirt that hung out over the red Bermuda shorts. 'How could anyone *not* be taken in by such a clever disguise?'

'I detect an unseemly note of sarcasm, which I will ignore like the gentleman I am,' Trout said. 'The true test is about to begin.'

He stowed the fishing rod in a socket with several others

and made a great show of trying to start the outboard engine. The fact that he had disconnected an ignition wire may have had something to do with his failure to get the engine going. Act 1. Then he and Gamay stood out on the deck and waved their arms in a convincing show of a heated argument. Act 2. Finally, they dug out a couple of oars, placed them in the boat's oarlocks, and began to row toward the island. Act 3.

The powerboat was not designed to be rowed, and they made slow headway, but eventually they came within a hundred feet of a long dock where a big powerboat and a bigger sailboat were tied up. The dock was festooned with NO TRESPASSING signs. Enforcing their message was a security guard dressed in camouflage, who casually made his way to the end of the dock.

He flicked the cigarette he was smoking into the water and waved them away. When the boat kept coming, he cupped his hands to his mouth and shouted, 'Private property. You can't land here.'

Trout stood in the boat's stern and yelled back, 'We're out of gas.'

'We can't help you. Private property.' He pointed to a NO TRESPASSING sign.

Gamay said, 'Let me try, Mr Budweiser man.'

'He's probably a Miller drinker,' Trout said. He stood aside to make room for Gamay. 'Please don't use the hapless husband routine. I'm getting an inferiority complex.'

'Okay, I'll use the hapless wife instead.' Gamay spread her arms as if imploring the guard. 'We don't know what to do. Our radio won't work.' She pointed to the gas pump on the dock. 'We'll pay for fuel.'

The guard ran his eyes up and down Gamay's lithe body, then grinned and waved the Trouts up to the dock.

They rowed erratically up to the dock until they were close enough to see that the guard had a pistol holster attached to his belt on one side and a radio clipped to the other. Trout passed an empty fuel tank up to the unsmiling guard, who took it over to the pump and filled it while they remained in the boat. When he brought it back, Gamay thanked him and asked what she owed. The guard gave her a knowing grin and said, 'Nothing.'

She gave the guard a thick envelope. 'Then please give this to Mr Margrave in exchange for our fuel.'

The guard looked at the envelope and said, 'Wait here.' He walked out of earshot and spoke into his hand radio. Then he came back and said, 'Come with me.'

He led them past a steep flight of wooden stairs to the foot of the bluff. He produced a small remote control from a pocket, clicked it once and a section of wall swung open to reveal an elevator. He told them to get in and followed them into the elevator. Keeping one hand on his holster, he watched them during the trip of several seconds. The elevator door opened in a circular room. One look around told the Trouts that they were inside the lighthouse.

The guard opened a door and they stepped into the open. They were at the top of the cliff. There was a magnificent view of the sun-sparkled waters of Penobscot Bay. Three folding chairs had been set up, facing each other. A man was sitting in one chair, his back to the newcomers, peering into a spotting scope. He turned and smiled at the Trouts.

He had a slender saturnine face and strangely shaped green eyes that regarded the Trouts with amusement. He motioned to the empty chairs. 'Hello, Gamay. Hello, Paul. I've been waiting for you.' He chuckled at their expressions.

'I don't believe we've met before,' Trout said, settling into one chair while Gamay sat in the other.

'We *haven't*. We've been listening to you as well as watching all morning. Our electronic ears are far more sensitive than the listening devices you can buy from online spy store catalogs, but the principle is the same. We heard every word you said. I understand you brought me a gift.'

The guard handed Margrave the envelope. He undid the clasp and slipped out a computer disk. His smile disappeared when he read the label: 'The Dangers of Polar Shift.'

'What's this all about?' Margrave said. His tone had lost its phony warmth.

Trout said. 'The disk will tell you everything you want to know, and some things that you don't.'

Margrave waved the guard away.

'You really should play the disk,' Gamay said. 'It will explain the entire situation.'

'Why should I be interested in polar shift?' Margrave said.

'Simple,' she said with a sweet smile. 'You intend to cause the reversal of the earth's magnetic poles using extra-low electromagnetic transmissions, a process based upon the work of Lazlo Kovacs.'

Margrave cradled his sharp chin in his hand, pondering Gamay's words. 'Even if I had the power to make the poles shift, there is no law against it that I know of.'

'But there are plenty of laws against being the agent of mass death and destruction,' Trout said, 'although you wouldn't have to worry about prosecution because you'd be dead like the rest of us.'

'I stopped playing riddles when I was a kid. What are you saying?'

'That creating a magnetic shift will trigger an irreversible movement of the earth's crust with catastrophic results.'

'If that's the case, what would I or anyone have to gain from starting this process?'

'It's possible you're not in your right mind. More likely, you're just plain dumb.'

Margrave's pale cheeks flushed with anger. 'I've been called a lot of things, but never dumb.'

'We know why you're doing this. You're trying to stop economic globalization, but you've chosen a dangerous way to do it, and you'd be wise to stop.'

Margrave rose unexpectedly from his chair. He brought his arm back, then snapped it forward. The computer disk flew from his hand in a soaring arc that ended in the water hundreds of feet below the cliff. He waved the guard over and turned to the Trouts.

'You'll be escorted back to your boat. Move away from this island or I'll sink your boat and you can swim back to the mainland.' He smiled. 'I won't charge you for the gas.'

Moments later the Trouts were descending in the elevator. The guard marched them out to their boat, shoved them off and stood on the pier with his hand on his holster.

From the top of the cliff, Margrave watched the Trouts motor away from the island, then he undid the cell phone clipped to his belt and activated the voice dialing with a single word: 'Gant.'

Jordan Gant answered immediately.

'I just got a visit from some NUMA people,' Margrave said. 'They know a lot about the project.'

'What a coincidence,' Gant said. 'I was paid a visit by Kurt Austin, also of NUMA. He seemed well versed in our plans as well.'

'The people who came here said that what we're doing could trigger worldwide destruction.'

Gant laughed. 'You've been on that island for too long. When you spend some time in a snake pit like Washington, you learn that the truth is exactly what you want it to be. They're bluffing.'

'What should we do?'

'Speed up the deadline. At the same time, we'll slow them down with a diversion. The removal of Kurt Austin from the picture will derail NUMA and give us the time we need to make sure the project is completed.'

'Has anyone heard about Karla Janos? I don't like the idea that she might show up out of nowhere.'

'I've taken care of that. My friends in Moscow assured me that if I spread a little more money around Janos would never leave that island in Siberia alive.'

'Do you trust the Russians?'

'I don't trust *any*one. The Russians will be paid in full when they show me the evidence of her death. In the meantime, she is thousands of miles away from here, unable to interfere.'

'How do you plan to respond to Austin?'

'I was hoping I could borrow the Lucifer Legion for that job.'

'Lucifer? You know how undisciplined they are.'

'I'm thinking of deniability. If something goes wrong, they are simply a group of crazed killers acting on their own.'

'They'll need some supervision.'

'Fine with me.'

'I'll take my boat to Portland and catch a helicopter to Boston for the trip to Rio.'

'Good. I'll join you there as soon as I take care of some minor matters.'

After discussing last-minute details, Margrave hung up and barked an order to his guard. He went into the lighthouse and made a phone call. Then he piled a few belongings into a bag with his laptop computer. Minutes later, he was striding along the pier to the cigarette boat. The boat's powerful engine was warming up. He got aboard with two security men. They cast off, and he gunned the engine, launching the boat over the surface of Penobscot Bay with its bow high in the air.

The boat passed a speck of an island covered with a thick growth of fir trees. Paul and Gamay sat on a large rock in the shade of the trees and watched the fast-moving craft throw up a rooster tail of white water as it went speeding by the island.

'Looks like Mr Margrave is a man in a hurry,' Gamay said.

Trout smiled. 'Hope it was something we said.'

They hiked across the island to where their boat was tied up to a tree, got in and started the engine. Then they swung the boat around to the other side of the island, gave the motor throttle and followed in Margrave's vanishing wake.

35

The thirty-story tubular structure that houses the National Underwater and Marine Agency sat on an East Washington hill overlooking the Potomac River. Sheeted in green reflective glass, the building was home to thousands of NUMA's oceanographers, marine engineers and the labs and computers they worked with.

Austin's office was a spartan affair on the fourth floor. It had the usual accoutrements, including a desk, a computer and a filing cabinet. The walls were decorated with photos of NUMA research vessels, charts of the world's oceans and a bulletin board festooned with copies of scientific articles and news clips. On the desk was a favorite photograph of Austin's mother and father sailing on Puget Sound. It was taken in happier days, before his mother died of a lingering disease.

The office's plainness was partly deliberate. Because the nature of the Special Assignments Team's work was largely clandestine, Austin wanted to blend into the NUMA backdrop. The other reason for the purely functional nature of his office stemmed from the fact that he was often away on missions that took him around the globe. His workplace was the world's oceans.

On the same floor was the NUMA boardroom, an imposing space with a ten-foot-long conference table built out of a section of wooden hull from a sunken schooner. Austin had chosen a smaller and less regal space than the conference room to plot strategy. The small study lined with shelves that were stacked with books about the sea was a quiet place often used by those waiting to make presentations.

As Austin sat at an oak table in the center of the study, he thought about Churchill's war room, or the Oval Office, where decisions were made that affected the future of the world. He had no infantry divisions or powerful fleets, he mused. He had Joe Zavala, who would much rather be driving his Corvette convertible with a lovely woman at his side; Barrett, a brilliant computer nerd with a spider tattooed on his bald pate; and the beautiful and intelligent Karla Janos, whom Austin would have preferred to be talking to over cocktails.

'Paul and Gamay are on their way back from Maine,' he announced. 'They hit a dead end trying to persuade Margrave to call off his plans.'

'That means we have only one option,' Karla said. 'We've got to stop this insane scheme.'

Austin gazed across the table at Karla, studying the creamy, unblemished skin and perfect mouth, thinking how unfair it was for a simple threat to the world to intrude on the potential for romance. Karla noticed that she was the object of Austin's coral blue eyes. She raised a finely arched eyebrow. 'Yes, Kurt?'

Caught in the act, Austin cleared his throat. 'I was wondering how your uncle is doing?'

'Technically, he's my god-grandfather, but he's doing well. Simply exhausted and worn out. The hospital wants to keep him for a few days. He's got to stay off his ankle. But he'll probably escape as soon as he gets some rest.'

'I'm glad to hear he's doing well. I can drop you off at the hospital after our meeting. When we're through here, I'm driving down to an event near Manassas National Battlefield to brief Dirk Pitt, NUMA's director.'

'Is Pitt refighting the Civil War?' Zavala said.

'He's satisfied with the outcome, as far as I know, but he got roped into a charity deal near Bull Run. He'd like to get filled in before the White House session. What have you got, Joe?'

'Good news. I asked Yeager to scour the records of shipbuilders. I thought if we could figure out where the transmitter ships were built we might be able to track them down. But even Max drew a blank. Next I went after the dynamos. I thought they might be commercially made.'

'The generators we saw aren't the kind of thing you'd pick up at your neighborhood electrical supply house.'

'Only a few companies manufacture equipment that size,' Zavala said. 'I followed up on every one, checking their sales for the past three years. They all went to power companies except one order supposedly shipped to a factory in South America, which is owned by Gant's foundation. The same multinational company that owns the factory has a shipyard in Mississippi. Seemed a funny combination of property for anyone to own, especially a nonprofit lobbying group.'

'You're sure the foundation owns them?'

'Positive. I checked through the foundation's filings as a nonprofit. They own the shipyard through a straw company set up in Delaware. I had someone from NUMA follow up with a bogus story about retrofitting a big research vessel for us. The company itself is apparently legit. The management said they had just wrapped up a major retrofit job – they wouldn't go into details – and would be interested in making a bid.'

'So the ships are still there?'

'They left several days ago. I accessed the NUMA satellite archives. Four ships left the boatyard last week.'

'Four?'

'Three transmitter ships and what looks like a passenger liner. They seem to be headed toward South America.'

Barrett had been silent since watching the computer simulation. 'Thanks for your hard work, Joe. I'm feeling guilty as hell about all this. I can't stop thinking that this tragedy is my fault.'

'Not at all,' Karla said. 'You could never know that your work would be used in a destructive way. It's no different than my grandfather. He was simply interested in pure science.' Karla was shaking her head when a smile appeared on her face. 'Topsy-Turvy,' she said.

She laughed at the bewildered expressions around the table.

'It's the title of a bedtime poem my grandfather used to tell me. Not very good poetry, as I recall, but he said it was something that I would always have if I needed it.' She scrunched her brow as she tried to remember the words.

> *Topsy-turvy,*
> *Turvy-topsy,*
> *The world stands on its head.*
> *The sky's on fire,*
> *The earth's afraid,*
> *The ocean leaves its bed.*

Her recitation was greeted by a deep silence, which Karla broke on her own.

'Dear God,' she said. 'I've just described auroras, earthquakes and tsunamis.'

'A polar shift, in other words,' Austin said. 'Tell us more.'

'I'll try. It's been a long time.' She stared at the ceiling. 'Each rhyme starts with the same topsy-turvy couplet, and then the verse itself changes. The next one goes, "The key is in the door,/We'll turn the knob and hitch the latch,/To still the ocean's roar." It goes on for several verses, then ends with my favorite one: "Say good-bye to night./All's well once more,/As Karla dreams,/For all the world is right."'

Barrett whipped a ballpoint pen and notebook out of his pocket and slid them across to Karla. 'Could you write down every verse?'

'Yes, but —' Karla seemed flustered. 'Do you think all this gibberish *means* anything?'

'Just curious,' Barrett said.

'We should follow any lead, no matter how seemingly frivolous,' Austin said. He glanced at a wall clock. 'I've got to get moving. We'll meet back here in a couple of hours.'

He asked Zavala to talk to the Trouts and have them follow up on the transmitter ships, then turned to Karla. 'I can give you that ride to the hospital,' he said.

'I'll see Uncle Karl later. If I go now, he'll demand that I help him escape from the hospital. I'd like to go with you to see Mr Pitt,' she said.

'I don't know,' Austin said. 'It might be safer if you stay out of sight.'

'Maybe, but I don't feel like being stashed in a safe house. There's a good chance that whoever ordered my murder doesn't know that I'm still alive.'

'I'd like to keep you that way.'

'My grandfather's work started this nonsense. I owe it to him to stop his research from being perverted.'

Seeing the determined jut to Karla's jaw, Austin knew that no argument he advanced would be able to sway her.

Fifteen minutes later, Austin and Karla were picking up a car from the motor pool in the NUMA garage. As Austin drove out of the garage exit to join the Washington traffic, he and Karla were observed from behind the one-way windows of a van crammed with the latest electronic listening and watching equipment. The letter on the van's door identified it as belonging to the Metropolitan Transit Authority.

Doyle sat inside the van puffing on a cigarette as he and a helper monitored several screens that showed the street scene around the NUMA building. Hidden cameras in the van and a similar vehicle parked outside NUMA's main pedestrian entrance recorded the face of everyone leaving the building and compared it to images in its database. The facial recognition system was capable of checking more than a thousand faces a second.

The monitor alarm buzzed. The signal for a hit. A picture of Austin behind the wheel of a turquoise Jeep Cherokee that had emerged from the garage was projected on one of the screens. Below Austin's face was a summary of personal data. Doyle's hard eyes gleamed with excitement. *Bingo!* He had just ordered his helper to get into the driver's seat and follow the Jeep when a second monitor buzzed. The picture of the attractive young woman who was a passenger in the Jeep filled the screen. The database identified her as Karla Janos.

Double bingo!

A smile came to Doyle's thin lips. He couldn't wait to see Gant's expression when he told him that Karla Janos was alive and well and consorting with the enemy. As the van pulled away from the curb and tailed the Jeep, Doyle called a motel in Alexandria where six Harley-Davidson motorcycles were parked. Minutes later, six men emerged from the motel, hopped on the motorcycles and roared off to rendezvous with Doyle.

36

Karla surveyed the men in Confederate gray and Union blue who were crowding the suburban roads in their pickup trucks and SUVs.

'I must have been mistaken,' she said. 'I thought the Civil War was over.'

'You *have* led a sheltered life,' Austin said. 'The War of Northern Aggression is still alive and well. Holler the name of Robert E. Lee out the window and you'll recruit enough Rebel volunteers to reenact the Battle of Gettysburg.'

Austin followed the traffic to a parking lot adjoining a large open field of a dozen or so acres. After parking the NUMA car, they joined the throng of spectators and Civil War reenactors streaming toward the field. Signs along the way announced that the military demonstration and steam car parade were being held to raise money for the Friends of the Manassas National Battlefield.

Austin stopped a bearded man dressed in the butternut gray of an officer in Lee's army to ask directions.

'Stonewall Jackson at your service,' the man said with a courtly bow.

'Nice to meet you, General. You're looking well, considering. I wonder if you might know where the antique steam cars are gathered,' Austin said.

Jackson squinted into the distance, tugging thoughtfully at his beard. 'Technically speakin', cars weren't invented in 1861, so I don't know what you're talking about, suh. But if I did, I'd suggest that you might find what you're looking for near the Porta Pottis, which we didn't have back in my day.'

'Thank you, General Jackson. Hope you enjoy the battle.'

'My pleasure,' he said, tipping his hat at Karla.

As she watched Jackson melt into the crowd, she said, 'He really takes the part seriously, doesn't he?'

Austin smiled. 'Manassas was the first big battle of the Civil War. The Feds thought they were going to walk over the Rebels. People even came down from Washington with their picnic baskets to watch the battle, pretty much the same as they're doing today. The Confederates caught the breaks that day, but the Union eventually rallied.'

'Why aren't we at the actual battlefield?' Karla said.

'They tried a reenactment there some years ago. Things got kind of crazy, so they're holding it on private land.'

Karla looked around. 'I see what you mean about "crazy".'

Austin grinned.

'As old Stonewall might say, "Save your blood. The South will *rise* again."'

The six men who pulled their motorcycles up to the parked van looked as if they had been cloned in a lab. They all wore goatees, and their widow's peaks had been trimmed to arrow-sharp points.

Lucifer's Legion was an extreme group of neo-anarchists who felt that violence in advancing their cause was not only justified but necessary. Like their wild-eyed, bomb-tossing predecessors, they were the fringe of the mostly nonviolent anarchist movement, which wanted nothing to do with them. They traveled from city to city on their motorcycles, leaving a trail of chaos in their wake.

When Margrave became part of the neo-anarchist movement, he enlisted the legion's help. He reasoned that since the Elites had the police, who were empowered to use physical force, and, in some situations, kill, he and his supporters should have a similar option. He bankrolled the legion, using them as his personal Praetorian Guard. He was amused at first when they grew beards and cut their hair to affect a satanic look that Margrave had come by naturally. After several anarchist protests they were involved in became unexpectedly bloody, he realized that they were out of control.

He kept them on the payroll but used them less and less. He had readily accepted Gant's recommendation that he hire the security company for day-to-day operations. Margrave was initially surprised when Gant suggested that he use the legion to kill Austin and Karla, but he accepted the argument that in case anything went wrong the authorities would think that this was a rogue gang acting on its own.

Margrave knew the legion's psychopathic tendencies better than Gant, which was why he had insisted that Doyle keep an eye on them. Doyle had removed the stick-on METROPOLITAN TRANSIT AUTHORITY letters from the van. When the motorcycles pulled up next to the vehicle, Doyle stepped out of the van and inspected the odd crew dismounting from their bikes with a friendly grin that masked his disdain.

Doyle was a cold-blooded murderer, but with their glassy-eyed stares, fixed smiles and quiet-spoken voices these guys gave him the creeps. He hoped Gant knew what he was doing. He had worked, reluctantly, with the group from time to time. His own deadly expressions of violence were controlled and calculated. He killed for business reasons: to remove a competitor; to silence an informant. The undisciplined behavior of Lucifer's Legion offended his sense of order.

He pointed at a turquoise Jeep in an adjacent row. 'Austin and the woman are headed to the battlefield. We'll have to find them.'

The legion's members seemed able to communicate with each other without speaking, moving in unison like a flock of birds or a school of fish. Acting like a unit, they fanned through the parking lot. They sighted a panel truck owned by a company called Gone with the Wind Costumes. A company employee was unloading a rack of period outfits for the more casual reenactors who didn't own their own uniforms. He found himself surrounded by six grinning clones. One clubbed him unconscious with a telescoping blackjack while the others used their bodies to screen the assault.

They shoved the unconscious man into the back of the truck and rummaged through the collection until they found what they wanted. They carried their loot back to Doyle's van and changed into the costumes. In a short time, the bikers dressed in jeans and T-shirts were gone. In their place were three Confederate and three Union soldiers. They tucked sawed-off shotguns in their belts, then got back on their motorcycles and spread out like hungry wolves in search of prey.

Doyle left the van and joined the flow of foot traffic. As he moved through the stream of spectators and costumed participants, he scanned the crowd like radar. Doyle had near-perfect vision that was a valuable asset for a hunter and his sharp eye picked out Austin's white hair. A second later, Doyle saw the attractive blond woman by Austin's side. Her face was the same one the computer in the van had identified as Karla Janos.

He unclipped a hand radio from his belt and sent a quick message to Lucifer's Legion.

*

368

Austin had found the steamer cars. There were about twenty antique Stanleys lined up along the edge of the field. A middle-aged man with a clipboard in hand was moving along the line of cars.

'I'm looking for someone with a little authority,' Austin said, purposely setting himself up for the old gag.

The man grinned. 'I've got as little authority as anyone.' He proffered his hand. 'Doug Reilly. I'm president of the Virginia Stanley Steamer Club. What can I do for you?'

'I'm looking for a car owner named Dirk Pitt.'

'Oh sure, Pitt's the replica of the 1906 Vanderbilt Cup racer over there.' Reilly pointed to an open red car whose long rounded hood was shaped like a coffin. 'There were only two originals and neither exists as far as we know. Engines from a Stanley, though. Great hill climber.'

'Which one's yours?'

Reilly led them over to a shiny black 1926 sedan and pointed out the car's unique features like a proud father. 'You know anything about these old buggies?'

'I drove one at a steamer rally once. I spent more time watching the controls than watching the road.'

'That about sums it up,' Reilly said with a chuckle. 'The Stanley Steamer was the fastest and most powerful vehicle of its day. A Stanley with the "canoe" body broke the world's speed record with 127 miles per hour back in 1906. They deliver full power the second you hit the throttle. With their diesel drive, they could go from a standing start to sixty while most gas-powered cars were grinding through the gears.'

'It's surprising that we're not all driving steam cars today,' Austin said.

'The Stanley boys didn't want to mass-produce their cars. Henry Ford turned out as many in a day as they did in a year.

The 1912 Cadillac introduced the electric starter. These cars are all steaming, to save time. If the Stanley brothers had figured out how to make their cars start faster, and improved their production and marketing, none of us today would be driving what the Stanleys called an "internal explosion engine". Sorry for getting off track.'

'Don't be sorry,' Karla said. 'That was fascinating.'

Reilly blushed. 'All the other car owners have gone over to watch the reenactment. I'm keeping an eye on things here. When the battle's over, we're going to lead a parade around the field.'

Austin thanked Reilly, and then he and Karla made their way toward the battle reenactment. From the sound of musket fire and artillery, the fighting had begun. As they walked across the wide field, they could see a crowd watching skirmish lines of blue and gray advancing toward each other. The muskets made a *pop-pop* sound from a distance, and the smell of gunpowder drifted their way.

A couple of dozen other stragglers were headed toward the reenactment. Austin was giving Karla a history lesson on the Bull Run battles when, out of the corner of his eye, he noticed someone moving laterally rather than with the general flow of foot traffic. The man cut across their path, stopped fifty feet ahead and turned to face them. It was Doyle, Gant's henchman.

Doyle was close enough so that the unsmiling expression on his hard features was clearly visible. He stared at them a moment, then reached under his jacket. Austin saw the sun flash on metal in his hand. Taking Karla firmly by the arm, he guided her back the way they had come.

'What's wrong?' she said.

Austin's answer was drowned out by a guttural roar. Six Harley-Davidsons were speeding across the field in their direction. Three bikers dressed in Confederate army uniforms were closing from the left, and three in Union blue coming in on the right.

Austin yelled at Karla to run. They sprinted across the field with the bikers closing in a classic pincers maneuver but skidded to a stop before they closed on their prey. A police car with its lights blinking was flying across the field. The vehicle sped past Karla and Austin and stopped. The police officer got out of the car and waved his hands.

He was reaching for his book of tickets when a biker dressed in blue produced a shotgun from under his coat and took aim. The *pow* sound of the shotgun mingled with the noise of the musket fire. Shot in his leg, the policeman toppled to the ground. Without a look back, the bikers formed into a single line again and continued their pursuit.

Reilly was buffing the shine on his sedan when he heard the *pop* of motorcycle exhausts. He looked up and saw Austin and Karla running toward him. His smile turned to a puzzled expression of horror when he saw the bikers in hot pursuit.

Austin dashed up to the cars and told Karla to get into the red Stanley with the coffin nose. He slid behind the wheel. Reilly ran over to the car.

'What are you doing?'

'Call the police!' Austin said.

Reilly gave him a blank look. 'Why?'

'To report a car theft,' Austin said.

Austin heard the roar of motorcycle engines. The bikers were almost on them. He released the hand brake and unscrewed the throttle-lever lock on the steering post. Then he pushed the throttle lever forward. Steam flowed into the engine.

The bikers were only yards away when the car smoothly

accelerated with hardly any noise. Austin swung the steering wheel over. The Stanley narrowly missed the next car in line.

Austin slammed on the brakes and whipped the wheel over a second later to avoid hitting a family with two young children who were crossing the road. Austin drove onto the field. Doyle tried to cut off their escape. He stood directly in their path, aiming at them with his gun clutched in both hands.

Austin yelled at Karla to duck. Keeping his head low behind the steering wheel, Austin pointed the car directly at Doyle, who jumped to one side to avoid being hit. He tried to get off a shot. The car fender grazed his thigh, and the bullet went skyward.

The steamer raced across the open field. Austin remembered that in a steamer, it was necessary to accelerate slowly to get steam up. He had to use all his concentration to deal with the gauges and controls for a half-dozen different functions.

He glanced in the rearview mirror. The motorcycles were a hundred feet behind the car and closing fast. They were spread out at the start of a flanking maneuver that would squeeze the car between two lines of bikers. The car and its two-wheeled pursuers were approaching the crowd of spectators watching the military demonstration.

Austin leaned on the horn. A few people looked his way, but the horn was drowned out by the musket and cannon fire. He braked the Stanley and blew his horn again. Someone finally noticed him. The crowd began to part. By then, the bikers were coming up on both sides of the Stanley.

The steamer and its motorcycle escort raced across the smoke-filled open field between the Union and Confederate troops, who were drawn out in long lines facing each other.

The musket and cannon fire halted. Austin heard a sound he hadn't expected. Applause.

'Why are those idiots clapping?' Karla said.

'They must think it's part of the act.' Austin let out a blood-curdling screech as they passed between the opposing armies.

There was alarm in Karla's face. 'Are you all right?'

Austin flashed a grin. 'Hell, yes. I've always wanted to do a Rebel yell. Hold on.'

They were through the battlefield and headed toward a line of cannon brought in for the occasion. Austin braked so he could veer sharply off without a rollover. The bikers maintained their speed, and saw an opportunity to close in. The two leading bikers were only a few yards from the steamer's left and right fenders.

Karla looked at the rider on the right and shouted, 'He's got a gun!'

The biker was steering with one hand, and with the other he rested a gun on his arm with the muzzle pointed at Karla's head. Austin didn't think; he simply reacted. He jerked the wheel over and back.

The heavy bumper crunched the rider's right leg. The bike wobbled as it fought to remain upright. Then the motorcycle flipped, tossing the biker like an angry steer. Austin tried to nail the other motorcycle, but the rider saw what had happened to his pal and easily skated off beyond reach.

The car flew up a hill without slowing, then down the other side. Austin could see cars ahead, moving along a road that skirted the perimeter of the field. He had to dodge a stone wall and split-rail fencing, but, a moment later, the Stanley leaped over the berm and landed across two lanes of highway.

He straightened the steering wheel and increased throttle.

On the hard pavement, the car changed into a playful young filly that wanted to run. The hard rubber tires whirred on the macadam. He passed a couple of cars with the bikers hot on his tail, and once he was clear of traffic let the car's speed creep up to eighty. He saw a sign warning of a turnoff and feathered the brakes. The bikers fell back, suspecting a ploy.

Austin wheeled the car onto an access ramp. The Stanley shot onto the main highway. Austin weaved in and out, but each time he tried the maneuver the more agile bikers stayed with him. He tried to shake them by increasing speed. He was doing ninety, then one hundred miles an hour. He could barely see with the wind blowing in his face.

'Where's a traffic cop when you need one?' he yelled.

Karla was scrunched down in her seat, trying to avoid the full blast of air.

'What?'

'Do you have a cell phone?'

'You want to make a telephone call?' she said in disbelief.

'No, I want *you* to make one. Call the state police and tell them there's a maniac in an old red car being chased by a bunch of bikers in Civil War uniforms. *That* should get their attention.'

Karla nodded and dug in her pocket for a phone. She punched out an emergency number. When she got through to the police, she conveyed Austin's message. 'They say they'll have someone check it out,' she said. 'I'm not sure they believed me.'

The bikers were moving up again. Austin was pushing the car's envelope. He should have been dealing with the various controls governing water level, fuel pressure, pilot and other functions, but he was too busy staying on the road.

A moving shadow appeared suddenly on the highway.

Austin glanced up and to the side. A helicopter was pacing them. '*That* was fast!'

'It's not the police,' Karla said. 'It's a television station traffic helicopter.'

The helicopter easily kept up with the chase. Austin frantically scoured his brain for a plan, but he had exhausted all his options. The car flew past an off-ramp. Austin glanced in the mirror and saw the bikes slow, then make a turn onto the ramp.

'Our friends have deserted us,' he said.

Karla turned just as the last Rebel soldier turned off the highway. 'Why?' she said.

'Camera shy. They don't want to be on the six o'clock news.'

He slowed the car down to a manageable sixty. He and Karla waved up at the helicopter.

They were still waving when three Virginia State Police cruisers caught up with them. Austin heeded the phalanx of flashing lights and the wail of sirens and pulled off the highway. The Stanley was immediately surrounded by armed police officers. Austin suggested to Karla that she keep her hands where the police could see them. Once the police got past their nervousness and checked Austin's license and NUMA ID, they seemed more interested in the steamer than its occupants.

Austin told them about the bikers who had tried to force them off the road. At his suggestion, they talked with someone at NUMA, who vouched for Austin. The television station backed up the biker story. After about an hour, Austin got his license back, and was told he and Karla were free to go.

They stopped at a car wash to clean the grass and dirt off the car body. Austin was amazed to see that the car hadn't been damaged. People who were leaving the battlefield smiled and waved when they saw the steamer drive up a short while later. A tall man with dark hair and opaline eyes was waiting patiently for them.

Austin braked the car to a halt and smiled. 'Hi, Dirk. Thanks for the car loan.'

'I saw you go flying between the battlefield lines with the Hell's Angels on your tail. What's going on?'

'This is Karla Janos. Karla, Dirk Pitt.'

Pitt gave Karla his best smile. 'I was looking forward to meeting you, Miss Janos.'

'Thank you,' she said.

'How fast did you have her up to?' he asked Austin.

'Around a hundred.'

'Impressive,' Pitt said. 'I've only had her up to ninety.'

'Sorry to borrow your car without asking. We needed transportation in a hurry. Someone tried to kill us.'

'It's only a replica. Don't worry about it.' Pitt checked the car for damage, and, seeing none, said, 'Not everyone owns a car that was in the third battle of Bull Run.'

Austin's cell phone started playing the blues. He excused himself and put the phone up to his ear. Barrett was calling, and he sounded excited. There was a muffled engine roar in the background.

'I can barely hear you,' Austin said. 'What's that noise?'

'I always think better when I'm riding. I think I've got it.'

'Got what?'

'The nursery rhyme. It was code. I've got the formula for the antidote.'

Austin couldn't believe his ears. 'Say that again.'

'The *antidote*,' Barrett yelled, thinking Austin was simply not hearing over the noise of the motorcycle. 'I've got Lazlo Kovacs's antidote for polar shift.'

37

Shortly after the hot Brazilian sun dropped below the mountains, the handsome, 350-foot-long expedition vessel *Polar Adventure* slipped out of Rio de Janeiro harbor and headed on a southerly course toward the open waters of the Atlantic at its cruising speed of fifteen knots.

The *Polar Adventure* had been built by Danish shipbuilders in the late 1990s, and had enjoyed a busy schedule that took it to the Mediterranean, Europe, Greenland and most recently on Antarctic cruises. The ship had been purchased from its owners by a straw company set up expressly for that purpose by Gant's foundation.

The acquisition was purely an accounting device. On the books, the millions of dollars spent to acquire and refurbish the ship had been earmarked to build a factory in Santiago, Chile. The *Adventure* had been designed as a smaller version of the great ocean liners. The builders had lavishly decorated the decks and cabins with varnished wood and brass. Passengers could enjoy their voyage from the comfort of the outside cabins, the window-lined dining room, lounge, observation and covered promenade decks, or from an observation platform below the bridge.

As the ship plowed through the South Atlantic, Gant and Margrave stood on a balcony deep in the heart of the vessel. It overlooked a vast open space. A tall, cone-shaped metal structure, supported by extensive framework, rose from the center point of the space. Thick cables snaked out from the cone to four massive dynamos, two on either side of the structure. A covered moon pool below the cone allowed it to be lowered into the ocean.

'We essentially gutted every nonessential space below the main deck to make room for this setup,' Margrave said with a sweep of his hand. 'After our initial crude experiments, we decided that we didn't need four ships. One vessel, properly outfitted, could produce enough power to get the job done. We had been concentrating the low-frequency transmissions to a central point from the four ships.'

'Which, as I understand it,' Gant said, 'created a scattering of the electromagnetic vibrations along the periphery of the target area, setting off unexpected waves and whirlpools like the ones that sank our transmitter ship and the *Southern Belle*.'

'Right. We solved that problem by using the single transmitter you see here, with an increase in the power level. It also meant that we didn't have to build a new ship to replace the one destroyed in the initial experiments. We simply moved dynamos from the other three ships and added one.'

'Are you satisfied with the crew I got you?'

'They look like a bunch of cutthroats, but they know their way around a ship.'

'They *should*. They've cut their share of throats. I used my old business contacts to recruit them. They're all former pirates who went to work for an ocean-protection arm of our security company.'

The two men left the transmitter hold and strolled along the polished wooden floor of the promenade deck until they came to the observation deck below the bridge. Windows that wrapped around the outside of the comfortably furnished platform offered a view of the sharp bow cutting its way through the ocean.

'This is where the passengers would normally observe

wildlife,' Margrave said. 'We'll be watching the reversal with our electronic eyes.'

He pressed a wall button and a screen dropped down showing a diagram of the Eastern and Western Hemispheres. 'I've always liked home movies,' Gant said.

'You'll especially like these,' Margrave said with a chuckle. 'We'll have the entire target area under surveillance with our lead-shielded satellites. We'll be able to see the giant waves and whirlpools developing on the periphery of our target area. Should be quite spectacular!'

'Not *too* spectacular, I hope.'

'Don't tell me you believe those phony warnings from Austin and his friends.'

'I'm a political person, not a scientific one. But I do know that Austin was trying to torpedo this project with scare tactics.' He smiled. 'Maybe I'd do the same thing if I were in his place helplessly watching something that I couldn't stop.'

'We didn't take the Kovacs Theorems at face value. We've run the computer models dozens of times. The waves and vortices along the edge of the target will spin outward. We don't think there is much shipping in the area, but collateral damage is sometimes unavoidable in any great enterprise.'

'Our compasses will change immediately?'

'That's our estimate. Our navigation equipment will be recalibrated just before we start the reversal and will work off our shielded satellites.' He offered his most satanic grin. 'We'll be the only ship in the world able to navigate. Should be quite the mess out there.'

'Tell me more about the target area,' Gant said.

'You can see it up there on the screen. Our friend the South Atlantic Anomaly. As I've explained before, it's essentially a "dip" in the magnetosphere where there is less

379

natural shielding.' He pointed to an intersection where lines of latitude and longitude crossed. 'About three hundred miles off the coast of Brazil is this area of weakest polarity, where a natural polar shift would occur.'

'The new North Pole,' Gant said.

Margrave laughed. 'I can't wait to see the faces on the leading Elites when they discover that Lucifer's warnings had some teeth to them.'

Gant spread his lips in his warmest smile. He couldn't wait to see Margrave's face when he learned that all the work and fortune he had put into the polar shift project would benefit the very Elites that he despised.

38

Barrett sat in a quiet corner table of the dark-beamed taproom of the Leesburg country tavern. He was scribbling madly on a napkin, his head bent low over his work. The table was covered with dozens of crumpled napkins. An untouched mug of beer sat by his right elbow. He was oblivious to the glances the other customers were casting at the spider decorating his bald pate.

Austin and Karla sat at the table. Sensing that he had company, Barrett looked up with a faraway look in his eyes. He grinned when he saw their faces.

'You don't know how glad I am to see you. I'm about ready to explode.'

'Please don't do that just yet,' Austin said. He asked Karla what she wanted to drink and ordered two black and tans, a combination of Guinness and lager.

Racing around the Virginia countryside in an open car had made them thirsty. When the beers came, Austin slugged down half of his, and Karla blissfully buried her nose in the foamy head.

Before heading off to meet Barrett, Austin had given Pitt an update on the polar shift situation. Pitt had said he would call Sandecker, who was returning the next day from a diplomatic trip, and set up a briefing with the president when he got back from a tour inspecting tornado damage in the Midwest. In the meantime, he wanted Austin to meet with the Pentagon. As an added bonus, he gave Austin carte blanche with NUMA's vast resources.

'Sorry to take so long,' Austin said, savoring the cool brew that trickled down his throat. 'We came as soon as we could. There was background noise when you called, and I'm not sure I understood you correctly. You said something about the nursery rhyme, but I didn't get the rest.'

'After you left for Manassas, I started fooling around with Karla's bedtime rhyme. The title, "Topsy-Turvy," and some of the lines fit in with what we know about polar shift. It seemed too close to be coincidental.'

'I've found that few things are coincidental,' Austin said. 'However, it's a coincidence that I'm still thirsty and there's an untouched beer on the table.'

'I'm too cranked up to drink.' Barrett shoved the beer across to Austin, who shared half of it with Karla.

'We were talking about coincidences,' Austin said.

Barrett nodded. 'Kovacs was an amateur cryptologist. I started with the premise that the rhyme might be a cipher. I guessed that the topsy-turvy couplets were simply "nulls" – letters or words placed in a cipher to confuse – so I put them aside and stuck with the main body of the verse. A cipher is different from a code, which usually requires a codebook to make the translation. To unlock a cipher, you have to have a key, which is included in the message itself. One phrase jumped out immediately.'

'The key is in the door,' Karla said without thinking.

'That's the one! It seemed obvious, almost *too* obvious,' Barrett said, 'but Kovacs was a scientist who would have been obsessed with precision. It would have been more precise for him to have said that the key is in the *lock*.'

'The key was in the word *door* itself,' Austin said.

'That was my thinking,' Barrett said. '*Door* became my key word. You have to look at code breaking in a couple of ways. At one level, you're dealing with the mechanics of things, such as word or letter transpositions and substitutions. At another level, you're looking at the *meaning* of things.' Seeing his explanation greeted with blank looks, he said, 'What does a door do?'

'That's easy,' Karla said. 'It separates one room from another. You have to open and close it to pass through.'

'Correct,' Barrett said. 'The word's opening letter is D.'

He grabbed a clean napkin and with his ballpoint pen wrote:

DEFGHIJKLMNOPQRSTUVWXYZ
ABC

'This sets the pattern of letters for the plain alphabet. I took the last letter in *door* and used it in the same configuration for the cipher alphabet.'

'Let me try,' Karla said. Taking the pen, she wrote:

RSTUVWXYZABCDEFGHIJKLMN
OPQ

'I'm buying you a ticket to Bletchley Park,' Barrett said, referring to the British code-breaking headquarters during World War II.

'Using the alphabets to write the word *message*, you'd still get gibberish.' Karla stared at the word with disappointment in her eyes.

'Your grandfather didn't want to make it too easy. I came up with the same result. Then I went back to the key word. *D* and *R* are four spaces apart in the word *door*. I wrote down every fourth word in the main verse, but my gut feeling told me that it was too much. So I tried every fourth *letter.* Still nothing I could sink my teeth in. Then I thought, *D* and *R* are *fifteen* letters apart in the alphabet. I used that formula in the poem and picked out every fifteenth word. Then I used the plain and cipher alphabets to attempt the cryptanalysis. Are you still with me?'

'No,' Austin said.

'Yeah, that's what happened to me too,' Barrett said with a grin. 'So I cheated. I ran the whole bloody mess through a computer.' He reached into his jacket pocket and produced a computer printout. 'This is what I got.'

'A mishmash of vowels and consonants, but no words,' Karla said.

'I tried everything. I called up an MIT professor who spoke Hungarian and ran it by him. No go. Then I remembered Kovacs spoke Romanian, and called up a guy who runs the Transylvania Restaurant back in Seattle. He couldn't make heads nor tails of it. I would have torn my hair out, if I had any. I went back to the words that I had discarded, particularly *turvy-topsy*. I thought maybe it applied to what I was doing.'

'How could you turn the message upside down?' Karla said with skepticism.

'I couldn't. But I could interpret the words loosely, and run it *backward*, like the second line of the poem. Which is what I did. Still didn't make sense. Then I had an epiphany. As I rode around on my bike, I realized that it wasn't *supposed* to be words. It was exactly what it was, a string of letters, more or less. Once I jumped that hurdle, I figured that there were numbers in the message as well. Back to the computer. Certain letters were *indicators* that meant the next letter was actually a number. *A* preceded by another letter equals 1, *B* equals 2 and so on.'

'You've lost me again,' Austin said. From the puzzled

384

look on Karla's face, she was wandering around in cipher land as well.

Barrett set the computer page aside and picked up the napkin in both hands. 'This is an *equation*.'

'An equation for *what*?' Austin said.

'By itself, the message doesn't make sense, but we've got to look at it in context. Kovacs intended that the message would be seen by only one person: Karla. He said she would always have the poem when you needed it.'

'Are you saying what I think you're saying?' Austin said.

'I just figured this out a few minutes ago, so I can't be sure until I put it to the test,' Barrett said. 'But Kovacs could have given us a set of electromagnetic frequencies.'

'The *antidote*,' Karla whispered.

Austin gingerly picked up the napkin as if it would fall apart. 'This is the frequency that can neutralize a polar shift?'

Barrett's Adam's apple bobbed a couple of times 'Hell, I *hope* so,' he said.

Karla leaned over and kissed Barrett on the top of his bald head. 'You've *done* it.'

Barrett looked downhearted for someone who had saved the world. 'Maybe. I'm afraid we don't have much time.'

'What do you mean?' Austin said.

'After our meeting, I listened to the phone conversations transmitted by the electronic bug you planted on Gant's estate. He and Margrave talked. They've left the country by now.'

'Damn,' Austin said. 'Where did they go?'

'I don't know. Margrave never got around to telling me the plans for the final phase. But it's not where I'm worried about, but *what*. I think they're about to put their plans for a polar reversal into effect.'

'Any estimate on how long we have?'

'Hard to tell,' Barrett said. 'The target location is in the South Atlantic. I wasn't in on the final discussions, so I don't know the exact spot. Once they're on-site, it's only a matter of hours before they pull the switch.'

Austin handed the napkin back to Barrett. 'Can this equation be translated into something we can use to actually neutralize the reversal?'

'Sure. The same way $E = mc^2$ was translated into the Bomb and nuclear power. All you need are the resources and the time.'

'You'll get all the resources you need. How long will you need to build something that will do the job?'

'I'll need help. I provided the engineering and made the scale model for the trigger device, but others worked on the actual construction.'

'I'll get you help. How long?'

Barrett gave him a bleak smile. 'Seventy-two hours. *Maybe.*'

'I think I heard you say thirty-six,' Austin said. 'How big will this device be?'

'*Really* big,' Barrett said. 'You saw the setup on the transmitter ship.'

'Ouch,' Austin said. His unshakable confidence wavered for a second, but his agile mind was already cranking into gear. 'What do you do with this thing once you get it built?'

'It has to transmit electromagnetic waves covering roughly the same area as the polar shift.' He shook his head. 'We're going to have to figure out how to transport the neutralizer to the target area. Damn. I feel so responsible for this whole mess.'

Despite Barrett's biker appearance, he had a fragile psyche. Austin saw that guilt was tearing the brilliant computer whiz apart, and if that happened he would be of no use.

'Then I can't think of anyone who would be better at cleaning it up. Leave the transportation to me. I've got an idea that might work.'

He rose from his chair and put some bills down on the table for the beers. As they left the tavern, Austin saw Spider head toward his motorcycle and said, 'Where are you going?'

'To ride my bike.'

'I'll have someone pick it up,' Austin said, taking him by the arm. 'Too dangerous.'

Karla grabbed Barrett by the other arm, and they steered him to the Jeep. On the way back to Washington, Austin got on his cell phone, called Zavala and said he had an important job for him to do.

'I'll get right on it,' Zavala said after hearing the details. 'I talked to the Trouts. Good news. They traced the transmitter ship to Rio via satellite and are on their way.'

Less than an hour later, Austin pulled into the NUMA parking garage with Barrett and Karla and they took the elevator to the fourth floor. The corridors were silent and dark except for a shaft of light coming from the study next to the conference room. Zavala had brought Hibbet in as Austin had requested.

Austin said, 'Thanks for coming, Alan. Sorry for yanking you here a second time, but we need your help.'

'I meant it when I told you to call night or day if you needed me. Is there anything new since we talked the last time?'

'We've confirmed that the whirlpool and giant waves were side effects of an experiment in causing a polar

387

reversal. And that the magnetic reversal could trigger a geologic reversal with catastrophic implications for the world.'

Hibbet's face turned ashen. 'Is there any way to stop this from happening?'

Austin's lips tightened in a thin smile. 'I'm hoping that you can tell us.'

'Me? I don't understand.'

'This is Spider Barrett,' Austin said. 'He designed the mechanism to trigger a polar reversal.'

Hibbet glanced at the sad-faced Barrett and his tattooed head. He'd been around long enough to know that the sciences attracted their share of oddballs. He extended his hand. 'Brilliant work.'

Barrett beamed at the professional recognition. 'Thanks.'

Austin sensed an instant synergy between the two men. 'We want you to work with Spider, Joe and Karla to build an antenna capable of neutralizing the low-level electromagnetic waves that are being used to create a polar shift.'

'Building the antenna won't be a problem. It's nothing but metal and wire. But you could use it to hang laundry, for all the good it would do without the correct frequencies that would act to buffer those being used to stir things up.'

Karla smiled and slipped a folded sheet of paper from her blouse. Using infinite care, she unfolded the paper and slid it across the table to Hibbet. He picked the napkin up and frowned as he read the equation written on it. Then the light of understanding dawned in his eyes.

'Where did you get this?' he said in a whisper.

'My grandfather,' Karla said.

'Karla's grandfather was Lazlo Kovacs,' Austin said. 'He encoded his work before he passed it down. Thanks to

Spider, we've figured it out. Now that we've done all the hard work, can you build us an antenna?'

'Yes,' Hibbet said. 'At least, I *think* I can.'

'That's good enough for us. Tell us what you need. You've got all the resources of the US government behind you.'

Hibbet laughed and shook his head. 'That's a lot better than dealing with the NUMA bean counters. You don't know the trouble I've had trying to buy experimental equipment.' He paused in thought. 'Even if I can whip something together, we'll still need a platform to carry it to where it would do the most good.'

'How big would this contraption be?' Austin said.

'*Big,*' Hibbet said. 'Then you'd need the generators to power the antenna. And a way to transport something that weighs tons.'

'That's the bad news,' Austin said.

'What's the good news?' asked Hibbet.

Austin grinned. 'Necessity is the mother of invention.'

The phone rang just then and Austin picked it up. Pitt must have pulled some major strings. The Pentagon was sending a car over to pick him up.

The earth seemed to be on fire in a hundred different places. Volcanoes erupted like a virulent disease, spewing forth huge, glowing lava fields whose smoke cast a thick pall over the planet. Wind storms of unimaginable power whipped the massive cloud into twisting vortices that ranged across continents. Tsunamis slammed into the North American coastline on the east and the west and created a narrow continent squeezed by two angry oceans.

Then the image of the ravaged planet disappeared. The large screen in the Pentagon screening room went blank.

Lights that had been dimmed for the presentation went back on, to reveal Austin and the stunned faces of a dozen or so military brass and political people who were sitting around a long conference table.

'The computer simulation you just saw was prepared by Dr Paul Trout, a computer graphics expert at NUMA,' Austin said. 'It presents a reasonably accurate picture of the consequences of a geologic polar shift.'

A four-star general sitting across from Austin said, 'I would be the first to admit that was a frightening picture, if it's true. But as you say, it's a computer simulation, and could just as well be based on imagination as fact.'

'I wish it *were* imagination, General. We didn't have time to prepare a written summary, so you'll have to bear with me while I lay out the main points of what we're dealing with here. The first link in the chain of events that led to this meeting was forged more than sixty years ago with the work of a brilliant electrical engineer named Lazlo Kovacs.'

For more than an hour, Austin laid out the timeline, touching on Tesla, Kovacs's escape from East Prussia and the electromagnetic warfare experiments conducted by the US and the Soviets. He described his meeting with Barrett, the man who had translated the theorems into reality, the ship-sinking ocean disturbances and the plans to initiate a polar shift. Austin was aware of the fantastic nature of his story, so he left out a few details. Had he not seen them with his eyes he would never have believed in the existence of dwarf mammoths in a crystal city locked in an ancient volcano.

Even without the more unbelievable details, he faced a wall of skepticism. Austin made his case with the skill of a powerhouse attorney talking to a jury, but he knew he would be peppered with questions. An assistant secretary representing the Department of Defense cut Austin short when he was describing Jordan Gant's involvement with Margrave.

'You'll have to excuse me if I find it hard to believe that the head of a nonprofit organization and the billionaire owner of a respected software company are in cahoots to cause this so-called polar shift over some vague neo-anarchist cause.'

'You can argue about specifics,' Austin said, 'but this is far from a vague cause. Lucifer used the bright lights of Broadway to send its message to the world and shut down New York City as a warning. I think 9/11 proved that you ignore seemingly lunatic warnings at your peril.'

'Where are these so-called transmitter ships?' asked a naval officer.

'Rio de Janeiro,' Austin replied.

'You said there were four ships earlier but one sank?'

'That's right. We assumed that a replacement ship would be built, but we found no sign of it, so we're assuming they're going ahead with the trio.'

'This should be a slam dunk,' the assistant secretary said. 'I suggest we send the closest submarine to keep track of these ships, and if they engage in suspicious behavior we sink them.'

'What about diplomatic considerations?' the four-star general asked. 'Shoot first and ask questions later on the high seas?'

'It would be no different than shooting down a civilian airliner targeting the White House or Congress,' the secretary said. 'Can we do it?' he asked the naval officer.

'The navy likes a challenge,' he said.

'Then that's the plan. I'll run it by the secretary of defense and we can get the ball rolling. He'll brief the president when he gets back tomorrow.' He turned to Austin. 'Thanks for bringing this to our attention.'

'I'm not through,' Austin said. 'There's reason to believe we have something that will neutralize the polar shift. We may have found an antidote.'

Every eye in the room stared at him.

'What sort of antidote?' the general asked more out of politeness than interest.

'It's a set of electromagnetic frequencies that we think will counter the polar reversal.'

'How do you plan to administer this "antidote"?' the assistant secretary said. 'With a big spoon?'

'I've got a few ideas.'

'The only antidote I'd like to use is a torpedo right up their butt,' the naval officer said.

Everyone in the room except for Austin roared with laughter.

'Don't mean to be impolite,' the assistant secretary said. 'Why don't you work your ideas into a report and get it to my secretary.'

The meeting was over. As Austin was ushered through the labyrinth of corridors, he remembered his meeting with Gant, and his impression that he was not someone whose duplicity should be underestimated.

Slam dunk, my ass, he thought.

39

The Trouts had booked a beachside hotel room with a balcony that overlooked the harbor and offered an unimpeded view of the distant shipping docks. Since arriving in Rio, they had taken turns sitting on the balcony watching the transmitter ships.

Trout brought Gamay a cold glass of orange juice and pulled up a chair beside her. 'Anything happening?'

Gamay raised the binoculars to her eyes and studied a long shipping dock on the other side of the harbor. 'The transmitter ships haven't moved an inch since we got here.'

Trout borrowed the binoculars and inspected three ships tied up parallel to the dock.

'Did you notice that the liner is gone?'

'It was there yesterday. They must have left before we got up this morning.'

Gamay had wondered what a passenger ship was doing in a cargo vessel area. They had read the name painted on the stern: *Polar Adventure*. But neither one of them had given the vessel much thought. They had been more interested in the three cargo ships, which were named *Polaris I, II* and *III*, after the northern pole star.

'I think we should take a closer look,' Paul said.

'My thoughts exactly. I'm about ready to go for a ride.'

Minutes later, they were driving along the edge of the harbor. The resort hotels thinned out, and the neighborhood they were passing through became more commercial. Eventually, they came to a concentration of warehouses, shipping company offices and maritime buildings. They passed several containerships, and went by the empty berth formerly occupied by the ocean liner. A guardhouse had been set up near the three vessels they had seen from the hotel.

Standing outside the structure was a beefy guard who carried a side arm and a rifle. He was smoking a cigarette and talking to a longshoreman. Paul kept the car at the same speed so he wouldn't attract attention, but he drove slowly enough for Gamay to give the ships a quick but thorough inspection.

'Any other guards?' Trout said.

'Only the one, that I could see. There may be more on board.'

'Maybe not. They wouldn't want to attract attention by having too many security guys hanging around. This could be a golden opportunity to snoop around.'

'Yes, but he had a very big gun. How do you propose to get past that?'

Trout gave Gamay a lopsided grin. 'I was thinking that a beautiful woman could provide a, uh, diversion.'

'Here we go again. *Cherchez la femme*. The oldest trick in the book. Do you think he'd fall for a ruse like that?'

'You're kidding,' Trout said with a chuckle. 'We're talking about a hot-blooded Latin male.'

'Unfortunately,' Gamay said with a sigh, 'I think that you're right. Okay, I'll do my Mata Hari impression, but you're buying dinner.'

A half hour later, they were back in their hotel room. Paul mixed a couple of cool rum drinks, and they sat on the balcony sipping from their glasses and taking turns watching the ships through binoculars until the sun went down.

After a dinner sent up by room service, Gamay took a

shower, doused herself with perfume and slipped into a lowcut red dress. Beautiful women abound in Rio, but Gamay drew every male eye in the lobby when she and Trout crossed to the hotel entrance.

The shipping dock had undergone a stark personality change. The trucks, longshoremen and stevedores had left for the day, and the dock area had developed a rank, sinister atmosphere. Unevenly spaced pole lamps cast yellow puddles of light that were diffused by a fog that had moved in from the harbor. A foghorn moaned in the distance.

Gamay drove past the empty berth formerly occupied by the *Polar Adventure* and pulled the car over and parked under a lamppost near the guardhouse. She got out of the car, stood in the light and took a swig from a bottle of rum. With noisy fanfare, she raised the hood and poked her head underneath. Then, swearing loudly in Spanish, she kicked the fender, looked around and waved at the guard. Weaving as she walked, she made her way over to the guardhouse.

The guard was a dark-complexioned, muscular man with an expression of bored suspicion on his flat-featured face. Gamay spoke perfect Spanish, but for the benefit of the guard she slurred her words. She said her stupid car had stalled, and asked him to come take a look. He glanced at the car, which was partially obscured by the shadows, hesitating.

'Don't tell me you're afraid of me with that big gun you're carrying.'

She staggered and seemed to fall before she grabbed the guard's shoulder and gave him a blast of rum-soaked breath. The appeal of a sexy, drunk woman and the veiled insult to his manhood did the trick. He laughed lustily and put his arm around her shoulder. Gamay laughed too, and they made their way back to the car.

'I think they gypped me and there's no engine,' she said, placing her hands on her hips.

She was gambling that he would follow the male instinct to stick his head under the car hood. When he did, Trout stepped out of the shadows, tapped him on the shoulder, then dropped the guard with a powerful right cross. With Gamay's help, they gagged and tied the dazed guard with towels borrowed from the hotel, took his guns and stuffed him in the backseat of the car.

Trout put the man's cap on his head, slipped a flashlight into his windbreaker pocket and tucked the pistol in his belt. 'Call in the cavalry if I'm not back in twenty minutes.'

Gamay hefted the rifle. 'Be careful,' she said, giving him a peck on the cheek. 'You're *looking* at the cavalry.'

Trout would rather have Gamay at his back than a hundred John Waynes. She was an expert marksman, and anyone caught in her sights would have a short life. He swiftly climbed to the top of the gangway and looked around the deck. The fog that hung over the ship and dampened the deck lights would make him less visible, but it would also provide cover for any guards watching the deck.

He had seen the photos Austin and Zavala had taken of the ship exhumed by the whirlpool and had a general idea of the layout. He blindly navigated his way through the murk and managed to find the superstructure without slamming face-first into it. He felt his way along the exterior until his groping fingers came to a door. He stepped into a darkened space and flicked on the flashlight he had borrowed from the guard. A companionway led to a deck below.

Clutching the guard's pistol in his free hand, he descended the stairs and followed a maze of corridors. At the end of one passageway, he paused and put his ear against a metal door, then tried the handle. The door was unlocked. He opened it and stepped through.

His footsteps echoed as he slowly made his way to a railing and saw that he was standing on a balcony. He was in a cavernous space that must be the generator room Austin and Zavala had described. He flashed his light around and realized why there was only one man guarding the ships. There was nothing to guard. The room was empty.

Trout made his way back to the main deck. Austin had talked about a shaft that ran down through the hull from the deck to the water. He finally found it, along with the framework around the rectangular opening. But there was no sign of the cone-shaped structure. The ship seemed to have been stripped clean. He pondered the idea of checking out the control room, but decided that there wasn't time. Gamay would storm the ship in search of Trout if he didn't come back when promised. He headed for the gangway.

The guard had regained consciousness, and Gamay had to threaten him with his gun to quiet him down, but other than that there had been no incident.

'What did you find?' she said.

'*Nothing.* And that's what's so interesting. My guess is that the other ships are stripped down too.'

They dragged the guard from the car and left him in the shadows. He had started struggling against his makeshift bindings. With a little more effort, he would be able to free himself. About a hundred feet from the guardhouse, they tossed his guns into the harbor. There was little chance that he would raise the alarm once he got free. His employers would not be pleased if they learned he had fallen down on the job. He would have enough trouble explaining what happened to his weapons.

On the drive back to the hotel, Trout described his search of the ship and the surprising results.

'But *why*? And what did they do with all that stuff?'

Trout shook his head, picked up his cell phone and punched out a number from the directory.

'We'll let Kurt figure that one out.'

40

Austin reached into his desk drawer, extracted a dart from a board game and had his hand poised to throw it at the chart of the Atlantic Ocean pinned to the wall when the telephone rang. He picked up the receiver. It was Paul Trout calling from Rio.

'Hope I'm not interrupting anything important,' Trout said.

'Not at all. I was bringing my scientific training to bear on a knotty puzzle. How's the girl from Ipanema?' Austin said.

'Gamay is fine. But there's something strange going on with the transmitter ships. I snuck on board one a few minutes ago. It's been stripped of its turbines and the electromagnetic antenna. I suspect someone has done a similar housecleaning with the other ships.'

'Empty?' Austin raced through the possibilities in his mind. 'They must have done the housecleaning when the ships were in the Mississippi boatyard.'

'We should have figured that something funny was going on. The ships are just sitting there, tied up to the dock. No preparations. Nothing to indicate that they're going to sea anytime soon. Only one ship has left the dock since we've been here, and that was an ocean liner.'

Austin was deep in thought and only half listening to Trout. 'What's that you said about a liner?'

'The *Polar Adventure*. It was tied up next to the transmitter ships, but it left earlier today. Is it important?'

'Maybe. Joe says a liner left the shipyard in Mississippi about the same time as the transmitters.'

'Wow! Think this is the same vessel we saw?'

'It's possible,' Austin said. 'They move the transmitters into the liner. Then, while we're watching the decoys, the liner sneaks away with the payload in broad daylight. So much for the navy's plans to tail the ships with a submarine.'

'Classic "bait and switch" operation. Damned clever.'

'How long since the liner left port?'

'It was gone this morning.'

Austin did a quick mental computation. 'They could be hundreds of miles out to sea by now. That's a jackrabbit start.'

'What do you want us to do?'

'Stay put for now, and keep an eye on the ships in case their owners have another card up their sleeve.'

Austin clicked off. He was angry with himself for not anticipating that anyone intelligent enough to carry out a polar reversal would do everything possible to throw pursuers off their trail. He turned his attention back to the chart. It was a big ocean. With every passing minute, the liner came closer to losing itself in hundreds of square miles of open sea. He thought about calling the Pentagon with the news from Trout, but he was in no mood to waste his breath debating with the assistant defense secretary.

Sandecker might be more successful, but even he would have to deal with the Pentagon bureaucracy, and there was simply no time. Screw 'em, Austin thought. If the world was going to end, he would rather have the responsibility on his shoulders than those of an anonymous government functionary with an attitude. This was going to be a NUMA deal, through and through.

Ten minutes later, he was in a NUMA vehicle driving

through the quiet streets of Washington. He took the highway to Washington National Airport, where the guard at the gate of a restricted area checked his ID and directed Austin to a hanger in a far corner of the airfield. He could see the glow of lights, and easily made his way to where a Boeing 747 jumbo jet was parked on the tarmac.

Floodlights set up on stands ringed the huge plane and turned night into day. The plane was surrounded by drums of electrical cable and stacks of aluminum and steel. Workers crawled in and out of the plane like ants on a candy bar.

Zavala sat under the lofty tail of the plane at a makeshift table assembled from a sheet of plywood and a couple of sawhorses. He was going over blueprints with a man dressed in coveralls. He excused himself when he saw Austin and came over to greet him.

'It's not as bad as it looks,' he said. He had to raise his voice to be heard above the noise.

Austin glanced around and was relieved to see a semblance of order in what at first seemed to be total chaos.

'How long before the bird is ready to fly?' Austin said.

'We've had a few glitches, but all the stuff is here. It's mostly a matter of fitting everything in and connecting it. Seventy-two hours should do it.'

'How about tomorrow morning?' Austin said.

Zavala smiled. 'You should get a slot on Comedy Central.'

'Unfortunately, there's nothing comic about the news I just received from Paul.' He told Zavala about the missing liner. 'Could you assemble the rest of the setup while we're in the air?'

Zavala winced. 'Possible, but not advisable. It would be like trying to stuff a sausage on the run.'

'What if there's no choice but to try?'

Zavala looked at the hectic activity and scratched his head. 'I never could resist a juicy sausage. C'mon while I break the bad news to my right-hand man.'

The man Zavala had been reviewing blueprints with was Drew Wheeler, an amiable Virginian in his forties who was a NUMA specialist in the logistics of moving big payloads around the world. Austin had worked with Drew on a few projects where heavy equipment was needed in a hurry. Wheeler's tendency to think things through, as if he were mentally chewing on a plug of tobacco, could drive people who worked with him to distraction. But they soon learned that he had a knack for laying out complex plans in his head so they could be executed seamlessly.

Austin asked how things were going and got the typical Wheeler response. He cocked an elbow on one hip and squinted at the plane from under his eyebrows like a farmer trying to figure out how to remove a tree trunk from a field. 'Well,' he said, pausing before he answered. 'Things are going okay.'

'Are they okay enough to get this plane off the ground tomorrow morning?'

Wheeler chewed the question over for a moment before he replied. 'What time tomorrow morning?'

'As soon as you can make it.'

Wheeler nodded. 'I'll see what I can do.'

He ambled back to the plane as if out for a casual walk. Austin wasn't fooled. 'I'll bet you a bottle of Pancho Villa tequila that Drew's already figured out how to do this.'

'I know him well enough to recognize that's a sucker bet,' Zavala said.

'A wise decision. Where did you get the plane?'

'You'd be surprised what you can lease these days if you've got deep pockets. It's the 200F freighter, a modified version of the passenger 747. It's got a capacity of nearly 250 thousand pounds. The main problem was to get all the hardware you see lying around into the plane without having to crack it open like a can of sardines. We tossed the problem around awhile with Hibbet and Barrett,' Zavala said. 'I had it in my mind that we'd have to go with massive generators like the ones we saw on the transmitter ship. But Barrett said it wasn't necessary. We could use smaller generators, just more of them.'

'What about the coil?' Austin said.

'That gave us the biggest headache. I'll show you what we did.'

Zavala led the way to the nose of the giant plane. Two people in coveralls were bent over a dishlike structure set up on a platform. Al Hibbet smiled when he saw Austin and Zavala walking in his direction.

'Hello, Al,' Austin said. 'Having fun yet?'

'The most fun I can remember since I got an electric motor for my Tinkertoy set. Karla has been a big help.'

The other worker looked up and revealed Karla's smiling face under a baseball cap. 'What the professor means is that I'm a great help holding a screwdriver.'

'Not at all,' Hibbet said. 'Karla may not have a technical background, but she has an instinct for solving problems. She has obviously inherited her grandfather's genes.'

'Glad to hear you're working well together,' Austin said. 'Joe said you had a problem with the coil.'

'That's right,' Hibbet said. 'In the transmitter ships, they dangled the antenna below the ship. We were going to sling it under the fuselage.'

'Would that be a problem during takeoff?'

'You hit on the problem. This is the radome for the newly designed antenna. I got the idea from some of the setups

I've seen on early-warning aircraft. It was Karla's suggestion to redesign the cone to fit into the dome.'

'I used to have guppies in my fish tank,' Karla said. 'They have a pouch under their chin that gave me the idea.'

Hibbet whipped a plastic covering off a metal-and-wire construction about twenty feet across. The circular framework that sat in a wooden cradle was shaped like an inverted coolie hat. It was flat on top, with shallow sides coming to a point on the bottom.

'Ingenious,' Austin said. 'It looks like a squashed-down version of the cone antenna. Will it work as well?'

'*Better*, I hope,' Hibbet said.

'That's good, because we've revised our schedule. We need everything ready to fly out by tomorrow morning. Can you assemble the final stages while we're in the air?'

Hibbet pinched his chin. 'Yes,' he said after a moment. 'It's not the ideal way to do something this complex. We won't even have a chance to test the turbines. But we can start going down the punch list as soon as we mount the antenna and dome. We'd better ask Barrett for his opinion.'

They climbed a gangway into the 747's vast interior. A line of sixteen squat steel cylinders, spaced evenly apart, ran nearly the entire 230-foot length of the airplane's cargo space. A network of cables connected the cylinders and snaked off in dozens of different directions. Barrett was kneeling over a cable between two of the cylinders.

He saw Austin and the others and got up to greet them.

Austin glanced around at the complex arrangement taking up a good part of the plane's enormous interior. 'Looks like you've got enough power capacity to light up the city of New York.'

'Almost,' Barrett said. 'It was a bit of a problem hooking

up the power source, but we finally jury-rigged a system that should work okay.'

'I'm more curious about the dynamos. Where did you get so many at such short notice?'

'Special order from NUMA,' Zavala said. 'They were going to go into some new ships before I borrowed them temporarily.'

'New power source. New antenna. Is it all going to come together?'

'I think so,' Barrett said. 'That is, I'm ninety-nine percent sure, according to the computer models I've done.'

Austin shook his head. 'It's that *one* percent that worries me. Can we do it all by tomorrow morning?'

Barrett chuckled, thinking Austin was joking. Then he noticed the serious expression in Austin's eyes. 'Something going on?'

Austin relayed Trout's account of the mysterious liner.

Barrett slammed his fist into his palm. 'I told Tris months ago about my idea of using a single ship to concentrate the transmission. I even gave him the plans for the switch. He said it would take too much time. Guess I shouldn't be surprised he was lying again.'

'About that schedule?' Austin said.

Barrett's eyes blazed with anger. 'We'll be ready,' he said.

Leaving Barrett to his work, Austin and the others climbed back down the plane's gangway. Austin asked where he could pitch in. Zavala ticked off a short list of last-minute supplies. Austin walked away from the activity to where it was quieter and made his phone calls. In every instance, he was told that the material would be delivered quickly. He was walking back to the plane when he saw that Karla had followed him. She had evidently been watching as he made the calls.

'I've got a favor to ask,' she said. 'I want to go on the plane.'

'This is the part where the hero says, "It could be dangerous,"' Austin said.

'I know. But it was also dangerous back on Ivory Island.'

Austin hesitated.

'Besides,' Karla said. 'What could be more risky than riding with you in a Stanley Steamer?'

Austin would have to tie Karla up to keep her from boarding the plane. He smiled and said, 'Neither of us is going anywhere unless we get back to work.'

She threw her arms around him and planted a warm kiss on his lips. Austin vowed to devote more time to pleasure after this job was done.

As they made their way back to the plane, a car pulled up. A tall figure got out from behind the steering wheel and limped toward them. It was Schroeder.

'What are you doing here?' Karla said.

'I'm more curious about how you got past the gate,' Austin said.

'The usual formula. A combination of bravado and false identification.'

'You're supposed to be resting in a hospital bed,' Karla scolded.

'A hospital is not the same as a prison,' Schroeder said. 'They let you go if you sign a paper. Do you think I could stay in bed knowing you were doing this?' He gazed with wonderment at the plane under its bright lights. 'Ingenious. Do you really think you can neutralize the reversal from the air?'

'We're going to try,' Karla said.

'*We?* You're not going on this mission? It might be dangerous.'

'You sound like Kurt. I'll tell you the same thing I told him. My family is responsible for this mess. It's my responsibility to help clean it up.'

Schroeder laughed. 'You're Lazlo's granddaughter, without doubt. Stubborn, just like him.' He turned to Austin. 'Take good care of her.'

'I promise,' Austin said.

Schroeder glanced at the bustling activity in and around the plane. 'When do you expect to leave?'

'Tomorrow morning,' Austin said.

'This is one old dinosaur who knows when he's extinct,' Schroeder said. 'I'll be at the hospital waiting for your call. Good luck.' He embraced Karla, shook hands with Austin and hobbled back to his car. They watched the car's taillights until they were out of sight, then Austin turned to Karla.

'We've got lots of work to do.'

She nodded. Walking arm in arm, they made their way toward the huge aircraft.

While Austin's NUMA crew was in a frantic race to achieve the impossible, Tris Margrave was having no doubts about the imminent success of his project. Doubt was something foreign to him, and would never have entered his mind.

As the *Polar Adventure* plowed through the South Atlantic, he sat in his comfortable ergonomic chair behind a control panel built into the forward observation platform. His long fingers played over the controls like an organist in a great cathedral. He had started the dynamos as soon as the ship left port. Each generator was represented on the large computer monitor by a red symbol and number, which meant that it was active at a low level.

Red lines ran from the dynamos to the image of a cone. The cone was green except for its red point, indicating that a minimum amount of power was flowing into the huge coil lodged deep in the ship's hold. Margrave thought of it as the equivalent of idling a car motor.

On another screen, the console displayed a cutaway diagram of the earth that showed its layers. Special sensors in the ship's hull would be able to detect the electromagnetic penetration and the extent of ripple effect.

Gant had been on a tour of the ship, talking with his security people. Ever the perfectionist, Gant wanted to be sure that when Margrave had outlived his usefulness he would be quickly disposed of. As he entered the observation platform, Gant smiled and said, 'Not much longer?'

Margrave glanced at his GPS. 'We'll be on target in the morning. It will take another hour to position the ship and deploy the coil. The sea is calm, so it might not be that long.'

Gant went over to the bar and poured two tall flutes of champagne. He gave one glass to Margrave.

'A toast would be appropriate.'

'Here's to the defeat of the Elites,' Margrave said. 'To a new world.'

Gant raised his glass. 'And new world order.'

41

Zavala left the 747's cockpit and made his way back to the plane's abbreviated passenger section where Austin was working on a laptop computer. Zavala was smiling as if he had heard a joke.

'Pilots are funny people,' Zavala said with a shake of his head. 'The cockpit crew would be pleased if you could tell them where to fly the plane.'

'I'll have a definite position soon,' Austin said. 'For now, you can tell them to head in the general direction of the mid–South Atlantic.'

'That narrows it down,' Zavala said.

'This is the area we're looking at.' Austin pointed to the glowing computer screen. 'That's a NASA diagram showing data collected by the ROSAT spacecraft. That blob you see extending from Brazil to South Africa is our hunting ground, the South Atlantic Anomaly.' He tapped the keyboard and zoomed in on a cluster of rectangles. 'This area has the most pronounced dip in the magnetosphere.'

'Which means it would be the logical point to start a polar shift,' Zavala said.

'Yes and no. Here's where I think we should go.' He tapped the screen at a different location. 'The earth's crust is thinner here, allowing for maximum penetration with the Kovacs waves.'

Zavala puffed his cheeks out. 'That's still a lot of ocean to cover. A couple of hundred square miles at least.'

'It's a start,' Austin said.

He cocked his ear at the sound of an electrical hum coming from the cargo section. A moment later, Karla and Barrett came through the door. Karla's golden hair was in straggles, and she had dark circles under her large eyes. Barrett's hands and face were covered with grease.

Austin thought that even in her disheveled state, Karla could put the most pampered fashion model to shame with her graceful beauty. She raised the screwdriver in her hand like the torch on the Statue of Liberty.

'*Ta-dum!*' she said. 'Time for trumpets and drumroll. We're done.'

'The dynamos are all on track and running,' Barrett said.

Barrett had hauled the last cable in less than an hour before, and the plane was airborne within minutes of shutting the door. Al Hibbet had watched with a sad expression as the plane took off. He had wanted to join the mission, but Austin said they needed to leave someone with an intimate knowledge of the mission behind. Just in case.

The humming increased in loudness. Karla acknowledged the congratulations that followed, then stretched out on some empty seats and promptly fell asleep. Austin removed the screwdriver from Karla's fingers and tucked it on the seat beside her.

'Thanks,' Barrett said. 'Now, if you'll excuse me.' Following Karla's example, he yawned and crawled onto the next row of sets where he, too, stretched out and immediately fell asleep.

Austin made a note of the longitude and latitude at the position on his computer, then went up to the cockpit to give the plane's navigator the coordinates. He asked how long before they would be on-site and was told it would be approximately two hours. Austin looked out the cockpit window at the layer of cottony clouds that stretched out as far as the eye could see.

The crew was made up entirely of volunteers who were fully aware that they were flying on a dangerous mission. While the navigator laid out a flight plan, Austin and Zavala returned to the passenger cabin.

'From what you said in the cockpit, we'll arrive on target about the same time as the ship,' Zavala said.

'It's an even tighter squeeze. We'll be in the same neighborhood. When we get there, we'll have to launch a search pattern. I don't know how long it will take to find the transmitter ship.'

'Any delay could be fatal. That low cloud cover won't help.'

'I've been thinking about that. The Trouts reported that they saw a lot of electrical activity in the sky minutes before their boat was sucked into the whirlpool.'

'That's right. And Al said there were celestial fireworks when the US and the Soviets were fooling around with electromagnetic warfare based on the Kovacs Theorems.'

'Then there's every reason to think that we'll see the same phenomenon when Margrave and Gant gear up their zapper. I think we should be looking at the *sky* rather than the sea. The clouds might actually *help* us find the ship.'

'Brilliant! I'll alert the crew to look for fireworks.'

Austin reluctantly awakened Karla and Barrett. He gave them a few minutes to rub the sleep out of their eyes. As the plane sped toward the South Atlantic Anomaly, he brought them up to date on the situation. They agreed to split up when the time came, with Karla on one side of the plane, Barrett on the other. Austin would alternate back and forth and serve as liaison with Zavala, who would keep watch from the cockpit.

Zavala's voice came over the speakers. He said the plane would pass over the outer limits of the search area in fifteen minutes. Austin could feel the growing tension in the cabin. The atmosphere grew even tenser when Zavala announced that they were in the hot zone. They took up their positions at the aircraft's windows. Ten minutes passed, then twenty. Austin moved back and forth across the wide cabin, offering encouragement. It was hard to believe that a vast ocean lay below the thick layer of clouds.

Austin had suggested that the plane fly a series of parallel runs back and forth across the search area. It was the same lawn-mower pattern Austin would have used to search for a lost ship and would cover many square miles in a comparatively short time. They finished one run, then made another and were on their third when Austin began to wonder if he had made a mistake. He was checking his watch every few seconds.

The plane had turned to make another run when Karla called out, 'I see something. Around three o'clock.'

Austin and Barrett scrambled across the cabin to the other side of the plane and peered through the windows. The sun was low in the sky and its slanting rays had created blue shadows in the cloud cover. But off to the right, the sky pulsated with a golden-white radiance that was similar to the glow a thunderstorm would produce in the clouds. Austin grabbed a microphone connected to the cockpit. Zavala replied over the speakers that he had seen the glow in the clouds as well.

The plane banked into a turn and, like a moth attracted to a flame, began its long glide toward the light that bubbled in the distance like a giant witch's cauldron.

42

With time short, it had been necessary to opt for simplicity in setting up the control panel in the spacious cargo section. The console was a flat board that rested on supports raising it to waist level. The layout was deliberately uncomplicated, consisting of a main switch that controlled the flow of power to all the dynamos. Various dials and gauges kept tabs on different parts of the operating system.

Zavala's voice came over the speakers. 'We're going into the clouds.'

Austin felt a prickling on his scalp and his hair stood on end, not because of fear, but from the sudden electrical charge that saturated the air. Karla's long blond tresses were standing on end like the hair on the Bride of Frankenstein. She reached up and patted her hair down, with limited success. With his shaved scalp, Barrett had no such problem, although the spider tattoo had goose bumps.

The electrical show was only beginning. Every surface of the cargo section began to glow an electrical blue like the Saint Elmo's fire that sailors used to see dancing in the rigging of their sailing ships. The plane's interior lights blinked on and off, as if a child were playing with the switch. Then the lights went out completely.

Stroboscopic flashes from outside lit up the rows of windows and illuminated the bewildered faces in the cargo section like dancers in a disco. The plane seemed to be in the midst of a lightning storm. But there was no thunder, only the muted roar of the jet engines. The relative silence heightened the eeriness of the scene.

The intercom must have operated on a separate system, because Zavala's voice crackled over the speakers. His message was brief and to the point:

'We've lost the cockpit instruments.'

A second later, he relayed a message that was even more terrifying. 'Oh hell, the controls are gone too.'

Austin knew that a plane the size of a 747 wouldn't go into an instantaneous dive, but it wasn't built to soar on the updrafts like a glider. Once the aircraft discovered it was on its own, it would lapse into a tumble that would rip its wings off. He put his arm protectively around Karla's shoulders.

Something was happening in the cargo area. The electrical display seemed less brilliant. The cold fire playing along the walls and ceiling seemed to be dying down. Dark spots appeared in the shimmer and dampened the ghostly blue light. There was one last, brilliant burp of radiance. The interior lights blinked on.

A second later, Zavala's voice came over the speaker with a welcome announcement:

'The instruments and controls are back on,' he reported.

Austin removed his arm from around Karla's shoulders and went over to check the control panel. He was worried that the surge of static electricity that had put on such a dramatic light display might have burned out the switches. To his relief, everything was in order.

Karla had noticed a change in the light coming through the window and went to investigate. She pressed her nose against the Plexiglas and called the others over. Austin peered out a window and saw that they were through the overcast. Blue ocean was visible through the vaporous tatters of low-lying clouds. A flickering brilliance from

414

above caught his eye. Instead of the underside of the cloud cover, he saw an aurora of swirling whites, blues and purple that formed a luminous canopy. The very heavens seemed on fire; it was as if a hundred lightning storms were discharging simultaneous bolts.

The plane had made it through the electrical barrier in one piece, but they weren't out of the woods yet. Although the electrical assault was fading, the farther they dropped below the clouds, the more the plane was being buffeted by gut-wrenching turbulence. Power-packed winds slammed into the 747 from every direction. Despite its massive size, the plane pitched and yawed like a kite on a string.

The buffeting was only a softening up. The plane was slammed like a boxer on the ropes by a series of head-on wind gusts. The cargo space reverberated with loud bangs as the winds hammered the plane as if it were rolling along a road full of deep potholes. Just as it seemed that another pounding would pop every rivet in the plane, the blows became less violent and less frequent. Then they stopped completely.

'Are you all right back there?' Zavala said.

'We're fine, but you need a new set of shock absorbers.'

'I need a new set of *teeth*,' Zavala said.

'Tell the pilot that was a nice save. Are the wings still attached?'

'He says thanks, and who needs wings anyhow?'

'That's reassuring. Can you see the ship?'

'Not yet. Still a few clouds.' There was a pause, and when Zavala's voice came back on Austin could hear the excitement in it. 'Look to the port side, Kurt. Around nine o'clock.'

Austin looked out the window and saw the liner below. The ship looked like a toy boat in the ocean. There was no wake, which confirmed what Austin already knew from the turbulence and light show the plane had encountered. The ship was stationary, and the electromagnetic assault had begun.

The ship was surrounded by a ring of waves that were moving away from the vessel in an expanding circle. Although it was hard to judge the size of the waves, the fact that their foamy crests were so clearly visible at the altitude the plane was flying meant that the seas were monstrous.

Austin got on the intercom and asked the pilot to level out at ten thousand feet and to circle the ship, dropping one thousand feet with each circuit. He turned to Barrett, who was standing at the control panel, and told him to get ready. The scientist nodded and began to increase the power to the dynamos. An electrical hum like a thousand bee hives filled the plane's interior.

Something was burning. Austin looked down the length of the cargo space and saw a cloud of purple smoke and sparks coming from one of the dynamos. He yelled at Barrett to kill the power, and, with Karla right behind him, he dashed down the long length of the plane.

Barrett had seen the gauge signifying a problem and had already hit the kill switch. Austin found the source of the sparks was a lead into one of the dynamos. The connection had come loose while the plane was being bounced around by the violent turbulence.

He examined the connection for damage, found nothing serious and quickly reconnected the cable. Austin yelled at Barrett to power up. The humming of the bees began, and rose to a pitch where it drowned out the roar of the jet engines. Karla had joined Barrett at the control panel. Austin stood near the intercom where he could keep in close touch with the cockpit.

'How does it look?' Austin asked.

Barrett's eyes swept over the control panel and he smiled. 'Everything is on track.'

Austin gave him the thumbs-up, and called to Zavala, 'What's our altitude?'

'Eight thousand feet.'

'Good. Bring her down to four thousand, and then make a level pass directly over the ship. Let me know when we're starting the approach to the target.'

'Aye, aye, sir.'

As the plane dropped lower, the pilot had to contend with an unexpected burst of turbulence. He got the plane back on an even keel with some skillful flying. Zavala called to say that they were making their approach to the ship.

Austin called out to Barrett to give it the juice. He hesitated with his hand over the power switch, and for a second Austin thought he hadn't understood. Then Barrett stepped aside and put Karla's hand on the switch.

'This is in honor of your grandfather.'

Karla replied with a broad grin and threw the switch. Power flowed into the antenna, where it was converted to pulses of electromagnetic energy. Austin had no precedent or experience to work with, so he was laying down a pattern of energy bursts in much the same way a sub-hunter saturates the ocean with depth charges.

They were over the ship an instant later. Austin ordered the pilot to repeat the procedure, coming in at another angle. The 747 wasn't built for strafing runs, and the big plane seemed to take forever as it banked around in a wide turn and started back to lay down another series of charges.

Again Zavala yelled out the five-hundred-yard mark. Again Karla laid on the power.

Another pass, another barrage of electromagnetic pulses flowed into the sea around the ship.

'How long do we need to do this?' Zavala said.

'Until we run out of fuel, and then some,' Austin said with a steely determination in his voice.

The mood was euphoric on the observation platform of the *Polar Explorer*.

Margrave and Gant gazed up through the glass-paneled ceiling, their faces bathed in the pulsating, multicolored light emanating from the aurora high above the ship. Margrave's strange face never looked more satanic.

'Spectacular!' Gant said in a rare show of emotion.

Margrave stood behind the control consol. He had been gradually accelerating the dynamos to full power, and the console was lit up like a pinball machine.

'The aurora indicates we've reached critical mass,' he said. 'The electromagnetic waves have penetrated the ocean floor. They'll change the electromagnetic flux and nudge the pole over. Keep an eye on the compass for the big flip.'

Gant glanced at the compass dial, and then gazed out one of the big picture windows.

'Something is happening to the sea.'

The ruffled surface of the ocean immediately around the ship had gone flat.

'We're at the epicenter of the polar shift,' Margrave said. 'A ring of giant waves will spin off from around the edge of an expanding circle. There will be some vortices around the perimeter.'

'Glad we're not in the way,' Gant said.

'It would be unfortunate if we were. The area of disturbance is pretty random. That's what sank our transmitter ship. It's like the calm at the eye of a hurricane. We'll be fine here except for a slight mounding of the water.'

Gant stared out at the rising sea. He had never felt so powerful in his entire life.

Austin's mind-set was the opposite of Gant's. He was like a doctor trying to bring a flatlining patient back to life, only in this case the lives of millions lay on the table. He peered out the window as the plane banked for another pass, unable to tell whether the antidote was working or not.

Then he noticed a circular area immediately around the ship where the water seemed to go dull, as if it were being flattened by a helicopter downdraft. He could see striations on the surface of the sea like the grooves made by a strong current. Moments later, the water began moving in an un-mistakable swirl with the ship at its center. Within seconds, the area of disturbed water was at least a mile across, bordered by a ring of foam on its perimeter. As the current's speed picked up, the sea within the circle became lower than the surface around it.

Austin was witnessing the birth of a giant whirlpool.

The *Polar Adventure* only rose around six feet above the surrounding sea-level before it began to settle again.

Gant noticed that a depression seemed to be forming in the ocean around the ship. 'Is this another side effect?' he said.

'No,' Margrave said. His puzzlement changed to concern when the surface became even more radically dish-shaped. White-foamed rips indicated the clash of strong currents. He snatched up the microphone connecting him to the bridge. 'Full engine power. We're sinking into a whirlpool.'

Margrave shut down the dynamos.

'What are you doing?' Gant said.

'Something's not right. There shouldn't be this kind of reaction.'

The ocean hollow was deepening and swirling currents had begun to form, but the ship was under power by then, and moving toward the side of the vortex. Its bow was slightly elevated, and it had to fight against the currents that wanted to drag it sideways, but the ship was making slow headway.

The maelstrom was expanding at the same time, however. Margrave screamed at the bridge to give the engines more power, but the ship seemed destined to lose the race, not really moving from the center of the vortex.

Then the character of the water changed again. The currents weakened, and the surface began to rise back to sea-level. It was mounding again.

'What happened?' Gant said.

'A slight diversion,' Margrave said. He wiped the nervous sweat from his forehead, and he smiled as he again powered up the dynamos.

As the ship rose higher in the air, the water around the vessel began to boil. The ocean liner was twenty feet in the air, then thirty.

'Stop this from happening,' Gant said.

Margrave killed power again but the ship continued to rise.

Fifty feet.

'You fool! What have you done?'

'The computer models –'

'*Damn* the computer models!'

Margrave left the control panel and rushed to one of the big windows wrapped around the observation platform. Her stared with horror at the sea.

The ship was at the top of a huge, fast-rising column of water.

Austin had seen the whirlpool grow until it was around ten miles wide. Now he watched in fascination as the vortex leveled out, changed into a seething pool of white steamy water, and began to mound into a watery cyclone.

The mountainous mass sprouting from the center of the vortex grew in height and width as it spun like a whirling dervish.

The plane was coming around for another pass. Austin dashed up to the cockpit.

'Bring us up as fast and as high as you can. Get away from this area.'

The pilot put the 747 into a steep climb.

The water column reminded Austin of photos he had seen of the nuclear bomb tests in the Pacific.

A panicked voice was crackling over the radio. 'Mayday! Mayday! Come in, anyone! Mayday!'

Austin borrowed the radio microphone. 'Mayday received.'

'This is Gant on the *Polar Adventure.*' He had to shout to be heard over the rumbling in the background.

'Looks like you're in for a roller-coaster ride,' Austin said.

'Who *is* this? Where are you?'

'Kurt Austin. We're a couple of thousand feet above your head. Take a quick look because we won't be around much longer. Dr Kovacs sends his regards, though.'

After a pause, Gant said, 'What the hell is going on, Austin?'

'We've given you a dose of the polar shift antidote. I'd say that you and your partner are all washed up.'

Gant's angry reply was unintelligible, lost in a thundering clamor.

Austin peered out the cockpit window. The ship was at the top of the water column, where it spun like a top. Austin could only imagine the panicked scene on board. But he had no sympathy for Margrave and Gant, who had sown the seeds of their own destruction.

As the plane altered course and began to bear off from its target like a great lumbering whale, it encountered turbulence generated by the powerful forces that had been unleashed, but it was nothing compared to the earlier wind blasts. The plane continued to climb without incident to around twenty-five thousand feet, where it leveled off.

Karla had her face glued to the window even though there was nothing to see other than the normal cloud cover. She turned to Austin, a dazed look in her eyes.

'What happened back there?' she said.

'Your grandfather was right on the money with his calculations.'

'But what *was* that thing, that incredible waterspout?'

Austin wasn't sure what was happening but suspected that the push-pull of electromagnetic pulses from the ship and the plane had set into motion unimaginable forces.

'Nature doesn't like being messed around with. The combination of the antidote and the initial transmissions created a strong reaction.' He smiled. 'It's like taking something for an upset stomach. There's always a last eruption or two before things settle down for the better.'

'Then it's over, finally.'

'I hope so.' Austin called the cockpit, and asked, 'How's the compass doing?'

'Normal,' Zavala said. 'Still pointing to the north pole, more or less.'

Barrett hadn't moved from behind the control panel. When he heard Zavala's report, he slapped his hands together. He came over and gave Karla and Austin big hugs.

'We did it,' he said. 'By God, we *did* it.'

Austin replied with a weary grin. 'So we did,' he said. 'So we did.'

43

Doyle was glad that this would be his last trip to the lighthouse island. He had never liked the place. He had grown up in the city, and the remote beauty was lost on him. He would be even happier once he had disposed of Lucifer's Legion and left the island forever.

He landed his plane near the island, tied up to a mooring buoy and rowed to the dock where one of the Lucifer creeps was waiting to greet him. He could never remember their names and told them apart by hair color. This was the red-haired guy who, because he most resembled Margrave, seemed to have an elevated status in the group, although he was short of being a leader, anathema to the pure anarchists.

'Haven't seen you since our car chase outside Washington,' the man said in a soft-spoken voice that sounded like the rustle of a snake in dry leaves. 'Too bad your friends got away.'

'There's always another time,' Doyle said. 'We'll tend to Austin and his friends once we take care of the Elites.'

'I'll look forward to it. You should have let us know you were coming,' the man said.

Doyle hefted a canvas bag he was carrying. 'Tris wanted to surprise you.'

The answer seemed to satisfy the legionnaire. He nodded, and accompanied Doyle to the elevator that whisked them to the top of the cliff.

The other Lucifers were waiting on the lighthouse bluff, and when Doyle repeated his reason for coming to the island they gave him that unnerving grin. They all headed for the keeper's house. Doyle led the way to Margrave's kitchen. He got glasses and a beer and placed them on the table.

He pulled a bottle of champagne from the bag and poured it around. Then he opened the can of beer and held it high.

'Here's to the imminent destruction of the Elites.'

The red-haired man laughed. 'You've been hanging around with us anarchist types too long, Doyle. You're starting to sound as crazy as the rest of us.'

Doyle gave him a friendly wink. 'Must be catching. Cheers.'

He upended his beer and drank half the contents of the can. He wiped his mouth with the back of his hand, watching with pleasure as the Lucifers tossed down their champagne as if it were water.

'By the way, Margrave wanted me to give this to you.'

The package had come the day before. With it was a note, signed by Gant.

The note said: 'Plans for PS postponed until next week. Please give this gift to our friends in Maine after you share a *special* bottle of champagne with them. Say it's a gift from Margrave. Very important to wait until they drink their champagne.'

The red-haired Lucifer opened the package. It was a DVD disk. He shrugged and slipped it into the DVD player. A few seconds later, a still picture of Gant's face appeared on the screen.

'I want Lucifer's Legion disposed of,' Gant's voice said.

'And how do you propose we go about doing that?'

Impossible. It was the conversation he and Gant had after the foxhunt.

'Go up to Margave's island in Maine, tell them that you have a gift for them. Say it's from Margrave. Send them to hell, where they belong, with a glass of the bubbly.'

All eyes in the room were on Doyle.

'It's not what you think,' he said, brandishing his most charming Irish smile.

Doyle never had a chance. He'd been doomed the moment he got the disk. He would never know that disk came from Barrett, not Gant. And that the bug Austin had planted under the garden table had done its work well, picking up Gant's instructions to murder the Lucifers.

He got up and tried to make a break for the door, but one of the Lucifers tripped him and he fell to the floor. He got to his feet, grabbing for the gun in an ankle holster, but he was pushed back to the floor and relieved of his weapon. He stared up at the satanic faces ringed around him.

He couldn't figure it. The Lucifers knew he had poisoned them, yet they were smiling. Doyle would never understand that the opportunity to kill surpassed all other emotions, even fear of their imminent death.

He heard the knife drawer slide open, and then they came for him.

Epilogue

Two hundred miles east of Norfolk, Virginia, the NUMA research vessel *Peter Throckmorton* and the NOAA survey ship *Benjamin Franklin* cut their way side by side through the glassy green seas like a pair of modern-day corsairs.

While the bows hissed through the water and the decks became soaked by flying spume, the atmosphere was subdued in the *Throckmorton*'s dimly lit remote-sensing control room. Spider Barrett sat with his eyes riveted to the Mercator projection of the world displayed on the screen in front of him. Although the center was air-conditioned, perspiration gleamed on Barrett's tattooed head.

Watching Barrett's fingers fly over the keyboard were Joe Zavala, Al Hibbet and Jerry Adler, the wave expert Joe and Austin first met aboard the *Throckmorton*. Several of the ship's technicians were gathered in the room as well.

Barrett stopped and rubbed his eyes, as if he were about to admit defeat. Then his hands moved over the keys like those of a concert pianist. Blinking red dots began to appear on the world's oceans. He leaned back in his chair with a wide grin on his face. 'Gentlemen,' he said grandly, 'we have liftoff.'

The center echoed with applause.

'Remarkable!' said Dr Adler. 'I can't believe that there are so many breeding grounds for rogue waves.'

Barrett clicked the cursor on a dot. A display of statistics appeared, representing sea, weather and current conditions at that particular location. The most important information that appeared was a threat assessment detailing the potential and probable size of a giant wave.

The exercise brought forth another round of applause.

Zavala took a phone out of his pocket and called the *Benjamin Franklin*. Gamay was waiting with Paul for his call in a similar control center aboard the NOAA ship. 'Tell Paul that the eagle has landed,' Zavala told her. 'Details to follow.'

He clicked off and walked to a corner of the room where he had left a rucksack. He opened the rucksack and pulled out a couple of bottles of tequila and a stack of paper cups. He poured a round of tequila, and raised his cup in the air.

'Here's to Lazlo Kovacs,' he said.

'And to Spider Barrett,' Hibbet joined in. 'Spider has made a force for destruction into something good. His work will save the lives of hundreds and possibly thousands of mariners.'

Barrett had put his mind to work on the flight back from the South Atlantic Anomaly after he had seen the uncontrollable power that had been unleashed. He was trying to think of a way to use the Kovacs Theorems for beneficial purposes. After the plane touched down in Washington, he vanished for several days, then he showed up unexpectedly at NUMA headquarters and ran his idea by Al Hibbet.

What he proposed to Hibbet was breathtaking in its imagination and scope, yet remarkably simple. His plan was to use watered-down versions of the Kovacs electromagnetic waves to detect anomalies below the ocean floor that were suspected of causing surface disturbances. Every oceangoing vessel of a certain size would be outfitted with a Kovacs sensor mounted on the prow. The sensors would constantly broadcast information, which would be compiled with satellite observations and global electromagnetic field readings.

The data would be fed into computers, analyzed and re-broadcast as warnings of breeding areas for giant waves. Ships could then chart courses around dangerous breeder areas. It was decided to conduct sea tests in the vicinity of the giant waves that had sunk the *Southern Belle*. Because of its interest in ocean eddies, NOAA was asked to participate, which got the Trouts involved.

The two ships rendezvoused over the site of the sunken *Southern Belle*. A wreath was dropped into the water in remembrance of the ship's crew. Then the field tests began over a period of several days. The tests uncovered several glitches, which were quickly remedied. Now, with the system an obvious success, the mood in the control room had become downright raucous – especially after it had been lubricated with generous shots of tequila.

At one point, an ebullient and slightly inebriated Al Hibbet turned to Zavala and said, 'It's a shame Kurt can't be here. He's missing all the fun.'

Zavala smiled knowingly. 'I'm sure he's doing fine.'

Karla Janos came out of the tunnel blinking like a mole. Her face was dirty, and her one-piece jump suit was covered with dust. She shook her head in wonder, still impressed by the scene that confronted her eyes. A temporary village had sprung up on the grassy bowl at the bottom of the caldera. At least two dozen large tents housing facilities for sleeping, cooking and research were laid out in neat rows. Several helicopters were parked nearby.

The area around the tents bustled with activity. Access to the crystal city had been improved by drilling a tunnel and clearing away the rocky debris that was in the way.

Cables snaked into the tunnel from gas-powered electrical generators. A steady stream of scientists and assistants was moving in and out of the city.

Karla was elated and exhausted at the same time. The scientific crews had been working twenty-four hours a day on three shifts. Some, like Karla, had become so involved in their work that they had worked more than one shift. She tilted her chin back and gulped several breaths of fresh air. In the blue-gray light, she saw a speck come into view over the rim and begin a descent into the valley.

As the object neared, she could see that it was a large, colorful canopy with a human dangling below. *It couldn't be.* Hoping against hope, she walked away from the tents to a clear area and madly waved her baseball cap in the air.

The paraglider had been descending in a spiral, but it turned in her direction, swooped in low and landed only yards away. Kurt Austin unbuckled himself from the harness and rolled up the canopy. He walked over with a grin on his face and said, 'Good morning.'

She had thought about Austin a lot in the past few weeks. Their encounter had been short and sweet. Then she was off to Siberia. But there were many times she wished that she had gotten to know the handsome NUMA man better.

'What are you doing here?' Karla asked with a combination of joy and awe.

'I've come to take you to lunch.'

She glanced at her watch. 'It's three o'clock in the morning.'

'It's lunchtime somewhere. I didn't come all this way to have my invitation rejected.'

She shook her head in disbelief. 'You're *crazy*.'

Austin's blue eyes sparkled with amusement. 'Insanity is part of the NUMA job description.' He took her hand.

'As the old Sinatra song goes, "Come fly with me".'

She brushed a strand of blond hair out of her eyes. 'I've been working all night. I'm a mess.'

'There's no dress code at the joint I have in mind,' Austin said. 'Come on.'

He asked her to help him carry his new paraglider to an open area, where he gave Karla a quick lesson. They spread the canopy on the ground, buckled themselves into the tandem seat, inflated the canopy with the prop wash and jumped into the wind. Karla was a natural flier, and the takeoff was far smoother than the first one he had made with Zavala. Once they were airborne, Austin circled above the tent village and put the paraglider into an ascent.

'Quite the change in scenery in a few weeks,' Austin said as the earth slipped away below them.

'It's hard to believe that the world's leading paleontologists, archaeologists and biologists are down there working on the scientific discovery of the century.'

'A discovery you can claim credit for.'

'There were others involved, but thanks anyhow. And thank you for the ride. This is marvelous.'

'Yes, it is,' Austin said for entirely different and very male reasons. He was in close proximity to a beautiful and intelligent young woman, and he could feel the warmth of her body close to his.

The paraglider and its two passengers rose out of the caldera. Austin gave Karla some quick landing instructions, and he steered toward a relatively flat area on the rim. The landing was slightly rough but not bad. Karla slipped out of the harness and went over to where a checkered red tablecloth was spread out on the ground, anchored at each corner with a rock. In the center of the tablecloth was a miniature vase with a wildflower in it, and a waist pack.

Austin made a sweep of his hand. 'Table with a view, mademoiselle.'

She shook her head. 'You *are* crazy. But in a very nice way.'

Austin opened the pack and lined up several jars, cans and bottles. 'Courtesy of Captain Ivanov. *Mosliak* mushroom appetizer, beef *tushonka* and red caviar on rye bread for dessert. All washed down with a good Georgian red wine.'

'How did you get here?' she said.

'I heard that Captain Ivanov was bringing in a batch of scientists, including some from NUMA. I hitched a ride with them on the *Kotelny*.' Austin opened the jars and cans, and poured two glasses of wine. 'Now that you've had a chance to study things, what's your take on the crystal city?'

'It will be decades of study before we know the whole story, but I think the city was built during the Stone Age in the magma chamber after the volcano had been long dead.'

'Why go underground?'

'The usual reasons. For defense, or because of climate changes. They used mammoths for beasts of burden, which allowed them to move the cyclopean blocks.'

'What happened to the inhabitants?'

'Climate changes could have dried up their ability to grow food. A polar shift could have caused a flood or earthquake that created the partial collapse of the chamber roof, giving the caldera its odd shape. That road up the side of the mountain indicates that the usual city access might have been blocked for one reason or another.'

'Have you figured out how the mammoths managed to survive?'

'Sheer adaptability. As the food source diminished, they

became smaller to adjust to the change in environment. They seem to have the capability to hibernate during the coldest part of the year.'

'What about the city's inhabitants? Who were they?'

'An enigma. It could take decades of research before we figure out who they were and what happened to them.'

'How are the little woollies doing?'

'The mammoths? Just fine. They seem content in the corral we built for them as long as we feed them. Maria Arbatov is in charge. The hardest part will be protecting them from the outside world. We're getting lots of press attention as you can imagine, and we're trying to control it.'

He swept the island with his eyes. 'I hope this all survives our aggressive inquiry.'

'I think it will. These seem to be purer research endeavors than trying to clone mammoths.'

'What next?'

'I'll spend a few weeks here, and then head back to see Uncle Karl in Montana. I'll be coming to Washington next month to give a speech at the Smithsonian.'

'That's good news. When you get to Washington, how about getting together for cocktails, dinner and whatever?'

The smoky gray eyes gazed over the glass. 'I'm particularly intrigued over the *whatever*.'

'Then it's a date. I think it's time to propose a toast. Ladies first.'

She only had to think about it for a second.

'To Uncle Karl. If he hadn't saved my grandfather, none of this would have been possible.'

'I'll drink to that. Without Uncle Karl, *you* would not have been possible.'

She gave Austin a smile full of promise. Then, in the light

of the arctic dusk, they raised their glasses high and toasted each other.

Although death had been a close companion for much of his life, Schroeder couldn't remember the last time he had gone to a funeral. He wanted to bury Schatsky in fine style. The little dachshund who'd been killed by one of Gant's gunmen had been a great companion. Luckily, the temperature at his mountain log cabin had stayed low so Schatsky's body had been preserved while he'd been away.

He took the stiff little body, washed the blood away as best he could and wrapped the dog in its favorite blanket. Using the dog's bed as its casket, he carried it out to the woods behind his house. He dug a deep hole, wrapped the dog and its bed in a canvas, and then buried it with a box of dog bones and Schatsky's favorite chew toys.

Schroeder marked the grave with a boulder. He went back into the cabin and lugged a wooden crate back to the woods and dug another hole not far from the dog's grave. He dumped the load of automatic and semi-automatic weapons into the hole and covered them up. He had kept a shotgun back at the cabin, just in case, but he no longer needed the deadly weapons he had kept hidden under his floor.

It was his way of marking an end to one chapter of his life. There was always a chance that something unpleasant from out of the past would catch up with him, but that would become less likely as he grew older. Karla would be coming to visit soon, and he had plenty of work to do getting kayaks and canoes ready for his guide business. But without the little dog padding around after him the cabin seemed very lonely.

He got into his pickup truck and drove off the mountain

to his usual watering hole. It was still early in the day, and the bar was relatively quiet. Without some of the regulars to greet him, he felt even lonelier.

What the hell. He sat at the near-empty bar and ordered a beer. Then another. He was feeling sorry for himself when someone tapped him on the shoulder. He turned and saw a woman, probably in her sixties, standing behind him. She had long, silvery hair, large brown eyes, and her tanned skin was barely wrinkled.

She introduced herself as an artist who had moved to Montana from New York. She had a bright smile and infectious laugh and a keen sense of humor, which she displayed in describing the cultural differences between the two places. Schroeder was so taken with her that he forgot to introduce himself.

'I detect a slight accent,' she said.

Schroeder was about to go into his usual reply, that he was a Swede named Arne Svensen, but he stopped himself. There would have to come a time when he began to trust other human beings, and it might as well be now. 'You have a good ear. I am Austrian. My name is Karl Schroeder.'

'Nice to meet you, Karl,' she said with a demure smile. 'I'd like to go trout fishing, but I don't know where. Could you recommend a reliable guide?'

Schroeder gave her a big-toothed grin.

'Yes,' he said. 'I know just the man for you.'

Acknowledgments

In re-creating the events surrounding one of history's worst sea disasters, the U-boat sinking of the German refugee ship *Wilhelm Gustloff*, this book relied heavily on *The Cruelest Night* by Christopher Dobson, John Miller and Ronald Payne. A number of sources provided inspiration for the chapters on giant waves, but perhaps the most dramatic was the BBC production *Freak Wave*, which included interviews with scientists and mariners alike. Our thanks as well to Sue Davis, president and CEO of the Stanley Museum, Kingfield, Maine.